ISBN: 9798398339925

Cover design by: Erelis Design
Library of Congress Control Number: 2018675309
Printed in the United States of America

For Fiona, Sean, Rian, and Liadh.

THE RAVEN AND THE NINE

By Peter Gibbons

ONE

879AD.

T he warship Seaworm sliced through the river like an arrow shot from a bow. Hundr stood on her steerboard platform, staring ahead, hand on the tiller as the crew pulled at the oars. The warriors grunted with each heave, and the water rippled behind them to rise in small waves against the grass-covered riverbank. Bush, the grizzled shipmaster, stalked the length of the keel, barking at one man to pull harder and cursing another for a lazy whoreson. Bush scratched at his bald head, egg white and stark in contrast to his wind-darkened face, carved and etched by years at sea. They rowed on a sun-drenched spring morning under a sky half clear, the colour of the bluest eyes and half filled by dark swirling cloud the hue of an old iron cauldron. They were Viking warriors—come for vengeance and for blood.

"They'll see us coming, my lord," said Bush, turning to frown at Hundr.

"I know." He nodded, but he didn't care. He wanted them to see him coming, to know who had brought five *drakkar* warships into their river. Each ship carried thirty Viking warriors, Norsemen, Danes, and Svears. Each worshipped the many powerful Aesir gods, such as Odin, Thor, Tyr, Ran, or Frey. Savage gods for savage men who took to the Whale Road in search of silver, reputation and glory. Hundr was their Jarl, their Earl, and each man had sworn an oath to serve him, to fight and die for him. Such men flocked to Hundr's banner of the one eye because he would be their ring-giver in return for their oaths. He would make them rich with silver and gold arm rings, coins and plunder. Each man's shield, crafted from planks of linden wood riveted to an iron boss, hung over the side of the sheer strake facing out towards the riverbank. Most of those shields bore Hundr's sigil of the one eye upon their leather covers, but others bore painted wolves, bears, eagles, axes or other fearsome designs to strike fear into an enemy.

"They might bring another ship and block the river entirely."

"I know." Hundr fixed Bush with his good eye. The other had been burned out years earlier by Hakon Ivarsson in a Northumbrian fortress, leaving Hundr's face scarred and fearsome. Bush shrugged and scratched at his belly and swung around the mast post, lowered and resting now in a cradle along the length of the ship's keel.

The oars rose and fell, and glistening water droplets tumbled from the oar blades, catching the early spring sunshine. A cormorant spread its dark wings and watched them glide along the river, and Hundr rested his left hand upon the cool ivory hilt of the sword belted at his waist. He wore two swords, Fenristooth, a gift from a dead Jarl, at his belt, and Battle Fang, a blade he had stripped from a fallen foe, strapped to his back. Hundr wore a chain mail brynjar. He had slid on the heavy coat of armour upon entering the inlet at the river's gaping mouth, where it carved open the coast of Northern Frankia into a wide estuary. Hundr's five ships had followed the flood tide into the river, and at the first lazy meander, he had passed down the order to don armour and make weapons ready. They did not wear their mail and weapons at sea, for to fall into the white-tipped waves wearing chain mail armour was to sink into the sea-god Njorth's icy embrace and die without honour.

Hundr glanced over his shoulder to where Einar Rosti's crew rowed his ship, the Fjord Bear, close behind. Einar Rosti, the Brawler, was Jarl of Vanylven in Norway, and Hundr loved him like a brother. Einar was a landed Jarl and oath sworn to King Harald Fairhair of Norway. Hundr was a sea Jarl and lived with his friend, Einar, at Vanylven. Hundr owned no land, but he had five warships and men to crew them, which made him a wealthy sea Lord and a man to fear.

"Shall we take off the prow, my lord?" asked Bush, calling from where he leant over the bow to stare into the mirror-like water, checking the river's depth.

"Leave the beast's head where it is." When travelling inland, Norsemen would usually remove the snarling beast heads from the prows of their ships so as not to frighten the land's spirits. But Hundr wanted them frightened because he did not come to Frankia to trade. He came to raid and kill. "Spears," Hundr shouted along the deck, and every second man rose from his oar to collect his spear from where it rested against the mast post.

"Around the next bend." Bush crammed a dented helmet over its dark brown leather liner. It was a fine helmet with a carved boar traversing the nasal and Bush's prize possession. He had taken the beautifully crafted helmet from a battlefield in England when he, Hundr and Einar fought alongside the sons of Ragnar Lothbrok against the Kings of Northumbria, Mercia and East Anglia to wash that island in blood. Hundr nodded and raised his hand to signal to Einar, who signalled to the other ships. All along Hundr's fleet, warriors would make ready. Each man wore either a leather breastplate or, if he was skilled enough with a blade to hold on to one, a precious brynjar which would deflect all but the hardiest of blows. They carried axes, spears, seax blades, knives, and some even carried swords.

"Archers, to the bow," Bush called down the ship. Four men ducked between the rigging, clutching their yew bows, quivers of goose feather-fletched arrows rattling at their hips.

The men hauled on the oars, and the Seaworm surged forwards. Hundr lent on the tiller and guided her around a turn in the river. She came about through a clutch of reeds and a willow tree, which leant into the water like an ancient grasping monster, and Hundr smiled. A *snekke* ship sat there, high in the water. She was smaller than the Seaworm and lay with her stern facing towards Hundr's ships. Two twisted seal hide ropes, as thick around as a man's thigh, fastened the *snekke* to either side of the riverbank.

"Rollo was ever a clever bastard," called Bush, grimacing at the barrier the *snekke* created across the river. The ship blocked the river, the lifeblood of trade for merchants and traders in this part of Frankia. Rollo, the Duke of the lands surrounding the river, was indeed a clever bastard. No ship could get past his blockade without identifying themselves, paying a tithe to pass, or fighting their way through it. If a passing ship paid the fee, Rollo's men would lower a rope and punt the *snekke* to the riverbank to allow passage. If an enemy or a ship unwilling to pay Rollo's tax approached, they would need to fight their way past that *snekke* and her crew. She was an old ship, and even from this distance, one could see green mould and lichen shading her planking. She carried no mast post, and they had carved her oar plugs wider to allow her crew to loose arrows from the deck whilst crouched and protected from enemy missiles by the sheer strake. That last layer of clinker-built planking ran the upper length of the port and starboard sides, and on her port side, Rollo had built the strakes higher with extra planking so that the *snekke* became a small, water-borne fortress rather than a sea-going warship. Her high sides protected her crew, and before an attacking ship could get close, they could hammer that enemy with arrows and spears.

Hundr's heart quickened, and he ran his thumb over the ivory sword hilt. Battle was coming, and he longed for it, thirsted for that heightened sense of being that a man experiences when he dances on the fragile space between life and death. Rollo, Hundr's enemy inside the fortress ahead, had caused the deaths of Hundr's friends, men who had sailed and fought beside him. Good men like Valbrandr, Hekkr and others had lost their lives because of the chaos unleashed by Rollo the Betrayer, and now Hundr came to make him suffer for it. Rollo had sent the vicious 'Burned Man' to kill Hundr and his men, and that fight had taken them to far Novgorod and ended in a welter of death. Hundr did not pity his lost friends, for they waited for him in Odin's hall, feasting on roasted boar beneath its high roof crafted from fallen warrior's shields. His lost friends knew the risks when they took to the Whale Road. They lived and died as warriors. But as their Lord, Hundr could not let their deaths go unavenged, not if he was to keep his reputation.

"Death to Rollo the Betrayer!" Hundr roared, and he dragged Fenristooth free of her fleece-lined scabbard, the hard iron scraping on the scabbard's throat as he pulled her free to hold aloft. His men barked a single clipped roar in response to his war cry.

"Four more strokes, and we will ram her!" Bush shouted from the prow. And so they would, and to ram that ship meant death. The *snekke* would take such a blow, and her thick mooring ropes would hold her firm. The attacking ship would flounder; her warriors unable to board the *snekke* over her high sheer strake, and the *snekke*'s crew would rain down death upon their enemies to turn the river red with blood.

"We won't board her," Hundr called to his crew, their strained faces turning to look at him, drawn with the effort of rowing and surprise at his orders. "We shall sail past here and onto Rollo's hall. That is where we make ourselves rich and where we kill the bastard who sent the 'Burned Man' after us. So, sail on past, and hammer her crew with your spears."

Bush gawped at him, and Hundr rested his sword upon his mailed shoulder.

"Archers!"

Bush repeated the order, and the bowmen nocked their white feathered arrows to their bowstrings, then the air thrummed as they launched shafts towards the enemy ship. Hundr set his jaw and called down to Bush to take the tiller. They passed each other as they shuffled down the keel, avoiding tripping on the ballast stones hidden beneath the filthy water slopping in the bilge.

"Take care, my lord. You've always been lucky, and we need that luck today," said Bush, placing a purple-veined hand upon Hundr's shoulder.

"And you, old friend. If I fall, I will save a place for you in Odin's hall, where we will drink and fight together until Odin leads us out to battle on the day of Ragnarök."

Bush threw his head back and laughed. "Do you hear that, you lazy whores?" he bellowed to the crew. "We serve Hundr, the Man with the Dog's Name. Champion of the North. The man who killed Ivar the Boneless and Eystein Longaxe. The man who has sailed from Jutland to Wessex, from Orkney to Novgorod." They cheered and looked up at Hundr with eager eyes, grim men with braided beards and tattooed faces. Their shoulders and backs bunched with muscle grown over long years hauling on oars, battling against the surging power of the sea, hands gnarled and strong from gripping the smooth pine lengths of wood. They were warriors and seamen who braved the horrors of the Whale Road, who laughed for joy as the Seaworm's oak planking sped across the waves before the wind and sang their grim rowing songs into the spite of the wind and rain off the coasts of the Vik, Svearland and Norway where the ice in the rain flays a man's face raw.

"This is the home of Rollo the Betrayer, whom we defeated at the great sea battle at Hafrsfjord and who sent his war dog, the 'Burned Man' Kvasir Randversson, to kill our Lord," Hundr began. "But no man attacks us and lives, so Kvasir lies dead in Novgorod, and we come to wreak our terrible vengeance on the Betrayer and his people. Are we Vikings?"

"Heya!" they roared as one.

"Are we men destined for Valhalla?"

"Heya!"

"Then kill! Kill them for me. Kill and make yourselves rich with the blood of our enemies! Odin watches us. Let him see the men we are!" Hundr shouted. The crew bellowed their approval, slapping each other's backs, wide-eyed with furious battle fervour. Hundr marched to the prow and ducked as an arrow whistled across the rippling river to slam into the prow. They glided close to the *snekke,* within three ships' lengths, and bearded faces peered through her arrow holes. Hundr gripped the prow, searching through the riverbank's dark green ash and elm trees.

Where is that boy? Soon it would be too late, the Seaworm would crash into the *snekke*, and there would be a slaughter in a Frankish river. If that ship stayed where it was, then there was no way Hundr could win or take his revenge.

Just as Hundr thought it was too late, as he was about to call to his men to back oars away from the blocking ship, the roar of twenty men shook the hidden shadows of the riverbank forest. Small birds fled from the treetops, still bright green with fresh spring leaves, and Hundr nodded to himself. The Seaworm crew cheered again, as did the warriors on board Einar's Fjord Bear and the rest of Hundr's fleet, who followed behind in a line of ships. Immediately, a long two hundred Vikings roared their acclaim as Finn Ivarsson and his twenty men burst through the forest to hack into the *snekke*'s mooring rope. One of them, a huge Dane, swung a two-handed war axe at the rope. His long, golden hair flowed loose around his head like the mane of a beast. Three of Finn's men raced in front of the big man and brought their shields together to create a protective barrier just as half a dozen arrows thumped into the linden wood that otherwise would have killed the big Dane.

On the fourth swing of the axe, the thick mooring rope snapped, and the crew of the *snekke* groaned as Finn and his twenty men ran past them towards Rollo's stronghold.

"Brace yourselves," said Hundr, and his men curled up into balls or gripped the ship's side to protect themselves against the impact. Hundr wrapped his arms around the prow, and a heartbeat later, the Seaworm crashed into the *snekke's* stern. The larger *drakkar* used the force of its momentum to push the *snekke* wide, where the ropes would have held her firm in the water. The Seaworm crew whooped for joy and leapt to their feet, throwing their spears across the bows and into the arrow holes of the enemy ship. Bush winced as the Seaworm scraped past the *snekke*, and the sound of it was like a magnificent tree falling in a deep forest, crunching, rending, and tearing. Bush pulled an axe from a leather loop at his belt and threw the weapon across the bows. Its bearded blade turned as it flew like the flight of a butterfly dancing between the flowers in summer. But the axe did not flutter gently. Instead, it screamed as the air washed over its heavy blade, making a wet chopping sound as the axe blade thumped full into the face of a raven-black bearded enemy warrior. The Seaworm pushed passed the blocking ship, and now the high-sided sheer strake of the enemy ship was behind them. The crew of the *snekke* continued to pour arrows into the Seaworm, and Hundr counted ten men on board that blocking ship. Three fell with spears in their chests, and in the madness of impending battle, Hundr, without thinking, placed his boot on the side and leapt onto the enemy ship. He landed heavily, cursing as his shin cracked into a rowing bench, yet rising with Fenristooth held before him.

An archer with chestnut eyes and close-cropped hair brought a nocked arrow around, but Hundr slid his sword's blade under the bow and into the man's belly. He cried out, and as he bent double over the terrible wound, Hundr kicked him savagely in the face to drive him back off Fenristooth's blade. Hundr whipped the sword around to slice open the face of a short man and then took three long strides along the *snekke's* deck. All around him was shouting chaos. Men died with spears and arrows slamming into their flesh, and Hundr killed another man with a sword cut to his neck. Blood sprayed brightly in the spring morning to splash onto the deck and paint her timbers red. He leapt across the bows again, landing between two of the Seaworm crew, who laughed and clapped him enthusiastically on the back. The Seaworm slid past the *snekke*, her crew left in bloody ruin in the river, and the way to Rollo's fortress now lay open before them.

"Oars, shitworms," Bush bellowed at the crew, and the long shafts of pinewood bit into the river water to power the Seaworm towards the stronghold of Duke Rollo Ganger, the Betrayer. Hundr clasped each of the archers' forearms in the warriors' grip in salute for the men they had killed aboard the blocking ship. Ahead, Finn Ivarsson raced along the riverbank and leapt onto the timber jetty, which served as a riverside port for the stronghold.

"Wasn't so long ago that you killed some of Rollo's bastards in this very place," said Bush, grinning. Only a year earlier, Hundr, Finn, and Ragnhild had fled Rollo's feasting hall and escaped from the town as Rollo's men came at them with axe and spear. Hundr had killed men that day, and today would see more blood. Finn cut a man down with a slash of his sword and danced around another, leaving that enemy to the men running behind him. They were his men, and where he was young and lean with barely a fluff of a beard upon his chin, they were big, bearded growlers who had sworn an oath to serve Finn following their master's defeat in the Rus city of Novgorod. Hundr nodded to himself and braced as the Seaworm approached the jetty. Finn had done well in cutting the *snekke* loose, just as he had last year in his first summer a'viking. Before blindly sailing up the river towards Rollo's fortress, Hundr had sent scouts loping up the riverbank to look at Rollo's defences. So, he knew the *snekke* was waiting for them and had sent Finn and his fighters to cut the thick mooring rope and open the river. Now, Finn had one more task to complete. As the young warrior sprinted up from the jetty, the boots of his men thundered on the planking;

Hundr knew the stronghold would be his.

Rollo's men came from the gate in alarm at the sounds of battle cries and the screams of the dying, those who had not died but lay injured on the *snekke* moaning and calling out in pain, and six of Rollo's warriors came through that open gate armed with spears and axes. Finn and his warriors cut through them, hacking and slashing until the gateway ran with the blood of Rollo's oathmen. The fortress was a simple but effective ditch and bank topped by a stout timber palisade of sharpened stakes. Rollo's men had not thought to close the gate upon hearing the attack, so confident were they in the efficacy of their river blockade. Those men died, and as Finn reached the yawning gateway, he turned to Hundr and raised his blood-soaked sword in triumph. Hundr raised his own blade in salute.

Finn might be the youngest of them, of an age similar to Hundr when he had first become a member of the Seaworm crew many years earlier, but he was a skilled and savage fighter like his father. Finn was the son of the fearsome Viking champion, Ivar the Boneless, and the grandson of Ragnar Lothbrok, the most feared and respected of all Viking seafarers. Ragnar and sons were legends, spoke of wherever men sailed, and no Ragnarsson had died asleep in his bed. Hundr shuddered at the memory of Ivar, his odd-coloured eyes and viciously fast sword skill.

Three of the Seaworm crew made the jump

to the jetty and turned to brace the gliding ship with their legs as she brushed alongside it, preferring to risk a broken leg than see the precious planking damaged and incur the wrath of Bush, the shipmaster. However, Hundr didn't wait for them to tie off the ship. Instead, he leapt onto the jetty and ran across its planking and up towards the fortress. Behind him poured the men of the Seaworm crew, and then the rest of his ships, filled with his warriors—all had come for vengeance and plunder.

TWO

Hundr killed a stocky warrior with a tattooed face, gutting him with Fenristooth and slicing his throat open with Battle Fang. He paused, letting his warriors surge around him, their hungry faces feral like wolves amongst sheep. Men died, and women screamed, dashing between thatched houses of wattle and daub. A pig squealed and ran across Hundr's path, and on that bright spring morning, death had come for Rollo's people. It was a still morning, and the air was thick with damp wood smoke and tinged with the iron smell of blood.

"Where is the bastard?" asked Einar Rosti, striding through the gate, clutching his axe in one hand and a wicked seax blade in the other.

"Where is that snivelling piece of weasel shit?" Einar was an enormous man, a head taller than Hundr, with a hard, flat slab of a face burned like old leather by sea winds. His beard was grey, and his eyes fierce.

"Finn searches for Rollo," said Hundr, jutting his chin towards Rollo's high-gabled hall that rose above the smaller dwellings. A hall was the centre of any Norse settlement. It was where the Lord lived with his family, where a hearth burned on all but the hottest of days, and where that Lord feasted with his warriors.

A tangle-haired man burst from a building. He was bare-chested and bleary-eyed from sleep, and he charged at Einar with a spear held low in both hands. He bellowed his war cry, and Einar hooked his axe blade around the spear's head to divert the blow. Einar kneed his attacker in the stomach and drove his seax blade up under the man's chin so that blood sloshed out of his skull like ale from a barrel. Einar frowned and pushed the corpse away from him, shaking his head at the thick blood soaking his left hand and forearm.

Three more of Rollo's Vikings emerged from a building with faded, rotting thatch. One had a shield and carried a sword; the others came armed with axes. Hundr charged at them, his sword blade ringing like a bell as it clanged on the boss of the shield. Einar barged the shield man out of the way with his shoulder, and Hundr slid his blade over the shield's rim and into his throat so that the man died with a blood-gurgling cough. The second and third men struck at Einar and Hundr, swinging their axes with the fury of men protecting their homes. Hundr danced away from the blow, cutting his sword low across his attacker's calf. The man fell to one knee, his eyes flashing wide with terror. Hundr smashed the pommel of his sword into the fallen man's nose and then killed him with a thrust to the chest. Einar struggled with the remaining axe man for a moment before throwing him over his hip and pounding his axe blade into the man's skull.

"Bloody Rollo," Einar tutted in disgust. "His men are just like him, coming from the shadows like whipped dogs. There are no drengr here, no men who follow drengskapr, the way of the warrior. I hate the treacherous dog; I knew he was a rat from the first moment I laid eyes on him."

Hundr and Einar had rescued Rollo from his chains in the hall of Jarl Ketil Flatnose on the island of Orkney, and from that day, he was ever a man to mistrust. Rollo was hugely tall, a ferocious fighter, and had once served Hundr as a warrior. That was until he had fled with Finn as a hostage and then sent the 'Burned Man' to kill

Hundr and his men.

"If he's here, then he dies," Hundr said before turning to one of his captains, who marched towards him with his crew of thirty fighters following behind. "Asbjorn, scour this place for silver, weapons and anything of value."

"Yes, my lord," replied Asbjorn, bringing his axe to his chest in salute. He barked at his men, and the warriors dispersed in every direction. They ducked under the low door lintels of houses, workshops, and so on and would go through every building until they had made a pile of riches to take back home to Vanylven.

"About time we made ourselves rich again," said Einar. "We made nothing last year in Novgorod, and your crewmen are hungry mouths to feed."

"What we take from here should repay you and the folk of Vanylven. It's been a long winter, and your people have been good to us."

"My people are your people, brother. You know that." Einar smiled and clapped Hundr warmly on the shoulder. They were brothers of the sword, and although Einar was the Jarl of Vanylven, Hundr knew he and his men were welcome there anytime. Other than the sea, it was the only place Hundr could call home, and although Einar griped about the cost his people bore to keep Hundr's men warm and their bellies full, he loved having the warriors around.

A grizzle-bearded man from the Sea Stallion came tottering along the principal thoroughfare through Rollo's stronghold. He clutched at a wound in his shoulder, where a bloodstain blossomed on the jerkin beneath his leather breastplate.

"Rollo's men are coming... in a shield wall," gasped the warrior through clenched teeth.

"How many?" asked Hundr.

"Thirty men, my lord, at least."

It had all been too easy, first the removal of the *snekke* from where it blocked the river, then getting to the gate before the defenders had time to close it upon hearing of the river skirmish. Rollo was many things, but he was no fool, and Hundr expected there to be hard fighting before he could have his vengeance.

"Call the men. We make our own shield wall across this street," said Hundr, and he turned to Einar. "Take your men into the winding pathways between the dwellings. When you hear the fighting start, bring your men around their flanks."

Einar nodded and bellowed for his men to rally to him. They came clutching plunder, pouches of coins, knives, and jewellery. They tossed the loot into a makeshift pile and joined Einar as he disappeared into the snarl of lanes between the wattle and daub buildings, the stomp of their boots heavy on the earth and the iron of their weapons jangling as they marched. Bush took a curved horn from where it hung from a leather thong at his belt. It was a beautiful thing of black and cream-coloured horn, ringed and chased with silver, and Bush brought it to his lips and let out a long, sonorous song.

"I'll never tire of that sound," Bush said with a grin. Warriors came hurtling up the pathway from where the rest of Hundr's ships had moored alongside the jetty, and his men poured through the fortress' gate. "Make the shield wall, you turds," Bush growled at the men, hirpling amongst them on his bandy legs, and they smiled at his curses. "Make the wall and get ready to earn your silver. Kill as many of the bastards as you can and make your reputations."

Five men spanned the street's width. Five of Hundr's warriors overlapped their shields, and five more were behind them. They made the wall of linden wood and rested their spears on the iron rims of their shields, making ready to meet the charge. Once the wall was five ranks deep, Hundr sent more men into the lanes to join Einar and keep a lookout for any potential attacks from Rollo's warriors on the flanks or rear. Hundr carried no shield but braced himself with his two swords held ready. A battle song, deep and rumbling, echoed over the thatch. Rollo's men came on, their shields overlapped, and they sang to Odin of a glorious death. They, too, came in ranks—grim men who knew their business, come to kill the men who raided their fortress.

"I thought I had missed the fight," a familiar voice intoned, and Hundr nodded a welcome to Ragnhild. Her one eye blazed with the impending thrill of battle. They shared the Odin wound, having both lost an eye like the All-Father himself. Ragnhild was a priestess of the Valkyrie order of warrior-women sworn to serve Odin and send brave warriors to fill his corpse hall of men slain in battle. She was fierce, a skilled fighter, and Hundr's trusted friend.

"What took you so long? Were you waiting in the rear until the fighting was over?" Bush ribbed, yet no one laughed but him. To mock Ragnhild was to die, but she and Bush were old friends, and she gave what passed for a smile on her scarred, savage face. She held her recurved bow, made in the eastern fashion of wood, horn sinew and glue, and a quiver of arrows hung from her belt.

"I'll still kill more than you, ugly one," she said.

"That's Rollo's shield wall," pointed Hundr, gesturing to where the enemy slowly approached along the pathway towards their position. "But there are so few of them; there must be hundreds more elsewhere. Take your archers up onto the rooftops, Ragnhild. Rain death down on Rollo's men, and find the rest."

Ragnhild nodded and led her bowmen to the flanks. Hundr's men took up their war cries, beating axes on shields and winding themselves up into the frenzy required for men to meet in battle, where an enemy will try to cut and rend at you with axe, sword and spear. Where you can smell the breath of the man who comes to rip away your life, who you must kill before he kills you. That knowledge turned men's bowels to water, and Hundr felt his own guts churning despite his years of experience. Bravery, however, was overcoming that fear and using it to become fast and lethal enough to kill those who came to kill you. Hundr paced behind the lines, the swords comfortable in his hands, their weight familiar and welcome.

Rollo's men let out a roar to shake Asgard itself and then sprinted the final ten paces to crash into Hundr's shield wall with a sound like thunder in a summer storm. Shields came together, men grunted at the effort, spears struck, and warriors screamed in pain as blades slashed their faces, ripped their groins open, and pushed deep into their hearts. Hundr's ranks surged forwards, and Ragnhild's arrows slapped into the enemy from above as she took up her position atop the surrounding buildings. Hundr paced behind the lines again, eager for news of where the rest of Rollo's men were hiding. Yet that news did not come, and he cursed as his hunger for battle overwhelmed him.

"Boar's tusk," he shouted. His men knew that order. They practised it relentlessly along with all their other battle formations every winter when there was little to do but sleep to stay warm and practice with weapons in the ice and rain. Warriors formed up behind him like a spear blade, with Hundr at its point. His chest heaved, and the gut-wrenching fear turned into a fire of anger. "Tusk coming through," he yelled. The ranks in front of him gave way, and Rollo's men let out a roar of triumph as they believed Hundr's shield wall collapsed beneath their onslaught. But their joy was short-lived because Hundr charged. He charged at the tip of a wedge of his warriors and ran into a gap in the enemy line as they stumbled into the open space his front rank had created. Hundr leapt into them and cut at a blue-eyed man's face, cleaving off the lower part of his jaw with a monstrous overhand strike. Next, he drove Battle Fang's point into another warrior's belly and drove that man backwards into his men. The wedge behind Hundr propelled him forward, and he slashed his sword across the throat of a tall warrior who could not raise his shield in time to block the strike. Warm, iron-stinking blood spattered Hundr's face and brynjar as the war rage enveloped him.

Hundr stumbled as he punched through the enemy's rear rank. He turned and sliced his blade across the calf of a man in the last line, and Rollo's men died. Einar came howling from a side street, his size and savagery driving deep into the enemy as his axe crashed into faces and chests, carving a bloody swathe of death amongst them. In ten heartbeats, the fight was over, and Rollo's men lay dead or writhing in agony. The mud of that central laneway was now churned to a crimson slime with the blood of the fallen, and as men voided bowels in their death throes, the stench became overwhelming.

"He's not here," shouted Finn, striding from the hall with his hands on his hips, looking with a nod of appreciation at the slaughtered foemen. Hundr and Einar exchanged a long look of frustration and marched towards the hall. The skull of a magnificent stag rested over its doors, and Hundr entered its gloom to see a huge fire crackling at the central hearth. Finn's men had gathered the folk in the hall together at its centre, and they knelt next to the warmth of the fire.

"Where is he?" Hundr said to the prisoner closest to him. She was a full-figured woman with a big birthmark on her right cheek. The woman stared open-mouthed at Hundr's face, at the hollow where his eye should be and the grim scarring around it. She saw a blood-soaked lord of war, and her lips trembled in terror. He shook his head; she was too afraid to be of any use to him. Hundr pointed his sword. The blood from the men he had killed lay thick on the blade, and the glow from the nearby fire danced on the bright steel beneath the scarlet wash. He levelled it at an ageing man with a shiny, round face beneath long greasy crow-black hair. The man swallowed hard and shook his head.

"This one is Rollo's steward," said Mundi, one of Finn's men. One of those who had sailed with the 'Burned Man' and who, after his death, had sworn an oath to serve Finn Ivarsson. The 'Burned Man' had served Rollo, and so Mundi was familiar with Rollo's stronghold.

Hundr pressed the tip of his sword into the steward's gullet. "Where is Rollo?" he asked again, slowly.

"Gone, Lord. Gone to be married," answered the steward, his fearful eyes flicking across the hard-faced killers who had stormed the hall.

"Bastard has escaped us again," snarled Einar before he grasped a horn cup of ale from a feasting bench and threw it across the room into the darkness at the hall's edges, where it clattered upon the hard-packed earth.

"Rollo is getting married?" Hundr asked.

"He marries the daughter of a great Frankish duke, Lord." The steward grinned, exposing a mouth full of blackened teeth.

"No doubt this daughter comes with a vast dowry." Hundr sheathed his sword and paced the hall, the floor rushes rustling beneath his boots, understanding in that moment why there were so few of Rollo's warriors within the fortress. Rollo would have travelled to his wife with most of his forces as a show of his strength and power. Leaving only enough men to defend the stronghold's sturdy palisade in the event of an attack. "We have come all this way, and Rollo is gone."

"He's a lucky bastard," hissed Einar. "If he fell into a pile of horseshit, he would come up smelling like the fairest maiden. Where is his hoard?"

The steward shook his oily face. "There is no hoard. Lord Rollo is but a humble merchant who only has enough coin to feed us poor folk. There is nothing left after a long winter."

"Rollo is a murderous bastard with more deep cunning than a starving wolf. We left him after the battle of Hafrsfjord with only four ships, and he turned himself into a Duke of the Franks. He has a hoard here, and we are going to steal it." Einar grabbed the steward by the scruff of his jerkin and hauled him to his feet. "Tell me where it is, or I will cut off your fingers and feed them to the pigs."

"No need for that, Lord Einar," Mundi intervened. Einar stared at him, but Mundi just shrugged. He was a big man with a heavy beard woven into a thick braid wound about with silver wire. He was bald with a writhing dragon tattooed across his skull. "Rollo keeps his hoard beneath his top table. Move it, and there is a pit there beneath the boards."

"So, he learned something whilst he was emptying old Ketil's shit pail then." Einar let the steward go, and the man crumpled to the floor and scampered back amongst his kneeling people.

"What do you mean?" asked Finn. He wore a shining brynjar, and his youthful face was sharp but handsome. He was shorter than Einar by a head and of a similar size as Hundr.

"We found Rollo shackled in Ketil Flatnose's hall when we raided Orkney. I wanted to kill him, but Hundr let him live in exchange for showing us where the old marauder kept his silver. Ketil, the sly old sea eagle, had dug a great pit in the ground beneath his high feasting table and filled it with enough silver and gold to make a man weep."

Hundr's men moved the high table aside, and beneath it, the hard-packed earth gave way to dusty floorboards, which Einar smashed to kindling with his axe. In that hole was a hoard to put even Ketil Flatnose's riches to shame. Finn brought a flaming branch from the fire and held it as they all peered into the hole beneath the boards. A murmur of awe resounded from the crowd as the firelight glinted off bowls full of silver coins, some with images of Frankish and English kings, others with the strange writing of the Musselmen from the south of Spain. There were objects of gleaming gold, boar's head brooches, cloak pins fashioned to look like a horse's head, and rings that flickered with red and green stones. There were plates stolen from Christ God churches and even a torc of golden wire interwoven and as thick as a woman's wrist.

"Well," said Bush, scratching at his bald head. "We won't be going home empty-handed, anyway."

"Load it all up and take the ship we saw docked against the jetty," Hundr instructed. The hoard was vast, but Hundr would keep little for himself. Rather, he would choose something beautiful for Sigrid, his wife, who waited for him at Vanylven with a belly full of baby. He would give a third to Einar in payment for his hospitality, and the rest he would share amongst his men. His duty as their Lord was to keep their pouches full of silver. That was why they followed him and swore oaths to be his men.

"What shall we do with this place?" asked Finn.

"Let your men loose. Burn it all. Nobody harms the women and children, or they answer to me," said Hundr. "Let Rollo come home to find his fortress in ashes and his hoard stolen. Let him also know who did this to him. Leave my banner here to remind him."

THREE

Einar pushed open the hall's heavy oak doors, the callouses on his shovel-like hands pressing against the rough wood as the doors swung open on their iron hinges. A wave of hot air washed over him, and Einar smiled. He breathed deeply, taking in the earthy smell of timber burning in his hearth; the musty old ceiling rafters stained the deepest brown from years of winter fires burning beneath their long timbers. Herbs and spring flowers adorned the walls and feasting benches to mask the smell of the floor rushes, and Einar laughed long and loud because he was home. It had been but moments since the Fjord Bear and the rest of

Hundr's fleet had secured their mooring ropes to the stout posts on Vanylven's harbour. The townspeople had flocked to the port to welcome home the warriors, and Einar had leapt from the deck onto the harbour, feeling as young and lithe as a man half his age. He had met grinning faces, and men clapped him on the back as he strode through them. They were proud of their Jarl and his reputation and cheered to see the safe return of the fleet, which bore Hundr's one-eyed sigil. The ships and their warriors meant protection and safety for the folk of Vanylven. Without them, they were like prey to wolves. No hungry Viking hunter would dream of attacking a coastal town protected by five crews of fair-famed warriors.

"Woman of the house!" he bellowed, and a serving girl brought him a cup of frothing ale in a wooden drinking cup. He took a long pull, enjoying its cool refreshing taste as it washed the sea water's salty dryness from his throat. Einar wiped the froth from his beard on the sleeve of his jerkin. "Where is the lady of the house?"

"Here I am, my love. No need to roar the place down like an old bear," said a tall woman who came striding from the rear of the hall. She wore a green gown the hue of a summer meadow, and a stole of fox fur covered her shoulders. "Woman of the house? Since when do you talk to me like that?"

"Hildr." He gulped down the rest of his ale and handed the empty cup back to the serving girl with a wink. She smiled and shuffled away, and Einar hurried to Hildr. He swept her up into his arms and spun her around, laughing again like a drunken father on his daughter's wedding night. "Frigg's tits, but you are beautiful."

"Put me down," Hildr said, chuckling. "You smell like a boar."

"Just the way you like it."

Einar put her down, and Hildr laughed, then reached up and kissed him. Her lips were soft and warm, and at that moment, Einar wondered why he had ever left Vanylven to sleep wet-arsed on a warship as they sailed south to Frankia. He cupped his hands around her soft cheeks and drank in every inch of her face. She was still beautiful, and the crow's feet at the corners of her eyes, the lines upon her forehead and the wrinkles on her top lip told of their years spent together and Einar loved her as much as he had when she was young, lithe, and golden-haired. That hair still shone in the sunlight streaming through the smoke hole in the hall's thatch, but there was as much iron grey in it now as gold.

"Well, is he dead?"

"No, mores the pity. The bastard was off getting married, if you can believe that. But there was silver there, my love, and gold. I have something for you." Einar fished his hand into a pouch he kept beneath his armpit. The men of Hundr's crews were Viking warriors who carried everything they owned in a sea chest which doubled as a rowing bench. They were stout men in a fight, but Einar had been around men like that his entire life and had been such a man himself long ago. So, he knew to hide his wealth from their greedy paws. He pushed his tongue into his cheek as he rummaged in the leather purse, his fingers pushing between silver coins and pieces of hacksilver until he found what he was looking for. Einar freed his hand from the purse and hid the item in his fist. "Close your eyes and hold out your hand."

"Einar, please. We don't have time for this. There is a problem with a wool merchant, and…"

"Close your eyes." She sighed and shut her eyes tight, holding out one long-fingered hand and resting the other on her hip. He placed the ring in her hand and held his arms out. "You can open them now."

Hildr opened her eyes, and her pupils grew at the sight of the ring. It was a beautiful thing Einar had found in his portion of Rollo's hoard. A shining silver ring with a shockingly bright purple amethyst stone carved with the marks of the Musselmen. The stone shone, catching the light in the room, and Hildr smiled with joy. She slid it over her finger and held it up to admire the craftsmanship.

"Einar," she gasped and drew him into another embrace. "So, you have returned with riches, then?"

"Aye, we don't have the head of a sneaky, murderous bastard, but we stole his hoard and burned his hall. So, it wasn't a wasted trip."

She smiled again and held up her hand to stare at the ring. "Did we lose many men?"

"One man died. One of Ragnhild's archers fell with a spear in his chest. Ten men were injured; one of those will probably die from infection. He took an axe to his leg, and the wound stinks."

"Ragnhild?"

"She fought like a Loki demon, as usual. Do you miss it?"

"Fighting? Yes, of course I do. I am a Valkyrie, just as Ragnhild is. But who would run this place whilst you go off on your adventures?"

"Maybe I shouldn't go to sea anymore. I'm too old; my back aches. That wound I took in…"

"You will never stop fighting, my love. It's in your soul. It is what you are. You are a drengr, and I wouldn't have it any other way."

"One day, I might not come back." He swallowed heavily at that thought. Einar felt his years weighing him down. Glorious feasts in Valhalla filled his dreams on some nights, but on others, he was a wraith wandering Niflheim with other souls who had not died in battle. Most of all, he feared being apart from Hildr, whether that was in life or death.

"Don't talk such nonsense," she soothed, placing her hands on his chest. "When you die, Odin will welcome you into his Einherjar, and I will join you. We shall be together for all time. But now, I must talk to you of Sigrid."

"Sigrid?"

"Yes. She is heavy with child and having a miserable time of it. She, too, missed not sailing with you, and she missed her husband terribly. So, I promised that you and I would eat with her and Hundr this evening. To welcome you home."

"This evening? I had thought to feast the warriors and drink?"

"You can drink yourself into a stinking, snoring mess tomorrow. Tonight, we make Sigrid happy."

"That's Hundr's job, not mine."

"They will be here after sundown, and I won't hear another word on the matter. Now, wash yourself, and I will have clean clothes brought for you."

Einar grunted and unbuckled his belt. As he laid them down, the axe and seax banged loudly on a feasting bench. His men expected to be feasted, as did Hundr's warriors. Einar wanted to feast and drink with the warriors instead of enduring a night of baby talk, swollen bellies and thin ale. But he didn't have the heart or the inclination to argue with Hildr. It was still early in the summer, and there would be time for another voyage before the fighting season was over. So, Einar would pick his battles and save his arguing for when he broke the news that he would take to the Whale Road again.

Hundr and Sigrid arrived as the sun's disc sank into a flame-orange sunset, and a half-moon hung in the sky like a great shining earring of the gods. Hundr wore a plain leather jerkin and came without his brynjar, whilst Sigrid wore a long, loose, woollen smock. Einar gasped when he saw her because Sigrid was huge. Sigrid was a beautiful, golden-haired and fine-boned woman, just like Hildr had been. Disease did not scar her face; she was a stout fighter and had become skilled with a bow. She, the proud daughter of a famous Viking Jarl, had met Hundr in Orkney when Hundr and Einar raided her father, Ketil Flatnose's hall. Now, Sigrid looked thoroughly miserable as she waddled to the table set for dinner.

"Hildr, it does me good to see you," said Hundr, inclining his head in greeting.

"Please, sit." Hildr smiled, directing them to the feasting bench that Einar's servants had laid with fresh bread, ale, roasted duck and baked fish.

"How are you... coping?" asked Einar, uncomfortably waving a hand towards Sigrid's distended belly, which was as full and round as a bladder stuffed with barley. She frowned at him and manoeuvred herself onto the eating bench, sighing with relief as she shifted into as comfortable a seating position as possible.

"Forgive me, Jarl Einar," she said. "I am exhausted. If this baby doesn't come soon, I don't know what I'll do. I am glad to see you safely returned. How was Frankia?" Sigrid wore her long hair loose, with one side combed forward to hide the left side of her face. She noticed Einar looking at it and bowed her head so that her hair covered her face in shadow. Sigrid had taken a deep cut to her face in the brutal fighting in Novgorod's palace last summer, and though the wound had healed over the long winter, under Hildr and Ragnhild's expert care, the cut had left her with a terrible scar running from her left ear to her jawline. The scar marred her young, soft beauty, but the risks for women who took to the Whale Road were the same as for men. Sigrid had left her father's hall seeking war, glory and reputation. She had found all three in her love for Hundr and bore the scars as evidence of her experience in the flaming hot forge of battle. Einar looked away, turning his gaze to Hundr instead.

"Frankia was like plucking treasure from a Christian church," Einar answered, frowning at Hundr. "But we missed Rollo. He was not at home."

"And the spoils of war were plenty?" Sigrid pointed at the new ring upon Hildr's finger, and Hildr stretched over the table to let Sigrid inspect the magnificent craftsmanship. Hundr leant forward and grabbed a chunk of bread and a leg of duck. He took a deep bite, the juices from the meat running from his mouth into his beard. "You are lucky to have a husband who loves you so."

Hundr coughed, almost choking at her words. "You know I must give my share of the spoils to my men. They expect it. That is the price of leadership. I can get a ring for your finger, an arm ring, or a cloak pin if you like? Bush or Asbjorn would be happy to take a piece from their share."

"No, no. It would just be nice to be considered once in a while, that's all."

Hundr sighed, and Einar smiled. He stuffed a crust of bread into his mouth to stifle his laughter. He had seen Hundr break shield walls and kill fearsome champions. Together they had stormed fortresses and traded blows with the grimmest and most savage warriors in the world. Yet his friend sat before him, cowed by the woman he loved, and Einar knew that feeling. Being around an angry woman was like walking across a ship's plank hammered through with upturned nails.

"I apologise for my ill humour," said Sigrid, and she placed a hand on Hundr's arm with a wan smile. "It's so long since I got a proper night's sleep that sometimes I cannot control my words."

"The baby will come soon," assured Hildr. She waved for the servants to pour them some ale. "It will be a boy, we think. There has been heartburn and a long shadow on Sigrid's belly."

"A son!" beamed Einar, and he raised his cup of ale to toast those omens but quickly lowered it when Sigrid scowled at him. She rubbed a hand upon her breastbone. Clearly, the heartburn was nothing to be happy about from her perspective.

"Young Finn fought well again," said Hundr, changing the subject. "His men admire him, and the rest respect him."

"He will make a good Viking war leader," Einar nodded proudly.

"You have raised him well," said Sigrid.

"He has lived amongst us since he was a boy," said Hildr, "and now he grows into a fine young man. He has been like a son to you, Einar, and you should be proud of him."

"I am," Einar affirmed. "We will need to find a wife for him soon, one that befits the son of the Boneless."

"We missed you in the fighting," Hundr said to Sigrid, and she smiled.

"Next year, I will sail with you again. I miss the smell of the sea and the thrill of battle." Sigrid smiled again but then used her hand to cover the scarred side of her face.

They ate together and spoke of the raid, of the hoard they had found, and of the room Sigrid and Hildr had prepared for the new baby. Hundr and Sigrid would live in the great hall with Einar and Hildr for the next year, and Einar had been glad to provide a suitable room with its own small hearth for the baby to be warm and safe after its birth.

"Having a child is a great risk," said Hildr, wagging a long finger at Sigrid. "Akin to standing in the shield wall. Do you know how many women die in childbirth? Or how many bairns die in their first months?" She saw the shocked look on Sigrid's face and smiled nervously. "But you are as strong as an ox, and your baby will be the same. It will be a thrill for us to have a baby around the place. I cannot wait."

Einar raised his cup as a toast to that, hoping it was a more palatable topic to drink to this time. But, just as he did so, the enormous doors to the hall creaked open on their hinges, and Finn burst in, his cheeks red beneath his chestnut mop of hair.

"Einar, Hundr," he panted between gulps of air, his chest heaving. "Ships approach, flying the raven banner of the sons of Ragnar Lothbrok."

FOUR

"It can only be Bjorn Ironside or Halvdan Ragnarsson," said Einar, rising from the feasting table. He took a swig of his ale, and his eyes shone from the hard slab of his face.

"How many ships?" asked Hundr, thoughts of Sigrid and her uncomfortable pregnancy slipping away. Finn swept his hair back from his face and regained his composure, blowing out his cheeks and catching his breath from the dash from the quayside to the hall. The raven banner was known the world over as the sigil of Ragnar Lothbrok, the first great Viking raider. A man with the deep cunning to take the warriors of small Viking raids on churches and villages and forge them into mighty fleets and armies, leading them in the sack of great cities and full-blown war. The sons of Ragnar had taken up the famous banner, the white outline of a raven set in deepest black, and were just as vicious and warlike as their father. A memory sent a shudder down Hundr's spine of meeting that banner in a sea battle off Dublin's Irish coast. He had killed Ivar the Boneless that day, the mightiest son of Ragnar Lothbrok. Ivar had hated Hundr for killing his son, Hakon Ivarsson, yet Hundr now counted Ivar's son Finn as a friend. *Strange how the norns twist the strands of men's lives together at the foot of Yggdrasil, the great tree at the centre of the world.*

"Four ships, *drakkars* from the look of it, but it's hard to tell with the light fading," said Finn. "Which of my uncles can it be?"

"Four warships could be a long two hundred men or more," Hundr replied. "So let's hope it's Bjorn and not Halvdan."

"I have missed Bjorn," grinned Einar. "If it is him, we shall have to brew more ale and prepare ourselves for feasting worthy of Valhalla itself."

"Have the ships taken down their beast heads?" asked Hundr.

"I can't tell from this distance," Finn answered with a shrug.

"They can't pass the fjord chain anyway," said Sigrid. "So ask the sentries there to find out who approaches."

"We passed it," chimed Hildr flashing a wicked grin, which gave an inkling of the warrior she had once been. The Valkyrie order had raised their charges to be warrior priestesses, teaching them to fight with axe, spear and bow and to heal the wounded from the time they were girls. Hildr was right. Hundr and Einar had stormed Vanylven to take it for King Harald Fairhair. Vanylven lay within a fjord whose waters were as smooth as glass, and the previous Jarl had built two jetties which jutted across the fjord's width. They removed the great chain from between the timber-built towers at the end of each jetty for merchant vessels and friendly ships. An enemy's ships would flounder on that chain, and Einar and Hundr's warriors would pour arrows and spears onto the decks from the towers and jetty. So, to attack Vanylven was to die. When taking Vanylven, Hundr and Ragnhild had scaled one tower under a hail of enemy missiles and lowered the chain. It had been a hard fight. Rollo had fought alongside Hundr that day. His size and strength made him a formidable warrior and a man to fear.

"We did," agreed Hundr, "but we found the only way to do it, and Vanylven won't be retaken in our lifetime. Now, come, Finn, I will ride with you to the towers, and we shall discover which of your uncles approaches."

Finn nodded. "What if it is Halvdan coming to kill me?"

"We won't simply let him take you. And besides, you are not an easy man to kill. The last time Halvdan saw you was when you were a boy, and he tried to kill you then." Hundr's old friend Sten Sleggya, the Sledgehammer, had saved Finn from that fate when his mother Saoirse had led Finn into a Ragnarsson trap. Hundr smiled at Sigrid, and she reached up to grab his hand. He kissed hers and stroked her scarred face with his other. He understood her struggles with the baby. Sigrid wanted nothing more than to take to the Whale Road with Hundr and Einar, but they also wanted children. The gods had brought them luck enough to make Sigrid pregnant, and there was joy in that. Hundr loved her dearly, but as he ran from the hall behind Finn, he was secretly pleased to be away from her ill humour and hoped the baby would come soon.

"Take a crew with you," called Einar, "and if it is Halvdan, sound the alarm. He will die here in our fjord, and we shall add his ships to our fleet."

Hundr and Finn rode to where the eastern jetty joined the Vanylven coastline at an outcrop of slate grey rock. Thirty of Hundr's men rode at their backs, the sound of their hooves like thunder in the calm evening. The moon cast a pallid reflection of the fjord's gently lapping waters, and Hundr rode with his two swords, one in a scabbard at his waist and the other strapped to his back. They rode around the wide curve of Vanylven's bay. Beneath hills of swaying pines and beyond the great chain and twin towers were four warships rowing across the fjord. As he reached the point where timber jetty met rock, Finn leapt from the saddle in a fluid motion, and his boots landed heavily on the dark planking, which stretched out into the water's depths. He ran along the jetty and had almost reached the guard tower as Hundr dismounted from his own horse.

"It's been many a year since I was a lithe as that," quipped Bush. He slipped heavily from the saddle, grunting as his paunch pushed against the horse's flanks. Bush stepped awkwardly onto the jetty, and for a moment, Hundr thought he would stumble into the water in his brynjar chain mail coat, but the grizzled shipmaster righted himself and blew his cheeks out. He adjusted the axe at his belt and the seax at his lower back, and together they strode along the jetty, eyes fixed on the approaching ships.

"Drakkars," said Hundr. "Big ones." The ships had lowered their sails within the fjord's waters, protected on all sides from the wind by the hills. Oar blades bit into the smooth water,

THE RAVEN AND THE NINE

sending ripples dancing out from their hulls and powering the sleek war vessels forward. Hundr tried to count the oar blades, but between their rhythmic rise and fall and making sure he didn't step into the water as he walked, he lost count.

"Fifty-man crews, each of them," said Bush. "Fine ships, oak strakes and one-piece keels."

Fifty men meant two hundred warriors, enough to match Hundr's own force. But not enough to fight their way from their ships up to the towers, remove the chain, and storm the port whilst Hundr's and Einar's warriors rained arrows and spears down upon them. Should they make it through that hail of death and get ashore, those men would then meet a shield wall of Hundr's warriors, Viking veterans of countless fights and fearsome men. To do that, a man would need to bring a fleet of ten ships or more into Vanylven's fjord, and even then, it would be a hard fight.

They reached the tower and climbed the smooth timber ladders to the summit.

"They've taken off their prow beasts," said Finn, pointing towards the ships. They crept closer, having slowed. The lead ship came on as the rest backed oars to halt themselves safely out of range of the men upon the towers and jetty. The leading ship, which Hundr noted at this close distance, was larger than the others, with twenty oars on each side of her long keel. With no wind, the effect of the approaching raven sigil blown full by the wind was lost, and a small black triangle hung limply from the mast post bearing the white-outlined raven. At sea and in a good wind, those ship's sails would billow full with a gigantic raven, and all who saw that symbol would know fear. Still though, to see even the small version of that banner was to know that a Ragnarsson approached, a scion of that family feared from the azure waters of Ispania, across the coasts of England, Ireland, and Frankia, and as far east and southeast as the distant lands of the Rus and the Khazars.

Hundr ground his teeth, searching the deck for any sign of Halvdan Ragnarsson, against whom he had fought a terrible and bloody battle on Dublin's walls. He had lost friends in the fight, like Sten Sleggya, a man who he had loved like a father.

"If it's Halvdan, don't let him in," Bush warned, shaking his head. "No matter what slippery words slide off his tongue to pour his deep cunning into our ears. He's as sneaky as a starving stoat."

"I lived with my uncle Halvdan for a long time," said Finn, frowning at Bush.

This surprised Hundr because Halvdan had tried to kill Finn during that dreadful fight on

Dublin's high walls, and Finn was but a pup at the time.

"Do you remember him?" asked Hundr.

"I do. He was a harsh man, cruel even. But he treated me well. He allowed my mother's priest to teach me the ways of Christ and the teaching of Lord Jesus."

"You were the son of his brother Ivar, who was King in Dublin. So, he wanted you close. He wanted to rule as your regent in Ireland, and then he tried to kill you and take the crown for himself." Hundr spoke savagely and saw a flash of anger in Finn's brown eyes. However, at that moment, the deep wail of a war horn pealed out from the lead ship, as long and clear as though sounded by Thor himself from his hall Thruthvanger deep in Asgard. The sound broke the tension, and though the night was casting a dark shroud over the water, Hundr caught sight of an enormous man making his way to the lead ship's prow. He ducked beneath rigging and came to stand with an arm hooked around the prow post, strangely low with its snarling beast head removed. Hundr smiled because there were few men in the world who could boast such great height and breadth of shoulder, and one was his friend, Bjorn Ironside.

"Ho there!" called the man in a deep voice, almost as stirring as the sound of the war horn.

"I am Erik Bjornsson, a Lothbrok; come to see my father's friends. I seek the Man with the Dog's Name, Einar the Brawler, and Finn Ivarsson, my cousin."

"I didn't know Bjorn had a son?" Bush lipped, a frown creasing his wind-darkened face.

"Look at him," said Hundr, smiling. "He is every inch his father's son. Let him in."

"Welcome, cousin!" called Finn, cupping a hand to his mouth as he shouted across the water.

"We'd best ride back to Einar," said Bush, rubbing his hands together. "If this Erik is his father's son, we had better be ready with plenty of ale and food to welcome him."

Four men hauled the mighty chain towards the western tower and opened the fjord entrance to Vanylven for Erik's ships. They slid in through the towers under slow oars, Erik standing proudly at the prow of his ship and waving greeting at the warriors in the towers. Hundr, Finn and Bush rode back to Einar with the news, and although Sigrid and Hildr's faces soured at the impending feast spoiling their evening meal together, the people of Vanylven buzzed like a beehive in deep summer at the approach of friendly ships. It meant ale, food, and merrymaking, all at their Jarl's expense.

"Bastards will eat me out of hall and home," Einar grumbled to Hildr. "We shall likely starve for weeks afterwards, and it will cost me a small fortune to buy in more ale and food to replenish what Erik and his men will consume." Although he complained, there was a glint in Einar's eye, and once she recovered from the shock of the news, even Sigrid seemed to have the weight of her long pregnancy lifted from her shoulders. She strode around the hall with Hildr, ordering feasting tables to be set with cups and plates, for bread to be brought, and for casks of ale to be rolled in.

"I must change," Sigrid muttered, hooking her arm through Hundr's. She smiled at him, her cheeks red with excitement.

"You look wonderful as you are. This suits you," Hundr said, laying a hand gently upon her swollen belly. "You glow like the embers of a hall fire on a winter morning. The baby will come soon, Sigrid, and I couldn't be happier."

She smiled again and kissed him on the cheek before striding away to fuss over how a servant set up an iron spit over the fire. The hall doors creaked and opened slowly, and in the torchlight, a big man walked through and stood with his hands upon his hips. His men paused behind him, and not one of them came higher than his shoulders. His head was crowned with a wild, curly shock of red hair, and a long, thick beard of the brightest orange, like a flame, was held in a thick braid woven with little metal trinkets that sparkled in the firelight. A shining brynjar covered him from neck to knee, and from his shoulders hung an extraordinary cloak of white bear fur, so thick it made his wide frame seem even more impressive. He pulled a huge, long-handled war axe across his shoulder and held it out for one of Einar's men to take. That was a mark of respect, for men did not bring weapons into a feasting hall. Ale and axes were never a wise mix amongst the Northmen. Erik passed it over in one hand, but when the servant took hold of it, the mighty weapon proved too heavy, and the servant's two hands dropped so that the butt of the axe's haft banged loudly upon the ground.

"Careful with that, man," Erik boomed, white teeth showing beneath the bush of his beard. "Dwarves forged my axe in the days when the gods walked the earth. Tyr himself would be proud to wield such a weapon. If he could lift it." Erik turned to all in the hall and winked, and they erupted in peals of laughter. The servant dragged the weapon away. Its head gleamed, carved into two wide sweeps like a single wing of a butterfly.

"Welcome, Erik Bjornsson," said Einar, and he strode toward him with open arms. "I am lucky to count your father, Bjorn Ironside, son of Ragnar Lothbrok, as a friend. You are most welcome here in Vanylven."

Erik came forward and accepted Einar's embrace. They held each other in a small test of strength, each man hugging the other as tight as a bear, and the crowd in the hall chuckled. Erik was a half head taller than Einar, and Hundr had seen few men top his old friend for height.

"The skalds are right about you, Einar," said Erik as he pulled away from Einar's embrace. "You are as big as a bear and strong as an ox. My father sends his greetings. Now, where is the Man with the Dog's Name, whose fame flies across the world upon the wings of Odin's ravens?"

"I am Hundr." He stepped forward and raised a hand in greeting. "I fought back-to-back with your father once in Frankia. We thought we would die there, and what a death it would have been. How is Bjorn, King of the Svears?"

"He is well, and he talks of you often. Although I expected you to be a bigger man." Erik threw his head back and laughed, and Hundr couldn't help but laugh along with him. Erik stepped forward and grabbed Hundr's wrist in the warrior's grip. His hand was huge, like a beast's paw, and a stale smell wafted from his bear fur cloak to fill Hundr's nostrils. "Last we heard, you were in Novgorod, causing mayhem, no doubt?"

"There was some hard fighting last summer, and we lost many friends and brothers of the blade. But such is the life of a Viking."

"Come, drink with us," said Einar, leading Erik to the high table, cleared now of the earlier feast and laden with fresh bread and pots of ale. "You and your men are welcome. I must introduce you to my wife, Hildr, and Hundr's wife, Sigrid Ketilsdottir."

"The daughter of the great Ketil Flatnose, no less," smiled Erik, taking Sigrid's hand and kissing it. "I am honoured to meet the daughter of so famous a warrior." He placed his giant hand upon Sigrid's belly, and she winced at the over-familiarity. Hundr smiled to himself. It was ever the way when a woman was with child. People believe her condition grants them permission to feel the swollen bump of her belly, which contains the deep magic of a new life growing within. Yet they would never dream of touching the stomach of a woman who was not with child. "A son, I can sense it. I will pray to the gods, to Odin, Thor and Frey, that this child is born healthy and for your safety, my lady. I will pray that the child grows up to be just as feared and well-known as his father." Erik flashed a wide grin, his teeth the pure white of a child's teeth, and that smile creased his broad face into such a mischievous look that Sigrid placed her hand over Erik's and laughed fondly at him.

"Erik," piped Finn, sidling around a thick timber post which rose high into the rafters. Finn frowned at Einar and Hundr as if they had slighted him by not formally introducing him. "I am Finn Ivarsson."

Erik turned to Finn and eyed him up and down. He nodded and then darted forward to pull Finn into a deep embrace.

"Well met, cousin," Erik said, and he leant back so that he lifted Finn off his feet. "It is an honour to meet the son of my uncle Ivar."

"Well met indeed," said Finn, and he clapped Erik on the back before shaking himself free of the bear hug. Erik was a head taller than Finn and far broader in both chest and shoulder. "You are most welcome here, Erik Bjornsson. I hope we shall become friends."

"I, too, hold that hope. For I come to you seeking aid."

Hundr glanced at Einar, and the Jarl gnawed at his beard, returning Hundr's gaze from the corners of his eye. For the son of the King of Sweden, perhaps the most famous Viking in the North, Bjorn Ironside, to come to Vanylven for help felt like the work of the Norns; those three sisters who sit at the foot of the great tree Yggdrasil where they weave together the threads of men's lives at their whim. They cackle at hopes and dreams, cast great men asunder, and raise the lowest to the peaks of glory. Hundr had felt their presence in his own life. He had risen from a homeless wanderer in the lands of the Rus to join Einar's crew of Viking warriors aboard the Seaworm and then had become a fair-famed sea Jarl in his own right.

"Tell us, Erik, what could have happened that you have sailed from your father's lands and armies to seek our help?" asked Einar, the cliff of his face creased into a suspicious frown.

"My brother, Refil, fought and was lost in Ireland. Men say he is a captive there, and I will sail to free him. So, I come to the Man with the Dog's Name and Einar the Brawler for your help."

FIVE

The hall fire burned and crackled, and smoke swirled up through the hole in the roofing thatch to disappear into the night sky. Men drank and laughed, the noise of it rumbling around the rafters in a constant roar like a storm at sea. More bread, cheese, and meat from Einar's stores came out on platters. His servants rummaged deep into Einar's larders to keep Erik's men fed, along with his own warriors who had crammed into Vanylven's hall. Einar's eyes washed over the burly warriors supping his ale, beads of it in their beards and more jugs coming out of the kitchens to slake the fighting men's thirst for its thick, comforting taste. Einar winced at the amount of silver he would need to spend to replenish his stores but then smiled to himself that it would be Rollo's silver and not his own. This was the price of Jarldom, and it was the custom of all Northmen to welcome guests with hospitality, which meant lots of food and ale.

Einar sat in his chair at the high table, his hands curled around the smooth wood of its carved arms. Hildr sat to his right, and Erik sat in the place of honour between Einar and Hundr. Erik took a drink from a curved horn, a beautiful thing chased with silver at its widest end, one which Einar kept for only his most important guests.

"You brew fine ale here in Norway, Jarl Einar," Erik said, licking his lips and smiling in his red beard. "And I thank you for your hospitality."

"As the son of Bjorn Ironside, there will always be a warm welcome for you in my hall, Erik. How is your father?"

"Fat and happy. He has wealth, warriors, power, land and women of such beauty to dim the sun."

"So, he has achieved what all Vikings dream of."

"Just so, the raven banner controls the seas between Sweden and the trade route south to the lands of the Rus. My father's ports see such wealth, Lord Einar. Pelts, silver, gold, amber and soft silks from further east than any Viking has sailed."

"Tell us then of your brother's troubles."

Erik frowned and took another drink from his horn. "My father and my elder brother do not see eye to eye. Refil yearns to sail and fight just as my grandfather, Ragnar, and my father and uncles did. He is a Viking and would take to the Whale Road with my father's ships. Refil sees himself as the Ragnarsson who can emulate all that has come before, the sacking of Paris and conquering of Dublin, York and the Danelaw. He would fight harder, sail further, and forge a reputation greater than any in our family."

"I knew your grandfather and your uncles. I served Ivar for many years as his shipmaster. Ragnar was a man to both fear and love, and I was fortunate to have grown up around him. A ferocious man capable of great cruelty and also great kindness. Your brother has set himself a task worthy of the gods themselves. The days when Ragnar and Ivar sacked Paris, Dublin, and York were different times. Saxons, Franks, and the Irish were not ready for us. Their soft Christ god had brought them to their knees, and to them, it was unthinkable that men would attack their churches. Now, they protect rivers with ships and bridges, and churches have warriors close by." Einar leant forward across the feasting table and beckoned to Hundr, who was in conversation with Sigrid and Finn. Hundr's one eye flicked to Einar. "Did we not hear that King Alfred of Wessex builds fortresses all across his lands to protect them from our raids?"

"Aye," said Hundr, raising his voice to be heard over the din inside the hall. "The Saxons call them burhs, and they are under construction in estuaries and rivers. Alfred will fill the burhs with warriors, and his people can flee to them whenever an enemy sail is sighted. He is clever, this King Alfred. He is also brave. I saw him fight at Ethandun, which was a savage battle."

"So, Erik, I think your brother sets himself an impossible dream. But, as I say, I knew Ragnar, and he, too, was a dreamer. For what takes us to the Whale Road but dreams of reputation and glory?"

"I envy you that, Jarl Einar. You must tell me a tale of my grandfather before this night is over. My father humoured Refil for a time. He granted him ships and lent him his shipmasters. I sailed with them, and there were great days. We sailed across to the islands of Jutland and raided great sea Lords. We harried the Wends and killed the Rus. Refil is a warrior, daring and skilled. But he is also my father's heir. And no son of Ragnar has died peacefully in his bed. So, the King would keep Refil at home and keep him safe and ready to sit on the throne one day."

"A small price to pay, to be King of the Svear when Bjorn dies."

"For most men, yes. But Refil took three of my father's ships anyway and sailed to Ireland. He sailed away on an ebb tide hidden by darkness. That was a year ago. News came to us this spring on the lips of Saxon merchants that Refil had become embroiled in a war in Ireland. A war between my uncle Halvdan and an Irish king. There are rumours he was taken, others that he is dead, and one more fearsome." Erik leant in close, and Einar's nose filled with the rank stink of his bear fur cloak. The whites of Erik's eyes grew large like full moons, and he fixed Einar with a piercing stare, placing a huge hand upon Einar's forearm. "We heard that an Irish Witch-Queen has bewitched Refil, and he now fights for her against Halvdan."

"Halvdan still rules in Dublin?"

"He does, last we heard. But Ireland is like England was, filled with small kingdoms, and each king believes himself to be as powerful as an old emperor of the Rome folk. A man with three goats and a flea-bitten dog can call himself King in Ireland."

Einar sat back in his chair and nodded grimly. He had fought in Ireland and lost friends there. Hrist, a Valkyrie warrior beloved of Hildr, Sten Sleggya and Kolo. It was a place of striking beauty and savage Irish warriors who were as wild and untamed as the grey seas that lashed its coast's crags and cliffs. "Bjorn will not send men to find his son?"

"He will not. My father was furious that Refil took three of his ships. He denounced Refil as a thief. But he has given me ships and his finest captains to bring Refil home. A king must save face, but a man would do anything for his son. My father even sent his champion, Styrbjorn the Dancer, along with me to seek my brother."

"The Dancer?" said Einar and spat out a mouthful of bread he was chewing.

"Aye, it might not seem like a name fit for a warrior. But wait until you see Styrbjorn fight."

"I shall have to see this man. Show him to me."

"There." Erik pointed to three men, two giant Vikings with beards covering their chests, their arms thick with rings, and a smaller man dressed in a leather breastplate with a lean, clean-shaven face. Light from a torch fixed to the wall bathed them in an orange glow, and the big men were front rankers for sure, thick-chested men strengthened by years pulling an oar, wearing heavy mail brynjars and hefting weapons. Any man would fear fighting such scarred growlers.

"The big one with the scar on his cheek, or the

bigger one with the silver torc around his neck?"

Erik chuckled. "The small man, that is Styrbjorn. He is the greatest swordsman in the world." He shrugged and then reddened as Einar threw his head back and laughed.

"You have not seen Hundr fight yet, Erik. But I like your little man. Maybe we will have him fight one of my men with practice swords?"

"If you wish, Jarl Einar." Erik's tone became serious, his humour melting like ice under the sun. "But will you sail with me? Help me rescue my brother from whatever fate has befallen him in Ireland?"

Einar frowned. The memories of that far-away island sat heavily inside his thought cage. He glanced at Hildr, who shrugged as if to say *don't ask me.* Einar held out his cup for a servant to fill it with ale, and he took a drink. To get to Ireland, they would need to brave the dangers of the Whale Road from the coast of Norway to the Orkney Islands and sail around the wild northern coasts where savage Picts lived beyond the high cliffs and crashing seas. They would sail ever westwards, hoping for fair winds, but when those winds did not come, they would lower their oars and heave their warships through the swell, praying to Ran and Njorth for calm waters. Einar peered over at Hundr, but he was deep in conversation with Finn and Sigrid. Hundr had loved an Irish Queen once. They had met amidst a desperate ambush in the forests of Northumbria when she was a Princess, but in the end, she was destined to marry Ivar the Boneless, and their love turned to hatred and bitterness. So Hundr would not relish returning to Dublin. Undoubtedly, there was wealth in the city, it was one of the major Viking slaving ports outside of Hedeby, and for enough silver, a man could buy a woman with skin the colour of rich chestnut or a skilled healer from the distant east with knowledge of potions and herbs that can make a man travel to the otherworld. Einar and Hundr had left Ireland with little but the clothes on their backs, barely surviving a brutal war with Eystein Longaxe and Halvdan Ragnarsson. That had cost them a season's raiding, with silver for their warriors and their friends and lovers cut down and lost forever amidst the brutal fighting.

Einar reached under the table and held Hildr's hand. She squeezed his in return, and her touch made him smile. Erik stared at him, but Einar could not answer his request. The hearth fire warmed him, and his cloak was thick and comforting. He loved Hildr. Waking up with her each morning was a joy. They would spend their days walking through Vanylven, dispensing justice in the hall, or dealing with the myriad problems arising from running a large town. So, Einar's head told him to refuse Erik, to wish him luck, and to send barrels of dried fish and ale to his ships for the long journey ahead. He would wave to Erik from Vanylven's fjord bridge and return to his fire and his love. Einar's heart, however, longed for the crash of the sea, for the thrill of sailing a long-keeled *drakkar* through surging waves. His soul hungered for the challenge of war and the joy of battle. For Einar Rosti was a Viking, born and raised to axe and tiller. He did not stay warm by the fire whilst other men risked all for glory. The gates of Valhalla would not open for a man who died peacefully in his bed, holding hands with his wife and swathed in soft furs. For men who wished to go to Odin's corpse hall to fight all day and drink ale from curved horns with heroes for eternity, they must die in battle clutching axe, spear or sword with fallen foes crushed beneath their boots.

"We will help you find your brother, Erik," said Einar. The words spilt out before he could control himself, and his heart quickened at the thought of sailing out once more to battle and an unknown fate.

Erik Bjornsson slammed his hand down on the tabletop, spilling ale and making platters of food jump. "My father said Jarl Einar was ever a great man for a war. Will you all sail? What of the Man with the Dog's Name and the son of the Boneless?"

Einar ground his teeth and winced. He was Jarl in Vanylven and had his own warriors to bring to a fight, but only the Fjord Bear belonged to him. The Seaworm and the three remaining *drakkars* belonged to Hundr, as did the warriors who pulled her oars. "I will talk to Hundr and Finn. Now, what about a show to stir the lads' souls, eh?"

"What do you have in mind?"

"Your man, The Dancer, I want to see his sword skill you boasted of. Let's match him against one of our men and see what he can do. Wooden swords or real ones wrapped in cloth?"

"Very well," Erik grinned, wagging a thick finger at Einar. "But warn your man that Styrbjorn is as fast as a Saxon running from a Viking blade." Erik rose and placed a hand on Einar's shoulder, bending to look Einar in the eye. "I thank you for your friendship and your courage, Lord Einar."

Bjorn honoured him by calling Einar 'Lord'. The Ragnarssons were as close to a royal dynasty as you could get in the North, where the strength of a man's arm made him King rather than his birthright. Erik strode from the high table towards Styrbjorn and his companions.

"Will you come with us to Ireland?" asked Einar, turning to Hildr. "We could use your bow?"

She smiled and shook her head sadly. "I'm afraid those days are far in the past, my love. Don't just stay here with me because I will miss you, but because I'll worry about you when you're away. I will watch the fjord, hoping to see your ships rowing across the water to bring you home to me. One day, Einar, you will not return, for that is our way. The Viking way. But I want you to go. You are not a man to spend a summer at home whilst other men fight and take their ships to where there is danger. But with danger comes wealth, so bring us back silver and gold and stories of brave deeds and enemies killed."

Einar felt a slight tug in his throat. "What did I do to deserve a woman like you? A Valkyrie priestess and shield maiden of Upsala. I will return, my love, or I will save a place for you in Odin's hall."

"I shall go to Sigrid, for she will not take it well that her husband will be at sea when their first child is born." She stood and moved gracefully along the raised dais towards Sigrid. Hildr took her hand and led her through a small door at the hall's rear.

I haven't asked him to go yet.

"Jarl Einar," Erik called in his deep voice. "Styrbjorn will fight, so pick your man. He has his own sword, a blade forged in Frankia by the finest smiths, so the fighters will use their own blades wrapped in cloth."

"Very well, Lord Erik." Einar nodded. He beckoned to his men as he rose from his chair. "Make some space, lads. There's going to be a fight."

The men cheered and erupted from their feasting benches like bees from a kicked hive. They dragged the benches to the hall's sides, the timber legs scraping on the hard-packed earthen floor. Einar followed Hundr and Finn down to where the men formed a tight circle, pressing close in to get as close to the fighting as possible.

"Is that his champion?" said Finn with raised eyebrows, pointing at Styrbjorn, one of the smallest and slightest-built men in the room.

"That's him," said Einar. "They call him The Dancer."

The three men watched Styrbjorn rolling his shoulders and shaking his arms loose. He stretched one leg before him, leant low to stretch the muscles, and then repeated the move for his other leg. He took a sword from Einar's steward, for Erik and Einar's men had all left their weapons at the hall door out of respect for Norse custom.

"That looks more like a long knitting needle than a sword. Surely the thing will break?" Finn tutted. "I'll fight him, Einar."

"No, lad," said Hundr, and he ran his hand along his beard. "Any man that small but considered to be the champion of Bjorn Ironside's warriors is a man to be wary of."

"What? Look at him. All I need to do is…"

"Bjorn's crews are made up of men who have fought for Ivar, Bjorn, and Ubba. They are the sons of men who fought for Ragnar Lothbrok. These warriors are raised to be skilled, vicious, and merciless. Look at them." Hundr cast his hand around the hall. It was filled with big men—men with thick chests and brawny arms. Scarred men of reputation, men to fear. "And this is their champion. Without question, he is a killer. He must be fast and lethal, so don't fight him, Finn. If you lose, you will lose face in front of your men. They revere and respect you at the moment. Don't squander that in a fight for nothing. Let someone else fight him."

"You don't think I can win?"

"Hundr is right," said Einar, stepping in before Finn became angered. "We will let Amundr fight him. Let's see how The Dancer fares against the giant."

"I can beat him," Finn huffed, crossing his arms, and Einar noticed the withering look he threw at Hundr. Luckily it was on the side of

Hundr's dead eye, so he did not see the anger there.

"Amundr!" Einar called. Men moved apart on the hall's western side, some of their own will, but an enormous man who elbowed his way through them thrust the rest out of his way. Of a size with Erik, Amundr's arms were like two hams, and his hands were the size of feasting platters.

"Yes, Lord Einar," he said in a deep, rumbling voice.

"You can fight him, but don't kill him."

Amundr turned and cocked an eyebrow at the little man, who continued to perform various stretches. "Is he a dwarf?"

Einar laughed. "No, he is not. But he is fast, so be careful."

"Can I use my axe?"

"No, a sword wrapped in cloth."

Amundr shrugged and nodded. Einar raised Amundr's hand, and the men in the hall cheered wildly, roaring so loud that the thatch almost lifted from the roof beams. A man handed a cup of ale to Amundr, and he downed it in one go, the dregs spilling down his braided beard, dripping into the floor rushes. He stalked to the centre of the circle of men, and Einar's steward handed Amundr a sword wrapped in an old, faded cloak.

"So, what does Erik want?" asked Hundr as they watched Styrbjorn take up his sword and swish it through the air in three broad strokes.

Einar leant in to speak quietly to Hundr, almost whispering so that Finn would not hear. "He wants us to go to Ireland with him. His brother is lost there. Bjorn and the missing son, Refil, are estranged after a public falling out. But Bjorn still wants his son found and brought home; he just doesn't want to send a force of his own warriors and lose face."

"So, he sends Erik with his ships and asks us to go with him?"

"Aye. Halvdan still rules in Dublin, and there is talk of a Witch-Queen of the Irish." Einar glanced at Hundr from the corners of his eyes without turning his head. Hundr's face flushed a deep crimson.

"We have a score to settle with Halvdan. Do you think it's her?"

"Could be. Last we saw of Saoirse was her falling wounded, with Ragnhild's arrow in her belly. She could have lived."

"Fate was not kind to us the last time we sailed to Ireland. Do you think it's wise to test the Norns again by returning?"

"Dublin is rich, and last time we left with nothing. This time we could leave that cursed place as rich as merchants from Serkland."

"If she is alive, she is Finn's mother and will want him back. Halvdan still wants him dead. After all, Finn is Ivar's heir and the rightful King of Dublin."

Styrbjorn waved Amundr on and strode to the centre of the fighting circle on the balls of his feet, his sword held loosely at his side. Amundr grunted and marched towards him, his blade like a twig in his monstrous fist.

"I know all of that," said Einar. "But I still think we should go; it's early summer, and over three-quarters of good fighting season is still left of the year. So let's find Bjorn's son and make ourselves rich whilst the kings of Ireland are at war. They won't be watching for us if they are too busy watching each other. There are churches there and wealth to be won."

"There is a strange warp and weft to this, Einar. I can feel it."

"But will you sail?"

Hundr smiled and shrugged. "Of course, I will."

Einar laughed, throwing his head back and holding his shaking belly. He clapped Hundr on the back because he knew his friend better than most, and there could never really have been any doubt that Hundr would sail. Einar called for more ale, and a servant filled two cups, the contents sloshing over the rims as Einar passed one to Hundr. Einar felt alive. The prospect of returning to sea always filled him with joy. There was little in life to compare to the surge of the sea beneath his hand on the tiller or the thrill of battle, even though his longing for Hildr would cut him like a belly wound.

Amundr lunged forward with his sword, deceptively fast for a big man, but Styrbjorn skipped away on his toes, not even bothering to raise his blade. Amundr kept moving, turning that lunge into an upward flick, and the tip of his wrapped sword sang close to Styrbjorn's face, but the little man leant back and spun away. He jogged lithely to the other side of the square and swung his sword in wide arcs as though he was still warming his muscles for the fight. Amundr turned and grunted, his lip curling.

"Not much drengskapr in this," said Hundr. Which was true. The way of the warrior was to stand and fight, not to take a backward step before an enemy. But The Dancer was something else, and Einar feared for Amundr's pride.

Amundr stalked across the open circle, and now he held his thin blade before him, its tip flickering like a serpent's tongue. The warriors huddled around the fighting space roared, the Vanylven men shouting their rage at Styrbjorn because he would not stand and trade blows, and Erik's men bellowing support for their champion. Amundr raised his sword to strike, but the slight man darted inside him and flicked his sword up to slash at Amundr's ribs, and the big man jerked his blade just in time to deflect the cut. Styrbjorn kept moving, ducking under Amundr's tree-trunk arms. He came up with his sword held in a reverse grip, dragging the blade across Amundr's thighs. In a proper fight, that cut would have come below the line of Amundr's brynjar chain mail coat and sliced open his legs, and Amundr bellowed with fury. He thrust a paw out to grab Styrbjorn, but the little man skipped away as though on winged feet. As he moved backwards, Styrbjorn struck out with his sword, and Einar's jaw fell open because the strike was almost too fast to see. The cloth-wrapped sword slapped across Amundr's face, and then Styrbjorn stepped in to rap his blade across Amundr's wrist. Amundr yelped in pain, as effeminate a sound as Einar had ever heard come out of a warrior, and his sword clattered to the ground. The hall fell silent, stunned at the speed and skill of the slight swordsman. Styrbjorn twirled his blade and brought it to a stop behind his back before bowing deeply to Amundr. He held out his hand, and for a moment, Einar thought Amundr would rip his arm off, but then the big man laughed, clasped Styrbjorn's arm in the warrior's grip, and pulled the smaller man into an enormous bear hug. Amundr lifted

Styrbjorn from his feet, then dropped and raised his hand in salute.

"Bring some ale for the Champion of the Svears!" Amundr roared, and the hall erupted into a cheering mess of ale-swilling Vikings.

SIX

Eight ships sailed out from Vanylven. They rowed through the fjord bridge, where the townspeople thronged the twin jetties to wave them off. Young lads climbed the towers to call and wave at the warriors, dreaming of the days when they, too, would sail out on such magnificent drakkars armed with axe, spear, sword and shield. The wind filled the ships' sails as they headed southwest along the coast of Norway, the one-eye sigil stark upon heavy woollen sails pulled taut by gusts of rain and whipping sea gales. Hundr had cut the throat of a goat and let the blood drip over the Seaworm's prow and hull, praying for such weather, and Njorth had heard his prayer.

The ships kept close, racing across the heaving mass of the Whale Road. Their hulls sliced through towering waves, crashing into troughs and rising on peaks, men laughing at the sheer joy of it. The warships raced to the vast cliffs of the Shetland Islands, spending two nights anchored in a hidden cove where waves smashed against the unforgiving coastline, which rose from the sea as though the lands had been carved open by a god's giant axe in the time before men roamed the earth. Men ventured ashore to fetch water, search for birds' eggs, and steal sheep from the rugged people who lived there. Stealing was a gamble, for such men were Vikings themselves, welcoming of visitors for a price, but also men to be wary of. The islands were wind-whipped places of hard weather and even harder people, carving a living out of rock, ice and storm-lashed hilltops. But Shetland and Orkney were the thoroughfares for ships sailing from Norway, whether they meant to sail southeast to Northumbria or Frankia or southwest along the ragged Pictish coast and down to Ireland.

Malevolent squalls swallowed the fleet off the northern coast of Lachlainn, sheets of driving rain and skies as dark as ash drove ships off course. The Seaworm, Fjord Bear, and two of Erik's ships waited for two days searching islands and finding vessels from the fleet repairing torn rigging or damaged hull planks.

Ships would come to look at them, wolves looking for easy prey in dangerous waters, but their captains banked away in wide sweeps once they saw the size of Hundr and Erik's fleet. Sea monsters also came to peer at them with grey faces and canny eyes, rolling in the white-tipped waves and dancing in the wake of the wind-borne warships. The moon changed from a bright crescent to a half-full circle of silver light in the time it took them to reach Ireland's coastline. The shipmasters like Bush and other experienced sailors in Erik's fleet knew that coast well, it being a major route for merchants and warriors alike. Goods could pass easily from Northumbria, which spanned the north of England, across to the markets in Dublin and then north and east to Norway, Jutland and the Vik. The fleet made the crossing to Ireland's rugged coast against a savage wind which blew from the north, as cold and hard as an eagle's heart. Clouds fled before that wind like hares running from hunting dogs, and the sun died over the distant, brooding coastline. The sea surged in a grey-green mass in that channel, and froth flew off the waves to lash the men's faces in a salty whip. Waves thundered like galloping horses in a mad charge, racing to roar and shatter on the jagged Irish cliffs, the undertow sucking and ripping at the seabed before it was crushed again by another galloping rush of violent waves.

Erik brought his ships close to shore at an inlet a day's sailing north of Dublin. He had called to Hundr across their bows complaining of lack of water and food, and so he would send men ashore to fill barrels and hunt for meat. Hundr waved him on and put his own fleet to anchor in a curved bay, protected from wind and the worst of the sea by steep hills on each side. Hundr let his men rest for the day, and they lolled on the decks, drinking the dregs of their ale barrels and eating hard oatcakes and dried fish. It had been an arduous journey, and the wind had not always been favourable. Hundr's back ached, and his shoulders burned from the turns he had taken at the oars, but such work was good for a warrior's strength. Einar's Fjord Bear rowed close, and the crew lashed the two ships together with seal hide ropes, allowing the men to jump between ships to share stories and trade provisions. So, on a bright day where the sky was as pale blue as Sigrid's eyes, Hundr rested his arms on the sheer strake at the Seaworm's stern. He rolled up the sleeves of his jerkin, and the sun warmed his neck and forearms.

"We should start forcing the men to wash themselves," said Ragnhild, her scarred face creased into a frown. She leant away from Sigvarth Trollhands as he swung past beneath the rigging, and whilst Hundr caught a waft of Sigvarth's pungent odour, he knew he smelled little better himself.

"There aren't many opportunities to bathe at sea unless a man falls overboard," said Einar, lowering his chin to smell his own jerkin. Their weapons and armour sat beneath rowing benches wrapped in oily fleeces to keep out the sea's salty spray, which turned iron and steel to rust and ruin.

"Some of these bastards want throwing overboard," Ragnhild quipped, and Hundr laughed. She had also come aboard from the ship she captained, the Wind Elk. "At least they are good in a fight, I suppose."

"We shall wait here for Erik," said Hundr, "and enjoy the rest after a hard journey. We are lucky we didn't lose any of our ships, and only one man lost."

"Old Fjolnir died of the coughing sickness, and it's a pity he didn't get to die with an axe in his hand," sighed Einar, reaching for the hammer amulet at his neck to ward off that bad luck.

"The last time we saw this coastline, we barely escaped with our lives," Ragnhild murmured. She leant on the smooth ship's timber next to Hundr and stared towards the shoreline. A single, low house roofed with dark green turf was visible above a grey cliff face. Smoke wafted from the building in thin tendrils to drift into the vastness of the pale sky.

"Kolo was a good man and a fine warrior. I still miss his laughter," said Hundr. He shifted his hand and placed it upon Ragnhild's, and at first, she flinched at the gesture but then nodded slowly and let his hand rest there. They were brother and sister of the blade and not so used to sharing emotions or physical contact beyond the punch and kick of weapons practice or the clinch and throw of wrestling back on Vanylven's shore.

"He was..." she said, struggling to find the words. "The only man I have ever loved. I broke my oath to Odin for him, and he died here on Dublin's walls. But he died in battle, and I love him all the more for that."

Kolo had been an enormous warrior whom Hundr had fought a Holmgang against when Kolo served Jarl Haesten. Haesten had bought Kolo as a slave during the legendary journey he and Bjorn Ironside had made south around the unknown coasts of far Ispania. His skin was the colour of the darkest night, and he had fought like a demon. Hundr and Kolo had become friends, and Kolo and Ragnhild had become lovers. She had forsaken her oath of chastity to Odin, sworn when she joined the Valkyrie order of warrior priestesses. But an oath was worth breaking for a love which burned so bright as that of Ragnhild and Kolo.

"We have had little luck with the sons of Ragnar," said Einar. "Let's hope that changes with his grandson."

"If Erik's brother is with Halvdan in Dublin, then he shouldn't be hard to find."

"Halvdan won't simply welcome us with open arms. He will not have forgotten how we fought his men and stole Finn away before Halvdan could cut his throat. Halvdan is King in Dublin, a wealthy trading port, and we are bringing the rightful heir back within his grasp. If Erik's brother is with Halvdan, then we should sail away before Halvdan tries to kill us."

"We owe Halvdan a blood debt," said Ragnhild, and if Halvdan Ragnarsson had seen the look on her one-eyed face, he would have shivered in fear.

"We do," agreed Hundr. "And we haven't sailed all this way to see Erik reunited with his brother and then sail away singing songs and cheering our success like fools. We came to fight, raid, and win silver."

"Are you saying we should attack Halvdan?" said Einar, his eyebrows raised so high that they almost leapt from his face.

"I'm saying that Ragnhild is right. We ran from Dublin once. Friends died here. Men like Sten and Kolo, warriors like Hrist and Blink.

Halvdan should feel our vengeance."

Einar shook his head and rubbed his eyes between his thumb and forefinger. "Well, whilst we are reminiscing about old times, what about this bloody Witch-Queen Erik keeps talking about?"

Hundr felt their eyes upon him, burning into him, waiting for him to say what Einar and Ragnhild both knew but refrained from giving voice to in front of him. He looked out to sea, where the Fjord Bear banked away from the coast, her oars biting gently into the calm waters and taking her out to sea towards where the Wind Elk and the Sea Stallion sat beam-on to the Seaworm. The *drakkars* bobbed lazily on the ebb tide, her crew searching for more of the grey beasts who leapt and danced in the waves or more of the wide-eyed seals they had seen since reaching Ireland's coast. The animals were like dogs of the sea, and the men would point and try to throw them food so that the sea creatures would follow in the ship's wake.

"You both think it's her. Saoirse," Hundr said. He voiced that name, so long left unsaid but which had been forever etched into his thought cage.

"Who else could it be? There is a wyrd to this place. I've said it before," grumbled Ragnhild.

"She was never a witch. Women do not suddenly become völvas overnight. Besides, she fell to one of your arrows when we fought Halvdan on Dublin's palisade. So she is probably dead."

"You climbed the walls of York's fortress just to get to her. You loved her, and there's no denying it." Einar jammed his thumbs into his belt and pushed his shoulders back as though he had spoken some profound truth or wisdom of the gods. "She was an Irish Princess. We saved her life when The Saxons ambushed Hakon Ivarsson in that bleak Northumbrian forest. Then she betrayed you to marry Ivar instead."

"I know, Einar. I was there."

"Then the rancid bitch came to us and asked for our help to save young Finn from his uncle," added Ragnhild. "We did that. Einar here almost died getting the boy out of England. Then she betrayed us again. Sten died, Kolo died, as did my Valkyrie sister Hrist and our old friend Blink. If she lives, then she must die."

"Saoirse is not the Witch-Queen," Hundr insisted, even though he felt her stirring deep in his soul. He sensed she was alive, the woman who had changed his life.

"There has been plenty of time for her to become a witch; that's all I am saying," Einar

THE RAVEN AND THE NINE

said, his mouth rolling beneath his beard as though he chewed a mouthful of pebbles. "And there's more than one kind of witch."

"Really, Einar? I didn't know how well-versed you are in the world of völvas and seers. I remember Harald Fairhair's Sami sorcerer well enough, but he is the only one I have ever met."

"People know about such things in the north. The gods work in mysterious ways." Einar frowned at Hundr, taking offence at the belligerent questioning of his knowledge of witchcraft. Hundr had not forgotten those days, nor had he forgotten Saoirse's startling beauty. He had loved her then and thought of her often at night when sleep would not come, even when he lay next to Sigrid. In his memories, Saoirse was still young and pretty, as she had been when they were young together in York, not the bitter older version of herself who had spat hate and poison at him at the battle inside Dublin.

Hundr sighed, thinking of Sigrid and wondering if the baby would come whilst he was away, which it probably would according to the wise women who fussed around Sigrid and her swollen baby, women who had given birth themselves and knew of such things. He loved Sigrid. Differently perhaps than he had Saoirse, for that had been a wild and obsessive love, whereas his feelings for Sigrid ran deeper and were more meaningful. One thing was for sure: Saoirse hated him. She blamed him for how her life had turned out and told him as much with terrible venom and a face twisted with malice and spite. She blamed him for killing Hakon and Ivar. Saoirse would have been a Queen of Ireland and England had either or both lived. Hundr could only imagine the depredations and darkness of her treacherous climb to becoming a Queen. If she was alive, her hate would burn all the brighter for losing Finn, but if Hundr and Einar had left Finn behind, Halvdan would have slit his throat that very day to rid himself of the rightful heir to Dublin's throne.

"Sails, Lord Hundr," came a shout from amidship. "Off the port bow."

Hundr stalked along the Seaworm's deck, ducking beneath rigging and stepping carefully over ballast stones and around rowing benches and barrels of food, water and ale. Men crowded at the prow, so much so that Einar barked at them to get back before the ship tipped off balance. Hundr weaved through his men as they made way for him and came to stand next to Thorgrim, a hardy warrior and the son of a famous Viking voyager.

"What is it, Thorgrim?" asked Hundr.

"There, my lord," he said, pointing to shore, where a wide island topped by dark brush and a line of weather-beaten trees, bent and twisted by Njorth's relentless fury. The island rose as high as two masts at its highest point and then tapered down into shale beaches at both ends. It was only as wide as ten ships laid bow to stern.

"I can't see any ships?"

"They have passed behind the island, my lord."

"*Drakkars, knarrs*, or fishing boats?" asked Einar, standing high in the prow and staring hard towards the island.

"They weren't *drakkar* warships, Lord Einar. And they weren't fat-bellied *knarrs* either. They were smaller, *snekker* maybe."

"So, Viking ships then?"

"Aye, unless the Irish *lombungr* have learned to build keel and stem," said Thorgrim, and the crew laughed nervously.

"Maybe they have learned," Hundr uttered, and the laughing stopped.

"There," said Einar, pointing to the island's northern end. A prow poked past where the treeline gave way to the sloping beach, and it was a snarling beast head, sure enough. "Two of the bastards. What's their game?" Then, as the first ship sailed clear of the island, another mast became visible behind the first, and both vessels suddenly shipped oars, and the shouts of their captains rippled across the sea, carried on the wind's breath.

"They know their business." Thorgrim nodded, and he turned to look where the rest of Hundr's fleet floated out at sea. "They came about the island to row into the wind. I think they are going to attack us."

Hundr's heart stopped. Einar licked a finger and held it up into the air.

"The wind is in their favour, and we are sitting here like a beached walrus. Oars!" Einar bellowed, pushing men, kicking them up the arse and back towards where the oars were stowed securely in the bilge whilst the ship rested. "Lower the oars, you lazy whoresons."

"Get my mail and my swords," Hundr said to Thorgrim, and the big man nodded. The two ships unfurled their sails, black squares emblazoned with a white-winged raven. The raven banner of the sons of Ragnar. They were Halvdan Ragnarsson's ships, smaller than the Seaworm but faster in coastal waters. They were still large enough to hold forty warriors each and perfect for patrolling along coastlines. Such ships would return to port daily and would not need to carry supplies. All those sleek warships carried was death. The points of their spears sparkled beneath a bright sun, and their sails filled, driving towards the Seaworm like two wolves closing in on lamed sheep. Hundr's best hope was that his three ships would see the charging vessels before it was too late, but even once they had, the Sea Stallion and the Wind Elk would need to untie themselves from one another, lower their oars and come about. By that time, the *snekker* would be alongside the Seaworm, and her warriors would launch spears across the sheer strake from both port and starboard sides. Then, the forty fighters on each ship would hurl grapnels over the Seaworm's sides and pull themselves close so that eighty bloodthirsty Ragnarsson warriors could clamber aboard and slaughter Hundr and his crew. The Fjord Bear was under oar, and now, Hundr could only pray for her shipmaster to notice the enemy vessels soon and come about. However, until that moment arrived, they'd have to fight to stay alive.

"Here, my lord," said Thorgrim, handing Hundr his heavy brynjar and his swords, Fenristooth and Battle Fang. Hundr nodded his thanks. "Find armour and weapons for Ragnhild and Einar." His friends had come aboard in only their jerkins. No warrior wore mail at sea in fear of provoking the Norns and risking falling overboard to be dragged to the bottom and die beneath Ran's icy embrace. Hundr shrugged on his brynjar, which slithered over his head and shoulders like the scaled skin of a serpent.

He strapped on his swords and glared at the charging ships, the raven banner sending a shiver down his back.

"Blow the horn. Alert the other ships," Hundr ordered, sending Thorgrim scrabbling for the horn hanging from a rusty ship's nail hammered into the mast post. Hundr's ships weren't likely to make it in time to warn the *snekker* off or to stop them from slaughtering his crew, but they would come if he and Einar fell, then the men on board those attacking Ragnarsson ships would die in a bloody slaughter at sea.

"Shields and spear!" Einar roared. He turned towards the oncoming ships and raised his own shield and spear in defiance, and the Seaworm crew bellowed with him. Each man retrieved his shield, spear, axe, or seax and prepared to stand against their attackers. They stowed oars, with no time to make any sort of manoeuvre to evade the ships racing across the waves leeward and with all the speed and ferocity of a charging boar.

Hundr breathed deeply and raised his good eye to the sky. "Hear me, Odin," he called, and the crew fell silent, reaching for the silver hammers, spears, or fish at their necks. "Men come to kill us, and we are ready to stand outnumbered. We are men who fought and killed heroes and champions across Midgard, at Hafrsfjord, Ethandun, York, Novgorod and Frankia. So grant us victory, and grant us your battle luck. Or let us die with honour and feast this night in your hall with the brave men who have fallen to our blades. We are ready for victory or Valhalla!"

The men roared again, and the enemy ships came on. A gigantic man leant over the prow of a ship whose prow beast was a growling bear. He was red-bearded and hung by one arm so that the blade of his twin-bladed war axe skimmed the water's surface. The men in that ship peered at Hundr from beneath their helmets and over the rims of their shields, killers' eyes both narrow and hard. They saw an easy target in their waters, a ship with her oars tucked away and at rest. Their leader saw a fleet outside formation and a chance to dive in, kill and steal weapons, arm rings and glory. They were warriors of Halvdan Ragnarsson, experienced fighters from Halvdan's garrison in Dublin, but with sails furled, Hundr doubted they knew who they came to kill.

The red-bearded brute leered over the prow of his ship, close now, white teeth showing in a rictus of hate. Hundr braced himself and knelt tight against the bow; his warriors did the same. Only Einar stayed on his feet, roaring his defiance at the enemy, war fury banishing all fear and thoughts for his own safety. Einar had earned his reputation as a fighter of Holmgang duels, as a killer, and as a captain of the Boneless.

He feared no man. A sickening crunch came as Red Beard's ship scraped along the Seaworm's port side, and Hundr held tight onto her timbers to avoid being thrown into the bilge.

"I wish I had my bow," growled Ragnhild through gritted teeth. She crouched next to Hundr and screamed her war cry to Odin as she sprang to her feet and launched a spear into the enemy ship. Ragnhild was a deadly archer, and in a fight at sea, she would usually take up a position near the mast and rain her arrows upon the enemy like death. Hundr pulled himself up by the sheer strake plank but then ducked back down with a gasp as a spear sang past his head. The weapon flew right across the Seaworm's prow to land in the blue-green waters. He cursed. Fighting at sea was a treacherous business. The men would have to bring the ships together in order to board. Missiles alone would not settle a fight. You could barge a ship with your prow, but no man would risk damaging his own vessel. Few things hold the great value of a ship, and only the wealthiest Lords and Jarls could afford to keep a *drakkar* in the water with men to crew her.

"Spears!" Einar bellowed, still standing at the prow, enemy shafts whistling past him. Einar raised his shield, and a spear crashed into it with a dull thud. He threw his own spear into the enemy ship and yanked the other one free of the linden wood of his shield.

"What are you doing down there?" Einar said, frowning at Hundr and Ragnhild.

"Bastards!" Hundr cursed and forced himself to rise. He swallowed, trying to take in the surrounding fight. To hesitate was to die, and all the men aboard the Seaworm would perish if he could not lead them to victory. One of the enemy *snekke* scraped along the Seaworm's hull, and her captain waited until they were fully alongside before his men threw their hooks over the side and pulled the two ships close. The second *snekke* was almost upon them, and once she was near, Hundr and his men would be outnumbered and trapped. A war horn blared, Thorgrim holding it to his lips and blowing it towards the heavens. The Fjord Bear was already turning, but too slowly. By the time Einar's ship reached the fight, it would be too late, and Hundr would be lying dead in the bilge with a Ragnarsson axe in his skull.

"Board that ship," Hundr said before the thought had fully formed in his mind.

"What?" Ragnhild intoned, mouth agape.

"Board that ship and kill the whoresons. If we wait here, then they will board us from both sides. Board the closest one and fight them first, then we can turn and fight the others face to

face. A shield wall at sea. We have done it before."
And so they had, at the famous sea battle at
Hafrsfjord. If they could fight off Red Beard's
crew, they could then make the shield wall
and face the second ship's men without being
surrounded. Then, it would be just like fighting
on land, and Hundr would back his experienced
warriors against any in Midgard. "Board them
and kill them fast. Otherwise, we face larger
numbers in front and rear. Ragnhild, with me."

She laughed at the sheer madness of it, but
it was their only chance if they wanted to live.
Einar shook his head at them both but then
grinned, leaning away from a spear which would
have taken him in the chest. Instead, the weapon
slammed into the prow behind him and quivered
there. Along the deck, spears were being thrown
by both sides, men shouted their anger at each
other, and the screaming had begun. One of
Hundr's own men writhed on the deck with a
spear in his guts.

"Valhalla," Einar said. He passed his axe to
his shield hand so that the haft sat behind the
handle, which spanned the bowl at the rear of the
iron shield boss. Einar winked, took two steps
and placed his right hand on the top sheer strake
plank and in one fluid motion, he leapt over the
side and onto the deck of the enemy *snekke*.

"Board them, Board them!" Hundr roared at

his men. They had to make the daring leap aboard the attacking ship before the *snekke's* crew realised their plan and before the two vessels came fully alongside. If not, it would be a time-consuming fight across the bows as men exchanged blows behind their shields, and before that fight was over, the second ship would be upon them. War was all about trickery and surprise, and the joy of war was in killing men who came to kill you first. In outthinking an enemy and casting them down, of not being the man lying in a pool of his own blood screaming with flesh ripped and torn by sharp, deadly blades. Hundr ran down the length of the Seaworm's hull, urging his men to jump to the enemy ship and kill her crew. He ducked beneath the rigging rope and tried to ignore the spear shafts clattering around him before he reached the stern and drew Battle Fang from the scabbard at his waist. Thorgrim slashed his axe at an enemy warrior who swung a grapnel hook and then jumped onto the enemy ship, followed by a score of Hundr's men along the length of the Seaworm. Hundr himself made the leap, and he landed on the enemy deck. His boots skidded as he did, and he grabbed for a length of rigging to catch his fall. A shoulder crashed into Hundr, throwing him backwards, and he saw the red-bearded warrior snarling at him, bringing around a giant double-bladed war axe to slice Hundr from neck to groin. Hundr kept his hold on the rope and let the momentum of the jolt swing him in a wide arc. The seal hide rope burned in the palm of his hand, but the axe swung through the space where Hundr had been. Hundr came back to his feet, too close to bring his sword to bear, so he grabbed the haft of his enemy's axe and punched him in the face with the pommel of his sword, feeling the man's lips crushing beneath his knuckles. Hundr punched him again, and Red Beard jerked away. He pulled against Hundr's hold on his axe, and he was strong, dragging Hundr into a vicious headbutt. The blow sent flashes of light spinning around Hundr's head, and he dropped to one knee.

Death was close at that moment, its shadow heavy upon Hundr's shoulders, but he had a wife and an unborn child to return to, and he would not let his men die so ignominiously after their glorious victories. He sliced his sword across the shins of his enemy and rolled backwards. Red Beard yelped in pain and swung his mighty axe overhand to crash into the deck. Hundr lunged with his sword, and the point punched into Red Beard's belly, but his hard, leather breastplate held the blow. Then, with gritted teeth, Hundr pressed the sword's pommel with his left palm and forced it home. Red Beard's eyes went wide, and a gout of blood sprayed from his mouth as he coughed.

Hundr ripped his sword free and spun to bring the sword around across his throat, and where only moments earlier Red Beard saw himself winning a quick victory capturing a valuable *drakkar* and taking all her crew's wealth, now he was dead, dark blood pulsing from the terrible wound in his neck. In less than a heartbeat, another enemy came for Hundr, a weasel-faced man armed with a spear. Hundr deflected the strike with his sword, whipped his seax from its sheath at the small of his back, and punched its point into the man's chest in three quick stabs. Hundr saw the battle unfold ahead of him. The *snekke's* crew were outnumbered, and his champions, fierce warriors of renown, rolled them up in a bloody slaughter. Einar, Ragnhild, and Thorgrim rallied the crew, cutting, slashing, and sending their attackers to the afterlife. The fight was over before it had even begun, and the surviving men of Red Beard's crew dropped their weapons and knelt in the bilge to beg for mercy. Ragnhild keened her war prayer to Odin and slit a man's throat so that his blood sprayed the sea air with crimson, a sacrifice to the All-Father she was sworn to serve. The second *snekke* came alongside the Seaworm, following the enemy's original plan, and Hundr smiled at the confusion on their faces when they found the Seaworm empty and a battle already lost on their sister ship.

"Shield wall and get the ships together," Hundr instructed, marching through his men and clapping them on the shoulders. Immediately, his crew threw the grapnels and brought the *snekke* close to the Seaworm, for the two ships had drifted a spear's length apart during the fight.

"Here," said Einar, handing Hundr a shield. A leather cover stretched across the shield's boards, painted with a crude white raven. Like rubies in his beard, Einar's face was spattered with red droplets of blood, and his eyes were still wide with battle fury. "Did we lose many?"

"Hrafn was thrown overboard and sank like a stone," Thorgrim answered. He held Red Beard's double-bladed war axe, turning it over and admiring the skill of the smith who had made it. "Five more are injured, three of those too badly to fight."

"Make a shield wall and wait for them to come on to us," said Hundr, overlapping his shield with Einar's. Ragnhild overlapped hers with his, and Hundr's men made a wall of shields along the bow of the captured ship. The second *snekke's* crew stepped gingerly aboard the Seaworm. They clutched axes and spears and gave each other nervous glances. They should have stormed the Seaworm and crashed into Hundr's men before they recovered from the first fight, but they hesitated and now faced a wall of shields and an enemy which outnumbered them. Finally, a tall man in a helmet crested with black horsehair stepped forward onto the Seaworm beyond the line of his men. He wore a leather breastplate with a raven carved into the chest.

"I am Toki Leifsson," the man shouted across to Hundr and Einar at the centre of the Seaworm crew line. "And you have fought well today."

"Jarl Einar of Vanylven," Einar responded, "and Hundr, the Man with the Dog's Name."

"I have heard of you." Toki allowed, and he pointed to where the Fjord Bear had begun to beat her oars towards the fight. "We came to kill you, and you won instead. We shall leave now, and one day we might fight you again to avenge the deaths of our friends."

"Who is your Lord?"

"King Halvdan Ragnarsson."

"So, you sailed out from Dublin?"

"We did, only this morning."

Hundr lowered his shield. "Go, then. Return to Halvdan. There has been enough blood spilt today. Take these nithings with you," Hundr gestured to the men kneeling in the captured *snekke's* bilge. "They threw down their weapons whilst others died. We will let them swim to you."

Toki nodded and raised his spear in salute. Then, he led his men back to the ship, and they backed oars away from the Seaworm.

"Strip them and throw them overboard," Hundr ordered, pointing at the kneeling enemies with his blood-drenched sword. He had captured an enemy ship, but the Seaworm had taken damage in the clash of vessels. Thorgrim, Einar, Ragnhild, and the crew pushed the starkly white naked prisoners overboard, and they gasped and flailed in the cold seawater, striking out for the other ship. Hundr reached for the amulet at his neck and stared up at the vast sky, wondering if his return to Ireland would bring him more luck this time.

SEVEN

Erik Bjornsson's fleet glided about a sharp angle of green-topped cliffs carved into the Irish coastline. They came with the raven banner full and proud upon their sails and tacked through the wind towards where Hundr's fleet made for the shoreline. The Fjord Bear, Sea Stallion, and Wind Elk flanked the Seaworm as she limped under oars towards a sheltered beach of dark shale below a dense forest. Hundr sifted through the pile of plunder his men had stacked beside the mast, leather breastplates, silver amulets, arm rings of silver and copper, and a few of gold, all taken from the defeated ship. In addition, there were a handful of rune-carved rings and thirty leather purses cut from the closely guarded places where sailors hid their coin.

"Not a bad haul," said Einar, watching Hundr and leaning against the mast with his brawny arms folded across his chest. "Considering they caught us with our breeks down, and we probably should have died."

Hundr looked up at Einar and nodded at the truth of that. The ships had come on fast and unseen, which should never happen to a Viking seafarer. Hundr pushed the takings into small piles, a share for each crew member who had fought so hard for their lives.

"Take this for Hildr." Hundr flicked a silver ring towards Einar, and he caught it, biting the ring to test its quality. He shrugged and tilted his head from side to side before secreting it away in his own purse behind his jerkin. Hundr, remembering the mistake he had made in not taking a gift of his own to Sigrid, picked out a beautiful arm ring made of silver and inset with gold. He had stripped it from the red-bearded captain, along with two other arm rings and a purse full of silver, which had been added to the pile to be shared between the crew. Hundr slipped the arm ring over his wrist and up his forearm to join his other finery. Arm rings were considered one of the most prominent symbols of a warrior's success, alongside the quality of

THE RAVEN AND THE NINE

their weapons and armour. It spoke to others of a man's fighting prowess and success in battle. To kill such a man would make a warrior rich and grant him reputation, but such men were not easy to kill.

"Take your share, Ragnhild," Hundr said, gesturing to the pile so that Ragnhild could choose something for herself. She crouched against a rowing bench, cleaning her knife with a cloth before sliding it back into the small scabbard at her belt.

"The souls we sent to Odin's Einherjar are enough for me," she replied, reaching up to rub the spear amulet at her neck. "Some of them fought well, but most were sailors and not fighters."

"Here." Hundr reached out with a fistful of amulets taken from the dead and defeated fighters. "Add these to your collection, then."

She smiled and took the amulets, her scar-ravaged face twisted around her mouth and nose. Like Hundr, Ragnhild had lost an eye. The skin around the empty socket was drawn and puckered, and an eyelid drooped there beneath a long and jagged scar. She had taken to wearing the amulets of the men she killed in her hair, weaving them into the braids hanging down her back, and she sifted through the new collection, tossing the inferior ones back into the pile of treasure and keeping others to add to her grim war jewellery.

"I think the Norns are laughing at us already for returning to these shores," said Einar, jutting his chin towards Erik's ships. "One moment, we are fighting bastards under Ragnar's raven banner, and the next minute, we are welcoming friends under the same sail."

"There is a strangeness in this place." Ragnhild nodded. "So, we should be wary. It is not like us to allow two ships to sneak up on us like that."

"Aye," agreed Hundr. "We have become too confident. We shall be more vigilant from now on. Perhaps we should not have let Toki's ship sail back to Halvdan." He stood and watched the shore grow larger. One of his men leant over the forward bow searching the sea bottom for sand shelves or rocks beneath the surface, and the warriors rowed the Seaworm in slowly, pulling only gently against the ebb tide.

"Now he knows we are here. No doubt he also knows that Finn lives and that Einar is like a father to him," said Ragnhild.

"Let him come," shrugged Einar. "Halvdan is a bastard we should have killed years ago. We have eight *drakkars* in our fleet, and I doubt his warriors outnumber ours."

"But four of our ships belong to Erik, and

Halvdan is his uncle. Erik has not come to Ireland to kill Halvdan; he sails to find his brother. Who is to say he would join his uncle under their shared banner if it came to a fight?"

"You don't trust Erik?"

"I don't trust anyone."

Ragnhild and Einar crossed their arms and frowned at him.

"Apart from you two, of course. And Bush. Hildr and Sigrid. Finn too."

"Well, that isn't no one…" said Ragnhild, and Einar chuckled, a deep chortle from his chest.

Tiny stones crunched beneath the Seaworm's keel, and Einar winced at the sound. Men leapt over the bows and hauled the warship up the beach, struggling against the tide.

"She's taking on too much water," tutted Einar, frowning. He stamped his boot in the seawater pooling in the bilge. A ship always took on water, especially a *drakkar* which sat low and sleek in the water, and the constant bailing was ever the bane of seagoing men. "Might have to replace some of the planking. Bush will know what to do to set her right." Einar ran a big hand along one of the Seaworm's smooth timbers. The ship had been his once, back when Hundr first joined the crew as a penniless, bedraggled bail boy.

Einar had captained the Seaworm for years in the service of the Boneless but had gifted the ship to Hundr following one of their many campaigns.

Hundr leapt over the side. The seawater was cold despite the clear skies and warm weather, and its sharpness snatched his breath away. He waded towards the hull and helped the men to heave the warship up the beach. Einar jumped in after him, holding a length of rope, and the men joined him to help pull the ship. The entire crew were in the water, and though the sea's monstrous strength would pull the ship back towards her embrace every time a wave went out, they gradually got the ship to shore.

"This will do," Einar huffed, falling onto his arse on the shale beach, gasping for air. "When the flood tide comes in again, she will float, and we can shove her off."

Hundr joined him, his arms and shoulders aching from the exertion. The rest of the fleet dropped their stone anchors in the calm sea waters, and the crews came ashore, wading through the tide as though they wore boots made of iron, stumbling beneath the pull of the waves.

"Were they my uncle's men?" shouted Finn, taking exaggerated steps over the retreating waves and then jogging up the beach to where Einar and Hundr sat.

"We are fine, thanks. I took a few bruises, and Hundr has a slight cut on his arm," Einar snipped.

"Sorry, Einar. We saw their sails but could not come about in time to get you. I'm glad to see you are unharmed. Were they Halvdan's ships?" Finn had been aboard the Fjord Bear during the fight, and though her crew had done their best to bring the ship about and race to the Seaworm, they couldn't have closed the distance in time to join the fight.

"They were Halvdan's ships," said Hundr, and he rose, bending his head forward to tip stinging seawater from his dead eye. He raised his hand to return a wave from Erik, who came striding from the surf, flanked by his warriors.

"So now he will know we are here," Finn intoned and looked from Hundr to Einar, a strange, wide-eyed look on his face.

"He'll know, lad. But don't worry about it. He will need an army to take you from us," said Einar, also rising to tower over Hundr and Finn.

"It feels good to be back in Ireland." Finn crunched a boot into the tiny beach stones and breathed in a deep chest full of Irish air.

"Do you remember anything of the place?"

"Not much," Finn shrugged. "I remember

Father Darragh, my old priest, and sailing away from Dublin on board your ship. I remember being afraid."

"Well, you are a warrior now with your own oathmen."

Finn smiled at that, and Hundr wondered what other thoughts swam behind those youthful eyes. Did he think of his mother, wondering if she was alive? If he did, he never spoke of it. Did Finn wonder what his father, Ivar, was really like, or blame Hundr for his death? Returning to Ireland must surely kindle the fire of those thoughts inside Finn, and Hundr sucked his teeth. *Perhaps coming here wasn't such a good idea after all.*

"There was a fight, and I missed it," boomed Erik, approaching with his arms spread wide. "But I see your legend burns as bright as men say, Jarl Einar and Jarl Hundr, for you have captured an enemy ship whilst we fetched water and hunted meat."

"One of your uncle Halvdan's ships," said Hundr. *Better to get that out in the open straight away.* The grin fell from Erik's face and was replaced with a puzzled look.

"Halvdan attacked you?"

"Not him, two of his ships flying the raven banner."

"They would not have attacked were I here with you. He might think we come as enemies now?"

Hundr felt Einar's eyes upon him at that comment, for they did come as enemies to Halvdan, even if Erik did not. "They took us by surprise, and you were not here. So, the fight was unavoidable."

"Did you ask them about my brother?"

Hundr cursed himself, for in the heat of the fight and its aftermath, he had forgotten to ask Toki or the prisoners if they had heard of Refil Bjornsson. "No. The opportunity did not present itself."

Erik pointed up to the forested hilltop behind Hundr, and he turned to look.

"No matter. There are riders there. Perhaps we can ask them."

Hundr squinted up at the hilltop where a clutch of five riders sat silhouetted against the sky, the spear points shifting and their horses plodding along the crest of the hill.

"Halvdan's men?" asked Ragnhild.

"No, it's too soon, and they are too far from Dublin. We are half a day away from the city," answered Hundr.

"Could be Irishmen then," Einar supposed.

"They have their own tongue. Most speak good enough Norse. We have a few Irishers in our crews."

"Aye," said Ragnhild. "There are two on the Wind Elk. Ailbe and Eochaid."

"Amundr…" Einar called, and the big man came lumbering up the beach.

"Yes, Lord Einar," Amundr said, frowning up at the riders.

"Fetch Eochaid and Ailbe from the Wind Elk."

Amundr marched up the beach, and Hundr watched the riders pick their way slowly and carefully down the hillside towards where grass-topped dunes edged the beach. Behind him, Bush, the shipmaster, barked orders at the men to get the Seaworm's repairs made before the tide came back in so that the sounds of hammers and saws mixed with the sigh of the sea and the cawing of gulls overhead.

"Could it be trouble?" said Erik with a gleam in his eye.

Two men came scampering up the beach, one with a shaved head save for a thick braid running from the base of his skull down his back and a clipped black beard, and another shorter man with brown hair and deep green eyes. They bowed their heads to Hundr, Einar, and Erik.

"We are north of Dublin, which means they could be Norsemen, Irish-Norse, or Irishmen," said Einar.

"I don't understand?" Erik responded, raising a thick red eyebrow.

"Eochaid, give him the short version before the riders get here," said Ragnhild. Hundr smiled at that. The two Irishmen were well known throughout his crews as great tellers of tales, almost as skilled as the skalds found at hearth fires across the Viking worlds. They told fantastic stories of the great Irish heroes and their old gods, those revered before the Christ priests came and turned them all into worshippers of the nailed god.

"Yes, my lady," said Eochaid. He had beady eyes as dark as the pool at the centre of Dublin, which gave the city its name. Eochaid ran a wiry hand along his clipped beard and glanced at his smaller shipmate. "If you don't mind me saying so, you Norsemen came to Ireland, raiding and killing just as you did to the Saxons and Franks," he began in his lilting Irish accent. "Before that, our own kings ruled us from the great clans. Then, Vikings came and raided our churches and monasteries and took our fair women as slaves. After that, you settled at Dublin, Vedrafjord, Vykyngelo, Limerick and Cork and founded great trading cities..."

"Holy Mother, preserve us, but they asked for the short version," Ailbe interjected. "There are full Norsemen here. There are then those who are half Irish and half Norse, and then proud Irishmen like my babbling friend here. We are both Irishmen of the Uí Néill clan in the north."

"I was getting to that," Eochaid said, giving his fellow Irishmen a dunt on the shoulder. "Amadan," he shot back in Irish, which earned him a punch to the shoulder.

"So, which of those would see us as their enemies?" asked Erik.

"All of them," Ailbe answered with a glint in his green eyes. "This is Ireland. Everyone is your enemy."

"If they speak only Irish, I want you to translate Ailbe," said Hundr. The little man nodded solemnly and then flashed a sly grin at Eochaid, who mumbled a jealous curse under his breath. The riders reached the beach, and their horses whinnied and walked with disturbed gaits because of the unfamiliar feeling of shale beneath their hooves. One rider wore a brynjar coat of chain mail, while the rest wore leather and slung the large, criss-cross patterned cloaks that Irish warriors wore over one shoulder. Each man carried a long spear and small buckler shield fastened to his saddle in front of his left leg. Hundr, Einar, and Ragnhild had taken off their brynjars following the fight at sea. It was unwise for a warrior to wade ashore while wearing full armour, as falling into the ebb tide risked being carried out by the undertow and drowned in the murky depths. And besides, seawater was ever the bane of armour and weapons, so warriors only donned their armour when there was a fight ahead. Otherwise, they protected their valuable brynjars by wrapping them safely in oiled fleeces to keep out the seawater's rot. Among the noble folk assembled on the beach, Erik was the only one who wore his shining brynjar and the same white bear fur cloak he had worn during his visit to Vanylven, so he appeared more like a lord than any of the others.

Hundr raised a hand to the riders as they fanned out into a line so that each stood alongside one another, facing Hundr and the rest. The rider in the brynjar urged his roan mare forward a few steps, and the horse skittered from side to side, snorting and dipping her head. He patted her muscled neck, eyeing the warriors he saw before him, offering Erik a lingering stare. His eyes wandered to the *drakkars* anchored in the shallow waters and to the Seaworm pulled up onshore. He had a round face and a grizzled beard, and he curled his lip at them.

The leader of the spearmen spoke in Irish. Hundr breathed a small sigh of relief at that.

Irish warriors were far less likely to attack them if they could convince them they did not come for trouble.

"He asks, what are we doing in his lands, and have we come to rape and steal from them?" Ailbe translated, leaning to whisper in Hundr's ear.

The warrior frowned at Ailbe and spat to his left in contempt at seeing a fellow Irishman sailing with Vikings.

"Do you speak Norse?" Erik asked, stepping forward with his hands on his hips.

"I speak your tongue well enough," the spearman replied.

"I am Erik, son of Bjorn Ironside, a Ragnarsson," Erik said, lifting his chin in pride.

The man spoke in his own tongue again.

"He says we are either fair heathens or dark heathens, my lord," whispered Ailbe. "I don't know what he's talking about."

"I seek my brother, Refil Bjornsson, who was last seen in these lands," Erik continued.

The spearman shrugged. "I saw you fighting with the dark heathens out yonder. You can stay here and fix your ship. But I know someone who will want to talk to you," he said in Norse.

"We do not come to make trouble nor to raid," Hundr reassured, holding his arms wide to show he meant peace. "We seek only to repair our ship and look for my friend's brother."

The spearman looked Hundr up and down, not bothering to conceal his contempt. Without his mail or swords, Hundr looked like any other scarred warrior. Only his arm rings marked him out as a man of any wealth or repute.

"We shall return tomorrow morning. You should wait here. We will ask for news of your brother," said the spearman nodding toward Erik. He did not wait for an answer but clicked his tongue and wheeled his horse around to trot back the way he came, followed by his men.

"Are they going to attack us?" asked Einar, the cliff of his broad, flat face creased into a scowl.

"No, Lord Einar," Ailbe shook his head. "We Irish are more cunning than we look. If they were going to attack us, they wouldn't come and talk first and exchange insults like you Norsemen do. The first we would know of it would be an army of them howling down the hillside in the dark of night or the fog of the morning."

"So, we'll repair our ship and stay here the night," said Hundr. "Get some lookouts up on those hills in case they come back for a fight."

"Why not just fix up the Seaworm and sail

away on the flood?" Einar grumbled. "I don't trust these Irishers. They hate us Norsemen just as much as the Saxons do. We can find some friendly Norse merchants to ask about your brother, Erik. Then we can decide what to do once we have news."

"We should stay," said Hundr. "They wouldn't suggest returning if there wasn't something for them to offer to us or ask of us."

Einar shook his head. "They want to offer us their bloody spears. That's all that's on their minds. Let's just go. We've already got into one scrape, and we haven't even been here for a turn of the sun yet."

"We stay," said Erik, nodding at Hundr. "I must have news of my brother."

Einar shrugged and threw his eyes up to Asgard. "Don't blame me when cursed *skraelings* charge at us with their spears and clubs in the night. I hate this place. There is ill luck in it; I can feel the seiðr of it even here on the beach. Nothing good will come of being here, mark my words."

118

EIGHT

Bush saw to the repairs of the Seaworm, and as the flood tide sneaked ashore beneath where the sun came down in a wash of flame orange dusted by cloud as light as freshly ground flour, the sea lifted her keel so that the warship bobbed on the gently lapping waves. The crews shifted up the beach as the tide came in and made driftwood campfires beneath the dunes where long grasses swayed in a light breeze.

Each of the crews of Erik and Hundr's fleet made their own small fires and ate whatever remained of their supplies from the long voyage. They ate dried fish and salty biscuits and drank ale thick with barley from the bottom of the remaining ale barrels. The crewmen laughed and told stories of distant voyages and desperate battles, and Hundr sat with Ragnhild, Einar and Bush, old friends and good friends, his brothers and sisters of the sword. Men held wrestling matches between the different crews, and Hundr laughed to see Amundr bellow in triumph as he bested a hugely muscled Svear from one of Erik's crews and restored his pride after the defeat by Styrbjorn, 'The Dancer', at Vanylven. Then, after the wrestling, storytelling, and drinking had died down, Hundr lay beneath a woollen cloak and watched the fire crackle and spit over the lengths of faded driftwood, and he fell asleep on an Irish beach thinking of Sigrid, wondering if he was a father yet and if his love and his child had survived the ordeal of childbirth.

Morning came with a brisk southerly wind, and Hundr awoke to the familiar sound of the quern stone as men ground out barley and oats for a morning meal. Fires were lit again, and men grumbled at sore heads and empty bellies. As Hundr pushed a mouthful of stale bread and thick porridge into his mouth, one of his men came running down the hillside, tripping in the dunes and scampering across the shale.

"Riders, Lord Hundr!" he shouted, his face red raw with exertion. "Lots of them, Irishers!"

Hundr sprang to his feet and pulled his brynjar from its fleece wrapping to shrug the heavy coat of mail over his head and shoulders. He strapped on his two swords and the seax at the rear of his sword belt and slipped his gold and silver arm rings over his wrists. Before the tide rose, Hundr had sent Erling, a young warrior from his crews, to fetch his war gear, determined not to meet the Irish as a common sailor but as a drengr. He had fought hard to achieve his status as a sea Jarl and would meet friend or foe in his war finery. Hundr marched across the thin strip of dry sand and shale patches to find Einar. The big Jarl wore his brynjar, as did Ragnhild, Bush, and Finn. Erik marched from the opposite direction in his bear fur cloak, flanked by two of his shipmasters, Gjalandi and Vigfus, both huge Svears from his father's, the King's, army. The Irish spearman who came to them the day before with arrogance seeing only salt-stained sailors and one nobleman would now see the warriors of Hundr and Erik's crews for what they were, successful and wealthy warlords with a fleet of *drakkar* warships anchored in the sea behind them.

"Here they come; let's see what the bastards want," Einar lipped. The brisk morning wind blew the iron-grey hair away from Einar's hard face, carved as it was with two deep lines across either cheek and chasmic wrinkles across his forehead. Crow's feet crumpled the skin at the corners of his eyes, and his face was wind-burned an intense brown by years of braving the fury of the Whale Road.

"I just want news of my brother," said Erik, wagging a thick finger at Hundr, Einar, and Ragnhild. The big man shifted on his feet, licking dry lips beneath his red beard. There was nervousness there. Hundr felt it on the man, and he smiled and nodded to show he understood. Hundr and Einar were dangerous, unpredictable and ever-ready for a fight. It was easy to forget the reputation he and Einar had built, the legend of the Man with the Dog's Name. Men feared that legend as much as they admired it.

At least one hundred mounted warriors popped up in ones and twos until the entire hillside around the beach was lined with mounted spearmen, and Bush gasped in surprise. Ten of those warriors rode down the same hillside as the Irish horsemen had yesterday, steeds treading carefully across the rough beach grass until they reached the sand. Hundr saw the man who had come to them yesterday at the group's rear. He spoke to the men in front of him, but Hundr could not hear the words from where he stood—they whipped away on the chill morning wind like a butterfly flown too far from the flowerbeds. The riders all wore the green plaid cloaks which marked out

Irish warriors, and one man wore a monstrous two-handed sword strapped to his back.

"Greetings from Lord Bárid mac Ímar, rightful King of Dublin," said a small man with a long, drooping moustache astride a dappled gelding. He wore his patterned cloak over his head like a hood to keep out the worst of the morning wind, but he was bald and thin-faced beneath that hood.

A broad-shouldered man with a handsome face at the centre of the group of riders dipped his head to Hundr, Erik, Einar, and the rest. He wore a thin circlet of silver on his brow and carried a spear. A small shield daubed with the raven sigil of the sons of Ragnar rested upon his saddle and over his left knee.

"I am Erik, son of Bjorn Ironside, and the Prince of the Svears," said Erik, raising his hand in greeting.

"So, we are cousins then, Lord Prince," said Bárid, a wide, white-toothed smile splitting his face. "For I am the son of Ivar the Boneless." He spoke in Norse with the sing-song accent of the Irish. There was a sharp intake of breath on Hundr's blind side, his dead eye side, but he fought the urge to look around, for he would have to turn his whole head and would thus alert Bárid to the fact that Finn had gasped to hear that he had a half-brother in Ireland.

"We are, indeed." Erik nodded, bringing a fist to his chest in salute. "I present to you Hundr, who men know as The Man with the Dog's Name, Jarl Einar of Vanylven, Ragnhild of the Valkyrie, Bush the Shipmaster, and Finn Ivarsson, who is your brother, it seems."

Hundr winced at that, for no prince happily welcomed a potential rival for his throne. Bárid let his eyes drift over them all, drinking in the quality of their brynjars, weapons, and arm rings before offering Finn a long, lingering, flat stare. There was no emotion visible on that face. The piercing blue eyes and chiselled jaw stayed still, and then he forced a half smile to play at the corner of his mouth.

"I have a brother," he said. "Welcome, Finn, son of Ivar."

"Well met, brother," Finn replied, copying Erik and bringing a fist to his chest in salute.

The big man with the two-handed sword spoke a short sentence in Irish, and the men with them laughed nervously, the laugh of men who knew they shouldn't do so but did it anyway. Some even shook their heads at the words. Hundr cursed himself for not bringing Eochaid or Ailbe with them but marked that he would ask the Irishmen to translate those words for him later. Hundr ground his teeth. The voyage to Ireland to find Erik's brother and to get rich in the process felt like it was slipping away. The warp and weft of the Norns was at work, and Hundr could almost hear them cackling at the foot of the great tree Yggdrasil.

"And the Man with the Dog's Name, I have heard of you," said Bárid, beaming. "And you, Jarl Einar. Men of reputation are always welcome in my lands."

"I come to Ireland seeking my brother, your cousin Refil Bjornsson," Erik spoke up. "We have received no word of him since he left my father's hall for Ireland. Have you any news of my brother, Lord Bárid?"

"Why yes," answered Bárid. "I met your brother, a big man like you but with golden hair. He was here last summer, though he was captured by your uncle, or so I heard."

"By Halvdan?" said Erik, stepping forward with wide eyes.

"By Halvdan, yes. Your brother fought alongside me against Halvdan. He is my enemy and is King in Dublin."

"Why would Refil fight my uncle? Why do you fight him?"

"Because he makes the people suffer, and he has tried to kill me many times. We fight him because he raids my allies, the Uí Néill clan. I can help you get your brother back, cousin. We are on the march now. North, where Halvdan plans to attack my allies. There will be a battle there, and we could use fine brave men such as yourselves. Will you join us?"

Erik looked at Hundr and then at Einar. The excitement upon his face was as plain as a tail-wagging dog. Einar frowned and sucked his teeth, not meeting Erik's gaze but keeping his eyes fixed on Hundr. They had come for Erik's brother, but Hundr had also come to be avenged upon Halvdan for the deaths of his friends Sten and Kolo. So, whilst it was strange for Bárid to offer them an alliance so quickly, it served Hundr's purpose.

"Thank you for your offer, Lord Bárid," said Hundr. "As you can see, we have men to feed and ships to sail. Can we not talk more of this battle and know your plans before we commit our men's lives to your cause?"

A gleam twinkled in Bárid's startlingly blue eyes as they locked with Hundr's one. There was a cleverness, a deep cunning there, and it recognised something similar in Hundr.

"I don't ask you to fight alongside us for the good of your health, Lord Hundr. We will pay you for your blades and your friendship and feed your warriors alongside our own. We march today, but first, we shall make a camp up yonder and talk more of our plans, and hopefully, you will agree to my terms. Will you eat with us?"

"Of course, Lord Bárid, you are most kind."

Hundr, Einar and Erik led their crews up the hillside, followed by Finn and Bush, but only after ordering Ragnhild and the crew of her Wind Elk to remain on the beach and protect the ships. Ten men from each crew would remain aboard Hundr's ships, and Ragnhild's crew would guard the beach and the Seaworm in case Halvdan's ships returned, looking for trouble. Ragnhild did not grumble at missing the chance of a midday feast. She was ever grim-faced and surly on such occasions, but her warriors groaned when she barked at them to use the time wisely and practice shield wall battle formations.

Eochaid and Ailbe came scuttling up the long grass, past Erik and his burly champions, to stand between Hundr and Einar. Hundr had ordered them up to the front and vowed to keep them with him so they could whisper him translations of any Irish words spoken by Bárid and his men.

"Did you hear what the big man said down there?" asked Hundr.

"Sneaky bastards talking in their own tongue so we can't hear," mumbled Einar.

"We heard, Lord Hundr," Eochaid chimed, his face lit up with excitement to be of use to his Jarl. "He said Ivar the Boneless must have whelped pups in every port, and Lord Finn was as beautiful as that Bárid. Forgive me, my lord, but he said that Finn's mother must have been a fine-looking slave."

"A slave?" barked Finn behind them. Hundr cursed silently, wishing the lad had not heard. "My mother was the daughter of an Irish king—and a queen herself. I had not heard of this Bárid until today. Who was his mother, I wonder?"

"Say no more, lad," said Einar, rightfully cautious about being overheard talking about their host's mother, whoever she was. "We knew your mother, and she was a queen, as you say, so be content with that. Men often talk ill of one another's mothers. You know that as well as I do."

"What else did he say?" asked Hundr. He could feel Einar's eyes upon him but refused to be baited to talk about Finn's mother. He did not want to be reminded of Saoirse, but he could not stop visions of her appearing in his thought cage unbidden, as she was when they first met, with golden hair and with such beauty that a man would die for her.

Eochaid slipped in the long grass but then righted himself. "The big one then said we are killers and murderers, my lord. He said that Bárid should be wary of us, that our reputations mean we are men to fear," Eochaid replied.

"He isn't as stupid as he looks then," said Bush, grinning. They marched up the hill, and its steep slope turned Bush's cheeks the colour of a summer apple. He removed the stained leather helmet liner he always wore on his head and ran a hand over his egg-white bald head. "Do you think Halvdan really has Erik's brother?"

Hundr waved a hand at Bush to remind him to talk quietly. The Irishmen were only a few steps ahead of them. Most of them had already reached the hilltop's crest. "I don't remember thinking that Halvdan Ragnarsson was a man to take any prisoners."

"But what if that prisoner was his brother's son, one of the Ragnarsson clan?" Einar intoned. Hundr turned and glanced behind him. The sea rolled in white frothing lines, and his fleet bobbed, anchored close to the beach. From this high up the hillside, the Irish coastline stretched away to the north and south, green clifftops curved and gave way to golden beaches hazed in the distance as a warm sun fought to break through cloud shifting on the breeze. Halvdan was a ruthless man. He had been King in Dublin these last years, and men said he ruled with an iron fist. Halvdan had fought with reputation during the years that the great Ragnarsson army had invaded England, toppling the kings of Northumbria, Mercia and East Anglia. He was a famous warlord, had raided and sacked many cities across England, Ireland, and Frankia, and Hundr agreed with Bush that Halvdan was not a man to take prisoners unless there was an opportunity in it.

The path became steep, close to the top, and Hundr grabbed a fistful of the long dry grass to haul himself up. A salt-tinged wind blew loose strands of hair away from his face, and he could taste the sea on his lips. Bárid's warriors made a long, winding column marching along the edge of a thick, dark forest. Alder and ash trees rose and intertwined, their leaves a lush, deep green as the wood swept away down into a shallow valley. Finn took three quick paces to nudge his way in between Hundr and Einar, and the young man ran a hand down his face, looking from one to the other.

"Spit it out, lad. What is it?" asked Einar.

"I was thinking," said Finn, "that I should ask Bárid for news of my mother. She was Queen, after all, and, well…"

Einar placed his heavy arm around Finn's shoulders. "Let him talk first. Let's see what this battle is all about. He's your brother, or so he says, and there will be time for the two of you to talk if we decide to join his fight."

"You don't think he is my brother?"

"If a man says he is the son of a great warrior, it gives him instant power and reputation. Who is to say if this lad is Ivar's son? He had the look of him, and Ivar was ever a man to seek pretty girls. But let's talk of war first, see what's going on here, and see if we can find Erik's brother."

Finn nodded and dropped back to walk beside Bush. Hundr's shoulders bunched, waiting for Einar to comment about Finn's mother and the trap she had set for them when she asked Hundr for help in Frankia. But the question did not come, and Hundr brooded on it himself, his mind flooded by how beautiful Saoirse had once been and how much of a fool she had made of him. Pulling on the rope of that thought led his mind back to Sigrid, and he stared across the sea again, reaching out for any feeling or sense from the gods to give him news of the birth of his child. None materialised, and after a short march, they came to a cleft in the headland, which cut back into the forest to make a natural bowl in the land. One side was edged with large rocks pitted with green lichen, and the forest side showed thick gnarled roots where the ground fell away beneath wide-trunked trees. Those roots reached out and twisted like the crooked fingers of a long-dead giant before plunging again into the earth within the crevice. Bárid's men ringed that grass-covered basin, and at its centre, a fire burned. They had taken large boughs from the forest and made a fire half as high as a man, Hundr could feel its heat from the edge of the crevice, and men fed more branches into it so that blaze crackled and spat as it ate the damp wood. Smoke billowed from the fire to be whipped by the wind and chased out to sea, and Bárid beckoned Hundr and his men to him, close to the fire where his own men had spread out cloaks for them to sit on.

"Sit, please," said Bárid, gesturing to a brown cloak laid out beside him. Bárid himself sat, reached for a skin of ale, and took a drink before passing it to Hundr. He sat and drank, nodding his thanks before passing the heavy, sloshing skin to Einar. "We are out of the wind here, and my men will cook some food."

Sure enough, a wiry man with a matted beard erected a spit over the fire's edge, and a huntsman with a bow slung across his back handed over a brace of rabbits.

"So, you say go north to fight Halvdan?" said Hundr, getting straight to the point. If there was to be a fight, Hundr's crews had value. He had four ships' worth of professional warriors, men who fought for silver, not farmers, millers or traders forced to fight for their lords whenever trouble arose. Erik sat opposite Bárid, and Hundr and Erik's warriors together were a long four hundred men and an army in itself.

"Halvdan is at war with my allies, the Uí Néill clan. They are a powerful family here in Ireland, not unlike the sons of Ragnar in their fair fame, but much older. Their kings stretch back to the times before men can remember. He would make himself King of this entire island. I will help the Uí Néill fight Halvdan."

"Because you want to be King in Dublin?"

Bárid smiled. "Because I want to take up my father's throne as King of Dublin."

Murrough, the giant with the double-handed sword, sat across from Bárid with his back to the fire, and Hundr noticed the big man's eyes flicked to Finn when Bárid mentioned the throne. Bárid and Finn looked of similar age, both young men who had not seen twenty summers.

"Are you sure Halvdan has my brother?" asked Erik.

"Your brother joined me, and others like me, to build a new kingdom of Norsemen. The Irish call us the *Finngaill*, the New Foreigners. We are half Norsemen, sons of Norse warriors, and Irish mothers—as much Irish as we are Viking. Needless to say, Halvdan and his kind, the old warlords who sit like bloated wolves in their slave ports like Dublin, Vedrafjord, and Cork, treat our Irish people like dogs. They raid, enslave, and rob our people at every turn, and we would change that. So, we fight against those men whom the Irish call the *Dubgaill*, the Old Foreigners. I know he took him as a prisoner, but I cannot say for sure that Refil still lives. But if he does, and we can defeat Halvdan, then your brother will be restored to you. I swear it." Bárid reached out to Erik with an open hand, and the two men clasped forearms in the warrior's grip. Hundr knew at that moment that Erik would fight alongside Bárid no matter what arrangement Hundr could make for silver or plunder.

"If we agree to fight for you..." said Hundr, "... what can I promise to my men as their reward? They are sworn to me. I am their ring-giver, and I am responsible for rewarding them for risking their lives."

Bárid flashed Hundr another broad smile. "Of course, Lord Hundr. Halvdan sails his fleet north from Dublin to attack the Uí Néill in one of their strongholds up there. That fortress sits within Loch Cuan, a long stretch of water not unlike a fjord in your homelands. If you agree to bring your ships and fight with us, any ships we capture are yours, and the wealth onboard those vessels and the men taken with them is also yours."

Hundr held out his hand and took Bárid's in the warrior's grip, for it was a fine offer. To own one warship made a man wealthy. In the far north, a man could call himself a Jarl if he owned such a ship and had men to crew her. So, if Halvdan sailed north with his army, then he must have a fleet much larger than Hundr's own, and to capture even three of those ships and sell them would make Hundr's men as rich as Lords.

"Now, tell us more of your Uí Néill friends and this loch where we shall fight."

NINE

E inar thumbed the blade of his axe, where it rested in a loop at its belt. His shield rested against the prow's curve within easy reach. The Fjord Bear lay behind a low island, only as high as the ship itself and barren of trees, so to remain hidden, he had lowered the mast post and secured it within its crutch so that it lay lengthwise along the keel. He turned and glanced at Finn, who sat on a rowing bench, oar in hand, along with the rest of the crew. The Seaworm, Sea Stallion, and Wind Elk sat alongside them in the calm waters inside Loch Cuan.

The loch reminded Einar of Hafsfjord in

Norway in that ships could only enter the sprawling expanse of water through a narrow slip of sea between the mainland and a long, low-lying finger of a peninsular to the east. Once that stretch of narrow water had been navigated, however, the loch opened into a vast and beautiful waterway, with countless small islands dotting its coastline and a formidable crag of a fortress at its northern end. Within that fortress loomed Mael of the Uí Néill, an Irish warlord Einar had never met, nor did he want to meet, after Bárid had told tales of the men Mael had captured from Halvdan a year earlier and whose skulls still stood on spears above the gate of his fortress, pecked free of flesh by ravens and crows.

"Will Halvdan come, Lord Einar?" asked Amundr, sitting across from Finn, huge and baleful in brynjar and helmet.

"So the scouts say," said Einar. "He sails up the coast with thirty ships and will arrive before the sun is above us." He glanced up at the sky, pale blue and covered only by trailing wisps of cloud. The wind blew north, and Halvdan raced north before it, or so Bárid had reported.

"What if Halvdan sends his men, and we don't get to fight?" Amundr spoke in his deep, slow voice. Einar almost lost patience with the man, having gone over the plan with his crew and the crews of Hundr's other ships for much of the day before. But he wanted them to be clear on what must happen, so he took a deep breath and turned to face them.

"Halvdan will sail his fleet through the channel," said Einar, raising his voice to the oarsman at the rear so they could hear him over the creaking of rigging and groaning of the ship's timbers as the boat rocked gently on calm water. "Halvdan believes that the Uí Néill have no warships in the loch and no fleet at all. So, he plans to sail right up the fortress, pour his men from his ships in a murderous charge and swarm the fortress in short order. We, however, will shit on his plan and turn his battle to bloody ruin by blocking the entrance to the loch once all of his ships are through."

"So he can't get out?" Amundr asked.

"Yes." Einar fought hard to keep his patience, as the big man had a habit of repeating the obvious. "So Halvdan will panic, turn his ships around and try to break out of the loch."

"But we won't let him."

Einar stared at Amundr but just nodded slowly. The faces of his men were stern. They wore whatever armour they possessed, be it a brynjar or leather breastplate, and the deck bristled with axes, spears, shields and swords. He bit at the beard below his bottom lip and looked across the smooth surface of the loch, disturbed only by the slightest ripples, protected from the worst of the sea by the land on all sides save for the narrow channel at the southern end.

"Lord?" said Amundr. Einar turned to him, and the big man's face looked as though he chewed on a wasp. "Why don't we just block the narrows so Halvdan can't get into the loch?"

Einar sighed. "Because then he will just sail away or land somewhere else. And we don't want that. We want to kill the bastard."

"Maybe I should have gone with Hundr and Erik," Finn suddenly piped up. Einar ignored him.

Hundr and Erik had taken warriors ashore to join with Bárid's men and those of the Uí Néill. The Uí Néill clansmen were positioned within the walls of the fortress, ready to burst out of the gates once it was clear what Halvdan would do. Bárid and Hundr were on the eastern side of the loch in case Halvdan put his warriors ashore there. The westward shore of the loch was left unmanned because that side of the shore was littered with dozens of islands of different sizes, and both Bárid and Hundr had agreed that Halvdan would not risk taking his ships into those low-lying islets because the surrounding water would be treacherous for a shipmaster unfamiliar with the waters. There would be sandbanks, rocks jutting beneath the surface, shallows, and other underwater challenges, making navigating without local knowledge impossible. Einar was surprised that the Uí Néill leaders had not wanted more say in the battle plan, but then he had been aboard the Fjord Bear all night and morning, and perhaps they had voiced their opinion during those hours. Their stronghold was a sturdy keep built upon a hill with both ditch and palisade or what served as a hill in this part of Ireland. The land surrounding the loch was low-lying, and Einar wondered how the folk who lived there would keep the wind out in the deep of winter when Njorth would hurl furious sea storms across the loch and its lands, scouring them with biting wind and driving rain. He thought then of Vanylven and his roaring fire and Hildr and her soft skin and golden hair.

"What if all the fighting is onshore, and we miss everything?" Finn asked, but again, Einar did not reply. Instead, he thought it would be a good day's work not to have to fight Halvdan Ragnarsson but still capture a few of his ships.

"If there is fighting on the shore," said Amundr slowly, "we can just row towards it and go ashore."

"Don't be so keen to fight your uncle, lad," warned Einar. "He is a son of Ragnar, both clever and fierce, and many men will die today. Don't be so eager to join them."

"But I want to fight," Finn insisted with an air of petulance in his voice. That feeling stirred within Einar, too—the lure of battle. The glorious feeling of pitting his strength and skill against other men, overcoming them, and being the greater warrior. That made a man's heart surge; the gods would see his valour. But Einar also wanted to return alive and in one piece to Hildr and his hall at Vanylven.

Torsten, one of the longer-serving warriors, moved along the Fjord Bear's deck to give each man a drink from a skin of ale and a fistful of hard bread. Einar frowned at the sky, for the sun had reached the highest point in its journey, but there was still no sign of Halvdan's fleet. He leant over the prow and caught Bush's eye where he leant on the tiller of the Sea Stallion. Einar looked up at the sun and then back to Bush, but the shipmaster just shrugged and scratched at his bulging belly. Einar stalked to the stern and waved to Asbjorn aboard the Wind Elk, and he also shrugged. Ragnhild was not aboard the Elk. She had left her in Asbjorn's capable hands and gone ashore with Hundr after deciding that was where the fighting would be at its fiercest.

Einar was about to shout to Torsten for a sup of the ale when the undulating sound of a war horn sang out across the loch. It came in a long, loud burst echoing around the bay and its low hillsides.

"Where did that come from?" Finn blurted, rising from his oar bench.

"Is that a signal?" asked Amundr.

Einar stood high at the prow, searching the loch for signs of trouble. There were no ships in the channel, yet he felt that familiar prickle down his back and hotness on his cheeks. That feeling the gods send when they want to tell a man that something was wrong, that there was danger close by.

"Look, there. To the east," said Finn, dashing from his position at the oars to lean over the sheer strake next to Einar. He pointed to the rolling hills on that side of the loch, and sure enough, Einar saw the glint of steel and movement there, yet he could not make out anything clearly from that distance. But it appeared the low hills moved as though the fields' brown and green grasses and briars shifted of their own will.

"It's Halvdan, the cunning old bastard," Einar hissed, and his hands gripped the ship's timber so hard that his knuckles turned white. "Thor's balls, but the battle plan has gone to shit." Which it often did. War was about planning and execution, outfoxing an enemy and trapping him into slaughter. But more often than not, those best-laid plans soured because enemies did not do what you wanted them to. Foes were not kittens rolling to have their furry bellies tickled. Men died in battle, and weapons tore and rendered at flesh, cutting and slashing. The injured often died days later, sweating and screaming from a wound that had gone bad. Or the injured survive but were too badly maimed to fight ever again and must beg for food and shelter like nithings. So men took care not to be trapped in battle, as there was much to risk.

"He isn't coming into the loch," said Finn, realising what Halvdan had done. "He has come ashore on the eastern coast and marched his men overland."

"He's tricked us," Amundr uttered. Einar turned to snarl at him but kept his temper.

"We can't sit here whilst the battle is on the other side of the loch," said Einar, his hand resting on the haft of the axe at his belt. He turned and scrambled along the deck, between rowing benches and ducking under rigging. Finally, he reached the stern and leant over the side. "Keep the Stallion, the Elk, and the Seaworm here. If Halvdan's ships do come into the loch, close the narrows as planned." Asbjorn and Bush nodded and passed the orders along the line.

"Do you think he will still come into the loch?" asked Finn.

"Who knows what the sneaky bastard will do, but if he does, I want him trapped. Now, row, lads. Get us across to that shore quickly." Einar marched back to the prow, clapping each oarsman on the shoulder, encouraging them on. Loch Cuan was wider and longer than the fjord at Vanylven, and it would take them time to reach the northeastern coast under oars. Moreover, the loch was a perfect shelter from the sea, and there was no wind in the place. But the tide was in flood, and so Einar barked at his men to pull, to bring their blades to Hundr and Ragnhild because as much as Einar wanted to get back to his Hildr and his fire at Vanylven, he was a warrior and had not earned his name, The Brawler, for being a timid man.

As the men hauled on their oars, the Fjord Bear pushed off. Her shallow draughted keel sliced across the smooth, glass-like surface of the water, and the prow sent ripples dancing towards the shore. Einar felt every pull surging beneath his feet, and after ten pulls, the warship raced across the loch, his warriors taking up the rowing song of the hero, Hermóðr, grunting at every stroke and powering towards the fighting. The Fjord Bear raced like a dragon, her oars beating like great wings, and the carved bear head upon her prow snarled at the enemy. The sound of battle rang out as they came closer, men roaring and bellowing, the injured screaming, and the thud and clang of weapons clashing filled the air. Einar drew his axe from its belt loop and picked up his shield. He slipped his hand through the leather strap until it pressed against his forearm and clutched the timber handle, which spanned the empty bowl behind the iron boss. Einar welcomed its weight, the supple linden wood board, the iron nails riveting them to the boss, and the thin ring around its outer edge. He rolled his shoulders and neck, loosening the muscles under the weight of the shield and weapons. Einar banged the bearded iron blade of his axe upon his shield rim in time with the singing of his rowers, and as they approached the shore, he raised his shield so the men could see the one-eye sigil of the Man with the Dog's Name on its leather cover.

The shore came closer, and on the sloping hillside, men fought and died. There were warriors in the green plaid of Bárid's men but more Vikings in leather and mail, hacking and slashing at one another in two long shield walls. At the rear of Halvdan's warriors flew the raven banner, the white raven on black cloth, high upon a spear, filling the Ragnarsson enemies with terror. Einar had fought under that banner himself for many years when he was Ivar's man. But now he came to kill, and his chest rose and fell like a running stag at the prospect of the fight to come.

"Shields!" Einar bellowed, and he braced himself as the ship raced towards the shore. He clutched the side as her hull scraped on the tiny stones and sand off the shore. Einar did not hesitate. He leapt over into the water. It covered his boots and trews, and its chill took his breath away as he waded towards the fight, teeth bared and ready to kill.

TEN

The axe beat down on Hundr's shield, hammering at the boards, each blow jarring his shoulder as a snarling Viking with a mottled face and greasy blonde hair tried to kill him. Hundr leant into the shield, holding the wall and keeping it tight to Ragnhild on his left and Thorgrim on his right. The ferocious fighting roared around him like a living thing. Battle cries mixed with the screams of the wounded and dying in an ear-shattering tumult of violence and pain.

"There are too many of the bastards," growled Thorgrim, grimacing as a spear thrust over the rim of his shields, only a finger's breadth from his face.

"Hold them," Hundr said. He flexed his fingers around the antler hilt of the seax clutched in his right hand. His swords were too long to be of any use in the awful closeness of the shield wall, where men pushed and heaved at one another, spitting, cursing and stinking. It was a pushing match and would remain so until one line broke or a brave man willingly broke a line to drive a wedge into the enemy shield wall. Another thud on his shield.

"Die, you piece of walrus shit," spat the mottled-faced man over the raging din of battle. His breath stank like a midden heap. Hundr shoved back, and then his boot banged into the mottled man's, so Hundr raked his heel down the man's ankle and instep, leaving the man howling in pain. The pressure on his shield relented for a heartbeat, and Hundr drove his seax beneath his shield's rim but found nothing to cut or tear. The man's face appeared again over the rims of both shields.

"Tried to gut me, didn't you, you bastard? But old Toki is too clever for…" He didn't get to finish because Ragnhild punched the tip of her spear into his face. The leaf-shaped blade cut through beside his nose, and his eyes clenched closed as she pushed the steel home, deep into his skull. Ragnhild twisted the spear and ripped it free. It left a terrible wound, ripping his eye so that its jelly slopped onto the gaping flap of skin, red and purple beneath it. The warrior stayed there, propped up by the men's shields on either side of him and behind him to hang there like a grizzly puppet.

"We need to break their shield wall," said Ragnhild through gritted teeth, her one eye blazing with anger. "They have the high ground and are pushing us back."

She was right. Hundr drove his shoulder into his shield again, bracing himself with his back foot, the force of his enemy pushing against him from the other side of the linden wood. His boots slid as the enemy ranks heaved their shield wall back towards the loch. Hundr's guts churned at the force driving him backwards. It was a terrifying thing, like pushing against something monstrous and inevitable. Soon, that same fear which curdled Hundr's belly would turn to fear in other men and then panic. Once panic set in, men would flee the shield wall. They would peer into the wide-eyed fury of their enemies; they would see the wicked sharpness of their spears, axes, knives and swords. Men's minds would fill with images of those blades slicing their skin or piercing their hearts, and they would run. Once men ran from the shield wall, the slaughter would begin.

Halvdan's men had come over the hills slowly, like a band of warriors out for a stroll. Bárid and the Uí Néill had placed scouts across the hills surrounding the loch, and they weren't even really hills, more like humps of grass-covered earth rising no higher than two halls stacked on top of one another. Those scouts were to watch for any surprises, but one or two must have fallen asleep or taken their attention from the seaward side of the peninsular, which hooked around the loch's eastern shore. Halvdan's warriors came from that side, marching slowly and carefully. Men had noticed them on the crest of the hillock, and first, a few shouts had gone up, men unsure who had ambled across the peninsular towards them. Then, the raven banner had crept up the hillside, and men's hearts had frozen in fear at the sight of the famous war sigil of the sons of Ragnar Lothbrok. For with that banner came death. It signified the most successful Viking warriors of all time, men who had conquered the majority of Saxon England and killed kings. They had sacked mighty cities like Paris and Hamburg. Without question, their reputations were legendary. So, to see that banner approaching, surrounded by spears, shields, and axes, made Bárid's men take steps backwards. Then, Halvdan's war horn rang out, and his warriors followed it up with a clipped roar and the formation of their shield wall. They moved deliberately and efficiently into the three ranks of shields, spreading further than Hundr could see. Hundr had then organised his crews into their own shield wall and heard Bárid's Irishmen doing the same thing.

"So much for an easy fight," grumbled Thorgrim, beads of sweat dripping down his face to run into his beard. The hook of a bearded axe blade clamped over the rim of his shield, but Thorgrim was a hardy fighter and experienced in the shield wall. He drove his knee into the bottom of his shield to stop his attacker from ripping it down or tipping it away from where it protected his neck and chest. If that happened, another blade would come to rip out his throat, and so Hundr braced his own knee against his shield, which overlapped Thorgrim's, and they held fast. They had planned to spring a trap on Halvdan, to let him sail into the loch and slaughter him on a bright day in early summer. But Halvdan was no pup new to the ways of war, and Hundr imagined the old wolf laughing at their plans before bringing his vicious Ragnarsson warriors to crush their play for victory and rip them to bloody shreds. Now, Hundr fought uphill against an organised foe who pushed them back slowly and inexorably towards the water's edge.

"I can break the wall," gasped Hundr, the terrible weight against his shield falling away momentarily. The dead man fell away, only to be replaced by a bigger warrior with a thick, braided beard who pushed and banged at Hundr's shield with an unseen weapon. Hundr wasn't speaking with arrogance, for he had broken many shield walls in his time. "But I can't see how long their line is."

Ragnhild grunted, dancing her right leg away from a spear point snaking underneath her shield before stamping down on the point to trap it beneath her boot. "If we don't break them, we will be waist-deep in the water, and half our men will drown."

Hundr risked a glance over his shoulder, and the water's edge was only ten paces away. The water lapped there softly as if mocking the fury of the fight in front of it. It was calm water, but it would drink them slowly in their armour and leather. Injured men would drown, and the slaughter would be disastrous. The weapon hacking into his shield scraped across the iron rim of his shield and thrust above Hundr's shoulder to nick his ear lobe. There was burning there and then wet blood on his neck. Hundr held his breath. Death was close. His one eye made it impossible to see how the battle unfolded around him, but he sensed in his gut that Halvdan was winning, and to lose was to die. Then, suddenly, a sound rang in his ears, and he risked another glance behind him. The kindling feeling of panic turned to joy because

THE RAVEN AND THE NINE

the Fjord Bear snaked across the water's surface, oars pounding, and Einar stood at the prow, enormous and baleful with his axe and his war-hunger.

"Einar has come," Hundr growled, and Ragnhild flashed him a fearsome grin. "Thorgrim," he said. The big man was hurling insults at the Viking opposite him, but the two warriors could not bring their weapons to bear in the crush of the shield wall. "Thorgrim!" Hundr shouted, and the warrior's head flicked around to him, eyes wide with fury. "When I go through them, you follow." Thorgrim nodded his understanding.

Hundr gripped his seax, the blade as long as his forearm with a single edge for slashing, and its dull side tapering into a wicked point. He took two deep breaths and did what no warrior should do. If one of his men did such a thing in their ceaseless practice of the shield wall, he would pull them out and roar at them, for to break the shield wall was to die. Hundr let go of his shield, but he did not do so because he wanted to run from the fight or because the muscle-burning fire in his shoulders screamed at him to let it go. Instead, Hundr released his shield because to win a battle, it took a lover of war, a man who craved victory and glory more than he feared death and pain.

The Viking with the braided beard roared with exultant joy as he sensed the force behind the shield opposite him give way. He saw a warrior in shining mail and glittering arm rings, and in a glorious flash, he saw his reputation soaring as the killer of a wealthy enemy. He saw fame and war glory. And then he died. Hundr bent at the knee and grabbed the bottom of the Viking's shield, ripping it towards his own body. The top end smashed into the warrior's face, mangling his lips and crushing his nose. In the same movement, Hundr plunged the point of his seax into the soft flesh inside the man's thigh, where there was no armour or protection. Hundr surged upwards with all the power in his legs and ripped the seax blade into the man's groin. He twisted the blade, and hot blood gushed from severed arteries to soak his fist. The Viking with the braided beard opened his ruined mouth, but no scream came. He died with his spear in his hand, and Hundr locked eyes with him, knowing that the man would wait for him in Odin's hall, where they would drink and laugh together about the battle and fight alongside one another every day until the end of days.

Hundr whipped a knife from the dying man's belt and pushed himself into the space created by his dropping shield. He stabbed and slashed with seax and knife; he cut at legs and faces, slicing at hands, fingers and necks. Shields, helmets, or armour caught most of his blows. But some cut flesh and his enemies pushed against each other to draw away from his fury. Men punched, stabbed and slashed at him with the full force of their strength. Battle was the fine gossamer line between life and death, and the force exerted there was of savage men fighting for their lives, total commitment to the slaughter and no compromise. Suddenly he was two ranks deep into Halvdan's shield wall. Ragnhild followed him, keening her battle prayer to Odin and savaging the enemy warriors with her axe. Thorgrim came then with his shield and his double-bladed war axe, and the three of them opened a wedge into the enemy shield wall. A blade scraped across Hundr's chest, yet his brynjar held the blow, and a shield boss punched into his shoulder. But Thorgrim held him upright. Hundr stabbed his axe into a bright blue eye, and a roar went up from Halvdan's warriors. That roar made Hundr shiver because it was not a shout of men who saw glory but of men who had dreamed of victory and now saw defeat and panic.

"What is happening?" Ragnhild shouted, fighting for her life at Hundr's side. He couldn't see above the throng of warriors and the press of those around him. There was no give in front of him, so whatever occurred was further along the shield wall. An axe came in a high arc towards his face, but Hundr drove himself into it so that the blow was too long and instead, the haft banged into his shoulder with a dull pain. He stabbed upwards with his seax and sliced at a snarling face, but the warriors before him held. Panic flared in Hundr's chest like a pot of boiling water because the Ragnarsson line stood fast. His plan to break through them and destroy their shield wall formation had failed. Now, the enemy pressed around him. The rank stench of their fetid ale breath, their sweat, and the leather of their clothes and armour filled his senses. His seax and knife were trapped; the seax held out before him and his knife at his side. Hundr had dropped his shield, and that folly now left him unprotected. The enemy, however, in their lust for his death, had pressed themselves too close, and the warriors behind pushed into the backs of those in front so their shields pinned Hundr. He shook and raged with his shoulders but could not move. Thorgrim roared next to him, his bearded mouth spitting and teeth snapping at those who had him similarly pinned.

"Spear," an enemy bellowed above the grunt and shove of the press. "Kill him with a spear. You there behind me, Rolfr, kill the bastard."

Hundr bucked and tried to stamp on enemy feet or bite at their faces, but he was stuck. Ragnhild screamed and howled for Odin's help, but Hundr knew that the Ragnarsson warrior had the right of it. It would be so simple to drive a long spear between the heads of their shield wall and tear out his throat. He was grateful at least to have hold of his weapons, and Hundr tried to control the fear and panic bursting out of him. Odin would welcome him, he hoped. His life had been one of battle and daring, and he surely deserved a place in Odin's Einherjar, but even with that knowledge, the fear of death was a mind-killer, and Hundr struggled again to get free of the enemy shields around him. The cold iron of a shield rim pushed into the soft flesh below his chin. It was jagged, and it rubbed and tore at him, his blood flowing over the pitiless metal.

The shield wall battle raged all around. Neither line had broken as yet, and Hundr was stuck in the press of men, three ranks inside the Ragnarsson army. The enemy spear came slowly at first, its tip shining and deadly. Men leant their heads away from it, and hands passed it through the press. One hand, the back of it thick with matted hair, jabbed the blade forward, but it stopped a whisker away from Hundr's good eye. He jerked his head backwards but could not get away from where it stopped, threatening him, surrounded by the growling faces of men who wanted him dead. Another hand took up the spear shaft, a closer hand, and just as it was about to stab into his face, the shields to

Hundr's left gave way, and he stumbled into Ragnhild. She gasped and slashed her axe blade across an enemy's stomach, and the purple coils slopped out of him onto the next man's boots. Hundr stabbed his seax into that man's armpit in five quick blows. There was confusion, men stumbling and dying, the iron stink of blood thick in the air.

"Die! Fight me and die, you shit-stinking whoresons!" came a familiar voice. Fear fell from Hundr like a discarded cloak because Einar the Brawler had come to fight. Einar was a giant man, tall, broad and powerful, with a lifetime of war skill in his ageing muscles. A long arm gripping a shield rose over Hundr and Ragnhild, covering them in shadow for a fleeting moment, and then it held the shield before them, protecting them from the enemy. Einar used his shoulder to barge between Hundr and Ragnhild. He grinned at them both before turning his flat, broad face to growl at Thorgrim.

"Are you going to fight or just stand there and die?" Einar said.

Thorgrim spluttered a response before hurling himself at the enemy once more. The crew of the Fjord Bear surged into the Ragnarsson line. Finn Ivarsson hooked his shield over Einar's, and they pushed the enemy back, breaking the shield wall. Then, the enemy showed their backs for the first time, fleeing from the force of Einar's charge. Finn killed a man with his spear and then launched the weapon overhand to take a running enemy between the shoulder blades.

Hundr sank to one knee, and Ragnhild did the same. They rested a weary arm on one another's shoulder and blew out their cheeks. No words were spoken, but both knew how close they had come to death. Ragnhild shook her head, her face spattered with flecks of red blood. The hillside was a mud-churned mess. The once green fields butting onto the loch had been trampled by hundreds of boots and turned to foul liquid by the blood and excrement of the dying. Hundr forced himself to rise to his feet, and all around him, the Ragnarsson shield wall crumbled, the enemy running back up the gentle slope pursued by his and Bárid's warriors, but surely Einar's attack had not been enough to break the enemy army? Then he saw it. To the north, a new army had entered the fray to turn the tide of the battle. Hundreds of warriors clad in plaid cloaks had poured from the Uí Néill fortress at the loch's most northern point, and they had smashed into the Ragnarsson flank. Those warriors, combined with Hundr's crews and Bárid's men, had beaten back Halvdan's warriors. Einar had disappeared from view, he and Finn taking the Fjord Bear's crew after the fleeing enemy, still hungry for slaughter despite the victory. Hundr strode after them, picking his way between enemy corpses, trying not to look at those men who begged for aid, those who writhed in the filth, injured in the fighting and in desperate need of a healer. They were mostly Halvdan Ragnarsson's men, and they knew the risks when they marched to war. They came for silver and glory, so Hundr spared them no pity, despite their reaching hands already crusting with blood and their eyes filled with desperation.

Hundr marched to the top of a hillock on the loch's eastern shore, and over the hill, he saw Halvdans's fleet in the grey-green sea. Many ships rowed towards shore when men had stripped themselves of armour and weapons to swim out to the safety of their boats. Men fought and died in the shallows, corpses floating face down in the lapping waves.

"Is that their Queen?" Ragnhild asked, coming to stand beside him to watch the gruesome end of the fighting. She pointed her blood-stained axe to where a woman sat astride a white horse. The woman wore a long black robe which billowed behind her as she rode along the beach behind the fighting warriors. Grey hair flowed from her head, the colour of a winter storm, and she brandished a long staff, keening war cries at the Irish warriors in their own language. Those Irishmen fought and killed with wild abandon, punishing the hated Viking invaders who raided their fortress and their homes. Hundr did not judge them for that unyielding slaughter, for Halvdan's men would have raped and murdered their way through the Uí Néill fortress had they gotten inside its walls. The men who killed down on the long strip of the beach did so with the relief of those who feared what would become of their wives, daughters and mothers if the Vikings had succeeded.

"She looks more like a völva than a queen," he said. "I can feel the seiðr magic pouring off her from here." The sight of that woman, in all black like a crow, and her pure white horse, the colour of summer clouds, made his shoulders shiver.

"Can you see Halvdan down there?" Ragnhild asked, bringing a hand to cover her eye from the sun as she searched for a sign of the raven banner. "He must die today."

Ragnhild's lover, Kolo, had died at the battle Hundr and Ragnhild had fought to escape from Halvdan and Dublin many years earlier. Of all Hundr's warriors, Ragnhild's desire for vengeance burned most brightly. Hundr's eye searched the battlefield but saw no sign of the famous war flag of the sons of Ragnar. The völva continued to thunder up and down the beach, spitting curses and howling her warriors on to kill the Vikings. Halvdan's men made a stand, knee-deep in the surf, brave men who rallied to make a last shield wall with the ocean at their backs and their enemies in front. Einar was down there, along with Finn and the rest of the Fjord Bear's crew. They made their own shield wall and advanced upon the enemy in an organised march three ranks deep. The Irishmen, however, hurled themselves against the Ragnarsson line in reckless attacks with swirling swords and axes. If he found the raven banner, Hundr would charge down into the blood-soaked beach at Ragnhild's side to exact her vengeance, but he felt no desire to fight again. His shoulders and thighs burned from the exertions of the shield wall. He had taken many blows to his chest and ribs, and his right shoulder throbbed where the axe haft had struck him. There were cuts to his face, ears and arms that had not hurt in the frenzy of battle but now stung and pulsed. With a sigh, he turned back to the loch, its water still and clear like a great sheet of ice, the blue sky reflected in its waters, and Hundr thought that this would make a fine place to live, as secure as Vanylven. The Loch was a natural harbour and shielded the place from the worst of the sea and its violent storms. He glanced then towards where the rest of his fleet had taken up position to trap Halvdan before that plan went awry.

Hundr's jaw dropped open, and he grasped for Ragnhild's arm. Unable to speak for a moment, he pulled her around to look in the same direction. He was horror-struck because ships came from the narrow entrance to the loch. *Drakkar* warships, sleek and flying across the water under oars. One entered at first, then more until ten ships were inside. Their oars bit into the glass-like surface, and their beast-headed prows reared and snarled northwards. They powered across the loch, oars pounding and the raven banner flying black and ominous from each mast.

"There could be five hundred men there," Ragnhild murmured.

"They go for the fortress. The old Ragnarsson wolf is a cunning bastard," said Hundr. Halvdan had sent his warriors to fight and die on the Irish hillside, drawing off the principal fighting force arrayed against him. Now, he pushed hard with his chosen champions towards his goal, the newly undefended Uí Néill fortress. Hundr charged down the hill's eastern slope into long coarse grass and onto the golden sand. He ran to the rear of Einar's warriors and roared at them to return to the Fjord Bear. Their first glances at him were incredulous, but once they saw the set of Hundr's jaw, they shouted the new orders to their shipmates. Hundr kept running, darting past big men in plaid cloaks who hacked into the enemy, turning the sea red with their fury, until he saw Bárid's huge Irishman, Murrough, swinging his monstrous sword with two hands, cleaving the enemy open like a butcher. Erik Bjornsson fought knee-deep in the water, laying about him with his axe, while The Dancer fought beside him, seeming to float on the surf as he darted and swiped his thin blade at the enemy like a deadly bee sting.

"Bárid," Hundr repeatedly called until he finally caught sight of the son of Ivar, soaked in seawater and splashed in blood. His feral eyes met Hundr's one, and he grinned in deathly appreciation of what he believed to be the slaughter of his enemies. "Halvdan is in the loch with ten ships. We need to march north now."

"We have won. The enemy is in flight. We can finish them here," said Bárid, pointing his sword towards where his men hacked into the remnants of the Ragnarsson army.

Hundr stepped forward and grabbed Bárid's shoulder. "The raven banner is in the loch, flying from the masts of ten *drakkar* warships. There is another army on the water heading for the Uí Néill fortress. The fight here was a trap to draw our forces out."

Bárid shook his head at first but then followed Hundr as he dashed back towards the hilltop. He cursed in his Irish tongue when he saw the enemy vessels.

"Take your ship there and go back to your fleet," Bárid said, shaking his head in disbelief. "Follow the original plan. If Halvdan sees that he is trapped, he might turn around. They are too close to the fortress." He passed a bloody hand down his face, glancing from where the ships pounded their oars across the loch.

"What if he doesn't turn back?" asked Hundr. Even though he knew the answer, he wanted to ensure that Bárid knew the risk.

"We can't get to the Uí Néill folk in the stronghold before Halvdan. The fortress will fall if he attacks, and he will slaughter the women and children with no warriors to defend them. So pray, my friend. Pray to your gods that the old Ragnarsson snake does what we want him to do."

ELEVEN

"Pull," called Einar as the warriors in the Fjord Bear hauled on their oars. Hundr heaved on one himself as he sat opposite Sigvarth Trollhands, concentrating on keeping time with the crew. Initially, they had brought the long drakkar warship about, a painfully slow process using only one bank of oars, before the beast-headed prow swung around, and they could row back towards the rest of Hundr's fleet.

"Blow that horn as loud as you can," Einar barked, and Bush nodded. He took the curved horn from its peg on the mast and licked his lips. He filled his chest with air and blew a long, mournful song on the war horn. It sang out across the water as though it skimmed the glimmering ripples like a flat stone. Bush blew it again, and Einar leant on the tiller to steer the ship towards the loch's centre. For Hundr's desperate plan to work, they needed Halvdan to see that they had blocked the entrance to the loch. When following Hundr down the hillside, Einar had questioned Hundr's plan, but his cunning friend had shaken off his concerns. He might be reckless, Einar knew, but at least Hundr was decisive.

Einar's first reaction to the plan to block the loch was that Halvdan would simply not care. The son of Ragnar was no pup new to the ways of war. He had brought his ships and army from Dublin to sack the Uí Néill fortress and had made that possible by using the attack on the eastern shore as a diversion. Einar didn't fully understand the nature of the war between Halvdan, Bárid, and the Uí Néill. The wars in Ireland were ever complicated because of the multitude of kings, kingdoms, and Viking warlords wanting to be kings. That melting pot of ambition and violence became more complicated as the sons of the old Vikings, the children of the warriors who came to Ireland when Einar was a lad and forged kingdoms for themselves with safe harbours and thriving slave markets, grew ambitions for themselves. Einar waved at Bush to blow his horn again, and as it echoed out across the water, Einar peered from where he stood upon the steerboard platform and hoped that he had done enough to get Halvdan's attention. He pushed on the tiller and brought the Fjord Bear on a southerly wind heading towards the narrows, where Asbjorn had already been clever enough to see what unfolded in the loch and had brought the other ships from the concealed position to block the narrows. Einar wiped at a nick on his forehead with the back of his hand. A man he had struck down in the shallows had flailed with his spear in his death throes and cut Einar there. He should have worn his helmet, but Einar didn't like fighting with his helmet on. He knew it protected his skull from the dangers of being knocked unconscious, but he hated not being able to see around him. A helmet made him feel hot and blinded to his flanks, so he rarely cared to wear one. He also did not care that he hadn't taken the time to get to the bottom of the conflict he fought in. All he wanted to was to kill Halvdan in revenge for Sten and Kolo, get rich, and get back to Vanylven in one piece.

Along the eastern hills, Bárid's men and the Uí Néill warriors ran along the lowland crest towards their stronghold. Einar clenched his teeth, understanding the panic in the hearts of the Irish warriors who had charged from behind their walls, led by their howling völva to destroy the Ragnarssons, only now understanding that by doing so, they had left their loved ones unprotected in their homes, defenceless against Halvdan's savage Northmen. Each stroke brought the Fjord Bear closer to the narrows, where Asbjorn had brought the Sea Stallion, the Seaworm and the Wind Elk bows on so that they formed a wooden wall across the only way in or out of the loch's wide waterway. It would all be for nothing, though, if Halvdan did not take the bait—if he did not fear dying outside the fortress more than he believed he could take it. If Halvdan could storm the walls before the Uí Néill returned, then he could defend its walls with his own warriors and Einar, Hundr, and their ships would sit limply at the wrong end of the loch whilst Bárid and the Uí Néill stormed their own fortress.

Einar glanced over his shoulder. Halvdan's ships had not turned. They still rowed full speed towards the north shore. Finn marched with Bárid and Erik, and Einar cursed himself for letting the lad stay ashore. He hated not being there with Finn when there was fighting. He shook that worry out of his head. Finn had proved himself in battle last summer and now commanded his own company of warriors sworn to be his men.

"He hasn't taken the bait," said Hundr. He had relinquished his oar to Erling and now stood at the stern below the steerboard, peering at Halvdan's fleet. "Raise the sail."

"There's no wind," Einar responded, frowning at his friend. "Hoisting the sail now will only make it harder for us to row. Besides, we are nearly there now."

"I don't want it raised for sailing. I want Halvdan to see the one eye upon it. He hates you and me as much as we hate him. He will know that Finn has grown to young manhood now and that where we go, so goes the son of Ivar and rightful heir to Dublin's throne."

Einar grinned at the deep cunning of that. He nodded, and Hundr barked orders at the men to raise the sail. They stared at one another at first, thinking their Jarl had gone mad. But when he bellowed at them, they snapped to it, and they hauled up the yardarm, the halyard and brace rigging before long. The crew unfastened the reef ties, and the sail flopped open, spraying the crew with the foul, cold water locked within her folds. The one-eye sigil stood proud on the white sail, and all men who took to the Whale Road knew it was the sign of the Man with the Dog's Name. Einar leant upon the tiller, peering across the water. The crew bellowed at each other, securing the bowline and shroud. Oars had been brought aboard and rested in their crutches, and the Fjord Bear wallowed in the loch's calm waters.

"I can fart more wind than this," grumbled Amundr, and the men laughed. The sail hung limply on the rigging, but the one eye was still visible. Einar clenched his teeth and remembered Halvdan's fury beneath Dublin's walls, of his hate and his savagery. Hundr had killed his famed brother Ivar, and Einar had taken Finn away from his clutches. Now, Einar hoped that would be enough to lure the wolf away from the unprotected flock inside the Uí Néill fortress.

"They are coming about," said Hundr, steely determination in his voice.

Einar squinted, staring hard across the water. His eyesight wasn't what it used to be, but sure enough, Halvdan's warships were turning in the water. "Bastard has taken the bait," he beamed, clapping Hundr on the back.

Hundr looked up at him, his one eye flashing in the sunlight, the scarred side of his face a torn mess around a sunken, empty socket. "But now he comes to kill us with ten ships and five hundred warriors."

"Thor's balls," said Einar. He had forty warriors aboard the Fjord Bear and another one hundred and thirty aboard the other three of Hundr's warships. They had diverted Halvdan away from the fortress, but it was maddened fury that drove the son of Ragnar Lothbrok away from his target. He came for murder and to settle old scores, and Halvdan terribly outnumbered Einar and Hundr.

"Lower the sail, now!" barked Hundr at the crew. They repeated their earlier stares. Their mouths open like caverns, asking themselves if their Jarl had lost his mind. Hundr sighed. "We have his attention now, which is good," he said, speaking in an even tone, explaining what was about to happen to his warriors. "But Halvdan Ragnarsson comes for us with his chosen champions. He comes to kill us and to send us screaming to Niflheim. So get the bloody sail down, and bring the ship alongside the Wind Elk." Hundr pointed to the line of three ships across the narrows, and Einar understood his friend's plan. They would make a land bridge across the narrows. If they lashed each of the four warships together, then Bárid and the Uí Néill could march their warriors back along the eastern shore and join the fighting aboard Hundr's fleet. If they came.

The crew hurriedly tugged and pulled at the seal hide rigging, lowering the heavy sail they had raised only moments earlier. Einar did not have to shout orders at his men, for they were men of the Whale Road, Viking sailors all, and every man on board the Fjord Bear knew his job, which rope to haul on and which to tie off. They knew when to hop around the deck away from the lowering spar and which knots to tie where to secure the valuable sail. The timbers creaked, and ropes groaned as the crew worked. They snatched oars from their crutches and slid them through the oar holes. As the crew made that first, back-breaking heave, the Fjord Bear lurched forward slowly, then as oars bit and men grunted, she surged forwards. Einar peered behind him to where Halvdan's ships came about on the still water. They turned as one, like a flock of birds returning from their distant winter homes. Those ships glided across the water, and then Einar's stomach clenched as the ten warships came darting in his direction. He could not see at this distance, for the loch was both long and broad, but he imagined Halvdan in his prow, axe in hand, staring hard at him, coming for death and slaughter. Einar dropped his hand to his own axe and smiled to himself. Even at his age, and Einar was sure he had seen at least forty summers, he was not an easy man to kill. He had fought already that day, and his axe blade was red with the blood of his enemies.

"Bárid comes, and with him, Erik and the Uí Néill," said Hundr, pointing eastwards. A band of horsemen galloped ahead of the warriors, who had indeed turned from their march towards the Uí Néill fortress and now came south along the low-lying peninsular that fringed the loch's east coast. There were thirty riders, Einar thought, and he glanced from them to Halvdan's ships. The ships would reach him first.

"We will have to hold against Halvdan's warriors until Bárid arrives. The riders will help us," said Einar. "But it could all be over before Bárid and Erik get here on foot."

"Then I will see you in Valhalla," Hundr replied and flashed a grin. Einar shook his head, remembering Hundr when he was younger. Full of ambition and bravery, hungry to become the man he was today.

"Still full of piss and wind." They both laughed, for men could find humour even in the most dire of circumstances.

They brought the Fjord Bear alongside the Seaworm, not bothering to bring her about so that she lay fore to aft alongside the other *drakkars*, her prow facing into the narrows rather than into the loch itself. The crew lashed the boats together, and Ragnhild ordered men to make ready shields and spears. Einar gripped his weapons. Other men's blood was crusted upon his brynjar, and he readied himself to fight again. He looked over the side, and the Fjord Bear was three-arm spans away from land, and the sea beneath them was still a flood tide. Einar was unfamiliar with the loch's waters, but when the tide ebbed, he knew that being that close to shore meant his beloved ship would flounder, and she would need to wait for the next flood tide before she would float again. Ragnhild raised her eyebrows at him, gesturing to a shield, but Einar refused. He had fought aboard ships many times, and the shield was a hindrance to a killer. Ragnhild was right in what she did. They must form a shield wall and prevent as many of Halvdan's warriors from boarding them as possible. But Einar didn't plan to stand in the shield wall. The Ragnarsson ships drew closer, their beast heads snarling. They fanned out so that they came in two lines of five, and now Einar could see spear points glistening, bearded faces staring, and men coming to kill him. Einar wouldn't stand in the shield wall because he knew what he was. He was a killer, as were Hundr and Ragnhild. Whilst the warriors held their shield wall in place, the killers would strike around its edges, finding space across the decks to hit and stab with the weapons and take their enemies' lives.

The Ragnarsson ships sped closer, and for a horrifying moment, Einar thought they would not ship their oars, that they would plough right into the Fjord Bear and the other Vanylven ships and crush both those and their own hulls in a furious charge. But then the oars came up as one and were shipped on deck. A drum beat shook the Fjord Bear's deck, booming war music to stir men's hearts, and Halvdan's men chanted in time with it.

"Make ready," Einar shouted to his men. Ragnhild ordered them into position, the shield wall firm. She picked up her bow and tested the string. Then, she came to stand with Einar and Hundr behind the shield wall, and they exchanged a fierce look, ready to die beside one another, brothers and sisters of the blade.

A terrifying howl split the air like a knife, high-pitched like a fetch from a story to frighten children on a cold winter's night. Einar turned to see that the horsemen had reached the shore, and at their head was the völva, black robes flowing and her white horse rearing on its hind legs. She screeched and screamed, clinging to her horse's reins and as the beast kicked the air, the völva's hood fell back to reveal flowing iron-grey hair and a face with piercing green eyes. It was a ravaged face, cheeks sunken around missing teeth. It was scarred, terrible, and marked with black tattoos of writhing animals and dark symbols. Although Halvdan Ragnarsson bore down upon him with hundreds of Viking warriors, it was that woman who froze Einar's heart in his chest. Despite her markings and the ageing of her face, Einar knew her, and her wild eyes met his. That look rocked him back on his heels, pure malevolent hatred hitting him like a slap across his face.

TWELVE

A great crash threw Einar from his feet, sending him sprawling in the bilge. The witch had distracted him, and he didn't brace himself for the impact. One of Halvdan's ships thundered into the Fjord Bear's hull in a great crunch, and the opposing lines of ships came together in a rending of timbers and a roaring of warriors. Einar scrambled to his feet but lost sight of the witch, and a thrumming snapped his attention back to the fight. Ragnhild loosed an arrow along the deck, and Einar followed its low arc as it slammed into the chest of a Ragnarsson warrior, pitching him into the water as he tried to clamber aboard the Fjord Bear. Einar came up and charged towards where the fighting raged. Enemy warriors leapt from their ships to be met by a wall of shields and spears. But still, they came in overwhelming numbers, forcing the Fjord Bear's men backwards. A shaven-headed man scrambled over the Fjord Bear's side, around the flank of the shield wall, and Einar slashed his axe across the warrior's face. Blood sprayed from the wound, and he slipped into the depths of the loch to be met by the sea god Ran's welcoming arms. Hundr drove the point of his sword into another warrior's gullet as he placed one boot on the deck, and Einar kicked that man in the gut to send him sprawling over the side.

"Hold them!" Einar shouted. The thud of axe and spear on linden wood crunched like the sound of a forest being felled. Weapons rang off shield bosses and iron rims in reverberating clangs, and men roared at one another, desperate for victory and hungry for blood. Einar peered across the bows and saw a similar story of uncompromising violence. Ragnhild loosed her arrows with deadly accuracy, and men cried out in pain as her shafts found throats, chests and armpits. Einar ducked as a spear tore through the air and soared across the deck above him. One of his men jerked out of the shield wall, clutching at a terrible gash in his throat which pumped dark blood down his breastplate. Hundr dashed into the gap, taking up the injured man's shield, and Einar helped the wounded man to slump against a thwart. He stared at Einar with wide, desperate eyes. Blood pulsed from the wound and around the fingers which the warrior pressed against his torn flesh. There was too much blood, and the warrior knew it. His face turned from the flushed redness of battle exertion to the ashen white of a man who knew death was upon him. Einar pulled the warrior's knife from his belt and pressed it into his hand. The man smiled through bloodied teeth and stared up through the rigging as though waiting to see Odin's Valkyrie come riding down from the clouds to take his soul to Valhalla.

"There are too many," said Ragnhild, edging across the deck carefully as she continued to send her arrows into the enemy. "They have brought their rear rank of ships behind the first, and those men now climb aboard the ships lashed to our own. We will all die here, Einar."

Four warriors in shining brynjars leapt from the deck of the Seaworm onto the Fjord Bear. The men of the Seaworm were hard-pressed. Einar noticed their shield wall had shifted from the prow to amidships, and Ragnhild was right. There could be no successful fight here against so many of Halvdan's men.

"Uí Néill!" came a roar from over his shoulder.

A big man in a wet cloak of green plaid charged past Einar and drove a spear point into one of the Ragnarsson men's stomachs. He let go of the weapon and drew a seax just in time to parry an axe blow.

"Bastards," spat Bárid. He, too, shouldered past Einar and traded axe blows with one of the four warriors who had jumped onto the Fjord Bear. One had fallen already, and Einar followed Bárid into the charge. Bárid and the horsemen ashore had waded through the loch and climbed aboard to join the fight. Einar swung his axe at a stocky warrior with a long beard. The man caught the blow with the haft of his own axe and slashed a knife at Einar's face. He swayed away from that attack, and the enemy warrior kept moving, stamping on Einar's foot and bringing his weapon around to a killing blow. Einar stepped into it so that the blow fouled on his shoulder, and he headbutted the warrior full in the face. The man's nose crunched against Einar's forehead, but his knife jabbed at Einar's ribs so that only his brynjar saved his life.

One of Halvdan's chosen champions, Einar thought. Einar pulled back and swayed from another axe swing. He followed that strike, chopping his own axe into the warrior's wrist, and blood misted before his face. The man gasped in surprise, not used to defeat, likely a champion of some backwater town or village in Norway or Jutland, but now he fought with Einar the Brawler and found his match. Einar slashed his knife at the man's face, and as the brute jerked away from the blade, becoming off balance, Einar kicked him into the path of the warrior who fought with Bárid. Bárid did not hesitate and killed both enemies in a flash of blades.

More Ragnarsson men leapt or climbed aboard the Fjord Bear, and Einar's heart sank as Tostig, a man with a family at Vanylven, fell out of the shield wall with an axe buried in his skull.

"We have to fall back," said Hundr from the thick of the brutal skirmish. The enemy had pushed them along the keel, and there was no room to fight. More of Halvdan's warriors swarmed over the prow. "Send a runner across the other ships to fetch more men. We must retreat to the shore behind a strong defensive line. I will hold them here as long as I can."

Einar nodded, yet he didn't want to send another man charging into the maelstrom of fighting on the other three ships, so he went himself. "Help Hundr, hold them back so we can all retreat across this deck," he said to Bárid. The Irishman had heard the conversation between Hundr and Einar, and he called the order to his own warriors so that they took up positions alongside Hundr, picking up shields where they could and hacking at the enemy with desperate ferocity.

"I'll cover you," called Ragnhild. She moved away from the fighting, ducking under the halyard line, and sent arrows singing across the bows. Halvdan's men aboard the Seaworm shrank back once one of them fell with an arrow buried in his chest up to the feathers. Ragnhild's recurved bow was a thing of tremendous power at so short a distance. Einar took his chance. He slid his axe back into its belt loop and charged over the side. He leapt and landed on the Seaworm deck, his foot slid in a puddle of blood and filth, and he came up with a snarl.

"We can't hold here, Lord Einar," panted Asbjorn, turning from where he fought desperately in a shield wall. Ragnarsson's warriors thronged the deck before them, so much so that the ship canted in the water, overloaded at the prow.

"We go ashore," said Einar. "But wait until the crews of the Stallion and the Elk go past you first." To escape death, their warriors would have to clamber over the decks of the interlocked ships and reach the shore. Asbjorn would have to hold. If the warriors aboard Asbjorn's ship, which was closest to the shore, went first, then Ragnarsson's men would surround and slaughter those on the other ships. Einar set off again. He ran, put one hand on the sheer strake and kicked his legs over the side. He landed on the deck of the Wind Elk but hadn't even looked at what he jumped into. A fist crashed into his jaw, and an axe came for his chest. Einar grabbed a brawny wrist and twisted the axe from its hand. He grabbed his attacker close, a short man with a broken nose and beady grey eyes, and stabbed him in the throat and face five times in quick bursts. He used the man's body as a shield and was lucky because he felt the thud of blades through the man's torso. The dying man's body shook and shivered under the blows as though in a fit, and those blades would have hacked Einar to pieces but for his human shield.

Ragnarsson's men thronged the Elk's deck, and Hundr's warriors lay dead or dying in the bilge. Good men like Hrorik and Ulf, men who Einar had feasted and drunk ale with in his hall. "Get back to the Seaworm, then the Bear, then go ashore! Now!" Einar shouted at a cluster of warriors who formed a desperate shield wall around the mast post. Einar pushed the corpse away from him and into his attacker's blades. He scampered around the rigging to join the warriors at the mast. Torsten stood with those men and led them across the deck in good order, shields raised so that the rabid Ragnarsson warriors found only linden wood as they tried to hack at them.

Einar peered over the side, but the situation on the Stallion was no better. Halvdan's men were thick on the deck, and Bush led a brave defence. Most of his men still lived, but the ship held her crew of fifty warriors, and another twenty enemy warriors were aboard so that she sat overloaded and deep in the water, lower than the Elk, with the waterline almost reaching her sheer strake.

"Bush," Einar shouted over the fury of battle. His friend heard him, turning with a face drawn taut with anger. "We are supposed to get ashore —that way." Einar pointed back across the decks. But Torsten had already led his men over the side towards the Seaworm, and he had gone too early. Another plan gone awry. Einar dragged a bloody hand down his face.

"Cut us loose then," said Bush from behind a shield. "Untie us, and we can push ourselves off."

Einar grinned and drew his axe. He hacked into the rope which secured the Stallion to the Elk, and in four blows, it came loose. An enemy warrior charged from the space left by Torsten's retreating warriors, and Einar killed him with his knife, opening his guts in a vicious slash. Another man came, and Einar edged away from him, searching with his knife hand along the sheer strake for the second mooring rope. The warrior jabbed at Einar with a spear but was timid and would not commit to the attack. Finally, Einar's hand found the rope, though he couldn't turn to cut it because another warrior joined the first, and together they came to kill him. Einar batted the spear away with his axe, but a sword blade snaked out, and pain burst from Einar's face as the tip slashed across his cheek.

"Hold on," Bush said, close by but out of sight. Einar trusted his friend, and instead of striking out at his attackers, he clutched the side. The Elk rocked violently, throwing everyone on board from their feet. Bush had cut the second rope, and the two ships canted to opposite sides now that they were free from each other. Einar left his attackers sprawling in the bilge and jumped onto the Stallion. Bush caught him, and the two men dropped their weapons to snatch up oars from their crutches beside the mast post. Ahead of them, Bush's crew held the Ragnarsson men back, but most had stumbled and fallen when the ships rocked like fishing boats in the wake of a great warship. Einar and Bush pushed with the oars, and the Stallion came away from the Elk slowly at first, but more of the crew dashed to help them, and in heartbeats, they were away from the battle with only twenty enemy warriors on their deck, and those men gaped at the open water between them and their own shipmates for they faced the Stallion's entire crew of fifty warriors.

"Kill them all," Einar said, and so they did. They threw the corpses over the side, then Bush ordered his men to the oars, and they brought the ship about in the narrow water space leading from the sea to the loch. Einar led them ashore and brought a ship's crew of warriors to the fight unfolding on the banks of the loch's eastern peninsular. As Einar and Hundr had fought desperately aboard their ships, Erik and Finn had marched along the spit of grass-covered land to reach the shore. There was now an army facing Halvdan Ragnarsson's men. Halvdan's warriors poured from the deck of the Fjord Bear in dozens, wading through the water to take up a position facing their enemies. Once he saw Hundr had left the ships, Halvdan brought his rear rank of warships about and now unloaded more warriors so that he had hundreds of fighters ashore. Einar and Bush led the Stallion's crew in a wide sweep, away from the Ragnarsson men, towards where Hundr stood in the front rank, facing the enemy.

Einar barged his way through the shield wall, men turning to growl at him but quickly swallowing their anger when they saw his size, his blood-spattered brynjar, and the set of his slab-like face.

"Why don't we just charge the bastards?" Einar

lipped as he reached Hundr. Bárid was there in the front rank, as was his huge Irish warrior with the double-handed sword. Finn stood in the second rank, and Einar smiled to see the lad safe. Ragnhild stood with Finn, shield in hand, and the Uí Néill warriors all about them in their distinctive cloaks.

"There has been too much fighting already," Hundr said simply.

"I want Halvdan dead, so let the old wolf come ashore," Bárid seethed, a ruthless grin splitting his handsome face.

Einar licked at dry lips, the cut on his face stinging and his body aching from exhaustion. The faces of the surrounding men were scratched and bloody, their eyes sunken from the fighting on the beach and then aboard the Vanylven fleet.

"Hold this," said Hundr, handing Einar his shield.

"Why?" Einar replied.

"Halvdan only turned back from the fortress because he saw my banner. He came back to kill me and Finn and you as well... if he can."

Einar shrugged and laughed at that truth. Hundr stepped out of the line and drew his two swords. He stood between the lines of warriors who had drawn up behind round shields but had not yet found the courage to charge one another. Battle seemed like a simple thing when the tales of it slid from the silky tongues of skalds in fire-lit feasting halls. But the shield wall, and any fighting involving blades, was a thing of unimaginable horror. It took courage for men to join the shield wall and risk death or terrible wounds. Courage, hate, or ale. Often it took all three, and Einar had seen armies face off like this for an entire day before retiring to fight the next.

"Take this," Einar said, passing Hundr's shield to Bush. He, too, strode out of the line to stand alongside Hundr. Bárid came with him, as did Erik Bjornsson.

"Halvdan Ragnarsson," Einar shouted, sensing what Hundr was up to. Time to goad the bear out of its cave and end the fight. "I am Einar Rosti, Jarl of Vanylven. This is the Man with the Dog's Name, Bárid mac Ímair, and Erik, son of Bjorn Ironside. Show yourself, or are you too old to fight? Do you cower behind your men like an old whore?"

The grim-faced warriors in the shield wall facing Einar bristled, but their ranks parted, and a man strode through them. He removed his helmet, a shining thing topped with a tail of horsehair, and Einar recognised Halvdan, son of Ragnar. Halvdan had a white beard streaked with black like a badger. He was of average height and build, with stooped shoulders. He had bone-white hair close-cropped to his head and wore a shining brynjar and a belt studded with gold.

"So all the turds are gathered together," said Halvdan, his voice as rough and grating as a shipwright's plane. "Even this Bárid, who claims he is my brother's son but is nothing more than a *skraeling* son of a nithing Irishman using other men's names for his own ends." Four big men flanked Halvdan, each wearing chain mail brynjars and helmets with eye rings and closed cheek pieces that hid their faces, making them seem inhuman, like war demons from the otherworld. One held a long spear from which the raven banner hung limply.

"You stole Dublin's throne," Bárid spat, and Halvdan chuckled scornfully at the young warrior. He curled his lip and looked Bárid up and down as though he examined a horse on market day and found it wanting. Einar noted Bárid did not mention from whom Halvdan had stolen the throne, for Finn was surely the rightful heir and not Bárid.

"Surrender to us, and your men shall live," said Hundr. Halvdan was only ten paces away from him, but he shouted so Halvdan's men could hear.

Halvdan let out what passed for a laugh, but

it came as a grim wheeze. He was the last surviving son of Ragnar, the great Viking raider and sacker of cities. Ragnar had died in a snake pit, thrown there by King Aelle of Northumbria. As the snakes sank their fangs into his flesh, Ragnar shouted to the King how the little pigs would grunt when they heard how the old boar had died. And so they had. The little pigs were Ivar the Boneless, Sigurd Snake Eye, Ubba, and Halvdan himself. Ragnar's sons had killed Aelle of Northumbria, then the King of East Anglia, razing most of England. No Ragnarsson had died in his bed, and the power of his notorious family and his own legend pulsed from Halvdan like seiðr magic.

"Where is Uí Néill?" Halvdan said with a sigh, as though he grew tired of the parlay.

A man shouldered through the ranks behind Einar, a balding man with a grizzled beard, his plaid cloak thrown over one shoulder, clasped with a silver cloak pin, and he wore a heavy torc of twisted gold.

"Here I am, Dubgaill," said the Irishman.

"We can have peace, Mael. I have Dublin, and you have the north. Stop raiding my lands, and I'll stop raiding yours. But these three must die. Give them to me, and we shall sail away in peace." Halvdan pointed at Bárid, Einar and Hundr.

"You are afraid," said Hundr. He sensed that their lives hung on a knife edge, as did Einar. Mael, the leader of the Uí Néill clan, owed them nothing. Einar had never even met the man. They only fought together because Bárid had led them to the battle in search of Erik's brother and with the promise of Halvdan's ships if they were victorious. The Irishman could easily hand Einar and Hundr over with no guilt or oath broken. "You are old and a coward; your father would be ashamed of you."

Einar winced. Hundr was a great man for hurling insults before a battle.

"I killed your brother and his son. So, fight with me now. Just you and I," Hundr continued.

Halvdan smiled, the smile a serpent must offer to a mouse before it devours it. His beady eyes flicked to Mael, but Einar could not see the Uí Néill leader's reaction behind him.

"I don't need to fight you, dog. You have already lost."

There was a shifting behind them, and panic raised the gorge in Einar's throat. He imagined Irish hands clamping on his shoulders and leading him and his men to Halvdan in return for peace. So, Einar did the only thing he had ever been good at, the thing that had seen him rise from nothing to become Jarl of Vanylven. He fought.

Einar didn't even bother to draw his axe. He just launched himself at Halvdan. The old wolf gasped in surprise as Einar charged into the gap between them. One of Halvdan's guards stepped in, so Einar batted his spear point aside with his forearm and barrelled into him. Einar grabbed the man's head and jammed his thumbs into the eyeholes of his helmet. The warrior screamed and bucked, and the jelly of his eyes gave way to blood. Einar let him drop, roaring his defiance so that Odin himself could hear it. He ripped his axe free and buried it into the hip of another of Halvdan's guardsmen, and then chaos erupted all around Einar. Bárid stumbled away from Halvdan with a knife stuck in his thigh. Halvdan snarled at him, whipping his sword free of its scabbard and slashing at the Irishman, but Bárid was dragged away by his men, howling at the pain of the knife in his leg. Hundr pounced at Halvdan, and the two met in a clang of swords to shake Yggdrasil itself. Men instinctively stepped back from the two fighters, knowing that they witnessed something rare. The crowd watched as the two fair-famed champions confronted each other, a thing that would be remembered long after all the men on the shore were dead and gone. A thing of legend.

Einar, too, stepped away. The warriors he had injured writhed on the grass in pain, clutching at their wounds. Halvdan and Hundr circled one another. Hundr drew his second sword from over his shoulder, and Halvdan pulled a seax free of his belt. Halvdan struck out lightning fast, but Hundr parried the blow. Halvdan came up with his seax, but Hundr let the attack pass him. At that moment, a look passed across the old wolf's face, knowing that Hundr outmatched him. It was a long-faced look of sadness, quickly replaced by a snarl. Halvdan threw himself at Hundr like a man half his age. They blocked and parried each other's blows in a blur of sword skill, almost too fast to follow. Suddenly, Halvdan reeled away in a spray of crimson, and his sword flew out of his hand. Hundr stepped in, sliced one sword across Halvdan's face, and drove his second blade point into Halvdan's stomach. The links of his expensive mail burst and Halvdan folded over the blade, sinking to his knees. Hundr kicked him onto his back, and the seax fell from Halvdan's left hand. Hundreds of warriors on both sides gasped as the son of Ragnar fell without a blade. Hundr dropped his sword and leapt for Halvdan's own. He scrambled in the grass to pick it up and then leapt back to the son of Ragnar. Hundr pressed the sword into Halvdan's fist and bent to whisper in the dying man's ear.

Silence passed over the armies, and a chill wind kissed Einar's neck. Halvdan's body

THE RAVEN AND THE NINE

twitched as he died, and Einar shivered as though the Aesir gods were with them to witness the death of so great a warrior. A man who had sacked Paris, conquered Saxon kingdoms, killed kings and forged for himself a kingdom in Ireland. Einar swallowed, and his shoulders sagged, for Halvdan was the last warlord of an age which ended with his death, or perhaps Einar himself was the last of those men who had grown up around Ragnar Lothbrok, a man who turned village raiders and seafarers into the most feared warriors in the world. Einar had been a boy in Ragnar's home, grown up around the sons, and served as a sea Jarl for Ivar. Einar's own father had sailed with Ragnar, and their deeds will live on forever in the songs and sagas told by skalds wherever men's hearts yearn for tales of daring, bravery and drengskapr, the way of the warrior. He had wanted Halvdan's demise, but it made him feel no better about Sten or Kolo's deaths, friends who had died years ago at the hands of Halvdan's warriors. Einar's heart sat heavy in his chest, memories of the old days thick inside his thought cage like honey.

"Luck stealer!" a screeching voice cackled, destroying the reverent silence. Hooves splashed in the lapping water upon the shore, and the völva rode her white horse to the place where Halvdan died. She sat atop her warhorse, hood thrown back, and her ruined mouth twisted with hate. She pointed her staff at Hundr, clutched by a bony hand, and trinkets jangled from the length of wood, bones, silver pendants and other things of dark seiðr. "Kill him before he steals your luck for his own glory. Seize him."

Einar's jaw fell open then because he had indeed seen the völva before. She had been younger then and beautiful. It was Saoirse, the Irish daughter of a king. She, who had been the wife of Ivar, and the woman for whom Hundr's love had known no bounds.

THIRTEEN

Hundr took his hand from behind Halvdan's neck, laying the son of Ragnar on the trampled grass, where thick blood pooled from his death wounds. He stood and stared at the screeching woman on the pale horse. Hate poured from her in waves, a powerful thing which rocked Hundr back a few steps. Yet, beneath the dirt and filth on her skin and the greasy tangle of hair, it was a face he knew. A face he had loved so much that he would have died for her. It was Saoirse.

"What are you waiting for?" she howled, throwing her head back and screaming at the sky. She roared toward Mael and where Bárid lay injured amongst his warriors. Her mouth was a cavern of darkness, punctured by a handful of rotten teeth, her face lined and covered in writhing tattoos. "Strike him down, kill him. Even now, your luck drains into him."

Mael, the leader of the Uí Néill warriors, raised his hands for calm, and she spat into the water in disgust. She screamed again and grabbed her horse's reins, and for a moment, Hundr thought she would ride him down, but Murrough grabbed the bridle and spoke to her in hushed words, too quiet for Hundr to hear. Her malevolent eyes, which had ones so captured his heart, now flicked from Murrough to Hundr, dripping with malice. Saoirse shook her staff at Hundr and wheeled her horse around, its great hooves churning the loch's shallows. She cantered away from the shore and back along the hillside northwards. Men peeled away from the ranks to follow her. Each of those men carried a black shield and did not wear the plaid cloaks of the Uí Néill or Bárid's warriors.

"So, what now?" said Mael. He had taken the few steps unnoticed and stood beside Hundr, staring at the Ragnarsson warriors. Hundreds of those men stood dumbfounded, staring at the dead king before them. Mael was of a size with Hundr but had seen ten more summers at least. His thinning hair was brushed back from a face that was circular in shape, and atop his slim nose were two intelligent blue eyes. There were few scars on Mael's face, nor on his arms. So he was no fighter, but to lead an Irish clan famous for its ferocity, Mael must be a man of great cunning and one to be wary of.

"Keep their ships," answered Hundr with a shrug. "Strip their weapons, armour, arm rings and anything of value, and let them march back to Dublin."

"We should let Bárid decide," said Murrough. The big Irishman strode from the water's edge, his huge sword slung across his back and his flame-red hair tied in braids. He jerked a thumb to where Bárid lay on the battlefield. Men crouched with him, and Bárid shook with pain, beads of sweat running down his face and both hands clutching his thigh. Halvdan's knife was still buried in the meat of his leg, just above the knee.

"There will be a new King in Dublin now," Einar uttered, and he frowned at the big man before looking at Hundr.

In the surprise of seeing Saoirse in this place, so changed and so full of hate for him, and in the tumult of his fight with Halvdan, Hundr had not considered what would happen if Halvdan died. He had come to kill Halvdan to exact revenge for his long-dead friends, but Halvdan was the King in Dublin. That throne had been usurped from

Finn, the son of Ivar. Hundr searched the ranks of warriors behind him, and Finn stood with Erik just behind where Bárid lay. The young warrior had fought, the marks of battle clear upon his brynjar and his weapons. He did not even care to look at where the leaders spoke, where they would decide the fate of Dublin and Halvdan's army. Clearly, the thought had not occurred to Finn either that he had a claim to a throne and could be King of Dublin. If he could press his claim.

"Aye," Murrough nodded. He stared at Einar, then glanced at Hundr and back to Bárid. "All must be settled, for there are two sons of Ivar, or so it seems." There was already tension there. Einar now stared back at Murrough, keeping his eyes fixed upon the big man, a familiar hardness settling over Einar's cliff of a face.

Mael stepped between them. "We must celebrate our victory tonight in my hall," he said, placing a hand on both Einar and Murrough's shoulders. "First, though, we must deal with Halvdan's men."

Hundr sighed and nodded. He marched to where Halvdan's corpse lay and met the eyes of the Ragnarsson army, hard men who had come for victory and plunder, yet instead, they'd lost their Lord.

"I am Jarl Hundr, the Man with the Dog's

Name," Hundr said. He had no fondness for the moniker. His name, Hundr, meant dog in Norse. Einar's crew had flung the name upon him when he had joined the Seaworm as a bail boy. He hadn't wanted to give his own name, the one given to him by his mother in far Novgorod, so Bush and the others had called him Hundr, and the name had stuck. Hundr also knew the fair fame hanging from his byname, the fame he had sought when leaving his home as a boy with nothing. Hundr waited, noting how Halvdan's growlers recognised his name. There were mumbles and grumbles amongst them. Iron clanked and wood thudded as weapons shifted and came to rest on shields or over shoulders. This was a delicate thing, to ask an army to surrender. They had not beaten these men, and Halvdan had been winning the battle before he died. Only the shock defeat of their legendary King prevented them from slaughtering their way through Hundr's, Mael's, and Bárid's men. Vikings respected men with reputations, and they expected confidence and swagger from their leaders. Hundr had to have all of that to convince the Ragnarsson army of what must happen next. "You have all heard of me," he continued. "For I killed Ivar the Boneless and his son Hakon in Northumbria. I killed Eystein Longaxe in Dublin. I have killed Frankish Lords, Norse Jarls, and Prince Yaroslav of Novgorod. Many men say I am the Champion of the North, and now I have killed your King, Halvdan Ragnarsson. Two sons of Ragnar have fallen to my sword. How many of you can boast of such things?"

Hundr paused again, taking time to meet many of the hard eyes staring at him from the ranks. "There is no shame in what must happen now, for though your King is dead, you fought bravely, and your reputation as the finest warriors on the Whale Road stands true." The Norse warriors of Dublin carried no such reputation, but it did no harm to stoke their pride. "But I killed Halvdan, and we won the battle. The fight is over. Any man here can challenge me now, we will make the Holmgang square next to your Lord's corpse, and you can try your luck." He stepped forward, waiting to see if any of Halvdan's champions would take up the challenge, but none did. They had seen Hundr kill Halvdan and heard the völva howling about his luck stealing. Hundr pushed the wyrd of that out of his thought cage, for now. "Good," he said. "Who commands you now that Halvdan is dead?"

A murmur rose from them like a thick sea haar as the great amongst the army looked to one another for a leader. A burly warrior stepped forward. He held a long-handled war axe with blood crusting on the curved blade. The warrior wore a fine brynjar mail coat and a helmet upon his head. He pulled the helmet off and let it fall to the ground.

"I am Vandrad of Skaland," he intoned, his voice deep in a bushy beard which covered his face from just below his eyes. The beard fell into a thick braid across his chain mail. His head was entirely bald, as smooth as a goose egg. "I am... or was Halvdan's champion. I can speak for our men. We have heard of you, Hundr, and you, Einar Rosti."

"I killed Halvdan in a fair fight," said Hundr, choosing to overlook the warrior's lack of formality, keeping his eyes fixed upon Vandrad's. "So, I claim his fleet of warships as my own. You men, however, came to kill the Uí Néill and are at war with Bárid mac Ímair, so your fate rests with them. I will speak for you, for you fought bravely, and I will ask Mael of the Uí Néill to let you return to Dublin unharmed."

Vandrad raised a fist to his chest to acknowledge the fairness in that.

"You must now lay down your weapons. You can make camp here on this spit of land until all is decided."

The fight was gone from them, and the Ragnarsson warriors lay down their weapons. Many were still aboard Halvdan's ships, but Hundr left the mess of that to Mael and

Murrough, for it was an Irish war and an Irish problem.

They spent much of the rest of that day marching wearily northwards along the shores of the loch where men looked for food and ale from the Uí Néill. Mael and his folk were generous in their thanks for both Hundr's and Bárid's warriors. Ale flowed like water, and Mael had his people set up tents made of sailcloth for the warriors to make a camp outside his fortress's walls. Erik's men guarded the Ragnarsson warriors as they sat sullen and hungry on the peninsular where they had been defeated, and Erik questioned Vandrad and others about his lost brother. Finn stayed with Erik rather than joining the Vanylven crews in their celebrations. Hundr, Einar, Ragnhild, and Bush saw to the safety of their ships, and the new vessels won following the battle. Men rowed the boats safely away from the narrows and away from Vandrad and his warriors, who were still close to five hundred strong even after the brutal fighting. One of Halvdan's ships was ruined. Her hull caved in when she struck the Wind Elk, but there were nine good ships moored off the loch's northwestern shore. They were a mix of *drakkars* and smaller *snekke* vessels, and Bush went between each ship, appraising keel, lines and rigging, scratching at his head beneath his stained leather helmet liner, grinning to himself at some, and shaking his head at others.

Hundr sat with Einar and Ragnhild. Their newly enlarged fleet lay at anchor in the lee of the many islands scattered along the loch's western shore, and the three friends warmed their hands at one of many campfires dotting the northern lowlands like so many stars in the fading daylight.

"To Sten and Kolo," said Hundr, raising a cup of ale. "May they look down upon us from the afterlife and see their deaths avenged."

Einar banged his wooden mug off Hundr's, and frothy ale slopped onto the soft grass. They had taken a sail from one of the new ships and cut branches from trees to make a tent on the small island. From there, they could see the Uí Néill fortress, high ramparts with a timber keep behind it, shadowed against the setting sun, and the raucous celebrations drifted over the water. Laughter, singing and pipe playing intermingled into a constant rumble.

"Sten is in the Christ heaven," said Ragnhild. "I don't know if Kolo sees our deeds or if he has gone to Valhalla or to the gods of his own people." She stared into the crackling fire, the orange glow catching wetness in her one eye.

"We came here for vengeance and wealth. Halvdan is dead, and we have nine warships. We are not yet at midsummer and have done all we set out to do. Are you happy that Halvdan is gone?"

"It does not bring Kolo back," she murmured, sniffing before squaring her shoulders. She drank her ale and smiled at Hundr, a forced, wan smile. "But, yes. We have killed an enemy; it has been a good fighting season. Even if we did not kill that sneaky bastard, Rollo."

"Are you regretting not returning to the Valkyrie order last year?"

"No, I don't regret that. I could not go back now after so long. My place is with you two and Hildr. We are our own order now." She drained her cup and stared out across the twilight-darkened water. Ragnhild had returned to her order of Valkyrie priestesses at Upsala the year before. They had rebuked her before sending them all on a search for Odin's lost spear. Hundr and Ragnhild had recovered the spear, and the order would have welcomed Ragnhild back amongst them, but she had instead returned with Hundr and Einar to Vanylven.

"Well, I am glad you stayed with us," said Hundr, holding out a hand. She took it in the warrior's grip and finally gave a proper smile, one that made her cheeks lift into round balls. Hundr laughed warmly, and she rewarded him with a friendly punch to the shoulder.

"What in Thor's arse are we going to do with these ships?" Einar sighed. He leant over to take their cups and refilled them from the wooden keg Mael's steward had provided along with three loaves of bread, thick yellow butter, some cheese and a rack of pork ribs.

"Keep one of the best boats," said Hundr. "Take on more men to crew her. Sell the rest?"

"Do we need another ship?"

"We could always use more men. After all, Rollo lives, and he hates us more than Halvdan. That hatred will burn even more brightly now, given we attacked his hall."

"More men require more food to feed them all winter, less of a share for our current crews after every fight," said Ragnhild.

"True enough," Einar nodded. He stroked his beard. "We can't sell them in Dublin for obvious reasons. Maybe Mael or Bárid might buy a few? If not, then maybe King Harald?"

"Why not Dublin?" said Hundr. "Surely Finn will be King there now?" The words landed into an awkward silence. Finn's fate was heavy on each of their minds, but the warp and weft of it were like holding a loaf just out of the oven.

"Does he want to be King?" asked Ragnhild.

"I don't know," said Einar. "We have never

spoken of it. We just raised him to be a warrior, to follow the ways of the drengr. I never thought he might actually take up his father's throne."

"Seems to me that Bárid wants it, though," Ragnhild remarked, which was true enough. "Should we look for Finn now, keep him with us?"

Hundr stared at her and then at Einar, the thought dawning on each of them simultaneously. They barely knew Bárid. He could be as ruthless as his father. It would be all too simple to seek Finn in the night and slip a seax into his gullet, removing any competition for the throne.

"Yes, I'll look for him before we sleep," said Einar. "But first, there is another hard thing for us to get out in the open and speak of. The witch."

Hundr looked away, his turn now to stare wistfully into the crackling fire.

"It was her, the bitch who lured us into that trap in Dublin. All sweetness and soft skin on the outside, wicked cunning and ambition on the inside," sneered Ragnhild. She spat into the fire to ward off the evil of it all. "That bitch hates you still. She spoke of luck, and you stole hers right enough. No point dancing around the truth of that."

Hundr hadn't thought of it like that before,

but since meeting him during a Saxon ambush in a deep Northumbrian forest, Saoirse's life had taken a violently different path from the one laid out before her as a girl in Ireland. She was the daughter of an Irish king, sent to marry the son of Ivar the Boneless to make peace between him and his Irish enemies. Yet Hundr fell in love with her and then pursued her, even after she was returned to her betrothed, Hakon Ivarsson. She had never loved him back, not in the same way, and Saoirse had understood that her duty as Princess was to marry Hakon and bring peace to her people.

Hundr fed a branch to the fire, jolting the flames and held his hands up to the warmth before taking another drink of ale. He had been young then, full of ruthless ambition. Everything seemed possible for a lad who had fled Novgorod and made his own way north, scavenging food as he went, stealing and doing whatever was necessary to survive. Eventually, Hundr had made it to the coast, where Einar took him on as a bail boy. He was the lowest of the crew, taunted and poor in his tattered jerkin. But the one thing his father, Rurik, the Prince of Novgorod, had given Hundr was a childhood of lessons with Novgorod's weapons master. Hundr might have slept with the animals and had a northern concubine for a mother, but he had learned to fight with sword, axe, spear and bow.

Those skills had helped him rise within Einar's crew so that by the time Hundr met Saoirse, he was already a belligerent warrior, so sure that he could win whatever he wished with only sword skill and courage. She had been his first love, and it was the wild love of youth, fierce and overwhelming. Hundr had climbed the walls of Ivar's stone stronghold in York to see her, and she had told him she must marry Hakon, but her guards spotted Hundr, and all became chaos. Maybe he had stolen her luck, along with Hakon's and Ivar's. Because of his actions, both men died in the end, and they forced Saoirse to find other ways to survive and maintain her position in Dublin. Not the ways of the blade but a woman's ways of cunning and self-sacrifice.

"Did Finn recognise her?" said Hundr, still in his daze, drawn to the flicker and warmth of the fire.

"No," Einar replied. "She looks less like his mother than ever. But she must have seen him. What mother does not know her own son?"

"Then he is in danger."

"She might be mad, but she would not kill him?"

"No," Hundr allowed. "But she will want him back. He is the heir to Dublin's throne and her son. Imagine her longing and despair since he left these shores with us."

"I'd hoped the bitch had died under my arrow," Ragnhild muttered.

"Well, she didn't," said Einar. "And she has a different power now. A völva's power. There are such women in the North; they can stir men's minds and direct their blades."

"So, find Finn before she does," urged Hundr. "We should leave this place as soon as the ships are ready."

"We don't have the men to crew another nine ships."

"We have enough to get them to the Welsh or the Saxons. We can sell them there. Or take on men to get us to Frankia to find buyers. We are richer than we have ever been, but only if we can turn ships into silver."

Einar nodded, pushed himself to his feet and went off to find Finn.

"We won, and there should be more joy in it," lamented Ragnhild with a long sigh.

"There is a strange wyrd about it," said Hundr. "A heavy thing unseen. The sooner we leave, the better."

FOURTEEN

Morning came with a spiteful drizzle. Hundr awoke to the ever-present early dawn sound of grinding grain. Across the world, people met the day with pestle and mortar or stone and slab, grinding wheat or oats to break the night's fast. Only lords and kings escaped that inevitability, and only because they had slaves to do the work for them. Yawns accompanied the crunching and crushing of stone on grain, along with the burps and farts of men who had drank too much ale. People rekindled fires and threw oats into small pots or upturned helmets to make porridge. Hundr washed his face in the loch's shallows. Light rain dappled the water, pitting its surface, and Hundr pulled his cloak close about his neck. The cook fires hissed, and the sea breathed within the loch and over the eastern peninsular. Hundr took a wooden bowl from Thorgrim and ate the sticky porridge as he went to find Ragnhild. She sat with Bush and Amundr, cleaning her bow and listening to Bush grumbling about the new ships and how to sail them.

"Einar didn't return last night, then?" asked Hundr. He had searched their island camp on the western shore, but none of the men had seen Einar.

"I haven't seen him," shrugged Bush. "Hopefully, he didn't get drunk and thump a few Irisher heads together."

Hundr frowned because that was entirely likely. Einar was a great man, a kind and loyal friend, and a good husband to Hildr. But he was also warlike and violent, a brawler and a killer. "I'd best go and find him then. And Finn."

"I'll go with you," said Ragnhild. "Like as not, Finn is still with Erik."

"I'll come too," rumbled Amundr in his drum-deep voice.

So they climbed aboard the Seaworm, and ten men rowed them across the still loch towards the Uí Néill stronghold, which rose from the

213

drizzling haar mist like a great shadow, smoke rising from morning fires and the sounds of animals braying and men coughing came from it like distant echoes. The people behind the palisade no doubt thanked the gods, or the Christ god, that they awoke that morning as free folk. If Halvdan Ragnarsson had lived and had his way, then they would be dead, enslaved, or raped. But Halvdan was dead, and the defeated Ragnarsson army huddled on the loch's southeastern spit, waiting to learn their fate.

"Bush will have to get the ships washed out before we sail," Ragnhild noted, grimacing at the splatters and pools of congealing blood on the deck.

"A few buckets of seawater will sort that out," said Amundr.

Even after all his years at the blade, it still surprised Hundr how much blood a man's body held. The skalds sang of battle, and the glory of it, and there was glory in it. Hundr knew that more than most, but there was also the horror of the dead and dying. Now, it was the morning after the battle. Reputations burnished, men had celebrated their victory, and all that remained was the blood sloshing in ships' bilges and an army of defeated men to deal with.

"You should have gone to Mael's hall last night," said Ragnhild.

Hundr shrugged. "It's no care of mine what happens to Halvdan's men. We came to kill him, and he is dead. We have ships to sell to keep our warriors in rings and silver. Let the others decide what will become of them."

The Seaworm crunched into a shingle beach, and Hundr jumped into the loch's shallows, cursing that his boots would be soaked for most of the day. Ragnhild and Amundr followed, and the crew dropped an anchor stone with orders to wait until Hundr returned. The shore was thick with men. Mael was clever enough to keep most of the army outside his walls. Using up his stores of ale and food to keep them happy was far simpler than trying to contain hundreds of Viking warriors and preventing them from molesting his people.

Hundr marched through the camped warriors, fires flickering to life and men emerging from tents gasping for water or more ale after too much supped the night before. Men in leather armour, or as yet unarmoured in simple jerkins, and proud warriors in brynjars were thick on the land like fleas on a grizzled hound. Hundr had tied a strip of black cloth around his missing eye. Rain always stung the flesh inside the puckered socket. The hood of his cloak was pulled over his hair; he had tied it by a strip of leather at the nape of his neck. He wore his two swords and two thongs attached his seax to the rear of his belt. Hundr also wore his brynjar, washed free of blood and war-filth with a handful of loch sand, and his arms were thick with warrior rings. Ragnhild and Amundr went similarly garbed in their chain mail coats, arms jangling with silver and gold rings. Men bowed their heads as the three stalked amongst them. Hundr heard men whisper his name, or Ragnhild's, and he nodded greetings in return. Some men stopped him, extending their hands, which he took in the warrior's grip. Where he knew a man's name, Hundr would say it and recall an act of bravery or skill. One man pushed a crust of bread into his hand, and another gave Ragnhild a skin of ale. Hundr asked for Einar at each fire, but there was no sign. Eventually, a man of Erik's crew pointed to the fortress, saying that he had seen Erik, Einar, and Finn go inside late into the night and that they had not yet returned.

Hundr, Amundr, and Ragnhild doubled back and marched along the shore with the dark, wet timbers of the Uí Néill palisade rising before them, sharpened stake timbers high and well maintained beyond a steep ditch. Just as Hundr approached a bridge spanning the ditch, a band of men emerged from an open gate in the fortress wall. There could be no mistaking Einar, his size marking him out even in the drizzle of misted morning gloom. Einar was with Finn, Erik and Erik's men, Vigfus and Gjalandi, and Bárid's man, Murrough. Hundr paused and waited for the group to cross the bridge.

"A fine Irish summer morning," quipped Murrough. He rubbed his hands together and smiled through the red of his beard.

"It's bloody miserable," said Amundr, squinting up into the rain, and Ragnhild chuckled.

"So, what news?" Hundr asked. He looked at Einar, but the big man looked away, not wanting to meet Hundr's eye. He clenched his jaw. There was a turd in the ale barrel of whatever Einar didn't want to tell him.

"There is news about my brother," said Erik. He wore his bear fur cloak, and a dunt taken in battle had already swollen and purpled the left side of his face. "He was in Dublin but then lost in the wars beyond its walls, fighting Irishmen. So, I will stay and look for him and his men."

"And I will go with him," said Finn, smiling broadly, first at Einar, then at Hundr. "We shall go to Dublin with Erik and Bárid."

"And what of Dublin, now that Halvdan is dead?" asked Hundr, keeping his eye on Finn.

"We have agreed that Bárid will be King there. He is the elder son of Ivar and the rightful heir."

"I see," said Hundr, not seeing at all. Perhaps

Bárid was the elder son, and perhaps therefore, he had a stronger claim to the throne, but just as Halvdan had tried to kill Finn when he was a boy, Bárid was unlikely to rest with another heir and claimant to the throne alive and kicking for men to rally around should his rule prove unpopular. "How is Bárid?"

"The wound in his leg is grievous," Murrough replied, frowning. "Halvdan's knife bit deep."

"Let me take a look," said Ragnhild.

"She is a Valkyrie priestess, a skilled healer," explained Hundr.

"I thank you," Murrough intoned, bowing his head to Ragnhild. "Please, come with me." He strode back towards Mael's stronghold, and Ragnhild followed.

"I met my mother," said Finn brightly. Hundr fought to keep his face like a stone, fending off the worry of that like an enemy spear. Finn had often asked Einar and Hildr about his mother. He had left her at an age where he was old enough to remember her, but that parting had been a desperate escape from Halvdan's warriors, who were bent on Finn's death. Even before that, Finn had been Halvdan's ward in England, and Saoirse had come to Hundr in Frankia to ask for help to free the boy from his fearsome uncle. Hundr had obliged, but it had been a cunning ploy to lure Hundr to his death. Hundr stared up into the rain, wondering if the Norns laughed at him. Those three sisters had woven the threads of his own life together with those of Saoirse, Finn, Einar and the sons of Ragnar in a deeply tangled web of fate and death.

"Is she here?" asked Hundr, keeping his tone even.

"Yes, she joined King Mael's feast last night. He is the King of the Northern Uí Néill, and my mother has her own warband. She has power here, Hundr. She is a Queen."

"I saw her black shields at the battle."

"Yes, they will help us search for Erik's brother."

Hundr stared at Einar. He wanted to tell Finn to be careful, to leave Ireland and take ship with him for the lands of the Saxons or Frankia, and then home to Vanylven, where Hildr and Einar loved him, where he could be safe. Hundr had killed Finn's father, a thing never spoken of but which hung between them like iron, red hot from the forge, a thing not to be touched lest it burn, but something that could be moulded and crafted. Whether that was comradeship and understanding, or hate and resentment, Hundr did not know. The silence crept into awkwardness, Finn's eyes on Hundr and Hundr's eye on Einar.

"I will stay with the lad," Einar said eventually. He spoke quickly and with a wave of his hand as if it were nothing. "We'll take half the captured ships to Dublin and sell them there. Bárid assures us of a good price. I'll keep the Fjord Bear and her crew."

Hundr nodded slowly, his mouth in an upside-down smile. "Very well. So, I'll leave with the Elk, Seaworm, and the Stallion with four of Halvdan's ships, and we'll meet you back at Vanylven before summer's end."

"You will be a father by then," said Einar cheerfully.

"I'll sacrifice to Freya and ask for luck for your wife," chimed Erik, and he stepped forward to pull Hundr into a warm embrace.

"And I hope you find your brother."

Hundr wished Finn and Einar well and then returned to the Seaworm. His heart was heavy and full of fear for his friend and for Finn. Einar loved the young warrior like a son, and it did not surprise Hundr that Einar had stayed in Ireland with him. Einar would do anything to protect Finn, even if the young Ivarsson was more than capable of protecting himself. Yet, despite not being surprised, Hundr was still disappointed.

"I wouldn't stay here for a ship full of silver," Amundr grumbled as their boots crunched tiny shells on the beach. "Doesn't feel right. There's trouble here. Bloody place makes my arse wink."

"We'll leave as soon as we can," said Hundr.

They climbed aboard the Seaworm and took cover from the rain under the sail, which the men had stretched over the lowered yardarm. Ragnhild returned before midday, and they rowed back to the island camp, which was alive with men busy breaking camp and preparing the ships for sea. Hundr stood in the prow, and he cursed to himself as the ship advanced, for waiting on the shore was a clutch of warriors holding shields with leather coverings painted black, and at their centre was a small woman in a dark cloak and hood. She stood back from her warriors and well away from Hundr's camp.

"It's the Witch-Queen," said Amundr, clutching the Mjolnir amulet at his neck to ward off her evil. Hundr ignored him and swallowed the impulse to clatter the giant around the head for always stating the painfully obvious.

"I should just put another arrow into the bitch from here," Ragnhild seethed. Which was not a bad idea, other than for the storm it would cause. "What is she the queen of, anyway? As far as I can remember, she was a follower of the Christ god, and now, suddenly, she is a völva?" Ragnhild spat in disgust.

"Let's see what she wants. Then we'll leave," said Hundr. He spoke evenly as though Saoirse's presence was nothing to him. Yet, in reality, her presence balefully reached out to him, clawing an icy fist around his heart. Old feelings and memories swamped his thought cage like seawater in a drowning man's lungs.

The crew moored the ship close to the island, and Hundr jumped from the prow, made his way through the shallow water, and stalked up the beach, his hand thumbing Fenristooth's ivory hilt in its scabbard at his belt. The black shield warriors glared at him, dark leather breastplates and helmets with eye rings so that they seemed like faceless warriors of the underworld, big men armed with spears and axes. Like warriors before the terrible gates of Nagrind, the corpse gate entrance to the dark underworlds of Niflheim. Hundr ignored them, also refusing to meet Saoirse's gaze, although he had the shiver of it on his neck. His boots crunched on the shale and then trod soft grass as he marched to meet the woman he had once loved but who hated him with every fibre of her being.

"Fate brought you back to me," she hissed. Her voice cracked and whispery like a serpent.

"Erik Bjornsson brought me here," Hundr said belligerently.

"No. The gods brought you and my son back to me."

"I thought you prayed to the nailed god?"

"My son is returned, and he shall be King," she said, ignoring the question. Her eyes gleamed in her time-ravaged face. She was thin, cheeks sunken and eyes ringed with dark circles. Tattoos marked her forehead and cheeks, strange animals, and signs he could not make out without staring into her face. Considering how fair she had once been, she was hard to look at. But even now, there was a feminine power to her, and he felt himself drawn to her. It stirred in his manhood, and he thought of Freya at that moment. An all-powerful goddess, but one who used her feminine charms to bring that power. Hundr had heard once in a skald song how Loki had let slip that Freya had slept with every elf in Asgard and that she had laid with three dwarfen smiths to get the magical brisingamen necklace.

"Bárid is the new King."

"Finn will be King. And you have come here to die." A smile flickered at the corners of her thin-lipped mouth. "The true gods spoke to me of his ascent, of how Ivar was descended from the Aesir. Finn is of the god-born."

"I came here to kill another Ragnarsson, and he is dead. Just like Ivar and Hakon. They were not born or descended from any god. They were just men."

She flinched and bared her teeth. "Luck stealer, you are a thing of Loki, a thing of Ragnarök. I have cursed you to ruin, and I will dance in your blood before the end. You and all your oathmen. I will have my vengeance for what you have done to me." Saoirse's eyes were wide, her face twisted in a rictus of hate.

"You can try to kill me. Many have. But I am not an easy man to kill. Even with the power you have found in your gods."

"My gods? Such arrogance. Misplaced, I think. You have no idea of the ruin you left me in. First, after Ivar, then again after you stole my son. You have no home, no people. Even now, your whore feels the wrath of my curse, her and your foul, rotten pup. You will suffer as I have suffered."

Hundr stepped towards her, fists clenched, and anger flared in his chest. How did she know about Sigrid and her pregnancy? But Hundr mastered himself. It was common enough knowledge amongst his crews and easy information to extract from men supping ale.

"I pity you," he said. "For you had so much, and look at you now. Withered and sour like an old apple in a pigsty." *We could have been happy*, he wanted to say. But he was glad he swallowed the words, for they were weak and would offer a glimpse into the depths of his soul, his longings and regrets. "I am leaving. If any harm comes to me or mine, and I get an inkling that you are behind it, I will return here with all of my warriors..." Hundr stopped himself, fighting to contain his anger. She was a madwoman; that much was plain. Any semblance of the old Saoirse was long dead, but this new Saoirse was a thing to be pitied, not worthy of threats.

"Your warriors?" she spat. "I am Queen here, Queen of my father's people and more. We shall throw the Dubgaill, the old foreigners, from our shores. You will come back, for I have seen it. When you do, you shall find the fury of my people here waiting for you." She hissed at him again and strode away in a flurry of her dark cloak and a wave of her skeletal hand. The charms and trinkets upon her person clinked as she walked, and Hundr wondered at her power —if she merely boasted of her influence or if she truly was a Witch-Queen. The power of the gods was mysterious, and men had told Hundr throughout his life that the gods had blessed him with luck.

Saoirse glided away, and her black shield warriors marched behind her. Her malevolence had shocked Hundr, and he shuddered at the dangers Finn and Einar faced as they stayed in Ireland. They would not leave if Hundr told them of his fear of the völva. That would not be drengskapr. But there was a deep wyrd woven into the changes taking place in Ireland, a place notorious for the fighting between its rival clans. Now, suddenly, the Uí Néill were allied with the Finngaill, the new Norse foreigners, along with Saoirse's black shield warriors. She had been a princess and was now the queen of a kingdom to the south, near Dublin, so the warring Irish kingdoms aligned, which was something new.

"Ragnhild, Bush," he called, striding down the beach. "Get word to Einar to beware that Witch-Queen. She means to make Finn King, and their lives are in danger. Tell him we shall wait off the coast a half day south of here in case he sees sense and brings his ship to join us. We sail as soon as we can. Sell these ships and return to Vanylven. And Bush..." The older man was halfway gone but turned on his heel to look back at Hundr. "Take Amundr and Sigvarth and see if you can get a dozen or more of Halvdan's men to swear an oath to serve me. They are masterless men now that Halvdan is dead. Any drengr amongst them will see that, as will some of the spineless ones who fear death from their captors. Try to find the drengrs amongst them and bring them to me. We need men to crew and sail the new ships to England."

The summer was still young, with plenty of time left for another campaign to keep his warriors happy. Yet, a burning desire to return to Sigrid kindled in Hundr's stomach—to get back to his love and his unborn child.

FIFTEEN

Einar weighed the heavy leather purse in his hand. It was as big as his fist, and four more were stashed away in the Vanylven men's lodgings. Einar gnawed at his beard, mulling over the welcome problem of having too much silver. Dublin's market throbbed around him. Shouting merchants barked above the constant rumble from the throng milling about the narrow tangle of streets and its wide square where men came to sell their wares and profit from the crowds who came from far and wide for the city's famed slave markets. Dublin had grown since Einar's last visit when he had arrived with axe and flame. This time he was an honoured guest of the King. The foul stench of the slave pens across the square rose above the finer smells of roasting meat and the smoke from a hundred cookfires which hung above the city like a second covering of cloud. The ever-present city malodour of shit and piss punched through it all, and Einar longed for the wind and the open sea.

"We should hide it all on the Fjord Bear," suggested Torsten, staring at the pouch. The hard-bitten warrior sat on a stone wall outside a tavern. He spoke with a mouthful of blood sausage, his fair hair pulled back from his face in a long braid.

"Which is where anyone would expect us to hide it. We have more silver than I've ever seen in one place in my life," said Einar.

Torsten shrugged. "If anyone wants to take our silver, let them try. We always have at least ten men on board."

Einar nodded thoughtfully at that truth. The Fjord Bear sat idle in the protected harbour of Dublin, which curved off from the wide River Liffey and around the city to shield it from the worst of the Irish weather. He had sold the ships taken from Halvdan weeks ago to a Danish warlord from across the Irish Sea. The man had secured a foothold for himself on the northwest coast of King Alfred's Saxon kingdom, in an estuary in what used to be western Northumbria. The warlord, a short man named Kraki, sold a boatload of Saxon slaves and returned across the sea with two *drakkars* and a *snekke* ship which he could boast had belonged to Halvdan Ragnarsson.

"Will there be a fight here, Lord Einar?" asked Ottar, a young warrior from Vanylven who was skilled with throwing axes, which he wore in a baldric across his shoulder. He drank ale from a jug hooked around the back of his hand, as did most of Einar's crew. They lazed and drank daily in taverns, spending their new silver on ale and whores. Einar had sorted out the shares of silver after selling the ships and kept the amounts owed to both him and Hundr.

"There had better be," Einar answered. "You lot are as soft and fat as Frankish lordlings."

Ottar patted his stomach and laughed. It had been over a month since the battle at Cuan Loch and since Hundr had left with Ragnhild, Bush, Amundr, most of their warriors, and three of Halvdan's ships. Hundr had also taken fifty of Halvdan's defeated warriors to crew the new ships, much to Bárid and the Witch-Queen's annoyance. Ottar broke off a chunk of sausage and handed it to Einar. He bit into it, and it was warm and glorious. Fat dripped from his mouth into his beard. Einar swallowed and rested a hand on his own growing paunch. He sighed and glanced up at the high keep perched upon a small hill in the city's centre. Bárid loomed there, nursing the wound in his thigh and newly crowned as King in Dublin. Einar saw little of him, preferring to stay outside of the keep with his own men.

Finn, however, stayed in the keep, as did the Witch-Queen, and Einar had seen less and less of the lad as the weeks passed by. Finn had marched out days ago with Erik Bjornsson and the Witch-Queen herself, along with Erik's crews, her black shield warriors and Finn's own men. Scouts had come to the Witch-Queen from her own lands south of Dublin with news of a Norse army marching north from the coastal fortresses on Ireland's south coast. Such places were rich slave markets and thriving settlements. Vedrafjord and Cork were ruled by brutal Norsemen of Einar's generation, who marched north to quell the so-called Finngaill, the new foreigners, as the Irish called Bárid and the second-generation Norsemen. Einar had declined the offer to ride, wanting to keep his distance from the Witch-Queen, or Saoirse, as he had once known her. Before Hundr left Loch Cuan, he had sent Bush to warn Einar of the Queen and her intentions and to ask Einar to reconsider and sail away from Ireland and its troubles. But he had stayed. Einar loved Finn like a son, and no matter how much he missed Hildr and his hearth at Vanylven, he could not leave Finn. Saoirse had not deigned to talk to Einar, and that suited him, but she and Finn had slowly become closer. At first, they just walked together, then spent days off riding or visiting her lands around Vykyngelo. Finn had returned from that trip full of enthusiasm, speaking of vast meadows and fertile lands filled with folk who celebrated the overthrow of the Dubgaill, the old foreigners.

When the news came of the advancing army, Finn had leapt at the chance to join his mother on the march, and Erik, too, wished to march in search of news of his brother. Following the battle at Loch Cuan, Finn had become a warlord in his own right. Bárid had generously allowed Finn to take one of Halvdan's ships captured outside the loch. They were the ships from which Halvdan had launched his surprise attack from the sea. So, Finn was now the shipmaster of the Wave Eagle, a *snekke* not as long as the Fjord Bear but a fine ship nonetheless. Once the Witch-Queen learned Hundr had taken some of Halvdan's captured warriors, she demanded that Finn take the same amount for his own oathmen. Bárid allowed it, so Finn now commanded not only the men who had sworn to him after the fight in Novgorod a year earlier but also a ship's crew of Halvdan's chosen champions, grim Norsemen all, and happy enough to be sworn to serve one of the line of Ragnar. They sealed their loyalty when Bárid and Mael of the Uí Néill decided that the rest of Halvdan's men were to be sold as slaves. Within a week of returning to Dublin, Bárid sold hundreds of good Norsemen to slavers from the lands of the Rus, the Ditmarsh, Frankia, and most of all to the dark-skinned men from Serkland who would take them south around Ispania to their own lands scorched by the sun.

"Round up the lads, Torsten," said Einar. He stared up at the dark timber keep on its hill and then eastwards to the unseen sea. "Let's take the Fjord Bear out for the afternoon. Get some rowing strength into our backs."

Einar marched at the head of his crew, thumbs tucked into his belt. They crossed the square and avoided the side streets, narrow gaps between the wattle and daub buildings slick with mud and Thor only knew what and kept to the major thoroughfares. As he walked, Einar remembered fighting in those very streets when he and Hundr had burned the slave pens and set a fire in the heart of Dublin before fighting a desperate battle across its walls.

After weaving their way around a noisy forge and along a wide street of fine houses with fresh, golden thatch, they made their way down the docks around the dark water, or black pool, which gave Dublin its name in the Irish tongue. The Fjord Bear lay snug between two fat-bellied trading knarrs, her mast post resting in a crutch on the deck. Einar sucked in the salt and fish smell, closing his eyes and smiling as gulls cawed and swooped overhead.

Torsten hurried the men aboard and shook his axe at a merchant with a gruesome neck goitre so the man would move his knarr from the path. Einar took up his familiar position on the steerboard platform with his hand on the tiller's smooth timber. He waited for the men to use their oars and pull them away from the surrounding ships before they could get the oars into the water beyond the black pool and get out into the river itself. The tide was between the ebb and flood, so they would row out towards the wide estuary mouth with relative ease, and Einar could not wait to get out onto the white-tipped waves and feel a fair wind in his hair.

"Lord Einar," called a voice from the quayside. Einar's heart sank as he turned to see Murrough standing by the mooring posts with a hand held up in greeting, his double-handed sword hilt poking over his right shoulder.

"Hold," said Einar, and Torsten passed the order along the deck. Einar waved to Murrough. His belly soured, knowing that his dream of a day out on the sea was about to be crushed under the red-haired Irisher's boot.

"Riders have arrived," called Murrough,

cupping his hand around his mouth to make himself heard above the din of the docks. "There is an enemy army less than a day away. We march today, and King Bárid asked if you and your men will march with us?"

Einar sighed. Finn would be in that fight, and what choice did Einar have? He couldn't say no after he and his crew had enjoyed the King's hospitality for the last month.

"Take us back," said Einar, and the men groaned. For there would be a fight, after all.

The next morning, Einar stared across a grazing pasture at enemies tramping their way through a field of waist-high wheat to form their ragged shield wall. He frowned up at a cold sun, pale for late summer. It was a dirty-grey day, and heavy clouds cast dreary silhouettes across the fields and hedges where the enemy shuffled into position. The clanks and clangs of their spears and shields rattled up the slight rise to where Einar waited with his crew. The Witch-Queen's black shield warriors formed the forward ranks of the Finngaill army, which the Irishers now called themselves. Bárid was still too injured to fight. The wound he had taken at Cuan Loch had turned rotten, and men said that only the seiðr of the völva had saved his leg and his life. Einar touched the hammer amulet at his neck to ward off her evil spirits. He wasn't sure if she had true völva seiðr, but she certainly had power over her men and now over Bárid. He had seen otherworldly power before, in King Harald's Sami sorcerer at the battle of Hafrsfjord, and that little man undoubtedly had something of the gods about him. But Einar had known the Witch-Queen when she was young and a Christ worshipper, and there was little power in her then. Still, there was no doubt she knew her herbs and woodcraft. Queen Saoirse had brought her seiðr to Bárid and applied poultices, stinking potions for him to drink, and even spider webs to place in the open wound. Most grotesque of all, however, were the maggots she put on the festering wound, much to Bárid's protest, for no king wants to be known as a man with maggots writhing over him. But, sure enough, the little worms had grown fat, and the wound had healed. Below Einar, she went amongst her warriors on the battlefield with a ladle, a dwarf capering behind her with a small cauldron of steaming broth, and she spooned the stuff into her front rankers. The men were stripped to the waist, painted in dark tattoos and armed with huge axes.

"Berserkers," said Torsten, and he spat in disgust. "A drengr shouldn't need a potion to summon his courage."

"Berserkers or Ulfheðnar?" asked Ottar. The Vanylven men had seen both in their time.

"Bears or wolves, who cares," Einar grumbled. "A man shouldn't stand in the front if he doesn't want to fight. They are everywhere now, these berserkers. I'm sick of seeing the bastards. Running into battle, drunk on mushrooms and foulness."

"Lord Einar," said a cheerful voice and Einar's dark mood lifted when he saw Erik striding towards him, his red hair bright and the trinkets in his braided beard glinting. The Svear wore his brynjar and carried a shield bearing the raven banner along with his beautiful butterfly-bladed war axe. Erik's captains, Vigfus and Gjalandi, marched with him, wearing shining mail coats and helmets. "Do me the honour of letting me stand beside you in the shield wall?"

"The honour is mine, Lord Prince," smiled Einar, pointing his spear toward the front ranks twenty paces away. "Although by the time the fighting reaches all the way back here, the battle might be over."

"Finn is down there, is he not?"

"There." Einar shifted his spear and pointed to where Finn stood in the third rank. His own warriors were deep within the black shield fighters, and Finn himself was next to Bárid's man, Murrough, in line. The King of Dublin's warriors formed the ranks behind those of the Witch-Queen.

"He does not bear the sigil of the Man with the Dog's Name any more?"

"No." Finn had taken his own banner since the army had returned to Dublin. He was the leader of a crew now and had taken to using the raven of the sons of Ragnar on his men's shields, and one of those men stood behind him with a scrap of cloth daubed with the raven hanging from his spear.

"Ah, he has taken the raven. My father would be proud."

The Witch-Queen reached the end of her line of berserkers and scuttled away, her black shield brutes banging their spears upon their shields in salute as she mounted her pale horse and galloped away to take up a position at the rear. Horns blared from the enemy, and a drum pounded out rhythmic war music. They formed their shield wall and came slowly across the field, a moving thing of iron and linden wood coming to kill its enemies. The berserkers at the forefront of the Finngaill army felt the force of their madness-inducing potion taking effect and began to roar, slather, and beat their weapons. Some even chewed the upper edge of their shields, crowing like animals and full of battle fervour. The rest of the army took up that war din, and soon the army of five hundred men were all clashing weapons and roaring their defiance at the enemy troops, who came on in well-ordered ranks.

"Old Randvr Cranelegs knows his business," said Torsten with an appreciative downward smile. Randvr was King of Vedrafjord, a coastal fortress in an estuary on Ireland's south coast. Not dissimilar to Dublin and perfectly positioned for slavers looking to sell their wares captured on the west coast of Wales or from the southwestern tip of the Saxon lands.

"Aye, well, he has more men for sure. At least a long hundred more," Einar uttered.

"My father knew Randvr in the old days," said Erik. "A drengr of the old kind, a man who made himself King by his own hand."

"A shame to fight him, then."

Erik shrugged. "This is our way, for men who go a'viking, is it not? If Randvr is strong enough, he will defeat us and remain King. If he is not, we will defeat him, and another man will rule."

Einar grumbled at the truth of that. Finn wearing his new sigil upon his shield, surrounded by his new ferocious crew, and the lad becoming closer to his seiðr-tinged mother, soured Einar's belly. More than once, he had asked Finn to leave Ireland and return to Vanylven, but Finn had brushed him off each time. Using the excuse that they had still not found any news of Erik's brother. But Ireland pulled Finn away from Einar. In the last week, he had only seen the lad twice, and both occasions had been but a brief greeting as their paths crossed in Dublin. Also, Einar noted Finn had taken to wearing the black cloak of his mother's warriors, as had his men.

"Shields!" came a shout ahead of Einar. He glanced up to see a hail of arrows launched into the sky by Randvr's warriors. The missiles hissed and fluttered like birds, and for a heartbeat, they seemed to hang in the air as though held there by some unseen force. Einar quickly bent and picked up his shield from where it rested against his leg and half crouched to hold the heavy shield above his head. Arrows thudded into timber, flesh, and the earth around him. Einar's shield was not hit, but a man two ranks ahead of him screamed and clutched at a shaft sticking out of his cheek, and another man looked puzzled at an arrow which had pierced his shield and gone straight through the wood and into his forearm.

"Rotten wood," said Torsten, shaking his head. "Time to go."

The berserkers broke ranks in a wild howl, like wolves smelling prey. They ran from the army at full tilt, racing across the space between the two shield walls. Enemy spears flew from behind Randvr's front line of shields, and half a dozen berserkers fell under the force of the leaf-bladed weapons. No arrows came from the Finngaill army, so eager were they to get at the enemy that the black shield fighters followed their berserkers into an all-out run across the battlefield. Einar marched forwards with his shield in one hand and his spear in the other. His axe rested in its belt loop, and his seax hung in a sheath by two thongs at the belt's rear. Einar wore no helmet, though each of his men did, and they shuffled ahead together. Einar overlapped his shield with Torsten's, and Erik brought his over Einar's with a thud.

The battlefield shook with the crunch and roar of colliding warriors. Berserkers hacked into Randvr's front rank, all pale tattooed flesh and whirring axes, and, for the most part, Randvr's line held. The big men in the front ranks simply thrust off the wild men with their shields and then stabbed their unprotected bellies and chests with spears. In places, however, the berserkers crashed through the shield wall. Einar gasped as one lithe warrior leapt clean over the first rankers to land on the warriors behind, and then another followed him so that at that one point, Randvr's shield wall broke. The black shield fighters followed up that wild charge with their own running line of shields. Finally, linden wood boards came together in an almighty crash of timber and iron, and the battle had truly begun.

Einar expected to meet and halt at the backs of the men in front of him, his crew being six ranks away from the front, but the lines kept pressing forward. He could no longer see Randvr's men now that lines had joined in hacking and slashing at one another, but normally two shield walls would come together in a crush and heave until one gave way or broke through the solid lines of shields. Men ahead of Einar whooped for joy and ran forwards, breaking the lines, which was a sure sign that Randvr's Dubgaill army had broken and was in flight. As the press of ranked warriors gave way, sure enough, the battle broke up into pockets of fighting and the chaos of a broken army. Men ran for their lives, pursued by the black shield brutes and Finn's crews.

"Come, Einar," shouted Erik, grinning beneath his helmet. "If we don't hurry, the battle will be over before we have reddened our axes." Then the big man set off at a run, abandoning his spear and ripping his axe free. His men let out a clipped roar and followed him into the slaughter.

"Go on, Torsten, let the lads go," Einar said. Torsten led them on, and Einar slowed his pace to a walk. His crew surged past him, hungry to attack the broken enemy and find their own share of glory and loot. Soon, Einar reached where the battle had started, and the dead lay staring up at the grey sky, some with eyes open in terror, others gaping with terrified mouths.

An injured enemy reached a hand to Einar, unable to speak, his mouth ruined by an axe blow which had crushed his mouth and jaw. Einar stepped around him. He followed his men through the carnage until they reached a knot of enemy warriors who had formed a circle of shields and defended themselves against all attackers. The black shield fighters had moved on, looking for easier prey, and Einar's head turned at the sound of thunder rolling across the pasture. The Witch-Queen came upon her pale horse, and she howled like a demon as her mount galloped through the chaos. Four black shield riders flanked her, stabbing and slashing with swords.

The circle of enemy shields broke, and the warriors surged at Einar's men. A warrior with a shield painted with an axe dashed at Einar. He came with an axe already red with blood and wore a conical helmet; his long moustache drooped around a snarling mouth. The warrior's eyes set hard upon Einar, for he saw a lord in a brynjar and arms thick with rings. Einar braced himself behind his shield as the man came on, his own shield levelled to smash into Einar's. But at the last moment, Einar released his and twisted around the warrior, jabbing his spear between his attacker's ankles so that the man tripped and crashed to the earth in a clanking, howling thrash of weapons and fury.

Einar whipped his axe free from its loop and beckoned to the man to stand up. The warrior bellowed with rage and came up snarling, axe swinging. Einar caught his axe strike with the haft of his own weapon and punched his left fist into the warrior's throat and then again into his belly. The man gasped for air, coughing and desperate to recover. The strength went out of his axe hand, and Einar pulled his weapon away to swing it around to thud into the man's chest. It sounded like a chopping axe hitting a wet log, breaking through the leather breastplate and into the warrior's heart. Einar ripped his axe free. Blood poured thick from the wound, and the warrior died well, weapon in hand like a man should.

Einar strode through the broken battlefield, searching for Finn. He didn't feel part of the fight—as though it was happening around him, and he was a mere observer. He passed Erik and his men fighting a band of ten of Randvr's warriors and saw Bárid's man Murrough take a warrior's head off with his long sword. Then, finally, Einar reached the field of wheat where Randvr's men had mustered for battle, and the Witch-Queen was off her horse, crowing behind a line of her fighters, urging them on with screams and curses. Finn fought there with his champions, and the battle was fierce. A tall man with a pewter beard fought in the enemy front rank, adorned with a shining helmet, a white horsehair plume at his crest, and a sword. His men died around him. Big men with shields bearing the axe sigil. Finn killed one of those men with his two swords, blades flashing in a blur of skill. A groan went up from the enemy warriors as the tall man fell to his knees. One of Finn's swords had slashed open his thigh, and his knee was a ruin of blood and bone. But as Finn swung the killing stroke, a warrior surged before the tall man and forced Finn back. This man had long, golden hair and a beard so fair that it was almost white. With his axe, he killed one of Finn's warriors, and even the champions fell back from his ferocity. The golden-haired man fought with axe and knife, and Finn tried to slash at him again, but the man swayed away from the blow, and his axe blade scorched across Finn's chest, the mail screeching but holding the blow.

Einar roared and ran at the shining warrior. The man held his axe in mid-strike, just as he could have killed Finn, and turned to face Einar instead. He came on in a blur of blades, axe and knife, lunging and swinging. Einar did not try to match the man's skill, for he was a young man who fought like one of the Aesir, yet Einar kept ploughing forward. The axe sailed past Einar's face, so close that he could smell the iron tang of blood on the blade, and Einar crashed his forehead into the golden-haired man's face with a crunch. He fell to the earth, stunned. Einar punched him in the jaw with the haft of his axe, and the warrior fell into unconsciousness.

Finn raised his blood-soaked sword in thanks to Einar but then turned his attention to where Saoirse capered in front of the tall man, the shining warlord who, due to his war finery and glee of the Witch-Queen, could only be Randvr Cranelegs. She held her skeletally pale arm and fingers up to the sky, cackling and mumbling to Odin, Freya and Tyr. Saoirse took her gnarled staff from one of her warriors and shook it at Randvr. The charms and bones fastened to it jangled as she danced through the dead warriors. Finally, Saoirse cast her staff aside and dug inside her billowing black cloak. Her hands came out, and she held them up for Randvr to see. Einar gawped at the iron bear-like claws that sat within her palms, curved, sharp and wicked. The claws were hooked over her fingers by two rings, and she brought one hand down and slashed open Randvr's face so that his blood splashed upon the battle-torn earth. The Witch-Queen set about Randvr with her claws, rending and tearing at him like a blood-mad she-wolf. Einar turned away in disgust, for it was no way for a drengr to die, hacked to pieces by a völva. The surrounding warriors beat their weapons upon their shields and chanted in low, humming tones.

"Finn Ivarsson," Saoirse shrieked, and Finn

strode towards her, chin up and shoulders back. "With the blood of this man, I name you Jarl of Vedrafjord, a leader of the Finngaill and Lord of warriors!" She unhooked her claws and bent to run her hand through the bloody mess of Randvr's face and neck. The Witch-Queen then smeared the blood down Finn's face, and he raised his sword as his warriors roared their approval.

Einar swallowed hard; his mind rattled. Saoirse was Queen in Vykyngelo, Bárid was King in Dublin, and now Finn was a powerful Jarl in Vedrafjord. The so-called new Norse foreigners, the Finngaill, had the east coast of Ireland under their heel, and the warp and weft of the Witch-Queen's schemes came to Einar like a ship through a fog. She was building enough power and enough warriors so that when the time was right, she could topple Bárid and forge a kingdom for her and her son that could rule all of Ireland. Finn soaked up the elation of his warriors, his face red with the blood of Randvr Cranelegs. Einar's heart sank, for he loved Finn. The time spent with Finn as a boy had been the happiest of Einar's life. He had no children of his own and had doted on the lad. Teaching him weapons, riding fine horses, talking and playing together. He had to get Finn away from Saoirse the Witch-Queen and get him home to Hildr, where he was safe. Even if Finn was now a powerful Lord in his own right, Einar had to try.

SIXTEEN

Five mornings after the battle with Randvr
Cranelegs, Einar marched through the
mud-slick lanes of Vedrafjord. It had
rained for two full days—a hard, driving
rain despite warm summer weather—and Einar
cursed as his boots squelched in the filth. The
leg bindings around his calves were filthy, and
he would likely need to buy new ones before his
time in Finn's new jarldom was over.

"I thought it was supposed to be warm here,"
grumbled Ottar, looking up at the driving rain.
The folk of Vedrafjord clung to the sides of wattle
buildings as they went about their business,
scurrying along the walls to keep out of the

wet. Vedrafjord stood on flat, lush farmland overlooking the broad, curving river, which led into a tidal river estuary thick with small fishing boats and faerings. The shallow valley was flat and verdant. Clutches of trees, crop fields and pastures dotted the riverbanks in broad sweeps leading away to distant, shadowed hills. The people had wisely opened the gate in the high timber walls, and so Finn had ridden a black mare into his new town, trailed by his own crew, without a fight but also with no fanfare of greeting. It was as though the people simply did not care. They had exchanged one Norse Lord for another, and Einar presumed that as long as the folk were glad to avoid any violence at the change, then they would welcome Finn as their new Jarl and continue to pay whatever taxes or levies were customary.

"If I hear another Irisher tell me this is the sunny southeast, I'll dunt his skull for him," Torsten griped. He adjusted the fine new cloak brooch he had bought with an arm ring stripped from a dead man following the battle. The brooch shone silver and bronze, shaped like a tusked boar's head, and it held his woollen cloak in place at one shoulder. Torsten pulled up the hood and mumbled something about hating the rain.

"We'll be out of here soon, lads," said Einar. The summer grew long, and his mind nagged him about the need to set sail before it turned swiftly into winter, making the voyage to Vanylven too perilous to attempt. Seas would churn, storms would rage, and sailing a *drakkar* was a summer business.

"It might be a miserable arse of a place," Ottar intoned, "but it has made us rich."

"It has," allowed Einar, "but most of our silver is still on board the Fjord Bear in Dublin." The three warriors marched through the rain-pattered mud towards Finn's hall. Its gable rose high above the town's buildings, most of which were single-storied and roofed with earth and grass rather than thatch. Einar rounded a corner, and the hall reared up before him, faced with a pair of enormous doors carved with whirling patterns and painted in blue and yellow. Torsten hopped up the timber-planking steps between the raised hall's entrance and the muddy street and banged on the heavy door before returning to stand with Einar.

"I hope there's pork," said Torsten through the side of his mouth, rubbing his hands together. Einar had sent a message to Finn asking to talk, and the new Jarl had sent him an invitation to eat with him that evening.

The doors eased open, and a slave in a plain brown woollen jerkin bowed and then beckoned them to follow. He was a short, wiry man with a balding pate and walked in a quick shuffle along the timber floorboards through a narrow passage beyond the door. Einar followed, and the passage was dark, lit only by a sputtering torch on one wall, but there was a fresh smell of cut pine in the place, which made it less foreboding. At the end of the corridor, two mail-clad warriors stood with spears held at the same angle away from their bodies.

"Lord Einar. All weapons stay with us," said the taller man, a broken nose mashed across his face. It was customary amongst Northmen not to allow weapons into a Lord's hall, and so Einar gave up his axe and seax, as did Torsten and Ottar. He kept only his small eating knife in a little sheath at the side of his belt. The guard on the right passed their weapons to the slave, who held them awkwardly in two hands before opening a small door in the wall to place weapons safely inside. The guards turned and marched further along the corridor, brighter now with more torchlight. Einar marvelled at the walls, iron spirals set within the timbers, and here and there, spikes jutted out. It gave Einar the sense that this was what it must be like approaching Odin's hall Valhalla, or Thor's mighty hall Thruthvangar. The walls shone and seemed alive in the flickering torchlight. Finally, they came to a high door, again set with iron spirals, but the hinges were crafted from actual spears. The spear points rested within the door itself, and Einar nodded appreciatively at the craftmanship and expense Randvr Cranelegs had put into his mighty hall.

The guards pushed open the spear-set doors, and the corridor's closeness opened into a long room twice as large as Einar's feasting hall at Vanylven. Torsten whistled at the high beams and the fine carvings on both roof and wall posts. There were horses, boars, sea monsters and images of the gods all etched into the timbers and painted in glorious colours which caught the shimmering light of the wall torches that made the figures seem as if they were moving, as though they watched Einar as he walked across a floor of long timbers covered with floor rushes. There were no windows in the hall, so the only light came from the many torches held in iron callipers upon stout posts or from the smoke hall cut into the roof. A fire crackled beneath that hole, and the smoke got whipped away by the draught so that the hall itself, although dark, was not choked by it. In the wintertime, that fire would fill its large stone hearth, fed with logs by slaves or stewards, but in summer, it only burned fierce enough to cook upon. A deep cauldron broiled upon it, and meat roasted there, skewered on a spit, its fat hissing as it dripped into the fire. The smell of the food filled Einar's nostrils, and his mouth watered. There were few better smells to fill a hall than roasted pork.

"Einar," came a familiar voice from the far side of the hall. Finn marched across the floorboards in long, confident strides. He wore a fine green wool jerkin above supple boots, and his chestnut hair fell loose around his shoulders in curls. "What do you think?" Finn held his arms out wide, turning to take in the breadth of his new hall.

"It is magnificent," Einar replied. "I congratulate you on your new position. Becoming a Jarl is no small matter."

Finn strode to Einar and brought him into a warm embrace. "You are most welcome," he said, pulling away and smiling broadly. "Old Randvr certainly knew how to live. His stores are full of food, the people are prosperous, and trade taxes fill his coffers."

Einar smiled along with Finn. It was hard not to be happy for the lad. He had become wealthy and powerful, the dream of any man who took to the Whale Road. Einar squeezed Finn's shoulder, as he used to when he was a boy. Two figures loomed out of the shadows to stand behind Finn. Big men in mail brynjars, armed with spears and axes that hung from their belts.

"Do you need guards to meet me?" said Einar, bristling as the two men stared at him. He knew both as men who had once served their enemy, Kvasir, the 'Burned Man'. They had sworn oaths to serve Finn to save their lives the day Kvasir died in Novgorod, and Finn had made them rich. So, they served him with loyalty and fervour despite his youth. The warrior over Finn's left shoulder was Udvarr, a Dane with two fingers missing from his left hand. The man brooding over Finn's right shoulder was Farmann, a Svear whose front teeth were carved with grooves and dyed with resin, giving him a fearsome appearance. Both were big men, almost as tall as Einar and broad in the shoulder.

Finn glanced at the baleful warriors. "You are right. This should be a meal for just the two of us." He inclined his head towards Udvarr. "Take Torsten and Ottar to the back of the hall and make sure they are well-fed and given as much ale as they can drink." Finn reached over to take Torsten's hand in the warrior's grip and then repeated the action with Ottar. They thanked him and followed the guards to the hall's rear. "Come, sit." The benches which would fill the vast space on feasts were gathered around the edges of the hall, save for one close to the fire, which was already laden with jugs of frothy ale, baked loaves of different shapes and sizes along with platters and drinking mugs carved of smooth wood.

Einar sat, groaning at the aches in his back and

knees. "I grow too old to march to war through bogs and shit-strewn cow fields."

"Not too old for the sea, though, eh?"

Einar chuckled. "I'll never be too old for that, lad."

Finn flinched around the eyes at Einar's use of the word lad, and Einar sighed. The young Ivarsson was a Lord of warriors now and of equal rank as Einar. So Einar would have to remember not to call Finn by the names he had when he was a boy.

"We have come a long way since I first met you and Sten. I was a boy then, wet around the ears and still learning of the nailed god."

"You were a good lad. It was a hard fight getting you away from your uncle Halvdan. I thought I was a dead man in that bloody Saxon forest." Einar remembered it well. He and Sten Sleggya had taken Finn from Halvdan's camp and fled through a forest pursued by Halvdan's warriors. Finn had broken his leg, so Einar carried him through the trees and briars whilst also fighting off their pursuers.

"It was my mother who bade you rescue me, was it not?"

"It was. She came to us in Frankia and asked Hundr to help get you back from your uncle."

THE RAVEN AND THE NINE

"I have thought a lot about that recently." Finn took a drink of his ale and ripped a chunk of bread from a loaf twisted into ropes like a torc. "How she went to him, even though he killed my father, her husband."

"She wanted you back," Einar said. "And she wanted us dead. So she led us into a trap, and men died."

Finn's eyes snapped up at Einar, and there was anger in the tightening of his mouth and the frown forming upon his brow like a gathering storm at sea. Two servants came to the table with platters of steaming pork and bowls of a thick barley broth. Their arrival broke Finn's instinctive anger, and Einar took a long draught of ale, wondering at the poison the Witch-Queen had poured into her son's ear. Finn smiled again and filled Einar's ale from a large ceramic jug.

"The old Norse lords of this island are all but gone now," said Finn, deftly changing the subject. "The Uí Néill rule in the north, Bárid rules in Dublin, my mother in Vykyngelo, and me here. Each of us is at least half Irish."

"Are the people happier?"

"I think so. Better to be ruled by those of your own blood, no? The gods are happier, or so I am told."

"I see you have relinquished the nailed god

fully now?" Einar pointed at the silver arrow-shaped runic amulet around Finn's neck.

"I was never really sure what gods to pray to or give thanks to," Finn shrugged. "When I was a boy, my mother and her people followed God and Christ. But you and Hildr were followers of the Aesir. Now that Mother is a devout worshipper of the Aesir, I feel I should be too. The gods bring me luck." He gestured for Einar to help himself to the food, and Einar pulled his eating knife free of the small sheath at his belt and took two thick slices of pork.

"And what does your mother say of Hundr and I?"

"She talks little of such things. When we eat or ride together, she talks of Ireland, its heroes and legends, and her people, who are also my people. She tells me about my father, Ivar. She talks of the need for the Irish to rule their own."

Einar ate his meat, and it was delicious. The pork was juicy and hot, and he mopped up his plate with a chunk of bread before stuffing it into his mouth. Finn kept his eyes down, looking at his food as he spoke, and Einar knew he had not spoken truthfully. Saoirse was a ball of hate and bile, and the white-hot centre of her anger was Hundr, the man she believed had stolen both her and the Ragnarssons' luck.

"It will soon be time to return to Vanylven before the weather breaks," said Einar. "I'll have to march the crew back to Dublin and back to the Fjord Bear unless you can spare a ship to take us there?"

Finn sat back, wiping his hands on his breeches. He smiled broadly. "Why leave? Stay here with me. Look how well we have done here in Ireland. You have been so good to me, Einar, and I wish to repay you. Stay here for the winter. We can send a message to Hildr with a merchant ship to let her know. A winter here, away from the duties at Vanylven, might do you good. You can help me look over this place and get things in order. We can hunt and fish and sail on the river?"

Einar reached over the table and placed his calloused hand over Finn's hand. He shifted in his seat, the show of affection as foreign to Einar as the Irisher language.

"Finn, I talk to you now as a man who thinks of you like a son. As you know, I have no children of my own, and I have tried to raise you as best I could. I am not your father, but Hildr and I have loved you like a son. So, what I say, please know I say not to hurt you, but because I could not sleep at night if I don't speak my mind."

Finn moved his hand away and fixed Einar with a flat stare. "You can speak freely here,

Einar, and I know all you have done for me and will be forever grateful for that." The muscles beneath Finn's jaw worked as he ground his teeth, sensing what Einar was about to say, the knowledge of it already bitter in his throat.

"Bring your crew and your ship back with me to Vanylven, Finn. You can be a Sea Jarl, like Hundr, and like I once was. You will be safe there, and we can all be together."

"I am safe here and a landed Jarl."

"There is a wyrd in this place for you, lad," Einar winced as he said the word. "You were the heir to the throne in Dublin, but yet it passed to Bárid, and your mother did not object. Who was Bárid's mother? Surely his claim is no better than yours, even though he seems the elder. Your mother has changed. She is not herself. She has become devoted to the Aesir, but not in a good way. There is a foulness here, something twisted and full of hate. I don't say this to hurt you, just to keep you away from harm."

"Harm?" Finn rose from his seat and rested balled fists on the table. "I am a warrior, Einar, as are you. Harm is my trade. There is nobody here who wishes me ill other than my enemies. Why would I leave? Look at all I have accomplished. I am a Jarl and still a young man. Bárid is welcome to Dublin, for I have my own lands and warriors to fill my hall." His voice rose steadily as he spoke, shifting into a shout. "Are you jealous of me, Einar? Why do you insist on referring to me as a boy? You want to run back to Norway so you can rejoin that luck-stealing bastard who killed my father?"

"Easy, la... Finn. I meant no insult. Stay here if that is what you wish. But I will leave for Vanylven as soon as I can. Hundr would not hurt you. Did he not teach you the cuts of the sword?"

"He killed my father!" Finn roared and banged a fist so hard on the table that the plates shook, and the jug of ale toppled to smash upon the floorboards. "Don't choose him over me, Einar." Finn's face was twisted, teeth bared, and brows furrowed. He leant over the table and pointed a ringed finger at Einar's face. Udvarr and Farmann loomed up out of the shadows, their mail and weapons chinking as they approached.

Einar rose slowly and stepped away from the table. He looked down at Finn and across at his two guards. "I would choose no man over you, Finn, and you will always have my love."

"But yet you run back to him like a dog."

"Careful," said Einar, trying to quell Finn's fury before it warped into a thing that broke their bond.

Finn roared in anger and threw the table over, its contents skittering over the floorboards and the bang of the table echoing around the rafters. The guards stepped forward, spears in hand.

"Take one more step, and I'll kill you both," Einar warned. "Right now, or we can make the square. I am Einar Rosti, Jarl of Vanylven, and no man who isn't ready to die squares up to me."

Udvarr and Farmann stood still, eyes flicking from Einar to Finn. They had sailed with Einar and Hundr for a year and knew Einar's reputation well. He was not known as the Brawler for being a timid man, and in his younger days, Einar had been a famed fighter of Holmgang duels. Torsten and Ottar stalked carefully around the guards, moving slowly. The tension was taut and ready to kindle to violence at any moment. They stood behind Einar, and Einar could almost hear the quickening of their heartbeats.

"Thank you for your hospitality, Lord Finn," Einar said, and he bowed his head graciously. Finn seethed, hands curled into fists, his cheeks flushed. But the newly minted Jarl held his tongue and simply glowered at the three Vanylven men. Einar walked backwards, keeping his eyes fixed upon Udvarr and Farmann until he reached the hall doors. Once through the spear-clad timbers, he marched briskly through the dark corridor, the whorls and spikes seeming to close in upon him as his thought cage spun with the unravelling of his relationship with Finn. Finally, Einar pushed through the double doors and sucked in a huge breath as his face met the fresh air.

"Round up the men," he ordered. "We must leave this place as soon as we can. The Witch-Queen looms within these walls, and her seiðr has turned Finn against us. We are not safe here."

SEVENTEEN

Hundr sat on the pine-built porch, running a whetstone along Battle Fang's blade. It was already sharp enough to shave with, but the activity at least stopped him pacing up and down, impatient for news from the wise women inside the building. They had come from across Vanylven's environs. Women who had birthed babies themselves and helped countless others do the same. They knew the charms a pregnant woman should wear to bring the luck needed for a safe birth and healthy child. They knew how to feel a woman's swollen belly and check for problems, and they knew how to perform a delivery not only from their own experience but of that passed down through countless generations of women.

Sigrid suffered. Her stomach was hugely distended, and the wise women said the baby was overdue. She could barely walk, and her feet and ankles were terribly swollen so that her once shapely legs were now like timber logs. It had been three days since Hundr had returned to Vanylven. He had led his fleet, including the ships taken from Halvdan Ragnarsson, north around the lands of the Scots, past the Orkney Islands and to Norway's rugged coastline before reaching the calm surface of the fjord at Vanylven. But, through squalls, raging storms, and thick haars off the northern Scots isles where the Seaworm lost sight of the fleet for three days, all Hundr could think about was the Witch-Queen's curse. He had not even stopped to sell the new ships. Instead, Hundr had spread the crews of the Seaworm, the Sea Stallion and the Wind Elk amongst the new ships so that he had trusted men sailing alongside Halvdan's warriors who had taken Hundr's oath.

The curse whipped across the white-tipped waves, the völva's voice howling on the winds which filled the heavy sails. Even when the ship's timbers creaked as she soared through chasmal troughs and over mountainous peaks, Hundr heard the spite Saoirse had spat against Sigrid and his unborn child. Hundr did not believe in seiðr magic, but he feared it. Like he feared the god's displeasure, as did all men. Many crews sailed with a *godi*, or man close to the Aesir, who would offer sacrifices for calm seas and good winds and pray to the gods for cures for men's ailments or dilemmas. Ragnhild served that purpose for the Vanylven crews, for who better to call out to Odin than a Valkyrie priestess? Ragnhild, however, gave no credibility to the Witch-Queen's venom. She had known Saoirse for as long as Hundr and had been there at the ambush in Northumbria when the Norns had twisted the fate of all three of them together in bloody war. Ragnhild saw Saoirse as a monster created by her own craving for power and vengeance, a woman who would do anything, and likely had, to survive and increase her influence. She had forsaken the nailed god for the Aesir and would stop at nothing to achieve her ambitions or quell the fire of her hatred. Maybe Ragnhild was right, but the curses of a völva, real or not, were not to be ignored when they involved all that was precious to Hundr.

Hildr had met Hundr at Vanylven's harbour. She asked where Einar and Finn were, and her shoulders had slumped and her arms folded at the news that they had remained in Ireland. Hildr had quickly packed up the sorrow of that in a fixed jaw and a long sigh before leading Hundr silently by the hand to a house next to the main hall. It was a low longhouse with a thatched roof which came so low that its bottom was less than a child's height from the ground, and inside, Hundr found the thing he had dreaded during his long voyage home. Sigrid lay abed, thick beads of sweat rolling down her face. Her beautiful features were drawn and sharpened by pain, and the scar on her face lurid red. The baby would not come, the child trapped inside her womb, unable to free itself from its mother to be born into the world. If the baby stayed like that much longer, Sigrid would die. Hildr and Ragnhild were as competent in the arts of healing as they were in the arts of war, but they knew little of how to help Sigrid. There was, however, a way—a last resort. Ragnhild and Hildr could cut Sigrid open and free the baby, but Sigrid would surely die. Ragnhild had shaken her head at even the mention of the procedure. Even if they took a blade to Sigrid's stomach, it was unlikely that the baby would survive. Hundr told them of the curse and the Witch-Queen's spite, so they had sent for the wise women.

Women came from villages and hillsides around Vanylven, riding in on donkeys and ponies. Wrinkled women in naalbinding headscarves and drab, heavy clothing. They were simple folk of Norway, the wives and daughters of fishermen or farmers. They knew the land and the sea, and the secrets of plants, poultices and charms, passed down through generations since the first days of distant times when the children of ash and elm first walked the grass of Midgard. The women came with pouches stuffed with roots, plants, and strange liquids in painted wooden jars, and the people of Vanylven bowed to those women just as they would to Hundr's warriors. The wise women fussed around Sigrid inside the longhouse. Hundr had made an unsuccessful sally to check on her, but they had scoured him out of the doorway with greater steel than the defenders of many a stout palisade. So, he sat and ran the whetstone along his blade, the sound comforting, the whorls and patterns in the shining sword a pool in which to drown his melancholy thoughts and worries.

He sat up with a jerk as the door burst open; the figures emerging from the gloom chased by another of Sigrid's awful howls of suffering. Hundr winced at the sound, the agony of it surely akin to the sound Loki made when his wife Sigyn ran to empty the pot she used to catch the venom a great serpent dripped onto his face. Loki lay fettered against a rock, lashed there by the Aesir with the entrails of his own son, destined to suffer the snake's venom, and whenever Sigyn emptied the pot, he would roar and writhe in such pain that the earth shook. Hildr strode from the longhouse, her face sheened with sweat and her lips thin and drawn.

"The baby will still not come," Hildr said, a shaking hand rising to brush a loose strand of hair behind her ear.

"What can we do?" asked Hundr. "There must be something?" He swallowed at the lump in his throat, his war skill, reputation and wealth useless now that the woman he loved needed him most.

"There is another we could try. A galdr-woman. In a cave high in the mountains, she was driven out of Vanylven by the old jarl long ago. This woman knows the Nine Charms of Odin, and if there is one who might be able to lift the seiðr, then it is she."

"Can she lift the curse?"

"That hag in Ireland has no power. She uses our gods as a tool for her own purpose. She cannot call upon the power of the Aesir to lay a curse upon Sigrid." Hildr paused and straightened her dress. "Not at such a distance, anyway."

"We must find this galdr-woman and bring her to Sigrid. How do we find her?"

"You must ride into the hills to the highest cave to the north. You will find her there and must convince her to come with all haste. But be warned, she will not come easily. There will be a test. She will want something from you."

Hundr's dead eye pulsed. "Keep her alive for me, Hildr." He wrapped his arms around her, and she held him close.

Within the hour, Hundr rode out with Amundr and Bush. They took seven horses, two each so they could push one mount hard whilst the other rested without a rider and a spare for the galdr-woman. They rode around the great fjord, past the eastern jetty of the fjord barrier and up into pine-dappled hills. They slowed their pace, and they rode in silence before Bush called for the horses to rest. Blown horses were ever the danger of a hard ride, and Hundr reluctantly stopped where a brook babbled across moss-covered stones, winding its way down the hills towards the fjord below.

"All this talk of seiðr and galdr makes me nervous," said Bush as he rummaged in his pack for a fistful of biscuits to share between them.

"What's the difference?" asked Amundr through a mouthful of biscuit.

"Galdr is runes and songs, the old ways of healing and magic from back when the world was young. Seiðr is wicked magic, dark and malevolent."

"Enough," snapped Hundr, pacing along the slick rocks around the brook. The water breathed down the hillside, and Hundr's thought cage rattled with the battling echoes of Sigrid's cries and Saoirse's curse. "No more talk of this, bad enough that I have a curse upon me and mine without you two rambling on about things which cannot be real."

"Such things are real," said Bush, and he slipped off the leather helmet liner from his head, wringing it between his fists. "As real as the birds and animals of this forest. You don't have such things in the east?"

"No," Hundr replied tersely, hoping that it couldn't be real if he denied the curse's magic. "We have wasted enough time here. We must push on."

They fed the horses from a bag of oats and rode ahead, slower as the slope grew steeper and the pines thicker. There had been such women in his father's court at Novgorod back when he was Velmud, a bastard son of a Rus Prince and a Norse slave. He had not been aware of it because runes and talk of luck did not reach the stables where Hundr had slept. His life then had been simple: an everyday battle to scrounge enough food and training with the weapons master. As he rode, Hundr let his hand rest on Fenristooth's ivory hilt, the coolness of it giving him some comfort. He worried about meeting the galdr-woman and what she would want from him or what she would take. Hundr was not used to this. He lived by the strength of his sword that had seen him rise from nothing to his current status as a Jarl and leader of men. A problem he could not resolve with a blade was unfamiliar. But now, as much as he hated to admit it to himself, he was frightened—not for himself, but for Sigrid and his unborn child. He would give up everything for them to live and be safe. He would take all of Sigrid's pain and suffering for himself; he would die if necessary.

The evening drew in, and the trees became thinner, casting spiteful shadows across the needle-sheeted hillside. Grass, moss, and bracken gave way to iron-dark rocks, at one end smooth and curved like a woman's hip and then jagged and sheer like an axe blade.

"There," said Amundr, pointing a thick finger to where a black slash showed in the face of a steep crag. It was a cave, and the hairs on Hundr's neck bristled as they rode past animal skulls laid upon the rocks. Other bones littered the place, along with the rotting corpses of crows and other animals. Hundr's horse shied and pawed as the earth turned into pebbles and rock, forcing them to leave the animals tethered there as they climbed higher towards the black crag. As they clawed and scrambled over rocks, the stones were carved with runes, lines and arrows, which could have been warnings or prayers, yet none of the three could read the carvings. Amundr cursed as he touched one, and then he let out a yelp, a child's scream of terror, as he reached for a high gouge in the rock to pull himself up and came away with bloody fingers from the corpse of a raven. As they approached the crag, there were more dead things—birds, squirrels, and a weasel. There were also more runes, but they were now smeared in blood across the rocks as the crag reared up before Hundr, like a gateway to another world. The underworld.

"I go alone from here," Hundr said.

"I'll go with you," Bush put forth. "There could be anything in there."

"It must be me alone. It's just a woman who knows which plants and shrubs to use to make Sigrid better," Hundr said, but the cavern yawned from the cold rock like the lop-sided maw of a jotun giant. Amundr would not meet Hundr's eye. The huge warrior clutched the hammer amulet at his neck and shook his head in a quick twitch.

Hundr found a winding path through boulders and chips of rock, and as he approached the cave, he noticed tendrils of smoke drifting from its upper edge, and a foulness hit him like a slap across the face. Rot came from the blackness, like the breath of a dragon or monster. Hundr gagged, and his guts broiled. He resisted the urge to draw his sword and pressed on, taking small steps into the void. He kept to the edge, a hand always upon the greasy, wet cave wall, his mind screaming at him to turn and run, but his heart urging him on for Sigrid and his child. There was a glow in the darkness, a sputtering cough of orange in the terrible gloom. Hundr's boots skittered and slipped on crunching things lying on the rock beneath his feet, and before the fire, there was a hunched figure sitting low and covered with a hooded cloak. Wan light danced from the small flames, for brief moments illuminating the cave walls where Hundr glimpsed more bird corpses and bones on stone-hewn shelves, along with other blood-curdling things of tooth and claw in the shadows. His stomach tightened, and he came about the huddled figure. It turned to him, revealing a wizened face with a complexion reminiscent of smoke-darkened oak, deeply lined yet adorned with bright blue eyes flecked with gold, and it fixed its gaze upon Hundr. The flames danced in those eyes, and she smiled mirthlessly in a mouth as dark as the cave's stygian depths.

"Sit," came a woman's voice, cracked and croaking like a dry hinge. Hundr hunkered down, noting the beads hanging from her ears. Something boiled on the flames, a pot from which the rotting smell spewed, dry and earthy. She reached to him, a gnarled hand with large, aged knuckles over thin bones, skin so wrinkled it was like cracked ice. She handed him a horn of liquid, warm and stinking. "Drink."

"I am here…"

She raised a crooked finger to shush him, and a sound came from her, a creaking cough which juddered her shoulders. She was laughing.

"Drink if you want my help."

Hundr had no choice. Every moment he wasted here was a moment of unspeakable pain for Sigrid. He brought the horn to his lips and forced down the vomit that crept up his throat at the smell of decay and wrongness. He tensed, swallowing the fluid, and it was like drinking a forest. Moss, fungus and rotting leaves, all mixed into one. It tried to come back up, but he kept it down. The blue eyes searched him, piercing his eye and travelling into the depths of his soul. His vision blurred, and he sat back against the cave wall. Flames and blue eyes swirled about him. The gods were close, and their terrible power was upon him.

EIGHTEEN

Searing heat and the ring of a hammer on iron. The impact rang up Hundr's arm to burst through the darkness, a muscled arm shining with sweat. Hundr jerked with surprise. He looked upon a glowing forge through two eyes, but the eyes were not his own. The hammer came down again, and he wielded it with deft skill. Hundr knew little of smith work, but the mind and body he now inhabited knew more of ironwork than any in Midgard. The orange fire within the forge burned bright like the sun. He could feel the ferocity of it on the face that was not his own. The brawny arm came down to beat the final blow on a forge-hot piece of iron, a pin only the length of his hand. It was delicate work. Too much force and the pin would mash out of shape; not enough and its shape would not be perfect. Hundr laid the hammer down and grabbed the pin with a leather cloth. The quenching bucket was close, but he knew he could not walk to it as a normal man would. Hundr reeled at the horror swirling within the thought cage of the smith, the man whose body and mind he inhabited in the dream brought on by the galdr-woman's drink. Hundr tried to close his eyes, to wrench himself free of the other mind, but something trapped him there, forcing him to see what the smith saw and feel what he felt. The muscled arms propped up his broad-shouldered torso and shuffled around the forge, strong hand over hand taking his weight and then moving from forge to anvil, around objects placed so that he could move using only his arms, and Hundr realised his legs could take no weight at all. Hate broiled in the smith's chest, hotter than the furnace itself, so bright was that malice that it almost made Hundr vomit. His wasted legs dragged behind him as he moved, useless and heavy, and a memory forced its way into Hundr's mind. A clear picture of King Niðhad capturing the smith whilst he slept, of the brutal king snarling and slicing his hamstrings with a wickedly sharp blade, rendering the smith lame and making him a prisoner on the island of Sævarstöð.

His shoulders bunched as his arms brought him around the forge, and the pin hissed and smoked as Hundr thrust it into the cooling bucket. Steam billowed around the smithy, and the smith shuffled back to his workbench, again using the immense strength in his forge-strong arms to drag his crippled legs along. He propped his torso up against his workbench and carefully fastened the pin to the clasp he had made earlier, the last piece of work in his masterpiece. The smith's eyes widened as he looked upon his work, two long sailcloth strips covered in beautiful white feathers taken from birds who flew too close to his forge. He would feed them with scraps of his food and bring them close enough to grab and pluck their precious feathers. Over months of painstaking work, the smith had crafted the unthinkable. Wings, broad and strong as those of a gull or albatross, to be strapped onto his arms and clasped over his chest, wings that would see him fly away from his hated enemy and island prison. More of the smith's memories flooded into Hundr's dream-state awareness. He saw the magnificent rings, jewel-encrusted brooches, and shining weapons he had crafted at the forge for Niðhad, making the King wealthy beyond reckoning. Hundr realised who he was, a knowing of a story told at countless fires by myriad skalds down long years. Cut hamstrings, Niðhad, the island prison, a lay well-known among the people of the north. He tried to shake his head, to wake and escape the body and terrible mind where his consciousness was trapped behind the eyes of Volund, the lame smith.

Volund laughed as he stroked the soft feathers of his forge-crafted wings. The laugh was a pain-wracked thing of vengeance and spite, for the lame smith thought how the greedy King sat at his high table that evening, glorying in Volund's latest creations, the jewels and wealth Volund's skill had brought to his hall. However, unbeknownst to the King, the perfect drinking cups from which he and the Queen indulged in golden mead were, in fact, fashioned by Volund from the hollowed-out skulls of Niðhad's own sons. While the Queen played with the shimmering jewels on her ringed fingers, little did she know that Volund had meticulously carved those jewels from the eyes of the very same deceased boys. Meanwhile, the King's daughter grinned and squealed, gleefully admiring the splendid brooch crafted by Volund, for it was as finely a worked piece of jewellery as any in Midgard. Yet she was unaware that its intricate beauty was achieved by incorporating tiny pearls made from her slain brother's teeth. The young princess would come to him soon, Volund knew, to repair a ring that belonged to her. Volund knew because he had broken it, to bait the trap, knowing that her father would send Princess Böðvild to his imprisoned smith Volund to have it repaired. He was ready for her. Ready to add her suffering into the cruel warp and weft of his hateful revenge.

The ring Princess Böðvild so loved was the same ring left to Volund by his swan maiden wife before she had left him alone in the days before his capture. The ring was his most treasured possession, the last memory of his beautiful wife, and Volund would have it back before he flew away from his captor. Hundr screamed and clawed at the pain that it was to be Volund, desperately trying to shake himself free of the galdr-induced vision. He could not escape or even close his eyes as Volund opened the special chest he had made to hide his wings, the same chest where the sons of Niðhad had met their gruesome fate. Volund carefully folded his wings and placed them inside the chest. He caught his arm on the edge of the chest lid, and a trickle of bright blood flowed from the cut. The lid's edge was sharper than any sword or axe blade Volund had ever forged, and he was the mightiest smith there had ever been or ever would be, in Midgard. That morning the two princes had wandered into Volund's forge, wide-eyed and curious about what shining treasures the muscled smith hammered out on his blazing forge. He had beckoned to them, urged them to come in and peek inside his special chest. He had promised them that there were gifts inside, marvellous gifts for the precious sons of the King. But as the two boys had leant over the edge of the chest, their tiny white fingers curling around its rim and the heads leaning in to peer into the chest's darkness, Volund had slammed the blade-sharp lid closed with all the smith strength in his mighty arms. At that moment,

Hundr screamed at the vision of the decapitated boys and then at how Volund delighted in taking those heads, the thirst of his vengeance devouring their deaths like fire-eating dry roof timbers.

Only one part of the dreadful plan was left to execute, and then Volund would leave. He would have to don his wings and fly first to Niðhad's hall and glory in telling the King how he had slaughtered his sons and made the King and Queen's precious objects from the dead princes' skulls. Then, he would take to the sky and soar above Niðhad's warriors and their spears and bows and away to freedom.

A knock came at the forge's door, and Volund's heart quickened. He bade the Princess enter, and she peeked around the oak timbered door, and Volund waved her in. She held the broken ring out to him in her soft hand, and Volund moved around his forge, using the formidable strength of his mighty arms to swing from anvil to workbench, getting closer to her. He reached out, snatching a fistful of her golden hair and dragging her close. She did not have the strength to resist him, and gentle Böðvild howled in terror. Volund would not kill her. The malice of his revenge was altogether more terrible than that. He would fill her belly with a child and leave Niðhad's precious daughter ruined, spoiled for marriage and with a bastard for King Niðhad to raise. The Princess writhed and clawed at Volund, desperate to escape, but his monstrous strength was too much, and Hundr wept for her pain and for the dead princes. Darkness came again, a fog clouding the Volund vision, and Hundr tumbled away from the murderous forge and the legend of greed, imprisonment and revenge. This time Hundr welcomed the dark, relieved to be rid of the horror of Volund's mind. Blackness enveloped him like a smothering pillow, thick, heavy and tasting of rotten food, powdery and gagging.

Hundr woke with a start, his chest heaving and his mind pulsing with the horrors of his vision. The galdr-woman cackled, a pink tongue flicking out across two brown teeth in her gums.

"Why did you show me that?" he gasped, shaking his head to free it from Volund's wicked mind.

"I showed you nothing. You saw what the gods wanted you to see," she said. "I will help your woman, Jarl Hundr." She worked with a small chisel at a blackened rod, long like a walking stick used by the elderly.

"How do you know what I ask of you?"

"Do you think I learned the galdr ways by being a fool? That I live in this cave like an animal by choice? Warriors, pah! A lot of empty-headed spear shakers and boasters. You told me all while you slept. I know about Sigrid and the babe and of other things—your seiðr witch in Ireland and her curse. She has no power here. I will remedy whatever foulness she had laid upon you and yours, but not without cost. The gods tell me you have their favour. Odin, the betrayer, ever a lover of war and daring, watches you. You have sent many brave men to fill his Einherjar for the last battle at Ragnarök. He endows you with luck, Jarl Hundr. And I will help you, though you will pay my price."

Hundr staggered from the cave, and the crone followed behind him, her rune-carved staff tapping on the cold stone and her breath ragged. The cave was cloying, and Hundr had to master himself to not run out of the place, to flee his Volund dream and the gods' power. Finally, they reached the horses, and Amundr, the mighty champion of warriors and veteran of countless shield walls, backed away from the galdr-woman. She laughed at him, and Bush whispered a prayer to Thor as Hundr helped her onto a horse. Amundr and Bush asked no questions, and as they rode down the hillside, the strangeness and god-wrought wyrd of it all hung in the air. They reached Vanylven as night fell, stars shining brightly beneath a full moon hanging low in the sky and mirrored in the fjord water, casting the valley in glimmering half-light. Folk came from their houses to stare at the galdr-woman, at the tattoos on her face, a hint of those magical markings visible beneath her hood's cowl. They whispered and shrank back from her but also showed her reverence—for though they all feared her, they also needed her. Many of the townspeople, and those who lived in the farms around the valley, would go to her bearing offerings of food, milk, and silver. They sought her aid in various matters, such as mending broken bones, healing festering wounds, acquiring love charms, or even casting curses upon their enemies.

Hundr led the galdr-woman to the longhouse and found Hildr standing on the porch. As soon as she saw the riders and the cloaked woman, she ran inside the house. The wise women emerged, sweating from the heat and steam they had used to try to coax the baby free of Sigrid's womb. Hundr ground his teeth as Sigrid's wails fell through the open door to fill Vanylven with dread at so much pain and suffering. The galdr-woman kicked her mount forward, and the wise women bowed their heads at her approach. She nodded back at them in a mark of mutual respect. Hundr leapt from his horse and dashed to help her from the saddle. He held her skeletal arm, taking her weight, which was like that of a small child, and lifted her to the ground. The bitter-sweet smell of decay came from her cloak and skin, and as he placed her down, she raised her healing stick. It was as black as charcoaled timber, but the runes she had carved upon it seemed to glow in the moonlight.

Hundr let go of her arm, and she appeared to grow stronger, taking strength from the stick and standing upright. She held the stick aloft, and a low, melodic groan came from deep inside her, like a great war horn. She stalked towards the longhouse, her feet lost beneath the folds of her black cloak, and her body swayed in time with her chanting. The people surrounding the longhouse stared with wide eyes and slack jaws. The galdr-woman had berated the three warriors all the way down the mountainside, laughing at their lack of knowledge of the gods, warning them that the old knowledge was seeping out of the world, chased out by greed and Christ-followers, but there was a mischievous humour to her sharp tongue. Hundr noted the glint in her eyes and the smile playing at the corners of her wrinkled mouth as she shook her staff at some, and caught the eyes of others who stared at her in awe.

"From the mountain, I come," she said suddenly, in a voice too deep and loud for the frailty of her body. "With a staff carved with the runes of healing. Odin's nine-herb charm is my gift, and I come to release mother and baby from a Loki curse, from a spell cast by one destined for Niflheim." She made her low chanting again, ascending the steps up to the porch, and the wise women parted to let her through. The galdr-woman paused at the door's entrance and rummaged inside the folds of her cloak with her left hand. The arm shot upwards, clutching a leather pouch.

"Hear me!" she shouted into the house and shook the pouch. Her voice came now in the same low, guttural sound as her chanting.

"Stime this herb is named; on stone, it grew.

It stands against poison; it combats pain.

Fierce, it is called, it fights against venom, it expels malicious draugr, it casts out venom.

This is the herb that fought against the snake,

This avails against venom, it avails against infectious illnesses,

It avails against the loathsome fiend that wanders through the land.

Fly now, Betonica, the less from the greater,

The greater from the less until there be a remedy for both.

Remember, Camomile, what you revealed, what you brought about at Frysvjalmir:

That he nevermore gave up the ghost because of ills infectious,

Since Camomile into a drug for him was made.

This is the herb called Wergulu.

The seal sent this over the ocean's ridge

To heal the horror of other poison.

These nine fought against nine poisons:

A snake came sneaking; it slew a man.

Then Woden took nine thunderbolts

And struck the serpent so that in nine parts it flew.

There, apple destroyed the serpent's poison:

That it nevermore in house would dwell.

Thyme and Fennel, an exceeding mighty two,

These herbs the wise All-Father created,

 Suffering in Asgard while hanging.

He laid and placed them in the seven worlds,

As a help for the poor and the rich alike.

It stands against pain, it fights against poison,

It is potent against three and against thirty,

Against a demon's hand and against sudden guile,

Against enchantment by vile creatures.

Now these nine herbs avail against nine accursed spirits,

Against nine poisons and against nine infectious

ills,

Against the red poison, against the running poison,

Against the white poison, against the blue poison,

Against the yellow poison, against the green poison,

Against the black poison, against the blue poison,

Against the brown poison, against the scarlet poison,

Against worm-blister, against water-blister."

The galdr-woman entered the longhouse and pulled the door closed behind her. There was a silence over the crowd gathered to hear her words, a power and knowledge almost forgotten —of the gods and the old world. Sigrid's wailing suddenly stopped, and Hundr's heart stopped with it, breath held, fearing that death had come for her at last. But the galdr-woman's chanting came from the house instead, and Hundr knew he had come too far not to trust in her skills now, even though his head urged him to charge through the door and make sure Sigrid was safe.

"I need a drink," huffed Bush, blowing out his cheeks. Amundr nodded, his knuckles closed white around the hammer amulet at his neck. Bush marched off in search of ale, and Amundr trailed behind him, the big man casting nervous glances over his shoulder towards the longhouse as he went. Men took the horses away to be cared for, and Hundr sat with Hildr outside the longhouse. The people went to their beds, and the night grew long. Hundr and Hildr waited, a fleece blanket wrapped about their shoulders, and they held each other as brother and sister, fretting for Sigrid's fate. They sat silently, listening to the galdr song, their friendship and hope keeping them warm. Bush and Amundr sat across from them, sharing a skin of ale. That night was as strange to Hundr as his dream in the cave, uncertain of time, waiting to see if his love and his child would live. He thought of the dream and Volund, and of suffering and vengeance, both things he had known in his own life. There was a message there for him, but he could not see it through the veil of danger to Sigrid's life. Then, suddenly, as Hundr and Hildr held each other with heads bowed, a cry split the night air like an owl on the hunt.

"Was that...?" gasped Hildr, and she stood upright, casting the fleece off their shoulders. Hundr rose with her, and the cry pealed out again. The unmistakable cry of a baby, a new life thrust into the world and stricken with fear from bursting out of the warm safety of its mother's womb.

"Sigrid," exclaimed Hundr, fear enveloping

him, terrified that the galdr-woman had cut Sigrid open to free the baby. He moved towards the door, but Hildr grabbed his arm to hold him back.

"Wait. Do not break the galdr... Sigrid's life could depend upon it." Hundr pulled his arm free, frustrated but knowing that Hildr was right. He paced the porch back and forth, the baby's wailing rattling in his skull, the feeling of helplessness angering him. Then another cry, joining the first one.

"Can it be?" he said to Hildr. "That sounds like two babies?"

"It does," she agreed, and a smile split her face like the sun rising after a night storm. "Twins."

The door to the longhouse creaked open, emitting a cascade of putrid smoke heavy with steam and so thick with galdr that Hundr almost fell off the porch. The galdr-woman came forth, a wriggling pink baby in the crook of each of her bony arms.

"The curse is lifted, and you are luck blessed with twin boys." She smiled and cackled in her dusty voice. "You are indeed beloved of Odin, I think."

Hildr ran to her and took up the babies, swathing them in the fleece blanket and crying with joy at the sight of the children. Hundr ran to her and kissed the heads of his babies. Then, he turned to the galdr-woman and bowed deeply to her.

"You have my eternal gratitude," he said, taking her thin hands in his own. "Name your price."

She fixed him with her piercing blue eyes, and a smile creased her wizened face.

"A head is the price. The head of the völva in Ireland. There is power in her eyes, tongue, and bones. I can ground them into powders to cure madness, to shrink the growths that live inside people and waste them away. I want it, and you must bring it to me," the galdr-woman whispered, and she handed him a stone the size of his thumb with a hole at one end. "Use this to ward off the völva's seiðr. I want the head of the one who laid the curse."

He reeled, shaken by the weight of that price, for it meant cutting the head from Saoirse's body and laying it at the feet of the galdr-woman. The death of a woman he had once loved for the life of his children, and he hoped for that of Sigrid. Hundr burst through the door, and his eye stung at the putrid smoke, but there on the bed was Sigrid. Her golden hair was soaked with sweat, her face thin and wan, dark circles beneath her eyes, but alive. Hundr ran to her side and pulled her close. Overflowing with elation, he laughed with joy and kissed her neck and face. His wife and children lived, and Odin had granted him luck once more. But in the joy, there was also fury and a burning hunger for vengeance for the one who had inflicted such anguish and pain upon Sigrid, bringing her close to the very gates of death.

NINETEEN

Einar pulled his cloak around his shoulders to ward off the morning chill. Steam came from his mouth and nose to mist the air. He feared he had waited too long to leave, that winter had already arrived, that the voyage east and north would bring storms to make the Whale Road roll with thunder, and that he and his crew would be lost off the wild coastline of Shetland or Orkney.

"Are we loaded?" he shouted as his boots reached the timber of Vedrafjord's quayside.

"Almost, Lord Einar," said Torsten. He jerked a thumb to where men rolled barrels filled with food up gangplanks and onto the deck. "The ebb tide will take us out into the estuary."

Einar sighed, turning back to frown at the high walls. The sun broke through a haar of cloud behind the spiked palisade, casting a pallid glint of orange into the grey formless cloud of night. Finn slept inside, a newly minted Jarl and beyond Einar's warnings. He had delayed sailing for an entire week, ignoring the protests of his crews at the oncoming change in the season and avoiding Finn and his mother's black shield warriors. She was in there with the lad, brooding and scheming, pulling her son tighter to her bitter breast and closing her grip upon him. Hildr's heart would break when he returned without Finn, but there was no talking to the young Ivarsson now. Einar had tried and failed. He feared the lad was lost to him, and it felt like a death.

"Come, then. Hurry and get it all loaded quickly. Cast off and get us into the river."

Vedrafjord was an old Viking longphort, a riverside camp with jetties and fortifications to allow for ship safety and a secure base to raid inland along the long River Suir. The longphort had grown into a fortress in its own right, and it sat on a sharp bend in the river close enough to the sea that open water could be reached in less than an hour, and the port was protected from the sea's fury by the river bend. The fort also granted a wide view of any ship approaching from all directions, and the land around it was green and fertile.

"What is that sound?" asked Ottar. He stood on the Fjord Bear's deck, one hand on the rigging and another cupped around his ear as he leant into the darkness. Einar stopped still and listened. The sea breathed, and a dog barked within the town, but there was something else rumbling in the distance. Einar turned again to stare back towards Vedrafjord. The gate facing the river was open, as it had been since Einar had arrived at the place, for there was no threat of attack following the defeat of Cranelegs. He squinted. His ageing eyes were not what they once were, and anything beyond thirty paces proved ever more difficult to make out.

"Warriors, Lord Einar," shouted a Fjord Bear man from the stern. He pointed up the sloping walkway towards the gate, and even Einar's eyes could make out spear points and helmets as dull as pig iron in the wan morning light.

"Cast off. Now," said Einar. His hand dropped to the axe at his belt, and he pushed his cloak back from his shoulders. He was dressed in a simple jerkin, his brynjar wrapped safely in an oily fleece in his sea chest. Einar came to sail, not to fight, but he knew by the tingling at the nape of his neck that the warriors came not from Vedrafjord to wave him off. There was danger, and he had to get his men safely away. The crew leapt from the dock to the Fjord Bear's deck, untying mooring ropes and making oars ready to push the ship away and row her into the ebb. Einar waited on the jetty, hoping that it was Finn and his men coming to make amends for the harsh words they had exchanged in the new Jarl's hall, but dreading it was the Witch-Queen who had come to exact her vengeance upon him for taking her son away.

"Just two more barrels, my lord," piped Torsten.

"Leave them."

"One of them is salted pork, though?"

"Leave them," Einar repeated. The warriors marching down the hillside were the black shield fighters. They followed the path, a worn path of shingle leading from the riverside jetty up to the town itself. Their boots crunched on the small stones, and Einar could make out the raven banner on their shields, knowing them then for Finn's men. He strode forward to meet them, thumbs tucked into his belt, and glanced over his shoulder to where his men were still busy readying the ship to push out into the river. They needed more time to get the oars untied from their crutches, to settle the chests and barrels in the bilge so as not to overbalance the ship in the water.

The warriors halted ten paces away. There were fifty men, enough for a fight, and Einar felt exposed without his brynjar. But he did not want to fight. He just wanted to leave and get back to Hildr and Vanylven. The warriors parted, and Finn stalked through them, stopping in front of Einar, his brow furrowed and a dark expression on his face.

"Finn," said Einar, raising the palms of his hands outwards to show he wanted to make peace. "I think we both..." he stopped suddenly because behind Finn came the Witch-Queen. She strode through the warriors, her hood and cloak billowing behind her, tattooed face bright and chin held high in triumph.

"Where are you going?" asked Finn. He spoke softly, not meeting Einar's gaze and instead kept his eyes fixed on the jetty's timber planks.

"I told you I was leaving. I must go to Vanylven before the weather changes. Let us part as friends. Not like this."

"He speaks as though he loves you," spat Saoirse, the tattoos on her face writhing as she snarled and pointed a bony finger at Einar. "He does not. This is the man who took you from me, my son. What kind of man steals children from their mothers? He denied you your birth right. He is a minion of the luck stealer."

"That is not how it was, and she knows it." Einar fought to keep his voice even and his temper caged. Einar had taken Finn because Halvdan would have butchered him, and Saoirse knew that as well as he, for she was there on that terrible day when Sten Sleggya died so that Finn Ivarsson could live.

"We can't let you leave, Einar. Come with us peacefully, and you will be treated as your rank deserves," said Finn.

Einar shook his head and was then surprised to see Erik Bjornsson standing next to the Witch-Queen. He caught Einar's eye but looked away sheepishly. Panic swelled in Einar's chest, its heat making him thirsty. There was danger here for him and his crew. He paused, not wanting to look around for fear that Saoirse would guess what he intended and send her black shield brutes to attack the Fjord Bear. Einar listened carefully. He heard a barrel creaking and rumbling up the gangplank, and he cursed Torsten for a fool for not leaving the food, for not using these few delicate moments to get the ship away before the morning descended into a chaotic fight.

"I am leaving. I wish you well here, Finn. You have been like a son to me, and I only want good things for you. I will return and visit you soon with Hildr. We will feast together and laugh about these dark days. Let me and my men go. There doesn't need to be trouble here today. She is your mother, but her heart is sickened with hate. Listen to your own heart."

"Fool," Saoirse spat. She surged forward, barging past Finn to shake her fist at Einar. "You are nothing to me, a warrior, simple-minded and unimportant. It is your master who must die, and for that, he must return here. He must come back, and then he will fall under my knife." Spittle flew from her mouth, and her lips peeled back to show a ruin of a maw, with only a handful of rotting teeth left in it. Time slowed. Einar could kill her, he could whip his axe free of its belt loop, and she was within his grasp. With one strike, he could end her and run to his ship. But not before the black shield fighters charged after him and swarmed the deck. She wanted him to bait her trap, knowing that Hundr would come for him.

"You are part of this?" Einar said to Finn, peering over Saoirse's shoulder. "You would keep me a prisoner to lure Hundr back here to his death?"

"Hundr killed my father," Finn uttered, and for the first time, he met Einar's eyes. There was hate there and a change in him. Yet there was also doubt in the set of his mouth as his lips turned in against his teeth.

"This is not drengskapr." Einar left those words there for Finn and Erik to chew over for a moment, both sons of great warriors and both raised to follow the way of the warrior. "If you want to fight Hundr, you should have challenged him to a Holmgang. Not a trap like this."

"Will you come peacefully, or shall we make you?" said Saoirse, a smile playing at the corner of her wrinkled mouth.

"Let my men go."

"Take him," she ordered and waved to Finn's warriors. "Kill his men."

"Go, Torsten. Get the men to safety!" Einar drew his axe and the seax from its sheath at the rear of his belt. The Witch-Queen crowed and capered, moving backwards to allow the warriors to come on with spears levelled. Finn followed her, as did Erik, and Einar's heart sank like a stone in a fjord at the betrayal. He had raised Finn as his own son, and to see a person he loved turning his back, knowing that Einar might die, was like a knife between his ribs.

"We won't leave you, Lord Einar," Torsten shouted, and Einar edged back, using the few seconds he had to turn to Torsten and his men.

"You are my oathmen," he said. "I order you

to return to Vanylven. Tell the Dog what has become of the Brawler."

Torsten's mouth moved silently, the grizzled warrior caught between obeying his orders and leaving Einar to die or face imprisonment.

Einar turned back to the black shield fighters. Four of them came for him, helmeted and with spears levelled, shields held at their sides rather than before them. They saw an old man with greying hair and a grey beard, a man without mail, and thought it would be simple to capture, wound, or kill him. Now, the ebb tide had washed away from this part of the jetty so that there was no water beneath the timbers, only the slick mud of the exposed riverbank. He could fight, but the black shield warriors would just surround him and subdue him, wading through the mud to jab at him from the front, side, and back with their spears. Nonetheless, he was Einar Rosti, Jarl of Vanylven, and he could not let them take him without a fight. He risked another peek over his shoulder, and the crew shoved the Fjord Bear away from the jetty with their oars.

Einar slipped his axe back into its belt loop and reached behind him to slide the seax into its sheath. He raised his hands to show he would not put up a fight, and the two leading warriors looked at each other and grinned.

"We can handle the old bastard," scoffed the

man on the left, a tall warrior with a thin brown beard and a long nose. "Stop the ship."

The spearman came on, waiting for the front two to secure Einar before they could charge at the Fjord Bear. The tall warrior reached out to grab Einar's wrist. He wanted to lead him from the jetty and let the other warriors pass to charge the ship. The man's hand was cold as it touched Einar's thick wrist, and he did not have time to react as Einar darted forwards. Einar moved from the hips, driving his chest and shoulders forward and then slamming his forehead into the warrior's long nose. The gristle and flesh mashed against the rock-hard bone of Einar's forehead, and the warrior grunted and tried to reel away. Blood spurted hot on Einar's face, and he grabbed the warrior's spear, ripping it from his grasp. In a flash, he whipped the leaf-shaped blade around and across the eyes of the second spearman. Both men howled in pain, and Einar barged into the first man with his shoulder so that he toppled into the mud beneath the jetty and kicked the other one to fall the same way.

"Come fight with Einar the Brawler," Einar growled. He launched his spear at the next man in front of him, and the blade plunged into the meat of his thigh. The warrior fell back into his own men, clutching at the spear shaft and groaning in pain. Einar looked back to see the Fjord Bear was away from the shallows and had moved into the river's ebb. Oars sprung from her sides, and Torsten raised a hand to Einar from the steerboard. Two hands emerged over the jetty's edge, followed by a face, as a man scrambled over the planking to stand and run towards Einar. Ottar. Boots stamped on the jetty, and Einar turned back to face his enemies. He armed himself with his axe and seax and readied himself, for they came on now with shields before them and spears bristling. Men who knew their business, experienced Norsemen sworn to serve Finn Ivarsson. Ottar ran up the jetty and came to stand at Einar's shoulder with his axe drawn and a grin upon his face.

"I couldn't let you die alone, my lord," he said. "Not when there is a death worthy of Valhalla to be had. Besides, I am not sworn to you. My oath is to Jarl Hundr." He winked and howled like a wolf before charging at the black shield bastards like a madman. He hacked at their shields, and his ferocity halted them. Einar joined him in the attack. He brought his axe down upon a shield rim to hook it down, stabbed his seax into the gaping mouth beyond, and twisted the point savagely to ruin lips, tongue and teeth.

A spear point flashed past his face, and Ottar grunted as a shield rim slammed into his jaw. A spear point punched into Einar's shoulder in a burst of white-hot pain, and another sliced across his side, ripping open his jerkin to tear into his flesh. Einar grimaced, but he hacked with his axe and stabbed with his seax, feeling resistance but unsure if he struck his enemies as he fell to one knee. He did not have his brynjar, and so the spear points carved him up like a roasted pig. Ottar stumbled and fell from the jetty, and Einar reached out for him, but a shield rim crashed into his skull. The iron rim connected with the top of Einar's head, plunging him into instant darkness. The shouts of the spearmen came to him as though through a fog. He was aware of boots stomping and kicking him, and he clutched the haft of his axe, determined that he would die with a blade in his hand. Soon, the darkness swamped him, filled with bursts of pain from the spear wounds and the impact to his head. The betrayal, however, hurt Einar far more than the wounds to his body. Finn, whose life he had once saved and then raised from boy to man, had turned on him. Erik's treachery stung, but not with the heart-thumping sadness that Finn would do him so much harm. The last thing he saw was a bittersweet memory of Hildr, sitting by their fire in Vanylven, before he succumbed to the enveloping blackness.

TWENTY

Einar huddled in the dark, shivering. The chattering of his teeth sent stabs of pain through the bruising and swelling on his face. He clutched himself, arms folded across his stomach, knees tucked up into his midriff. Time shifted, a strange mix of pain-wracked wakefulness, sleep, and a half-sleep of dark thoughts and fever. He did not know how long he had lain there amongst the floor rushes, stinking and filthy with his own piss and blood. Cuts, gashes and bruises littered his body, but he could not see them to understand how bad they were. Einar had been wounded before, even left for dead once, and knew well that the smallest of cuts could ache worse than the gaping gash. He knew some of his ribs were broken, for he could not unfold himself, and each time he moved, Einar's whole torso screamed at him. His captors had left him in just his trews, his upper body naked and cold with only a rag of a blanket crawling with lice to cover his shame.

"Ottar?" Einar said, his voice coming as a fractured croak. Through the pain and the wall of sadness at Finn's betrayal, Einar suddenly remembered that Ottar had disobeyed his orders and returned from the Fjord Bear to fight alongside him. He recalled only that Ottar had fallen but did not know if his shipmate had lived or died.

"Here," came a gruff reply, muffled but close.

"Are we alive?"

"I..." the voice started, then descended into a laugh, cut short by a groan of pain. "My jaw..."

Einar rolled over, wincing and grinding his teeth against the pain. He opened one eye, the other swollen closed. Dried blood was crusted across his face, and he tried to brush off its stiffness with his shoulder. Ottar's jaw was broken; Einar could tell by the shapelessness of his words like a man trying to talk underwater. But at least he was alive. Einar lay upon a hard-packed earthen floor, dusty and cold on the bare skin of his back. He was inside a room of some kind, stinking with excrement and sweat. There was a window, with shutters cast open but timbers secured to its outer side so that shafts of light sprang through them like sunlight illuminating a distant hill or valley through storm clouds. He shuffled himself towards where the sound of Ottar's voice had come from. The mewing noises he made as he moved despite the pain were not worthy of a warrior, and Einar hoped his enemies could not hear his whimpers. His hand touched warm skin, Ottar's foot, and then his shipmate reached over and grabbed Einar's hand. Ottar pulled him close, and Einar gasped and sweated at the effort like a man who had rowed through a squall upon the Whale Road.

"Water," Ottar managed through his injured jaw, though most of the word came as a lilting mumbling which resembled the sound of the word. Even in the half-light clawing its way through the window-barring timbers, Ottar's jaw was twice its usual size, swollen like an over-ripe vegetable. Ottar handed Einar a jug, and he drank deeply from it, the water thick with the iron taste of his blood as he washed down his parched throat.

"Are you injured?" Einar asked.

Ottar laughed and groaned. He nodded his head to spare himself the pain of talking.

"They put a hot iron to the worst of your wounds," intoned another voice from across the room, hidden by the darkness. "I could smell the burning flesh. Strange that they did that. She must want you alive."

"Who are you?" said Einar, squinting into the gloom to get a sense of the man. He remembered the cold spear iron piercing his unarmoured body in the fight on the jetty and the other wounds he had taken in the fight. His torso did sting with the burn of fire, long red and white welts lurid against the purple swellings.

"A prisoner. Like you. We are in a locked room in a house behind the main hall."

"We have not been tied or chained. We could fight our way out."

The dark figure let out a wry laugh. "It is not the walls or the door that hold us, friend, but the spears and axes which guard them."

"Who are you?"

"Refil Bjornsson. Believe it or not, I am a prince of the Svear, though you would not think it to see me now."

"Refil, son of Bjorn Ironside?" Einar shifted, shuffling forwards on the rushes towards the hidden voice.

"The same. Who are you that knows of my

father and I?"

"All men know of your father's reputation, but I more than most, for I had the honour of fighting alongside him in Frankia. I served your uncle Ivar and grew up with the sons of Ragnar. I am Einar Rosti, and this is Ottar Kjartansson."

"I have heard of you, Einar the Brawler. You sail with the Man with the Dog's Name? Strange you say you served my uncle because men say that it was the Dog's Name who slew him."

"The Norns weave a peculiar fate for us all. I came to Ireland with your brother to search for you. He is here, in this very town."

"Erik is here?" The man came forward, hope lifting the timbre of his voice. A shaft of light from the window illuminated his new position, a kneeling man with an unkempt beard and a mass of dark hair tousled upon his head. Refil was broad-faced like his father, but his cheekbones stood out like those on a skull above hollow cheeks.

"He is. But though I sailed from Norway to this luck-cursed island, Erik turned against me. We fought against Cranelegs, who was Lord here, and the young Norsemen defeated the old. Erik now marches with the Witch-Queen and the son of Ivar, whom I raised as my son."

"You talk too simply about such great events.

Cranelegs is dead, and Erik is here. Did he bring the ransom?"

"I know of no ransom."

"I came here with my crew, seeking reputation, but found only defeat and capture. Cranelegs held me here and sent a message to my father, asking for a hoard of silver for my release."

"I know nothing of that. I do not believe Erik knew you were here in Vedrafjord, only that you and your men were lost in Ireland."

"My men are dead, or slaves, or now serve another. I do not know their fates. I do not even know how long I have been here."

"Finn Ivarsson rules here now, and Bárid mac Ímair rules in Dublin."

"Much has changed, then. My uncle Halvdan ruled in Dublin when I was a free man, and Cranelegs had built this river fortress from where he ruled a wide swathe of this part of Ireland, a good place for trade and a high fort to defend."

"Have you tried to escape?"

"Many times. Once, I even broke free of the walls and into the open, but Cranelegs' men rode me down. You must have value if the new Lord here keeps you alive?"

"He was a son to me, but seeing the ruthlessness in his face, I know he would have killed me. However, it was the Witch-Queen who wanted me alive. She knows my friend, Jarl Hundr, will come for me. She hates us both and longs for our deaths."

"I have a young son, back in my father's hall in Sweden."

"Then I pray to Odin that you will meet him again."

The door to the room scraped open, its timbers warped by time scratched against the floor, and a man ducked under its lintel.

"Back against the wall, nithings," sneered the man. His brynjar clunked as he moved, marking him out as a warrior of wealth and reputation. He made to kick Refil and laughed contemptuously as the son of Bjorn Ironside flinched. "Back." He came towards Einar, and a shaft of light brought his face into view. Einar recognised him as one of the Witch-Queen's guards. Einar dragged himself back to sit beside Ottar. "Brawler, the Queen wants a word with you," said the guard.

Another burly warrior stooped into the room, striding forward to stand beside Einar, and the first guard stood beside Refil, ready to strike if either of the warriors tried to attack the Queen.

At that moment, she came through the door in a swirl of cloak and jangle of charms and bones.

"Two great lords," she chimed. "Living like pigs."

"You have Finn under your power then, witch," said Einar. He wanted to spring up from where he sat. He could be upon her in one leap, and her neck would break like a twig in his hands. He could rid Midgard of her foulness in a heartbeat. But he could neither spring nor leap, not with his ribs so injured and the burning welts of his wounds weakening him.

"He is my son; becoming a lord has always been his destiny. How I have sacrificed and prayed to the gods to see you laid low. They heard me, and here you are."

"The gods are fickle, and Odin has many by-names, witch. The All-Father is also known as Betrayer, bale-worker, and deceiver. You once worshipped the nailed god, and now you fancy yourself a völva. A few bones and amulets do not make you powerful, and nor do those markings which any can make." Einar flicked his finger towards her tattooed face.

"What do you know of my power, filth? Many times have I been cast down by ill luck, and each time I have risen again. Now I am a Queen and my son is powerful, Lord of Vedrafjord, and leader of men."

"And no doubt you whored yourself to every lord in Ireland to get there. Whore-Queen I name you, leader of nithings and…"

Saoirse lunged at him, fury erupting from her like venom. She scratched his face with her nails, raking his cheek with a hiss. "I am a Queen!" she seethed, a tear rolling down her face, the only hint of the truth of the hard life she had led, of the things she had done to rise amongst her people. "The Dog will come for you. You can live until then because I allow it. You are mine, jarl of nothing. And when he comes, you shall both die together, and I will dance in your blood and make cups of your skulls."

"Enough," said another voice from beyond the door. A figure ducked under the lintel to peer into the room. He came with a strange gait, and when the figure emerged from behind Saoirse's robe, Einar realised the man was a cripple. His right foot was missing at the ankle, and both hands were also gone. He leant upon a stick held in a groove of a leather cup on the stump of his right hand. The man was thin, bald and stooped. "They will suffer, and soon we will have our vengeance." The crippled man smiled at Einar, a darkly malevolent grin on his gaunt face. He turned slowly on his stick and hopped out of the room, his slender shoulders leaning heavily to his right side. Einar gasped at the wyrd of it, for he knew the man, and he had once been broad at the shoulder and a proud Irish warrior. He was Fiachra, Saoirse's brother from whom Hundr had cut hand and foot in their long-ago battle inside Dublin's walls. Hundr had left him a cripple and prayed to Odin that Fiachra would survive, and survive he had, but without either hand and only his left foot to hirple about on.

The Witch-Queen and the cripple left then, and she did not return. Men brought stale bread and water to the room each morning and took away the dented iron bucket the three men used for their piss and shit. Days came and went. Einar and Ottar healed slowly. Both men fell to fever, sweating and shaking on the cold floor as spear wounds, burns and bruising healed. Einar spent nights sitting with Ottar, holding him when the man wept for his mother like a child in the depths of his fever dreams. Refil went without food so that Einar and Ottar could strengthen, making his already thin face skeletal. Days turned into weeks, and though the three were not bound, they were never allowed to leave the dank prison of that room. Ottar's jaw healed, but it hung from the rest of his skull like a door left ajar, leaning to the left and slurring his speech. Refil recorded the passing days on the wall, etching a mark with a pebble he had chipped from the floor each time the sun came up to peek through the window timbers. Fiachra would come to the prisoners, shuffling into the room and chuckling with satisfaction at their bedraggled state. He would curse them for prideful Norsemen, curse them for the foul stench of their prison, and watch with a twisted satisfaction as he bade the guards to beat and kick them, relishing their grunts of pain while his own countenance soured with frustration at his inability to inflict the blows himself.

When Refil had made thirty such marks, Einar was well enough to stand. His head grazed the ceiling of roof timbers packed with daub, but he could walk the six paces across the room, past the window to the shit bucket and back again. Once Einar knew he could walk, he knew he could fight. So, the next time the guard brought food and water through the door, he found Einar waiting for him. Einar pounced upon the man, clubbing the warrior with his fists and elbows. Einar took the knife from the guard's belt and burst into the daylight, his bare feet cushioned by dew-soaked grass, and in that moment, his warrior heart soared, and Einar roared like a bear. Refil and Ottar followed him, but after two strides, shields and spears came for them in a wall of strength and brutal efficiency. They penned the three prisoners in like slaves. Einar was clubbed to his knees, and spear shafts cracked his head until he crawled back into the building like a dog. Fiachra came that night and had the guards take a knife to the three prisoners. The cripple watched with glaring eyes and a tight mouth as the guards cut Einar's chest in three long stripes. They did the same to Refil and Ottar, leaving them beaten and bloody. Fiachra returned again, haunting them many times over three days. He came with the guards, and because he had not the hands to wield a blade nor even to feed himself, he had those guards hurt the three prisoners. He would come at night, and by crackling torchlight, he bade the guards cut Einar, Ottar, and Refil. The cripple watched, eyes ablaze and his face sweating, as he took joy in their suffering. Blades ruthlessly scored Einar's flesh, cutting the skin from his body and peeling it away in strips while searing hot irons would burn their faces and hands, eliciting screams and sobs of excruciating anguish from Einar, Ottar and Refil. A big guard did the worst of the cutting, a green-eyed man with a close-cropped beard, and the three prisoners cursed both him and the cripple. In the days following the torture, when the shaking otherworldly fever took them as wounds scabbed and oozed with pus, the three swore that the cripple and guard would die.

After another ten of Refil's wall marks, Einar had recovered enough from his torture to claw his way through the roof, digging at the daub and tearing it out. The guards saw the damage when they came for the piss pot, and they subjected Einar to another flurry of fists, kicks and curses. The big guard came again and used a blacksmith's set of tongs to pull out two of Einar's fingernails. And on it went until so many of Refil's marks were scratched into the wall that Einar did not have the numbers in his head to count them. The cripple, at least, came no more.

Ottar and Refil warned Einar against any more attempts to escape, for the guards did not restrict their beatings to Einar alone. Indeed, all three of them suffered. Einar agreed not to try the guards any longer, and he started and ended each day with thoughts of Hildr and Vanylven. Torsten would have returned with the Fjord Bear by then. The journey would take no longer than six weeks, even in the worst of weather. Men had spoken of sailing from the lands of the Danes to that of the Saxons in less than a week. So, Hildr would know of Einar's fate, that he was last seen on the jetty, but would not be sure if he had lived or died. Hundr would also know, and the Dog would rage and bring all of his war skill and warriors to Vedrafjord to either free Einar or avenge his death.

Winter descended, transforming the lice-infested woollen blankets into precious treasures, rivalling the finest bear fur cloaks. Einar huddled within the tattered rag, his teeth chattering and breath steaming, and the three prisoners sat close together, relying on the warmth of their bodies as their only defence against freezing to their death. Refil dared to ask the guards for fire or simply a few more clothes but was rewarded with a dunt to the skull in response. Still clad in nothing but trews, the biting gnawed at them relentlessly, and Einar had never been as cold. Snow fell, drifting past the window timbers in a soft sigh. Coughs, shivers, and wheezes echoed in unison. Day by day, their strength dwindled, their once sturdy arms and backs withered, and their muscles honed over a lifetime of weapon work and rowing wasted away so that there was barely any meat on their bones at all. Ottar's chest grew so thin that Einar could see his bones through the parched skin. The coughing was a permanent bark, all three men spitting up green gobbets of infection and struggling to suck in gasps of ice-chilled air. Ottar's cough began as a persistent wheeze, transforming into a foul bark akin to the call of a walrus. Then it evolved into a drawn-out rasp that seemed to emanate from the depths of his heart and lungs. It would seize his muscles and wrack him with pain as though his body sought to expel one of its organs. One fateful morning, as heavy rain pelted against the window boards and cows lowed in a byre to the west, Ottar did not wake up. Einar shook him, yet his shipmate was as cold to the touch as the ice on a frozen water barrel.

The coughing sickness had taken Ottar's life, a man who had been a true warrior, devoted to drengskapr and living a life worthy of a place in Odin's Einherjar. The Witch-Queen had cheated Ottar of that afterlife, as had Finn's betrayal. Einar wept for Ottar, tears rolling down his face like a mother who has lost a son. He and Refil watched in gaunt silence as the guards dragged Ottar's body from the prison, each taking an ankle and pulling him across the floor like a piece of meat. Einar swore to himself that he would kill those men and as many black shield brutes as he could before his end. He swore it to Odin, Thor, and any god who would listen. They denied Ottar a glorious afterlife, fated instead to wander the Hel world with Odin's son Baldr until the end of days. With the shock of such sorrow, hate festered within Einar's heart like an open wound. The boy he had loved like a son was now his enemy, and the Witch-Queen would have to die.

Refil came close to madness in the frost when it became so cold that Einar thought it must be Fimbulwinter, that long foretold three-year winter without end which heralds the start of Ragnarök, the war at the end of time. Refil despaired that his brother Erik was so close but seemed unaware of his fate within the stinking hole of their prison. On a day when the wind howled across Vedrafjord with all the fury of

Asgard, Refil asked one of the guards to send word of his imprisonment to his brother. He promised the man wealth, gold and silver to dim the sun and that if he helped him, he could go to King Bjorn Ironside and be treated like the greatest of heroes. The guard just laughed and spat in Refil's face before leaving them for that entire day without food or water.

Einar and Refil immersed themselves in conversation, spending long hours in the dark reminiscing about past glories, battles fought, former loves, and tales of the gods. Refil loved the sea and would often talk of the joy of the Whale Road, of taking his ship and crew south to where the sun burned hot, to Ispania, where his father and Haesten had taken a great fleet years ago. Refil had sailed far and wide, encountering many strange peoples, and he spoke of trading beads, amber or furs with men from lands that nobody in the north had ever heard of. He was a trader and an explorer at heart, a man who found his purpose in the sea rather than in the glory of reputation and war. He wanted to surpass his forebears' deeds and be known as a discoverer of new lands. Einar understood that, for there were few pleasures in life to match the thrill of the sea's power beneath the tiller and the speed of a warship under sail in a fine wind. Refil had come to Ireland to seek the new Norse kingdoms and establish trade routes between Vedrafjord,

Vykyngelo and the Svear lands. Yet, instead of realising those ambitions, he had found himself confronted by a malevolent Witch-Queen and trapped in a dark, miserable, stinking prison.

Winter seemed like it would last forever, with short days and long, cold nights. Plagued by constant hunger, Einar shivered, his stomach empty and yearning. There were days when the memories of his past as a warrior and a respected jarl in shining mail seemed distant and hazy. Even the image of Hildr's beautiful face eluded him at times, overshadowed by his grim surroundings, feeling forsaken like a nithing destined to die in the shit-stinking dark. More days, however, were filled with hate. Einar nurtured the flame of that anger, for it kept him alive. He would talk to Refil of Vedrafjord —its layout, the size of the walls, the number of warriors it could hold. Einar built a ship of revenge in his mind, filled with his plans to bring the Witch-Queen down and thoughts of what to do about the young man who had betrayed him, a man who had once been a boy full of joy and laughter and who Einar had cherished as a son. Einar hoped Hundr would come, that he would come howling down from the north with ships and men, with swords, axes and spears. Then, when Hundr came, Einar would wield an axe again, unleash it upon his enemies, and be a drengr once more. When Hundr came. If he came.

TWENTY-ONE

The Fjord Bear limped into Vanylven just as winter took hold—when days began with steamed breath and frozen fingers fumbling with grain querns to make the morning porridge. Folk had brought animals in from pastures and pens to sleep in their homes, the smell a small price to pay for the warmth of their bodies. Sigrid and Hildr spent their days with the twins. The babies slept, screamed, ate, and shat in equal measures, and Hundr doted on their soft skin and tiny fingers. Hundr had expected Einar to return before the cold came when raiding and campaigning season was over. The seas became too treacherous to sail after that, storms too frequent, the fury of the waves enough to smash a drakkar into driftwood. Ragnhild shrugged off his concern. She believed that Finn and Erik would want to spend winter in Ireland and fight again there in springtime with silver and reputations to be won, and Einar would not return without Finn.

The galdr-woman was still the talk of the town—how she had saved both the twins and their mother, of the seiðr in it and the blessing from the gods. Hundr still feared the Witch-Queen's curse, even though Amundr, Ragnhild, and the rest scoffed at Saoirse's power. Childbirth was ever a danger to both mother and baby, and twins made that risk even higher. The galdr-woman simply knew the right plants and potions to make the babies come. There was no seiðr or galdr magic that could exert such power as to cause Hundr's babies to die. But even when people scoffed at the magic, they still touched the amulets at their necks to ward off the evil. Hildr missed Einar terribly, but she spent her evenings with Hundr and Sigrid, and Hundr was glad of that, for even though his newly born children were more precious to him than life itself, the crying was not a thing to be enjoyed. The babies kept Hildr from worrying about Einar and Finn, and Sigrid needed the help whilst she regained her strength.

On a day when cloud hung low upon the hills

surrounding Vanylven's fjord so that it seemed the highest peaks reached up to Asgard itself, Hundr was in the yard behind Vanylven's hall practising the strokes of the sword with Amundr and Ragnhild. The rest of his men worked on shield wall manoeuvres in a field beyond the hall. Ragnhild and Amundr came at him with wooden bladed spears, and he fought them with his two swords wrapped in cloth. Hundr ducked under a spear thrust and parried another strike with the blade of his sword. He swung at Ragnhild, but she wheeled away and brought her spear shaft low to swipe at Hundr's legs. He leapt over the attack and came down in a spin, striking his covered blade across Amundr's neck so that the big man grunted and frowned with frustration.

"How did you get me again?" the big man rumbled, and Ragnhild laughed.

Sweat sheeted Hundr's brow and trickled down his back beneath jerkin and brynjar. He breathed heavily and clapped Amundr on the shoulder, winking at him with his good eye. They took a break from practice to drink cool water taken from a barrel topped with a thin film of ice. Winter was a time for the men to practice and make ready for spring when campaigning season would begin. They would also bring the ships ashore and caulk them with a mixture of horsehair and sheep's wool together with a sticky pine resin. The burning pine smelled fresh and filled Hundr's lungs as he sucked in gasps of air to recover his breath from the fight.

A horn pealed out across the glass surface of the fjord, its low hum echoing around the hills. The three stopped still, glancing at each other and then out towards the fjord, waiting to hear another song on the great horn, but none came. One for a friendly ship, two for a trader, and three for an enemy attack. For a moment, Hundr thought it might be Rollo, come with his army in a surprise winter attack in vengeful fury at the burning of his hall in Frankia.

"A friendly ship," said Ragnhild after ten heartbeats, sure that there would only be one blow of the warning horn, and she ran to stow her practice spear in its rack.

"Clean and oil the blades," said Hundr, handing his swords to a young lad who grinned in awe at the beautiful weapons. Hundr set off at a run, Ragnhild at his shoulder, heading towards the fjord wall. As they ran past the main hall, Hildr burst through the doors, a cloth still draped over her shoulder from where she had been burping one of Hundr's twins. Her greying hair was swept back from her face and tied behind her head, and she stared at Hundr with a contrasting mix of hope and fear in her eyes. He waved to her, and the three friends took horses from the stable and cantered around the shore until they reached the western side of the fjord wall jetty. They rode in silence, each of the three wishing for it to be the Fjord Bear and that Einar would be at the steerboard, waving with one hand and another on the tiller. They hoped to see Finn standing in the prow with his chestnut curls falling about his handsome face. Hundr leapt onto the jetty timbers and raced towards the two towers between which hung the great chain barring entry to Vanylven's port to all but friendly ships.

"What ship is it?" Hundr called to the tower as he ran. He could see a ship in the fjord water to the north, sail lowered, and oars lazily stroking the water. The ship came on slowly without a sail raised, so all Hundr could tell about the vessel at such a distance was that it was a sleek hulled warship rather than a fat-bellied trading knarr. A helmeted head peered over the side and waved at Hundr.

"It's the Fjord Bear, Lord Hundr," the man shouted from within a cupped hand. Hundr's heart quickened, and he raced to the tower and ascended its steps, Ragnhild and Hildr close behind him. The guard reached down, grabbed Hundr's wrist, pulled him over the lip of the ladder, and did the same for the two Valkyrie. They leant over the tower's rim, hands on the smooth timber and watched the ship approach.

"Why so few oars?" asked Ragnhild. With only ten banks of oars biting into the water, the ship crawled towards the fjord bridge rather than racing towards home. There was little wind within the fjord, surrounded as it was by pine-covered hills on three sides, so any ship coming into the harbour did so under oars. It was the Fjord Bear, Hundr was sure. The men had removed her beast head prow so as not to frighten Vanylven's land spirits, but he could make her out from the shape of her hull and the red paint of her sheer strake.

"Maybe they are tired from the voyage?" said Hildr, her eyes searching the deck for any sign of the two men she held most dear. The ship edged closer, and Hundr's stomach soured as he noticed the odd cant of the hull in the water, something was wrong with the ballast in the bilge, and there was no way Einar would allow his precious ship to crawl into his jarldom like a whipped dog.

"Remove the chain," Hundr said to the guard. "We must meet them at the harbour." Hundr, Ragnhild, and Hildr raced to their horses and rode hard along the shoreline back to Vanylven. A crowd had gathered at the harbour, and the three friends dismounted and eased their way to the front, where their men waited, watching to greet their shipmates. Bush and Amundr stood at the forefront, Bush wearing the naalbinding cap he had taken to wearing lately rather than his leather helmet liner.

"She doesn't look right," Bush remarked, scratching his chin and squinting at the Fjord Bear's awkward lean.

"Any sign of Einar or Finn?" asked Hildr. She leant forward, almost to the point where she could topple into the water, so desperate was she to get a closer look at the deck and men who crewed her. The folk on the dock kept silent, leaving her question unanswered.

The oars splashed into the fjord, and Hundr felt a slight pang of relief to see Torsten waving from the steerboard, but as the Fjord Bear grew close and the crew slid their few oars from the oar-holes to let the ship glide into port, Hundr knew that neither Einar nor Finn was on board. He would have seen them by now, and Einar would not sail into Vanylven so quietly after being away from Hildr for so long. At that, Hundr stood next to Hildr, so he could be there for her when she understood that neither of the men she held most dear was aboard the ship. Eventually, the Fjord Bear came in, and the faces peering over the side were not the warriors Hundr had left in Ireland; they were half-men, white figures with wild beards, the skin of their faces pulled too tight over their skulls so that they looked like men who had returned from the

Skuld world.

"Thor, protect us," gasped Bush, and he moved to catch the lines the crew threw to shore and moored the ship so that the sailors could alight to the jetty. Torsten came first, his clothes stiff with sea salt, and he fell from the deck into Hundr's arms.

"What happened? Where are Finn and Einar?" Hildr stammered, her bottom lip quivering.

"Water," Torsten gasped, his lips cracked and his tongue creeping from his mouth like a piece of old leather. Bush handed the warrior a skin of water, passed along through the crowd gathered at the jetty, and Torsten took a deep gulp, groaning with delight as though it were ale brewed by the gods. He then passed the skin back to the thin, grasping hands of his shipmates, and he shook his head at Hundr before turning his wide, fear-filled eyes to Hildr. "They attacked Lord Einar." Torsten's voice came as a broken rasp. "We sailed away at his order; he commanded us."

"Attacked by who?" asked Hundr. Torsten reeled. His head bobbed to his chest, and his shoulder slumped as though he would pass out. "Torsten." Hundr grabbed the man by his shoulders to prop him up and ducked to meet his drooping eyes.

"Where are Finn and Einar?" asked Hildr, her voice shifting from concern to anger. She wore a blue dress clasped at both shoulders with bronze brooches and looked every inch the wife of a jarl and the leader of Vanylven. Yet, Hundr knew Hildr better as the fearsome Valkyrie warrior she had been, and it was with the steel of a warrior with which she now looked at Torsten and his crew. "Where is your lord?"

The crew looked at their boots, and Torsten raised his head to meet Hildr's fierce stare.

"Lord Einar was attacked, my lady, by Finn and the Witch-Queen. They came for him. Ottar stood with him, and Lord Einar ordered us to sail away and journey home to tell you and Lord Hundr of his betrayal."

"Finn attacked Einar?" she said, clasping her hands to her chest.

"Yes, my lady. He and the Witch-Queen. Finn is Jarl of Vedrafjord now, and I fear the witch has him under her sway."

"Does Einar live?"

"When last we saw him, he lived. Yet, they took him and Ottar, or so we thought."

"You saw him taken?" said Hundr, his fear for Einar tinged with anger, now knowing that Torsten had left Einar behind.

"We saw the black shield bastards swarm them, Lord Hundr, and beat them down with shields and spears. But I do not think they killed them."

"Where were you when they were taken?"

"Aboard the ship, rowing away as Einar ordered us to do."

A groaning murmur floated from the gathered crowd. Torsten looked across their faces, those people who whispered about him and his men. His jaw opened and closed like a landed fish. Their eyes accused him, and the whispers behind their hands spoke of cowardice and the forsaking of his lord. Hundr saw it too. He also saw the hurt on Torsten's journey-worn face as he saw their accusations. Torsten was a drengr, and to have his bravery questioned was the worst of all feelings.

"Einar ordered you to leave?" asked Hundr, raising his voice so all could hear.

"Yes, Lord Hundr."

"Then you did your duty, for you are oath-sworn to him and must do as he commands. Now, come and tell us more. Your journey has been hard, and you and your men need food and ale." Hundr put his arm around Torsten's thin shoulders and led him towards Vanylven's hall. Ahead of him, though, Hildr marched in the same direction with her hands clenched into fists at her side.

Hundr pushed the hall doors open and asked the steward to stoke the fire, which would now be kept ablaze during the long winter, the wood having been stockpiled throughout the year, guaranteeing that the flames would endure the bleak months, providing warmth to the inhabitants of the grand hall whilst the land beyond fell into frost and snow. Hundr then bade the steward bring benches for Torsten and his crew and mugs of warmed ale and porridge oats, which they ate with shaking hands before telling their tale.

They had left Einar with heavy hearts. Fights broke out upon deck as many of the crew wanted to return to Einar and fight and die at his side. Torsten, however, stood firm, and despite the heart-wrenching sight of seeing Einar and Ottar fall, he ordered the crew onwards, following Einar's orders and fulfilling his oath.

"Tell the Dog how the Brawler fell," Torsten told the folk gathered around the fire, and there was a collective gasp at the wyrd in those words. Hundr's hand searched for the stone hanging from his neck, the thumb-sized rock carved with runes by the galdr- woman. He held that rock and thought of Einar falling to Finn's warriors. The betrayal would have cut Einar deeper than any blade.

"How did it come to pass that Finn turned on Einar?" asked Hildr. All eyes turned to her, where she leant against one of the great hall posts with her arms folded.

"Finn had his own men, after the battle at Cuan Loch, added to the men who swore to him in Novgorod," Torsten answered. "We fought the Lord of Vedrafjord and defeated him, and Finn is Jarl of that place now. So the Witch-Queen rules in Vykyngelo, Finn rules in Vedrafjord, and Bárid rules Dublin. The völva and her allies run the east coast of Ireland. Einar asked Finn to leave with him, to return home before winter made the seas too treacherous. But Finn would not leave. He has grown powerful, and the Witch-Queen is his mother, after all."

"Saoirse wants you," Hildr said, jutting her chin towards Hundr. "She has hated you since you killed Hakon and Ivar. She hasn't killed Einar. I can feel it. He lives. She has cast her evil seiðr over Finn, just as she cursed Sigrid and your children. This harlot völva is a thing of hate and evil, and we must kill her."

"Just so," agreed Amundr. "We will kill all those Irisher bastards to get Einar back."

"But we can't sail now," said Bush. "The weather has turned. Look at Torsten and his lads.

We would never make it, or if we did, we'd lose half our ships and men and get to Ireland in no condition to fight."

"We cannot wait," Hildr insisted, striding towards Bush with her face set like the hardest stone. "Einar suffers, and our Finn is under a wicked spell."

"I wish to put out to sea immediately, just as much as you, Hildr," said Hundr, rising to hold her arm. He looked into the fury on her face, and she saw the same on Hundr's own. "This evil witch trollop tried to kill my children and my love, and now she has Einar. But to sail now is to die."

Hildr shook her head and snatched her hand away from Hundr, stinging him with a withering look, which she flicked to Torsten and his men.

"Are you all raven starvers like these men who would leave their lord alone in the hands of his enemies?" she exclaimed. Torsten surged from his seat, and Hundr tried to calm Hildr, but she had tipped her senses over into pure anger. "Are there no drengr in Vanylven who would put to sea with me to rescue Lord Einar?"

"Hildr," said Ragnhild, for even she, the most fiercely warlike amongst them, understood that the passage to Ireland was not possible this late in the year.

"No," barked Hildr. "I will not leave Einar and Finn there for the long winter suffering whilst we huddle by our fire, eating and drinking and safe."

"As soon as spring comes, when the first green shoots sprinkle the trees, we sail with all of our strength and bring red war to Ireland," said Ragnhild, "but we must wait."

Hildr turned on her heel and marched from the fireside, trailed by Ragnhild, who understood her sister of the Valkyrie order better than most. Hildr knew they were right, Hundr knew well enough, and she would regret how she had dishonoured Torsten and his men. But she had lost her husband and the man she loved like a son on the same day and must be forgiven for her rash words.

"Tell us of the voyage," said Bush, the shipmaster keen to understand the harsh voyage which had left them so ill-used.

The crew of the Fjord Bear looked at their boots, and the folk around the fire fell into a reverent hush as Torsten cleared his throat. All those packed into the hall were warriors and sailors, men who took to the Whale Road to go a'viking, seeking silver and reputation, knowing its risks and in awe of the fearsome power of Ran and Njorth, the gods of wind and sea who could reward a crew with favourable winds and calm seas, or curse them with mountainous waves and howling headwinds, with power enough to smash their *drakkar* warships to driftwood. The women huddled between the burly warriors and listened with wringing hands, for they dreaded spring, the time when their husbands and sons would take to the ships, not to return until the autumn. They were months filled with fear, the constant nightmarish worry that their men had died beneath crashing seas or been slaughtered by enemy blades on some distant shore. So, the people of Vanylven gathered close to hear Torsten's tale, still reeling from the news of Einar's fall and Finn's betrayal, the talk of seiðr and a völva like a tale a skald might tell before the same fire on a dark winter's night.

"We sailed north along Ireland's coast," Torsten began, hunched over with two hands around his wooden cup of warmed ale. He stared into the hall fire, eyes wide with the terrible memory and the flickering flames reflected in them as shadows danced on his gaunt face. "The gods favoured us, and we reached the lands of the Scots in mere days. But then the weather changed. A squall hit us as we rounded the northern tip of that wild land and came upon the islands. So, we tried to tack out to deeper waters, fearful of the sea's fury out there but seeking room away from the unfamiliar coastlines should the seas and winds toss us onto cliffs. There was no choice but to take down the sail and mast and secure the post in its crutch because the squall whipped into a frenzy, and we tried to heave-to. We sailed blind, clouds low and bleak, and the wind howled in our faces. We took on too much water and tossed our supplies and whatever else we could lose overboard to lighten the ship. The storm cleared, but we were lost, and without food or water, half our oars were gone, and our shields and weapons were lost. After two days of drifting, we got the mast and sail up again whilst we tried to get the rigging repaired. But we were cursed for seven nights with no wind and not enough oars to keep the Fjord Bear moving. The voyage was long, and we dared not risk going ashore, for all know the vicious men off that northern coast and how they would prey upon a warship fallen foul. After that week, the storm returned, but this time we ran before it downwind with no sail. Even with only our mast post up and rigging set, we clipped along, riding northwards and away from the coast, away from Orkney, and towards home. Waves came astern, and we spent a day bailing the bilge with raw hands, and when the wind changed, we dropped anchor for drag. Another week we lost rowing east, looking for land. Eventually, we found a familiar coast and limped home, fearful of attack, thirsty beyond description and starving. So, here we are and drengr we remain. Einar ordered me to go, to get to you, Lord Hundr so that we return with all of our strength and wreak our vengeance on his attackers."

Hundr stood and clasped his fist to his chest in salute to Torsten and his crew. "You have suffered much and followed orders. We spend winter preparing, and then in spring, we bring our blades for the witch." He thought of his Volund dream in the galdr-woman's cave, and part of him knew Einar was alive and imprisoned. Einar. The man who had taken him in when Hundr had nothing, a travel-stained boy with no silver or weapons to his name. Einar had granted Hundr a place on the Seaworm as bail boy, and he had never looked back. *Where would I be without Einar? He called me luck stealer once, just as Saoirse did. Maybe I am. But I will use whatever luck I have and the men under my command to punish those who have harmed my friend. One is a woman I once loved, and one is the son of a man I killed.* Hundr could almost hear the Norns cackling at the foot of the great tree, for they had truly woven a dark thread for him, Einar, and Finn Ivarsson.

TWENTY-TWO

Hildr raged. Neither Ragnhild nor Hundr could calm her, not Bush or any of the old Seaworm crew who had known her for many years. Even though Hildr knew the problem winter sailing posed, she still cursed them all for not taking to the ships immediately and sailing to Einar and Finn's aid. Only Sigrid and the baby twins could calm her. Hildr would soothe the crying babes and walk the hall floors, winding them and rocking them to sleep.

"She believes Finn has been done as much harm as Einar in all this," said Sigrid when she and Hundr ate a breakfast of hot porridge spooned from a cauldron over the hall fire. They were talking of Hildr, worried about her temper and her fears for the men she loved.

"I would not be so sure about that," Hundr remarked. They spoke in whispers because they had woken well before the sun that morning as the twins awoke screaming in the dark. Sigrid had fed them, and taking one each, they had walked the hall floors barefoot, shushing and rocking the babes until they fell asleep with full bellies from Sigrid's milk. The wise women of Vanylven had found a wet nurse for the children, but Sigrid preferred to feed the babies herself before resorting to that. So, the two children lay swaddled on a fur in front of Hundr and Sigrid whilst they ate the porridge prepared by the hall servants as they walked the floors, the grinding of the quern stones helping soothe the children. "He is what he always wanted to be, a jarl with his own warriors to command, men sworn to serve him alone."

"Is that not what you also wanted? Why you left Novgorod as a boy?"

"Yes, of course. But my mother was not a völva, and I did not attack the man who raised me. Einar is dead or imprisoned, and the witch could not have done that without Finn."

"Talk to Hildr. In spring, we shall sail to Ireland and see what has become of both Finn and Einar."

"We?" Hundr said without thinking it through. Sigrid fixed him with a flat stare. She had recovered some of her strength since the struggles of childbirth, but she was still afflicted with the injuries she had suffered delivering the twins and walked with a lingering limp.

"Am I not a warrior?"

"Of course you are. I just thought that..." Hundr looked down at the gently sleeping babies, their tiny, wrinkled hands close to their perfect faces.

Sigrid sighed. "I know, and I'm sorry. My place is here now. It's just difficult to accept. All of my life, I dreamt of becoming a famous warrior like my father. You gave that to me, and I love you for it. When you came to our hall on Orkney, I saw a way out, a way to avoid my arranged marriage, of being handed off by my father to whoever he deemed fit to further his ambitions. My worst fear was becoming a vessel for making babies and serving sons to powerful men. And now look at me."

Sigrid's father had been Ketil Flatnose, a warrior of fair fame across the north who had forged for himself a powerful jarldom in the Orkney Islands. Sigrid had been set to marry the son of another powerful warlord until Hundr raided Ketil's hall and became entranced by Sigrid's beauty. He reached over and stroked her head, moving a loose piece of her golden hair from her face to behind her ear. She was crying, and she wiped away her tears and smiled sadly at him. Sigrid was beautiful, blessed by the gods with a face unmarked by childhood disease and eyes as blue as a summer sky. She placed her hand over his, the wetness of her tears still upon her fingers. Sigrid had taken a savage cut to her face in the fighting at Novgorod a year earlier, and though its lurid redness had receded, she was ever conscious of the scar. Hundr traced its line with his finger.

"I see a warrior of reputation, a mother, the woman I love. We have men who can crew a ship, fight in the shield wall and die serving their oaths to Einar and me. There are few who can fight as fiercely as you and fewer with your bow skill. But there are certainly no others who can raise our sons as well as you can. There is glory in that, also. All men know of your battle prowess, and none will think any less of you for what you must do next. Once the boys are old enough, there will be a place for you on our ships. You have survived a witch's curse, freed from it by a galdr-woman and her songs and herbs. Now you have given birth to mighty twins who will one day take to the Whale Road themselves. You are no peace cow, Sigrid, no vessel for making babies. Yours is a legend which is already spoken of wherever men talk of warriors and fearsome deeds."

Sigrid smiled and cuffed away her tears.

"They are magnificent," she sighed, gazing at the babies. "Everything you have said is true, of course. It's just hard, that's all. A big change in my life. Find Hildr. She left earlier whilst we were settling the twins. She will listen to you."

Hundr kissed her and went from the hall. He gathered up a thick fleece and cast it about his shoulders before gently opening the wide hall doors. Hundr winced and opened them just enough to edge out, hoping that the hinges wouldn't creak and wake the babies. He couldn't quite get out and opened the door a little further. A gust of cold air blew in from the outside, rattling the wall-hangings and blustering the fire. The door hinges creaked, and a baby cried, so Hundr pushed himself through the gap and escaped out into the wind. It was still morning. Hundr frowned at a bleak sky with a fading hint of red in the distance. There was no sun, just a grey mass of sky and a fierce wind to ship the mountain pines and howl through Vanylven like the scream of a frost giant. Hundr pulled the fleece closer around him to keep out the worst of it. He wore a jerkin with a thick wool vest over it and heavy winter trews above boots and bindings around his calves and ankles. Vanylven was waking up. Folk came from their houses with puffy eyes and morning coughs. They went to fetch water from the well or to tend to their animals. Fishermen made their way to the shore to go out into the fjord and fish for the day's catch. A cockerel crowed somewhere out of sight, and a man bowed his head to Hundr as he shuffled past with arms full of firewood. Hundr didn't have to search for Hildr. He knew where she would go to vent her frustration.

He heard the thrum of the bowstring and the thud of the arrow before he reached the practice grounds. Hundr strode around a long stable topped with an earth roof, green with wild grass. A horse peered at him from the darkness of its stall, and Hundr reached out to stroke the beast's nose. Behind the stable stretched the long strip of grass where the warriors would practice their craft each day. Trees spotted the western side of the training ground, and the still waters of the fjord stretched away to the east. Mountains loomed in the misty distance, their peaks topped with clouds. A bow sang again, and Hundr walked towards the trees, where straw targets were set up for the warriors to practice archery. Hildr came into view, pulling her recurved bowstring back to her left ear and holding it there, the power in the bow stave stretching its horn, sinew, and wooden construct. She let a goose-feathered arrow fly, and it whipped through the wind too fast for the eye to follow before thumping into a distant target.

"As accurate as ever," Hundr called to her. Hildr turned to him, her face set firm and implacable. She wore her old war gear, trews below her brynjar, and a quiver hanging from her belt.

"I haven't kept up my training as much as I should," she said before sliding a white feathered arrow from her leather quiver.

"Your brynjar will rust in the damp."

"I need to get used to its weight again and the pull of the bow."

Hundr's armour was stowed in the hall, wrapped in an oily fleece just as it would be on board the ship. Safe for the winter, if not properly cared for, the expensive piece of war gear would rust, its hundreds of interlinked iron rings worth a fortune in silver and the mark of a successful warrior or jarl.

"You don't seem to have lost any of your strength."

She rolled her shoulders and shook her head. "I have. I used to be able to loose twenty arrows, each with the same power and accuracy. Now my back and shoulders are burning after six."

He smiled. "You know Torsten did as Einar ordered him, Hildr. If he had stayed, he would have broken his oath."

"His duty was to defend Einar, not leave him to be cut down, or worse, taken prisoner by that foul witch."

"Einar ordered him to leave, which likely saved both crew and ship. Torsten made it here through wild seas and heavy storms and brought us the news of Einar's fall. Now that we know, we can prepare over winter and be ready to strike. If Einar had stayed, they would have all perished, and we would think Einar and Finn happy in Ireland over the cold winter."

Hildr sighed and let her bow fall to her side. She looked up at Hundr with glassy eyes. "I know," she mouthed, the words dying beneath the lump in her throat. "What has become of my boy and my man? Has Finn really attacked Einar? They are so far away. I just wish we could go to them now, that I could help them."

Hundr moved to her slowly with his arms open. She was a hard woman, trained and raised to the blade since the time she could walk, and she could baulk at his attempt to comfort her, but she leant into him and sobbed silently into his chest.

"When spring comes, we sail to Ireland with all our wrath, and together we shall discover what has become of your boy and your man. I promise you that much, Hildr. If they have suffered, we will repay it tenfold."

Winter drew colder and harsher after that. In

the far north, the days become shorter and the nights longer still. Whenever there was light, the warriors were on the practice field. Shield walls moved against each other with cloth-wrapped blades or wood-carved replicas. They moved into line, overlapping shields and attacking one another until shoulders burned and arms ached. The warriors moved through advance and retreat formations, swine head wedge attacks, and how to encircle an enemy in an ambush. They wrestled, cold hands grasping for holds and men sprawling in the mud seeking leg locks, hip throws and arm locks. They worked with bows, casting spears, and held heavy shields out in front of their bodies with extended arms to build strength. Hildr never wore a dress after the day of the Fjord Bear's return. She was the first warrior out on the field each day and the last to leave. Whilst she still helped Sigrid with the twins when the day turned to dark, she spent most of her nights fletching feathers onto new arrows, and by the time of the midwinter Yule festival, she had sheaves of arrows fastened with twine.

Bush oversaw the caulking and repair of the fleet. The ships were brought up onto land, and pitch was heated, stirred through with horsehair and wool and spread between hull timbers to make the ships as watertight as possible. Sails were repainted with Hundr's sigil of the one-eye, and they crafted new shields. Vanylven's forges were alive with the hammer and flame of shield bosses and rims, of arrowheads and spear points. Vanylven prepared for war, and Hundr moved through the cuts of the sword each day until his body was sheeted with sweat. They sent word to villages and farmsteads surrounding Vanylven, and warriors came. Then, second and third sons with no land to inherit, and men seeking fame and fortune. They came with axes and knives, with old shields and spears used by their fathers and grandfathers long ago, men who had raided and become wealthy enough to buy land to settle on. Their descendants came eager to earn their own reputation and join the Man with the Dog's Name in his quest to rescue Jarl Einar, the Brawler of Vanylven. Hundr had berths for them all aboard the ships he had taken from Halvdan Ragnarsson, and as the warriors came in, Ragnhild put them through tests of their skill at arms. She made them form shield walls, and then she broke them with her Valkyrie ferocity. She had them fight her, Amundr, Erling, or Sigvarth so that she could judge their ability. Hundr allocated men to crews, and his small army grew until he had enough men to fill his ships with war-hungry Norsemen. The men who had sworn oaths to serve Hundr after the defeat at Loch Cuan kept to themselves for much of the winter were provided with a longhouse inside Vanylven's walls, and Hundr gave them a small share of the silver won in Ireland, even though they had been on the losing side. A leader emerged amongst them, a burly man with sallow skin and a top knot braid above a shaved skull. He was a Dane named Harbard and was a stout fighter on the practice grounds. He would bring their grumbles to Hundr, complaints of more blankets required for warmth or more food, or requests to go hunting in the mountains. Hundr tried to grant most of their requests. There was a danger that such men could turn into a problem. They were a surly bunch, stung from their loss and the death of their former lord, Halvdan Ragnarsson. Ragnhild advised Hundr to break them up and spread them throughout the other crews so that they could integrate with the Vanylven men and move on from their old lives. It was a good idea, and Hundr put seven of them with each of his crews, with Harbard joining him on the Seaworm.

Slowly mornings turned warmer. They no longer had to break ice from the top of water barrels to take a drink, and the nightfall receded, making days longer. Then, finally, green shoots appeared on branches, and the warships were lowered into the fjord, rigged and masted for war.

TWENTY-THREE

Seven ships made the journey west, and they flew before the wind with full sails, hulls crashing through the white-tipped waves like charging horses. The crews had to row for three days around the straits between the cliff-like islands close to the western territories of the Scots. One of the new ships became lost in a squall off the Suðreyjar islands but found the fleet again a day later and without damage. Bush led the fleet aboard the Seaworm as shipmaster, in which Hundr and Amundr sailed. Accompanying them on the seven warships was a formidable force of a long three hundred warriors, mail and weapons stowed in the bilge. All knew why they took to the Whale Road. They went to find Jarl Einar Rosti, who had been captured or killed by a völva, the same Witch-Queen who had cast her evil seiðr upon Sigrid and Hundr's children. All spoke in the dark nights about the legend of it, of the galdr-woman, and the Man with the Dog's Name who had now killed both Ivar and Halvdan Ragnarsson. In three weeks, they came to the Irish coast on a day when the sky was half bright, almost white to look upon, and the other half low and dark like an old nail. To the west, the sky appeared to reach out to touch far-off hills with tendril-like fingers as distant rain moved across the land like waves.

Hundr made camp a day's voyage north of Vedrafjord. As they tacked south in blustery gusts, they kept out to sea past Dublin and Vykengelo to avoid patrol ships along that stretch of Ireland's eastern coast. The ships dropped anchor on a long strip of golden sand, stretching as far as the eye could see and curving around to the south. The waters were still, waves barely lapping at the Seaworm's hull. Men wanted to go ashore and hunt for meat or steal it, their provisions growing stale and low after the weeks at sea. But Hundr kept them on board, not wanting his men to run into any of the enemy around the beaches or even Irish fisherfolk who would run to the Vikings with news of a fleet off their coast. Instead, they drank what remained of the ship's ale and Eochaid the

Irisher told them stories of Irish legend, of the times before the Vikings came, of giants and men with hunting dogs and proud warriors. Hundr took the first watch that night, listening to the sigh of the sea and the wind hissing through the coarse grasses beyond the sand dunes. The next day he would find Einar, dead or alive, and bring his wrath and vengeance upon those who had hurt his old friend. Saoirse ruled in Vykengelo, and she, the evil Witch-Queen, was the mother of all this suffering. Hundr had considered attacking Vykengelo before Vedrafjord, but there was no certainty that Saoirse would be at her fortress when she could be in Dublin with Bárid or in Vedrafjord with Finn. If Einar was alive, he would have spent a long winter as a prisoner, so Hundr would have to find Einar before hunting the völva. Hundr watched the black sea shifting beneath the night sky and was flooded by memories of Saoirse as she had been in Northumbria, young and beautiful. He recalled himself as a young man, foolish, ambitious and hungry for glory. Old faces smiled at him from the distant past, the broad, scarred face of Sten Sleggya, good shipmates like Brownlegs, Hrist, Kolo, Valbrandr and Blink. All dead, gone to the afterlife, having lived the life of a Viking.

Something splashed in the water close to the Seaworm's hull, snapping Hundr out of the memories of those faces that made him smile, despite the pain of their loss, for in life, he had loved them all. Hundr looked over the side, but there was nothing but the mass of shifting sea. He had left Sigrid holding their twins, one in each arm. She had returned to her old self after the birth; all her pregnancy troubles and problems were over. The womenfolk of Vanylven helped with the babies, caring for them as a community so that Sigrid had time to recover and regain her strength. There was joy in the children, a different joy to that of battle or the love of a woman. Hundr smiled at the thought of their soft skin and little hands. Sigrid had not asked him to take care or make sure he returned alive, but it was in the lingering look she had left him with in their home the morning he had departed. She had held his face in her hand, running her fingers across his dead eye and the raised scarring across his body, like runes cut into a rock to tell a saga tale.

Amundr came to take the next watch, and Hundr lay down to sleep. It did not come easily. He worried about what would become of his family if he died there in Ireland. Einar would provide for them, if he lived. But who would King Harald appoint to rule Vanylven if both men were gone? How could Sigrid provide for herself and the twins if Hundr and his men were defeated and lost on a distant shore? Hundr banished those worries with thoughts of

Vedrafjord, of how to attack the fortress and get inside, of those who must die for the pain they had caused.

Hundr left thirty men to guard the fleet, which they anchored off the eastern shore of an island that sat nestled in the curves of the River Suir. Spanning the three corners of a wide bend in the river, the island was large and wooded, with a fishing village on the northern shoreline. The tide was in flood, and Hundr sent one ship to secure the village with ten men to ensure the fisherfolk did not send word of their arrival to Vedrafjord. Hundr waded through the chill water to clamber up the riverbank and ventured through a dense spatter of gorse until he came into a grazing pasture sodden from showers of spring rain. He wore his brynjar, with Fenristooth belted at his waist in a fleece-lined scabbard and Battle Fang strapped across his back. Hundr's seax hung from the rear of his belt in a sheath held there by two thongs of leather. Although the day was cold and his breath misted in the spring air, he left his cloak aboard the Seaworm. The march and the fight to come would keep him warm. His warriors emerged from the water behind him, over three hundred Vikings in mail or leather, bristling with axe and spear, each man with a shield strapped to his back bearing the one-eye sigil painted in white on dark leather shield covers.

Throughout the long winter, Hundr and Ragnhild had repeatedly questioned Torsten about Vedrafjord, its fortifications and the surrounding land. Eochaid, the Irisher amongst Hundr's crews, knew little of the place, being from the west of the country. Vedrafjord was of the usual Viking fort construction, the tried and tested way of building a secure foothold in a hostile country, used by Viking raiders and invaders for longer than men could remember. They had built the fortification in a half circle, with the flat side facing directly onto the River Suir and the curved side facing landward. A ditch and a stout palisade built upon a raised earth rampart protected that landward side. Ragnhild had argued that they should attack Vedrafjord from the river, simply row their warships into the harbour and fight their way into the stronghold. To do that, however, they would first need to fight their way across whatever ships were docked on the riverbank, and Vedrafjord's defenders would simply fill those ships with warriors. It would inevitably be a bloody fight across the decks where many men would die, and to get to Einar, they would need to fight their way through an army.

Bog water soaked into Hundr's boots as he and his warriors marched through marshland and up towards a small hill crested with a clutch of hazel and alder trees. The warriors who followed him laughed and joked, as men tend to before a fight. They shared skins of ale, and their weapons clanked as they strode across the riverbank in loose formation. Hundr cleared the rise, and as the land stretched away into low grassland, bordered on the southwestern side by a boggy marsh, there stood Vedrafjord. There were ten ships moored on the riverside, where five jetties poked out into the waterway on stout timbers. Smoke rose from behind the palisade, coughing from the smoke holes cut into buildings roofed with a mixture of thatch and turf, greyed after the winter's cold and rain. There were cattle and sheep in pastures beyond the ditch, and Hundr's warriors came up behind him, the army of fighters he had brought across the sea to descend upon Vedrafjord in glorious, vengeful fury.

"Einar is in there," said Hildr, appearing at Hundr's side. She carried her bow unstrung, reserving the precious string for the imminent battle. The damp Irish air and the wetness of the bog would sap the bow's power, so she kept her strings dry and warm beneath her hood. Her axe rested in a loop at her belt, and she carried a knife on her left hip. There had been little talk of the fact that Einar could be dead, that Finn and the Witch-Queen could have butchered him the same day that Torsten sailed the Fjord Bear away from Ireland. Instead, it was an unspoken agreement between the warriors of Vanylven that they sailed under the assumption that Einar lived and was held in Vedrafjord.

"And we are going to get him out," Hundr replied.

"Are you sure this is going to work?" asked Ragnhild from Hundr's blind side.

He didn't want to say he wasn't sure because his men were close, shouldering past one another to get a better look at the fort. "It has to work. We use their hate against them," he said.

"What will you do if you come face to face with Finn in the fighting?" Bush pressed. Hundr winced because it was the question they had all avoided asking Hildr throughout the long winter. She had raised Finn as his foster mother, and a son attacking his mother was a thought best left alone.

"I am not here to fight Finn," said Hildr. "Only to get Einar back. But if I can talk to Finn…"

"It looks strong," piped Amundr, his shadow hulking over all of them and, as ever, stating the obvious.

"Let's hope they do what we want them to," said Hundr. "It's time to go. Bush, Amundr, you know what to do." They nodded in silent agreement, and Hundr set off down the northern slope of the small hill, heading back toward the river. Hildr, Ragnhild, Erling, and Eochaid came with him. From behind, Bush let out a long call on his war horn and their army marched down the hill towards the flatland grazing pastures and Vedrafjord's front gate. Then, just as Hundr ordered, they shouted their challenge to the enemy and banged their axes upon their iron shield rims so that a din to shake the sun ripped across a quiet Irish morning.

Hundr led his small band in a run along a line of hedges separating two fields. The river glistened ahead of him, and fear kindled in his belly like kindling sparking in a smith's forge. War meant risk. He risked the lives of his men and the lives of his friends, and his plan had to work. Hundr was a sea Jarl and a war leader; his men trusted and depended on him. He had spent many nights staring into the fire at Vanylven, wondering how to free Einar, and had decided that his enemies' hate was a weapon he could use against them. As ever in war, so much could go wrong, and he knew well from his long years at the blade that a plan rarely went smoothly. He needed Saoirse, Finn, or both to be at Vedrafjord for it to work. Hundr knew the völva hated him, and she could not refuse an offer of battle, even if it meant marching her warriors out of their secure fortress to fight in a shield wall battle. A sensible commander would laugh at Hundr's army from behind Vedrafjord's walls and wait for them to attack. Such fortresses worked because an attacker had to charge the walls, descend into the ditch under a hail of spears and arrows, climb the high earthen rampart and then scale the palisade walls, all under constant bombardment. On the other side of the palisade would be a fighting platform, from which the defenders would lean over the sharpened stakes of the walls to hack at the attackers with axes and spears. To attack those walls was to die. Yet, Hundr's hope was that Saoirse would lead her men out as soon as she saw his one-eye banner, her hate for him clouding her judgement, sacrificing her deep cunning at the altar of vengeance. Finn, however, was a different story. Hundr relied on Torsten's view that Finn had fallen under his mother's influence and that she had stoked Finn's own pot of hatred. Hundr had killed Finn's father, Ivar the Boneless, and the boy was ever proud and careful of his reputation. So, even if the Witch-Queen was not in Vedrafjord, Hundr hoped Finn would lead his warriors out of the gate, lost in a hate-filled madness and desire to kill the Man with the Dog's Name.

"There's the harbour," said Eochaid as they jogged along the riverbank. A soft breeze drifted from the river to rustle the briar and brush. The Irishman pointed to where the river lapped at weather-darkened timbers which emerged from the water to prop up timber-planked jetties. Men strode along the walkways, their boots banging on the wood, and the sound of their voices, garbled at this distance, mixed with occasional coughs and a dog's bark.

"Wait here," Hundr ordered, and he sank low, kneeling in the grass so that the soil, which was heavy and damp, seeped cold wetness through his trews to chill the skin of his knees. He looked back with his good eye to where Bush, Amundr and Sigvarth led the warriors onto the flat fields, spreading them out into six ranks of shields, fifty men across.

"They're looking," said Ragnhild, her breath coming in quick gasps after the run along the riverbank. Hundr wanted to get close to the river and away from the army before the men of Vedrafjord could see them. "But not at us."

She nodded towards the ramparts, where a gate faced east and a bridge spanned the ditch. Hundr and his band crouched to the north, with the river on their right, and spears appeared on the palisade, wobbling and shifting like heather in the wind. Men peered over the sharpened timbers at the army forming before them. Hundr wondered if Finn was amongst them and if the young Ivarsson felt fear knowing that Hundr had come for Einar or guilt at having harmed the old Jarl.

Bush blew his war horn again, and the

warriors of Vanylven clashed their weapons in unison, making the war music that would lift their hearts and steel their fears against the fight to come. They were three hundred of the finest warriors in Midgard, Hundr's own warriors who had fought across battlefields in England, Frankia, Norway and the lands of the Rus. Amongst them were Halvdan Ragnarsson's men, hardened warriors used to victory and keen to fight and regain their former reputations and pride, and then the men of Norway, who were a mix of old raiding veterans or young warriors eager to prove their worth. Hundr trusted their mettle and knew that if Finn brought his warriors out to fight, the newly minted Jarl of Vedrafjord would find himself up against a fearsome enemy.

"We wait until they march," said Hundr. They had been through the plan countless times, but the moments before a fight were the enemy of calm thought. His own heart pumped in his chest, and he wrestled with the urge to charge over the walls and find his friend—if Einar even lived.

More spears appeared on the battlements, and a roar rose within the fort like the sound of a sea rising to wrath in a growing storm. Voices shouted from behind the walls, challenging and defiant, but there were also screams. Women and children, word of the approaching army washing over the town like the tide. It was ever the women and children who suffered most in war, and they would fear the men in Hundr's shield wall, worrying at what would happen if their men-folk failed to protect them and allowed the attacking force inside the walls.

"They aren't leaving," Hildr uttered, her knuckles white around her bow stave. They waited, crouched in the bushes like wolves waiting for the shepherd to leave his flock unattended. Then the spears moved. Their points shifted from the battlements down from the fighting platform towards the gate.

"They are going to fight," said Eochaid in his Irish lilt. "Irishmen would never turn their backs on a fight. Sure isn't only my own blade begging to be let loose."

Hundr held them there, watching the fortress and waiting. If Vedrafjord's warriors did not empty the place to fight the offered shield wall battle, then his plan to search for Einar would be scuppered. There was little chance he could enter the fortress in broad daylight if it was full of Finn's warriors. Many of those men knew Hundr. The warriors who had sworn their oaths to Finn in Novgorod had spent an entire year with him at Vanylven, and many of the rest would have seen him at the battle of Cuan Loch. A one-eyed man would draw attention, especially when the best friend of the Viking world's most famous one-eyed man had been captured or killed by the fortress' lord. So, Hundr waited, his hand fingering the rune-carved stone around his neck, wondering if the völva, Saoirse, the Witch-Queen, was in the fortress. If she was, then he would kill her. Not only because of the suffering she had caused Sigrid or because she had tried to kill his babies before they had a chance at life, but also because he owed the galdr-woman a völva's head.

"Black shields," noted Erling, pointing towards the gated end of the fort. Men crossed the bridge over the ditch and marched sideways so that the black of their shields faced Hundr before turning to face their enemies.

"Young Finn was never a man to resist a challenge," said Ragnhild, and she grinned at Hundr. Her scarred face was grim enough to match his own. "Strings."

Hildr and Ragnhild fished their dry bowstrings from their caps and hooked one end around their bow's horn-nooked tip, stretching the powerful length of wood, sinew and horn across the back of one leg before nocking the other end of the string. They both carried quivers at their belts and were armed with axes and knives.

"For Einar," Hundr said. Hildr nodded at him.

Her golden hair shot through with grey pulled back from her face and tied into a plaited bun behind her hair. Her face showed wrinkles at the mouth and eyes, but she was yet strong enough to fight for the man she loved. "We find him and get out quickly."

"I hate to say it, Lord Hundr..." Eochaid began and then swallowed deeply as Hildr shot him a withering look. "But what if he isn't there, what if they... if he..."

"Once we get inside, we'll question a warrior and discover Einar's fate," Hundr said. He avoided Hildr's eyes, but it was time to speak truthfully, for they were about to risk their lives. "If Einar lives, we break him out. If he is dead, we search for the völva and her son and kill them both."

"Kill Finn?" Hildr gasped.

"You know deep down it has to be this way," Hundr replied. "He betrayed Einar, which means he betrayed you and me. No man can do that and live; I don't care who he is."

He didn't wait for her to respond but set off at a lope towards the harbour side of the fortress. The warriors facing off on its eastern side roared and clashed weapons at each other. The din was like rolling thunder undulating across a mountain range. Hundr's band came without shields, and Erling had a length of rope looped around him in case they had to climb the walls. Hundr leapt over a waist-high tangle of brambles, and his boots landed in the riverbank's mud. He was at the nearest jetty after two more laboured steps in its sucking sludge. The flood tide was not yet full, so the jetty's timbers were at head height from the river. The vertical timbers reaching from the riverbed were thick with green slime and lichen. Hundr reached up and pulled himself over its lip, turned and helped the others clamber over the edge until all five of them crouched on the jetty. He set off at a run again. The timber planks rattled beneath his boots, and fishermen in their small faerings stared at him with open mouths. The men had their families crammed into the boats, and more people ran from the fort's river-facing gateway. They came in ones and twos, a red-haired woman clutching a baby, a big-hipped woman dragging two scruffy urchins behind her. They came to board the ships in case the battle didn't go the way of the Dubgaill warriors. Hundr ignored them, weaving between each person, and they ignored him, oblivious to the fact that they were five enemies heading into their hometown.

"Two guards, black shields," said Eochaid. The two men stood on either side of the open gate, waving the fleeing women through. They were armed with black shields bearing Finn's raven banner and long spears.

"Kill them," Hundr snarled. The Valkyrie sisters didn't even break their stride, and the two guards died before they had the chance to notice Hundr and his band. The first took an arrow in his throat, and as Hildr's bow thrummed behind Hundr, the second succumbed to a shaft punching through the base of his skull.

The gate lay open, and Hundr dashed beneath its broad lintel as more women dodged around him, screaming now at the dead black shield warriors. Inside the palisade was a tangle of lanes, some thick with mud and others covered in small stones recovered from the riverbed. The buildings were all low, one-story houses and halls, and Hundr ran through the people who dashed about in panic, faces twisted in fear for the outcome of the battle outside their walls. Then, finally, he came about a strip of drooping thatch and saw two black shield fighters emerge from a doorway. They were mid-way through strapping on leather breastplates to join the battle, and Hundr charged at them. He drew Fenristooth in one smooth motion and back-cut the first warrior across his neck and face, opening up a gash that splashed blood onto the building's pale wattle walls. The second warrior turned to him in shock, mouth open and eyes wide. Hundr flicked the tip of his sword so that blood spattered the young warrior's face and held it a finger's breadth from the man's eyes.

"Norse or Irish?" Hundr asked in Norse. The man shook his head, eyes flicking from the corpse to the warriors gathered over Hundr's shoulder.

"You're an Irishman, and no mistake, look at the freckled head on you," said Eochaid in the Irish tongue, and the man nodded.

"Ask him about Einar."

Eochaid spoke again in Irish, and the warrior nodded and pointed down the lane, arching his fingers to the right.

"He says Jarl Einar lives. They keep him in a building close to the stables. It's this way," Eochaid translated, and Hundr's heart lifted because Einar was alive.

"Ask him if the Witch-Queen is here or Erik Bjornsson."

Eochaid spoke again in his own tongue, and the warrior shook his head, glancing nervously at Hundr and his grim face and then at his drawn sword, which ran with the blood of his dead comrade.

"The bitch isn't here," said Ragnhild, stamping her boot hard on the ground. "We'll have to wait to kill the mangy witch."

Hundr lowered his sword, but just as he was

about to set off after Einar, an axe flew past his dead eye to thud into the face of the Irish warrior. The blade slapped through flesh and crunched bone as it crushed the man's skull, and Ragnhild grunted as she wrenched her axe free of the dead man's head. She wiped her hand through the blood on her blade and smeared it across her face, mouthing a silent prayer to Odin. Hildr followed Ragnhild's lead, the two Valkyrie bloodied, ferocious and ready to kill.

The five warriors marched through Vedrafjord with weapons drawn. Hundr burst around every corner, expecting to run into enemy warriors, but there were none. Instead, all the fighting men in the fort had gone to the front gate to join the young Jarl's shield wall and his fight against the enemy. Hundr's thoughts were clouded as he strode with his blade in his hand. He was torn between frustration that the Witch-Queen was not at Vedrafjord and would need to be fought another day and relief that he would not have to bring his sword against the soft throat of Saoirse, a woman he had once loved so fiercely that he had been willing to die for her.

A great roar erupted outside the fort, followed quickly by a crunch like the sound of an ancient oak tree falling in a forest, its myriad branches crashing and snapping and shaking the very earth. Hundr followed the dead warrior's directions, and after coming about a long stretch of stables, he came upon an open field, the grass still twinkling with morning dew. At the far side of the field stood a small building guarded by four large warriors. The men faced away from Hundr, each of them armed with a spear. They stared towards the front of the fortress, no doubt cursing their ill luck at missing the battle. Hundr glanced over his shoulder, waiting until Ragnhild, Hildr, Erling, and Eochaid caught up to him. He watched the guards for a moment, their shoulders slumped. They would be downcast at missing the battle and thinking of the boasting they would be subjected to at the victory feast that evening. But they guarded Hundr's friend, so those men would have no victory or feast.

Hundr strode from the stables and into the open field. He held Fenristooth in his right hand and reached over his shoulder to pull Battle Fang out of her scabbard at his back. He curled his lip against his bottom teeth and whistled at them like a man might whistle for a dog. They turned, armed in leather, helmets resting on their spear points. Jaws dropped on the four guard's faces as they saw the five warriors approaching them, three men armed with swords and axes and two women in chain mail with blood-smeared faces.

"I have come for Einar the Brawler," Hundr shouted at them, holding his two swords out wide. "The Man with the Dog's Name is here to kill those who treated so great a warrior with such disrespect."

The guards looked at one another, then fumbled for their helmets and tried to level their spears. Hildr screamed and let fly a white feathered arrow from her bow. The missile thumped into a guard's shoulder, spinning him like a child's toy. Hundr ran at them; the long winter of frustration spent worrying about Einar and helpless to discover if he was living or dead burst out of him like vomit. He swayed away from a clumsy spear thrust and opened his attacker's belly with his sword, slicing beneath the rim of his leather breastplate whilst at the same time driving Battle Fang's point into the throat of a second guard, punching the sword's tip into the man's gullet and ripping it free in a gout of blood which steamed in the cold spring air.

Hundr kept moving, leaving the guards to the blades of his friends as he raced to the building.

"Einar!" Hildr shouted, following Hundr with long strides.

Hundr reached the door, made of stout timber and braced by a thick oak spar held by two crutches. He dropped his swords and lifted the spar. Grunting under its weight, Hildr helped him, and they hefted it free of its crutches and tossed it aside. Hundr retrieved his weapons and kicked the door in. Foulness surged from the gloom beyond the door, a smell of rot, stale sweat and shit. Hundr turned his head from it, but Hildr burst into the darkness with her bow slung across her back and a knife in her hand. Hundr squinted, struggling to get his one eye used to the darkness inside the room. He stepped inside. A shaft of light shone in from a barred window. Hildr sobbed, falling upon a huddled figure. It was a man with tangled hair and a wild beard. Hundr's eye cleared, and he realised the man was Einar, his face sunken against the hard lines of his cheekbones and jaw. He was terribly thin and dressed in stained rags.

"You came," Einar croaked, and a single tear rolled down one grim, smeared cheek. Hildr clung to him. He held out a bony hand towards Hundr, and he took it. Hundr lifted Einar to his feet and was surprised at how light he was. It was like lifting a child. He drew Einar and Hildr into an embrace. Then Hundr remembered his Volund dream in the galdr-woman's cave, Einar was the prisoner, and all that remained was vengeance.

"Of course, we came. We are as brothers, you and I. Let us leave this place," replied Hundr.

"Refil," Einar murmured, looking back into the darkness. Hundr peered into it, and another pitiful figure was hunched and emaciated in the darkness. Refil, the lost son of Bjorn Ironside.

TWENTY-FOUR

E inar clung to Hildr as she walked him out of the prison. His eyes creased as they stumbled into the daylight, and he laughed joyfully as Ragnhild killed a black shield guard with her axe. Vedrafjord was alive with noise, shouts and panic from within the town as folk hurried here and there, figures running between the buildings surrounding the field. He turned to ensure Refil followed, and his fellow prisoner hung from Hundr's shoulders like a starved bear, thick with matted hair and tottering on thin legs.

"Bastards!" came a shout across the field. Six black shield warriors came charging across the space, and each man bore a black shield emblazoned with the white raven. Hildr unhooked Einar's arm from her shoulder and let him rest against the building's wall. She slipped her bow from her back and, in one smooth motion, whipped an arrow from her quiver, nocked and loosed it. One of the warriors took the arrow upon his shield, but the power of it stunned him, and the others slowed their pace, forming a short shield wall to protect themselves. Ragnhild let more arrows fly, and Hundr ran past Einar, having lowered Refil to sit on the damp grass. Eochaid and Erling followed Hundr into the attack, and the three warriors tore into the enemy shields. Einar thought he would weep as Hundr broke their shield wall with deft cuts of his flashing blades. It was a thing he had dreamed of but thought never to see.

Einar knelt and picked up a spear from where it lay beside the body of one of his dead guards. He used the spear like a crutch, his body too weak to walk unaided, and he clenched his teeth with the effort of moving towards the fight.

"No, Einar, stay," Hildr said, but he waved her away.

Hundr killed a warrior with a sword thrust into his armpit, and Erling fought with a man wielding a shield pierced with three arrows.

Eochaid faced two of the black shield fighters and cut one man down with his axe. But the big man, the one who Einar wanted, plunged his spear into Eochaid's chest and roared into his dying face, piercing his armour. It was the guard who had beaten Einar so severely, the big bastard who had helped Fiachra torture him. Eochaid fell to his knees, and the big man twisted his spear to rip the blade free. The guard glowered at Einar and came on with his spear levelled. He tossed away his shield and lurched into a charge. Einar tried to steel himself and bring his spear to the fight but staggered with weakness and cursed his body for failing him. Einar watched the spearpoint coming for him and swallowed a lump in his throat. All that time spent in misery, now to die at the hands of his torturer, the man who had cut, flayed and burned his flesh to agony beyond reckoning. However, in a sudden flash of brynjar, iron burst in front of him, and Hildr turned the charging spear aside with her axe. She followed up with her knife, whipping it across her body in a backward grip so that the blade sliced across the big man's breastplate. He snarled and tried to bring his spear around, but Hildr chopped her axe down again to block the spear shaft and then fell down upon it with her knee. The spear's stave shivered and snapped, and Hildr plunged her knife into the big man's shoulder so that he fell to his knees, eyes closed and grimacing at the pain. Einar was enthralled.

Thor's balls. I love that woman.

Einar advanced on the big man, gripping his spear in two hands.

"Look at me," Einar said, his voice coming in a guttural growl. The big man shook his head, clutching at the knife stuck in his shoulder as blood pulsed from the wound. "Look at me," he repeated. The big man opened his eyes, and his mouth twisted into a rictus of hate. He opened his lips, his black beard shaking as he trembled with pain, and Einar rammed the spear into his open maw, twisting and ripping the leaf-shaped point inside the man's mouth, tearing his tongue, cheeks and throat open and turning his face to gore. The big man fell, and Einar almost fell on top of him before Hildr caught him. He wanted to hack into the big man's corpse and cut his limbs free of his body so that he would walk the afterlife as a cripple, but he had no strength. Einar turned to Refil, who grinned at the big man's death, and they laughed together, the joy of freedom mixed with the death of the man who had tortured them with starvation and the filth of their prison—a dream they had spoken of in the dark for so long now unfolding before them.

"My love," Hildr gasped and ran a hand down his face. "What have they done to you?" There were fresh scars, he knew. The big bastard had cut two lines down one side of his face and laid his cheeks open on more than one occasion.

"We must get out of this place," Ragnhild said. She moved slowly around them, an arrow nocked to her bow, turning carefully to each corner of the field and the buildings beyond, ready to loose at any more enemies who came close.

"Eochaid is dead," Hundr uttered, frowning, "and they have injured Erling." The young Viking bled freely from a deep cut to his thigh. "Let's get to the palisade." Hundr stopped dead as he looked upon Einar's face in daylight. He had greeted Einar in the dark of his prison and then launched straight into the fight with the guards, so he had not fully taken in his friend's terrible appearance. Hundr's swords dropped to his sides, and his eyes pored over the scarring on Einar's face. There was rage in that look, beginning as a jaw-clenching shock as he looked over the white scar tissue on Einar's face that turned into anger as he understood how Einar had suffered. Einar tore his eyes away, feeling a strange stab of shame that he hadn't been able to fight off his torturers. "Get those rags off Jarl Einar's back. Strip the big one and use his clothes."

Ragnhild leapt to the dead guard and cut free his brynjar. She stripped his jerkin and trews as Hildr peeled the ragged clothing from Einar's body, and both the Valkyrie and Hundr gasped at the marks on his chest and back. Einar tried to cover the scars, shame now washing over him like the tide. Terrible, unfamiliar thoughts ran through Einar's mind. Although he had tried to escape and fight back, he wondered if he could have done more. He feared being a nithing rather than a drengr. Hildr helped him with the clothes, but he shook his head at the brynjar, knowing that he did not yet have the strength to carry the heavy weight of the coat made of iron rings. Then, whilst Vedrafjord continued to churn with the fear of its residents around them, Ragnhild helped Refil don the clothes of another dead warrior. Folk ran between lanes and houses, desperate to know if their men had won or lost.

"Why don't we just go back the way we came?" asked Hildr, helping Einar to his feet.

"If our lads break their shield wall, the black shield bastards will flood back through the gate and charge through the town towards their ships. If they catch us between here and the river, then we die," said Hundr. He spoke in a low, flat voice. His chest heaved, the corded muscles of his upper body seeming to grow with each deep breath, lifting the chains of his brynjar with each inhalation.

"Our warriors are here?" Einar asked. He heard a clash of weapons and shields to the west but had only noticed it now that the guards were dead.

"Aye," Hundr replied. "They fight Finn's black shield men outside the walls. And I go to join them. Now, Hildr, stay with Einar, Refil and Erling. Find somewhere to keep them safe until the fighting is over. Do not go to the harbour. The enemy will flee there after we have crushed them."

"I can't fight," said Erling shaking his head, trying to rise from the grass with one hand clutching the gash in his thigh, but then he toppled backwards with a curse.

"Go to the stables or inside a house. Ragnhild, with me." Hundr approached Einar and took his forearm in the warrior's grip. "They will all suffer for what they have done to you."

He nodded in shame, knowing he was diminished and couldn't fight because of what he had endured. Now, he would have to hide with his wife whilst other men fought so that he could be free. Then he thought of Finn.

"Hundr, wait…" Hildr called as Hundr turned on his heel. There was a sadness on her face, and though she couldn't bring herself to say it, Einar wanted to say the same thing…

Don't kill Finn.

Hundr was beyond reason. His fury was

palpable. The Man with the Dog's Name just shook his head and marched towards the battle, a sword in each hand and filled with insatiable wrath.

TWENTY-FIVE

Hundr ran towards where the battle raged beyond Vedrafjord's walls. His boots pounded along the road leading directly from the harbour to the front gate. He ran because he was too angry to walk. Ragnhild was beside him, bow in hand and face smeared with dried blood. Ready to fight and kill. Einar had suffered. The great man laid low at the hands of lesser men. Finn, the boy Einar had taken in and raised to manhood, had betrayed him and allowed men of no drengskapr, nithings of no honour, to hurt and torture him. Filled with love for Einar for the chance he had given to him when he was nothing, for his friendship, honour and bravery, Hundr ran, his fists clenched about his swords, knuckles white. Hundr wanted to cut, slash, rend, and tear. He would be Einar's vengeance, the tool to bring suffering and death to those who had hurt his friend.

The gate was open, and there were men on the fighting platform, warriors with black leather breastplates daubed with the white raven. Two turned to watch Hundr and Ragnhild approach, but they did not understand. They saw two warriors running towards the battle from Vedrafjord, so they assumed they were on the same side. They were wrong.

"Kill them," said Hundr. Ragnhild did not even break stride. She sent two shafts flying in rapid succession, and the two guards fell. There was a man in the gateway, peering out to where the warriors fought, and as Hundr passed him, he reversed Battle Fang in his grip and cut the man's throat, cursing him for a nithing, for watching whilst other men fought. Hundr ran across the bridge spanning the ditch, the elm planking banging underfoot. Ahead, the scream of battle tore the land before Vedrafjord. Men roared, cried, and died in a field churned by blood, piss and the voided bowls of the dying. Two shield walls hacked at each other, his own one-eyed banner stood high and proud at the centre of the Vanylven lines, and the raven banner of the Ragnarssons flew amid the enemy force.

"Odin, grant me strength," Hundr prayed as he ran towards the enemy's rear. "Make me fast and deadly, and I will send you warriors for Valhalla."

Ragnhild loosed an arrow towards the rear of the enemy formation, aimed at the centre of their battle line, which stretched fifty shields across. A man fell with the goose feather arrow stuck in his back—a lurker, a raven starver standing at the rear of the fight whilst the drengrs, the lovers of war, the killers, fought in the front ranks, hacking at each other with sword and axe, making and breaking reputations in the shield wall where men fought for their very lives. Ragnhild let another arrow fly, and another man fell. The rear rankers at the centre turned and gawped at the two warriors dashing towards them, for they had thought themselves safe behind the fighting, waiting for the enemy shield wall to break so they could run into the fleeing men, and once the hard fighting was over, they hoped to wet their blades on the blood of broken men.

"Wait," Ragnhild barked. Hundr stopped, for Ragnhild knew the ways of war just as well as he, and she would not halt the charge for vengeance lightly. She steadied her breath and drew the last arrow from her quiver. Ragnhild took her time, nocking it carefully to her bow and raising the weapon. She pulled the string, muscles bunching to draw it back to her right ear. Ragnhild sighted her aim, her one eye honing in on its target. She released it in a thrum of power and turned and nodded at Hundr, not needing to look, certain that the arrow flew true towards its target. She let her bow fall and drew her axe and knife from her belt. "For Einar."

"For Einar," Hundr replied. They broke into a run together, and Hundr whooped with ferocious joy as the raven banner toppled, the warrior holding it killed by Ragnhild's bow skill. A roar went up from the Vanylven warriors when the enemy flag fell. Their hearts lifted, and enemy hearts sank. The banner was the army's symbolic heart, filling them with pride, a thing to give a man purpose, but to lose a banner had the opposite effect.

Hundr reached the first of the rear rankers, and one of those skulkers tried to run from him but moved too late. Hundr whipped Fenristooth across his face and kept going, slicing open the hamstrings of a warrior facing away from him towards the battle. Ragnhild screamed her Valkyrie war cry to Odin, and she cut with her axe. Hundr clutched his two swords close, and like spears, he drove them into the spines of the third rank of the Vedrafjord shield wall, cutting deep into the backs of two warriors who twisted and cried out at the unexpected pain. Ragnhild launched herself into the air, diving between the men stabbed by Hundr, and she crashed into the second rank, where a warrior was about to lift the fallen raven banner. She slammed her axe into his unprotected neck, and blood spurted bright against his mail. Hundr pulled his swords free of the dying men and hacked into the warriors surrounding him, men turning in shock and trying to bring shields about to meet the attack from their rear. A blade punched into Hundr's shoulder, but his brynjar absorbed the blow, and he drove his sword into the attacker's belly. A short man with blonde hair coughed up a gout of dark crimson as Battle Fang tore at his innards, and then Ragnhild began rolling on the ground, hacking at enemy legs with her axe and knife. There was chaos in the Vedrafjord ranks, and their line buckled. A great heave of Vanylven shields pushed into the gap Hundr and Ragnhild had created, snarling men roaring and stabbing with spears at the enemy. Hundr grabbed Ragnhild's brynjar and hauled her back before she became crushed in the charge of their own men.

There was a collective moan, a cry of despair as the Vedrafjord shield wall broke. Hundr jostled backwards, ducking beneath an enemy axe blade as he and Ragnhild scrambled to safety. Hundr cut at the axeman, but his sword blade scraped across strong chain mail, so he drove the point of his second sword up into the warrior's bearded chin. Blood poured from that wound in a hot rush, splashing down the sword blade and across Hundr's hand and arm. He yanked Battle Fang free of the dying man and shouted joyfully as shields bearing his one-eye sigil broke the enemy shield wall in half. Warriors stumbled into the space behind the enemy, and a giant man growled from behind a Vanylven shield, stabbing a spear at Hundr. He leapt back, and then the shield lowered, a broad, surprised face staring back at him.

"It's you, my lord," said Amundr, his eyes staring out of the eyeholes of his helmet.

"It's me," Hundr nodded and clapped Amundr on the shoulder. Then, Hundr slipped Battle Fang back into its scabbard strapped to his back and drew his seax with his left hand so that he went armed with sword and seax.

"Now we find the son of Ivar," said Hundr. He could not think of Finn as the boy he once was, for that would lead to pity and open the door to forgiveness. So, instead, he was merely the son of Hundr's greatest enemy and would follow his father into the dirt.

The Vedrafjord warriors broke like a dry branch in a summer forest. Once Amundr and his chosen champions forced their way through the splinter created by Hundr and Ragnhild, fear spread through the enemy ranks. Warriors peeled away from the battle, first in ones and twos, backing away from the fighting with open mouths and wide eyes. Then, once the mid-rankers felt the men behind them fade away, the open space became panic and rout.

"No mercy," Hundr bellowed at his men as they charged into the opening spaces in the enemy line. "Kill them all." He wanted them all to pay for Einar's pain, and so they would. He struck out at a warrior in a dented helmet, slashing at his ankles and then plunging his seax into the falling man's back. The running enemy avoided Hundr, Ragnhild, and Amundr's men like water around a river eyot. They charged in a howling flood towards the gate, now half open, as the folk inside the fort witnessed the collapse of their army and tried to close the two wide gates to stop the enemy force from entering the town and laying waste to wealth, women and anything they could get their hands on. The fleeing warriors pushed into the gates, and they closed no further. What had been a shield wall of two opposing sides of warriors had broken into a chaotic scene of men desperately running for their lives while clutches of braver men formed defensive circles, fighting fiercely behind their raven-daubed shields to protect their lives, their pride, and their reputations.

Hundr cut down another fleeing warrior and then held his anger. Usually, he wanted to pursue those fleeing warriors, for they were easy prey when the battle was over. In battle, most of the killing and wounding happens after one shield wall breaks—when one side runs and the other pursues, and the fear was replaced with unbound savagery fuelled by the joy and relief of survival. But now, Hundr wanted Finn, not some running whoreson bolting to find his wife and meagre belongings before they were all swept up by the victors.

"Finn Ivarsson!" Hundr roared, searching the battlefield for his enemy. He charged towards a clutch of five enemy warriors, desperately defending themselves from behind their black shields as Sigvarth Trollhands and eight Vanylven men hacked at them. Thorgrim swung his double-bladed war axe with such wild ferocity that he was as much a danger to his own men as the enemy. Hundr smashed into the shields, a spearpoint flashing past his face as he drove his seax into a gap between the shields' iron rims. Its tip punched into something soft, and Hundr yanked the blade upwards. An enemy screamed, and Hundr searched their bearded faces with his good eye, but Finn was not amongst them. He pulled away, leaving Sigvarth and the others to the kill. Ragnhild fought a broad-shouldered man, axe against axe, two vicious warriors weaving and swinging at each other with full, uncompromising force and violence. Hundr left Ragnhild to her fight and turned just in time to see a snarling face coming at him, helmeted and bushy-bearded with a sword in one hand and a shining brynjar coat of mail. The man swung at Hundr, yet he darted away from the sword, but the man was no fool, and his swing turned into a lunge at Hundr's chest. Hundr brought his seax up and turned the sword aside. He gasped, the swordsman following his strike up with a punch to Hundr's guts and a knee in his ribs. Hundr grunted and pushed the man away. He tried to thrust his sword up the enemy's arm and into his armpit, but the warrior lunged forward and headbutted Hundr full in the nose. The light turned to stars. Pain flashed through his skull, but to falter was to die. So Hundr dropped his sword, grabbed a fistful of the enemy's beard, and held him close. The acrid stench of his sweat and the earthy smell of the leather beneath his armour filled Hundr's nose as he drove his seax up with a shout and cut the swordsman's throat with so much force that the blade scraped on the man's spine.

"Dog," came a shout on Hundr's blind side. He turned, and there, holding two swords, tips dripping thick scarlet blood, was Finn Ivarsson. Hundr bent and picked up his own sword, and the two men circled each other like great war dogs. "You killed my father, and now I am going to kill you!" Finn spoke through clenched teeth, and Hundr saw a lifetime of hate in his youthful eyes. He had always suspected that hate was bubbling under the surface, a thing held back but straining at its fetters like Fenris longing for freedom on the day of Ragnarök. How could a son ever forgive or learn to live with the warrior who killed his father? Hundr thought of himself in that situation, of the malice that would have loitered in his heart growing up with the man who killed his father, and he knew it would have twisted and torn at him, forging an unquenchable longing for retribution.

"Betrayer! How could you do that to Einar? After he saved you from your uncle, raised you as his own and gave you ships and men?"

Finn used both hands to remove his helmet and tossed it away. His guards, Udvarr and Farmann, flanked him, and they formed a guard, keeping any men back who sought to attack the Jarl of Vedrafjord. He wiped the sweat and flecks of other men's blood from his face with his upper arm and looked around at the chaos of the battlefield, where his army collapsed, and his oathmen fled for their lives. Hundr saw a dream die in those young eyes, the tired face of a man who tried to emulate the great deeds of his legendary father, the warrior who men had called the Champion of the North until Hundr killed him and took that title for himself. He saw a man who had risen to become a Jarl so quickly that his own fame must have dazzled him, akin to stepping out of darkness into blinding sunlight, and now it was all in ruin.

"My uncle would not have killed me," Finn said, speaking calmly, the viciousness gone from his voice and replaced with a tired sadness. "My mother says Halvdan was my guardian, looking after Dublin's throne until I came of age. Halvdan raised me and gave me a priest to teach me the ways of God and Christ. Then Einar and Sten Sleggya took me away, and you killed my father and my mother's life was destroyed. For that, you must both die."

"You have kept Einar prisoner like a dog."

"To lure you here." Finn darted forward, stretching out his foreleg and flicking out his right arm so that the tip of the sword in that hand snaked at Hundr's face almost too fast for him to see. It came as a blur, and he felt the wind from the blow in the wet of his eye as the blade flashed a finger's breadth from his face. Hundr reeled away and brought Fenristooth up just in time to parry a follow-up swing from Finn's other side. He was fast, just as his savage father had been, and Finn walked away, rolling his shoulders and grinning wolfishly, exulting in his weapon skill and deadly speed. The crumbling battle rolled past the two warriors, men surging towards Vedrafjord's open gate pursued by Hundr's men hungry for plunder and pillage earned by the shield wall victory. Finn's two growlers were fearsome, and being armed in brynjars, shields, and axes, their appearance was enough to deter any interfering warriors, the victors moving towards easier prey. Ragnhild and Amundr fought alongside Sigvarth, Thorgrim, Bush and a clutch of Hundr's most vicious warriors. They clashed with the last remaining knot of Finn's fighters, a snarl of twenty men too proud to run, men who had spent a lifetime building their reputations and would rather go to Valhalla in their war glory than flee from their foes. Hundr was aware of that fight on his blind side, where weapons clashed, and men roared their battle cries, but he focused his good eye on Finn Ivarsson. He recalled teaching Finn the skill of fighting with two blades, of instructing him in the confidence and lethal speed needed to fight without a shield. Even then, there had been a nagging in the back of Hundr's mind that he had taught weapon craft to a lad who might learn to hate him.

Finn came on again, closing the space between them in a rapid sprint. He twirled his blades around him like the wings of a dragonfly, then took a heavy step to his left, feinted right and lunged the point of his sword at Hundr's chest. Hundr sidestepped the blow and danced around Finn, keeping his balance on the balls of his feet. Finn turned and ducked as Battle Fang scythed through the air in the space where Finn had been a moment earlier. Fenristooth blocked a low slash and clanged like a bell as it caught the edge of Finn's blade, sending a jarring ring up Hundr's arm. Hundr swung again, but Finn crouched low and skipped away. They came up to face one another again, both swordsmen sweating, two men equally matched.

"Where is your mother?" Hundr said, and Finn's eyes glittered with spite.

"In her own lands, where she will rejoice when I bring her your head."

Hundr pointed Fenristooth at Finn and smiled. "I will kill your whore mother like I killed your nithing father. Her head will swing from my ship's prow, but only after I have given her to my men, although she may have grown too rancid even for them." He spoke cruelly, but war was no place for courtly manners. It was where men died, and Hundr needed an advantage against Finn's prowess.

"Bastard!" Finn bellowed, his face twisted with malice. He charged at Hundr, his two swords held high as he meant to bring them both down in a great sweep that would carve Hundr in two. Anger flowed through him, clouding his judgement, and Hundr stepped into him, stabbing downwards with Battle Fang and punching Finn in the stomach with Fenristooth's hilt. Finn cried out in pain as Battle Fang cut through his boot and toes, leaping backwards with blood darting from his injured foot. He stared at it, horrified, and surged at Hundr in a limping lunge, all desperation in the attack. Hundr raised his sword to block the strike, but at the last minute, Finn rolled his wrist, and his blade scraped across and over Hundr's sword, slicing into his cheek and neck. Hundr gritted his teeth at the pain, stinging and bright, and his own blood oozed from the wound to soak his chest beneath his brynjar. The cut opened up the cheek on the side of Hundr's good eye, and for a harrowing moment, he feared Finn had taken that eye to leave him blind. But through the mist of pain from the wound, Hundr's vision cleared, and he snarled at his enemy. Hundr stamped on Finn's injured foot, the younger warrior doubled up with pain, and Hundr cracked Battle Fang's pommel across his skull. Finn fell scrabbling, dazed in the dirt, and Hundr stepped in, stabbing forward with Fenristooth to rip Finn's throat out. Suddenly, a shield crashed into him, sending Hundr flying backwards, sprawling on his back. Finn's protective growlers had seen their Lord about to perish and had joined the fight. They came to kill Hundr, beards bristling beneath eye-ringed helmets, shields before them and axes ready to strike.

Hundr surged to his knees, but Udvarr barged

him again with the iron boss of his shield to drive him down. Hundr scrabbled in the mud-churned filth of the battlefield, and Fenristooth fell from his grip as he tried to find purchase with his hand to push himself to his feet. An axe came for him, whistling through the air with all the brightness of a star, its bearded blade aiming to cleave his chest open. Hundr leapt away desperately, fear clenching his heart. The wound on his face pulsed, and his cheek was already swelling beneath his good eye. Another axe swung, and Hundr blocked it desperately with Battle Fang's blade. Finally, Farmann hammered the ironshod rim of his shield into Hundr's back; its force was like the kick of a horse. Hundr gasped, rocked with pain. He lay face down in the mud and could feel death closing in, wondering for a split second if the gates of Valhalla would open for him. Then he remembered Sigrid and his newborn twins. He remembered their love and how they would need him to provide for them.

I am the Champion of the North. I will not die like this in the shit-stinking mud at the feet of my enemies.

Hundr lifted his hips and twisted his legs around so that his body flipped over, and with the momentum of that turn, he swung his sword around in an arc, mere fingers above the dirt, and the blade cracked into Farmann with an audible crack as it hammered through boot, flesh and bone. He screamed and toppled like an oak. Udvarr shouted his war cry, swinging his axe for the killing blow, and died as Amundr caved his skull in with a mighty axe blow which sent the warrior's body rigid as blood and grey gore washed down his face. The fight with Finn's last warriors had ended, and Hundr's men came to his aid just in time. Ragnhild leapt upon the ankle-cut warrior and slashed his throat with brutal efficiency.

"Where is Finn?" Hundr asked as Bush reached out with a calloused hand to help Hundr rise to his feet.

"There. Gone, dragged off inside the walls. Borne by three of his warriors," said Bush, pointing towards the gateway where a mass of warriors, black shield fighters, and his own men rushed into the town for safety or plunder. The left side of Bush's face was swollen and red, the eye already puffed and half closed where a weapon or shield had struck his head.

"Back into the town," Hundr barked at his men. "Kill as many as we can. Any we don't kill today, we will have to fight again." Vedrafjord was his now, but the war was far from over. Einar was free, and Finn was defeated, but the Witch-Queen yet lived, and Hundr owed the galdr-woman her head.

TWENTY-SIX

Hundr found Einar, Refil, Erling and Hildr in a stable close to Einar's prison. Three black shield corpses lay at the opening of that stable, killed by Hildr's bow, their dried blood dunging the earth of Vedrafjord. Hundr's victorious warriors had run amok in the town, and he had gladly let them. They found a hoard of silver, gold, amber, and ivory in the main hall, and the warriors ransacked every dwelling until there was a pile of treasure to be shared amongst the crews. However, amid the frenzied bloodlust of Vedrafjord's downfall, some of Finn's ships had escaped.

After his fight outside the walls, Hundr joined

the vicious combat within the town itself. Black shield fighters were scattered everywhere, desperate men accompanied by their wives and children trying to reach the harbour, while knots of warriors opted to make a last stand in narrow laneways. Hundr's warriors had slaughtered them without mercy, cutting the enemy down in vast numbers. The fiercest fighting, however, took place at the harbour. Finn's warriors and their families scrambled to board their ships and escape their enemy's wrath, but only three ships had made it into the river. Hundr had led the charge against the mass of people desperately pushing to get to their ships whilst Ragnhild, Amundr, Thorgrim, and Sigvarth hunted black shield warriors in the twist and turn of Vedrafjord's streets. Hundr's men easily broke the shield wall that the warriors at the harbour had made facing towards the town, as the hardest warriors had already fallen in the frontlines of battle outside Vedrafjord. The folk amassed in front of the jetties descended into a panicked, screaming throng as Hundr's men broke their warriors. The people overcrowded the timber structures, causing them to buckle under the weight and collapse, plunging the horde into the river, their howling cries echoing. Some tried to wade or swim away, others clambered back onto the bank, but the only ships that managed to escape were the three who cast off before Hundr could organise a force to stop them.

There was no sign of Finn Ivarsson amongst the survivors and captives. Hundr reckoned Finn's warriors had got him aboard one of the three escaping ships, and he considered sending runners to his own fleet, which still lay moored on the island along the river's wide turn towards the sea. The runners could have ordered his ships to block the waterway and keep Finn's ships there, but the runners were unlikely to have covered the distance in time. Besides, the tide had turned, and the ebb sped Finn's ships, so Hundr had reluctantly let them go.

Hundr sat on a milking stool outside Vedrafjord's main hall. He sucked his teeth as Ragnhild cleaned the wound on his face with a strip of clean linen smeared with honey. Hildr was busy boiling a pot filled with flour, barley and honey to make healing ointments to treat the rest of Hundr's wounded fighters.

"You squeal like a child," Ragnhild tutted when Hundr flinched as she pushed the linen deep into his wound. "The cut must be clean."

A line of warriors formed beyond where Hildr boiled her pot. Most were standing, with cuts to arms, legs and heads. Others lay motionless on the ground while their shipmates held blood-soaked rags to their belly or chest wounds, half knowing that such injuries were killers but unable to leave their friends without hope. Other men wept, contorting where they lay, incapable of bearing the pain of their wounds. Beyond the field, Amundr and Sigvarth heated iron in the smith's forge, and they cauterised the worst of the wounded—men who had lost hands, fingers, or even legs in the brutal fighting.

"I've sent lads to bring the ships around," piped Bush, walking with his bowlegged gait across the field, shaking his head at the injured. "They'll row our fleet to the harbour here when the tide changes again in the morning."

"So Finn got away?" said Ragnhild, squinting as she pressed the lips of Hundr's cut together, assessing how to stitch the wound closed.

"He did. He'll be off to his mother the völva," said Bush.

"Do we go after them? Now we have Einar back?" asked Ragnhild.

"We stay here, tend to the wounded, and let Einar recover," Hundr replied. "Then we sail for Vykyngelo. The Witch-Queen and her son will be there, and they must both die."

"Don't let Hildr hear you say that," warned Bush. "She still sees Finn as the boy he was…"

"When he has turned into a treacherous, ungrateful turd," said Hundr, finishing the sentence.

"Einar is in a bad way. He and Refil Bjornsson are as skinny as Frankish whores."

"But they are alive."

"Why did the witch keep Einar and Refil alive?" asked Bush.

"She kept Einar here to get me here."

"And the witch kept Bjorn Ironside's son alive because she used his blood for her dark seiðr," Ragnhild interjected. She turned and fished around in her pack for a bone needle. "Or so Hildr says. Whilst they waited for the battle to end, Refil told her that the witch would come and take his blood; she would have her men cut him and catch his blood in a horn cup. She would take it away to use for her curses and such. Prince blood has rare power in it, apparently."

"Like the curse she believed would kill my children," Hundr uttered.

"Erik Bjornsson must not know that his brother is here?" said Bush.

"No, and Erik is with Bárid in Dublin, and Bárid is allied with the Witch-Queen."

"So we have to fight the völva and the King of Dublin?"

"No. We just have to kill the Witch-Queen, and

let Erik know what became of his brother."

"Well," said Bush, rubbing a gnarled hand across his bulging stomach. "I'll leave all that deep cunning work to you. I'm off to find some food."

Ragnhild closed Hundr's wound and then helped Hildr tend to the rest of the wounded. Hundr went into Finn's hall and sat upon his high seat. The chair was high-backed and carved from pine wood. Soft pelts draped the hard wood, and Hundr eased himself into it, exhausted from battle. His face throbbed, and he gingerly touched the wound, wincing at the pain. The muscles in his shoulders and back ached from weapon work, and he thought he could sleep for a week. He needed time for his men to heal and time to think. Finn had been defeated but managed to survive, and Hundr had learned a valuable lesson from his experience with Rollo the Betrayer: not to let any enemy live. But to kill Finn and Saoirse, he would need to attack Vykyngelo, and his enemies would likely call upon their alliance with Bárid mac Ímair once Finn's ships reached his mother's lands. However, Hundr lacked the manpower to fight both Saoirse and Bárid, so hard thinking would be necessary before the hard fighting.

The hall door swung open, and Sigvarth Trollhands strode in, followed by Amundr's hulking frame. Amundr had a barrel the size of a child over one shoulder, and Sigvarth carried an armful of drinking horns.

"Odin's hairy arse, but there was plunder in this town, Lord Hundr," said Sigvarth. They approached Hundr's chair, and Amundr set the barrel down. He took his axe from where it hung from his belt and chopped a hole in the wood so that Sigvarth had to leap forward and catch the escaping golden, frothing ale in three horns. The liquid poured out onto the hard-packed earthen floor, but not before Sigvarth had filled his vessels.

"Why didn't you just cut a hole in the top?" asked Sigvarth, but Amundr simply shrugged and scratched his beard. "We are wealthy men and drinking ale from curved horns, no less." He handed Hundr a horn as long as his forearm, chased with silver and finished with a blackened tip. Hundr took a long drink, and the ale was cool.

"Where are the people of Vedrafjord?" asked Hundr.

"Outside the walls, my lord," said Sigvarth. He drained his horn, much of the ale dripping down his beard and across his brynjar, then he stooped and caught more of the emptying barrel. Finally, he stood and eyed Hundr carefully, thoughtfully choosing his words. "Lord Hundr...we all know you don't much like slaving or the lads having fun with the womenfolk, but…"

Hundr raised his hand to stop Sigvarth. "We don't have many rules, but I won't have women raped or children killed."

"Yes, Lord Hundr." Sigvarth looked sideways at Amundr, and the big man shrugged once more.

Many Viking crews made their wealth through slavery, and Hundr's ships were rare in that they did not capture and sell slaves whilst sailing and raiding across the Whale Road. Hundr had been close to a slave himself, and his mother had been a slave to his father, the Prince of Novgorod. He knew of a slave's suffering—the hunger, humiliation, the bleak life without hope or esteem. So, whilst he tolerated slavery in other Vikings, Hundr would have no part in it. Without the vast number of slaves across Norway, Denmark and Sweden, Viking raiding voyages would not be possible. They needed slaves to keep warships afloat. There were simply not enough people in the Viking homelands to tend the considerable number of sheep required to provide fleeces for sailcloth and clothing and to tend the all-important woodland. Without slave labour to replant trees used for shipbuilding or pollarding trees for fencing and spear shafts, Hundr and his men could not put to sea.

"Send them away," said Hundr.

"Who, my lord?" asked Amundr.

"The people of Vedrafjord. Just send them away. We can't feed them, and they can return after we have left. But for now, get rid of them. By force if you have to."

And so it was that the folk who had inhabited Vedrafjord marched away in a solemn column of women weeping for lost husbands, dirty-faced children and carts containing whatever remained of their lives in their ransacked homes. Sigvarth and a crew of warriors stood firm in the face of the pleas and tears as desperate mothers sought to protect their children from hunger and destitution. The warriors persisted, urging them onward, west across the rolling hills, sometimes with a guiding hand, yet often resorting to using the blunt end of their spears.

Hundr and his warriors remained in Vedrafjord for four weeks. The cut on Hundr's face turned from an angry, swollen gash to an itchy scab. Ragnhild tended the wound daily, and she smiled with a healer's satisfaction when, after three days, the wound started healing without pus or a foul smell. Erling was not so lucky. Though Hildr and Ragnhild had tried to heal Erling's wounded leg, he had died within a week. Alongside him, a score of men also lost their lives during the same period. Despite the

Valkyries' attentions, some men's wounds still festered and turned green with the foul stench of decay. Such men died in excruciating agony, sweating, and fever-stricken. Indeed, more died in the days following the battle than during the fighting itself. Hundr ordered that the dead be granted a hero's funeral. So, they took one of Finn's captured ships and placed their deceased on dry timber cut from Vedrafjord's houses piled in the bilge. They set the ship alight and pushed it out into the river, granting the dead the honour they deserved by sending them to Asgard. However, Hundr refused to extend the same honour to the fallen black shield warriors, many of whom were worshippers of the nailed god, not Odin. Instead, those men were left in a rotting heap outside the town walls without pity, to be buried or burned by their own people once Hundr and his crews departed. Many warriors, and the simple folk of Vedrafjord who had fallen into the river when the jetty collapsed, simply drowned, their bodies bloating and floating away with the tide. Ragnhild sang a prayer to Odin for those drowned people on a night brightened by a full moon. She stood on the shore keening to the All-Father, and the warriors gathered to listen, holding their amulets shaped into hammers, spears, phalluses, or fish, depending on the god they favoured. Men destined for Valhalla believed that at the end of days, in the battle of Ragnarök, Odin would send them out from his great hall to fight Loki's forces, and amongst that horde of Loki monsters and giants would be an army of the drowned on board the monstrous ship Naglfar. When Ragnarök arrived, this terrible ship, constructed from the fingernails and toenails of the dead and the drowned, would rise from the depths of the sea and take to the battlefield against the Aesir.

On a hot day in the third week following the battle at Vedrafjord, Hundr found Einar resting beneath a willow tree whose branches hung from the riverbank to dangle in the water. The Jarl sat in the shade, eating from a wooden plate heavy with cheese and cold pork.

"You grow stronger," Hundr smiled, strolling along the riverbank to sit beside his old friend.

"There was a heron here earlier," Einar said, offering Hundr a piece of cheese. "The land is good for crops and beasts."

"Ireland is a place a man could make his home. If it weren't for the constant wars, the Christ worshippers, slavers and völvas."

Einar laughed and stuffed the cheese into his own mouth. When they had found Einar, he had been as thin as a corpse. The bones of his shoulders and gaunt cheeks poked through his emaciated skin, and he was a third of his old size. He was a Viking who had seen almost forty summers, more than most men hoped to live. He had spent his life at the oar and hefting weapons and was one of the largest men Hundr knew. But the time he had spent imprisoned had whittled him down to nothing. Refil was the same, and both men bore heavy scarring from their time with Saoirse, the Witch-Queen. After a week of rest and lots of food, Einar and Refil regained some strength and picked up weapons. Too weak for shields or axes, they had started with spears, focusing on lunging, parrying, and simply holding the staves out in front of them until their shoulders burned to rebuild strength. That very morning, Hundr had watched Einar and Refil fight each other with shields and spears, and he noticed a rekindling of the Jarl's former vigour.

"We can be ready to sail in a week," said Einar. "Most of the men are ready to fight again."

"We can stay for longer if you think you need it. The witch isn't going anywhere."

"Next week we go." Einar looked away from Hundr and stared into the river water, where it babbled around the willow branches. "I won't be my old self for a while, but there is a price to pay. For the suffering."

"Was it bad?"

Einar kept silent for a time, keeping his eyes

on the water. His face was scarred, and Hildr had described Einar's torso as being carved and scored like a ship's hull after a summer's sailing. Finally, Einar turned to Hundr, and he smiled wanly.

"Yes." Einar fixed Hundr with his grey eyes, a deep pain within. Hundr held his gaze and nodded slowly, understanding that a man did not need to describe what he had endured for his friend to know that it had been beyond explanation, horrific and painful, like the man in Hundr's Volund dream.

"Did Finn ever come to you?"

"No. I fear the boy I knew is gone, and Saoirse has crafted a new man in his place. A man filled with her hate and darkness. She came to me once and her cripple brother many times."

"Which is why they must die."

"Hildr cannot accept it. She believes if we take Finn home, we can save him."

"Because she loves him."

"Because she loves the lad he was. But he betrayed me. Finn must suffer the consequences for what he allowed his mother and his men to do to me. We are drengr, and the price for that is war." Einar held out a hand, and Hundr took it, grasping Einar's wrist, which used to be as thick as two of an average man's wrists, but was now all bone and sinew. "Thank you for coming for me." Hundr pulled Einar close, and they held each other in a brotherly embrace.

"I will kill them all for what they have done to you. They tried to kill my wife and children with seiðr, and you, my friend, with torture. But, we are drengr, and so next week, we sail for Vykyngelo to kill a witch, a cripple, and a traitor."

TWENTY-SEVEN

Hundr watched the fortress of Vykyngelo through the branches and beams of a dense forest, thick with the dampness of rotting leaves, the sharpness of pine and the leather and sweat smell of his army. The Witch-Queen's fortifications were formidable. Vykyngelo was so named for the sprawling meadows surrounding the coastal fort, and on a hill to the southwest was the forest in which Hundr and his crews now hid. The north-facing side of the wood was a mass of stumps covered with a thick layer of soaked sawdust, no longer golden yellow but brown and heavy. They had evidently cut boughs and trunks to reinforce the walls surrounding the fortress, and amidst the darker, blackened stakes, there were noticeable strips of fresh, golden timbers.

Einar, Hundr, Bush and Ragnhild had seen Vykyngelo before from the sea, so they knew that launching an attack would be incredibly difficult, and many men would die in the process. The place was actually two fortresses at the summit of a crag of a headland jutting eastwards into the Irish Sea. The first landward fortification was a ring fort of stout staves with thatched longhouse buildings inside. Then, a second ringed fortification sat perched atop a monstrous rock which rose from the sea next to the land but separated from it by a distance of only four men placed head to toe. That rock was virtually sheer on all sides, so there was no hope of attacking it by ship. A short timber bridge, gated at both ends, linked it to the mainland structure. So, an army attacking Vykyngelo would need to breach the first palisade wall, fight their way through the landward town, open the gate, cross the bridge, and then face the challenge of penetrating the second gate to the island rock fortress. The defenders could, of course, abandon the first fort if they felt the attacker would gain the upper hand. They could retreat into the rock island, and by cutting the bridge loose, they would be as safe as a puffin in its lofty nest.

Hundr had come to kill Saoirse, the völva, the woman he had once loved with all the openness and longing of his young, lonely heart. However, he knew that directly attacking Vykyngelo's walls was to die. So, instead, he planned to use Saoirse's white-hot hatred of him to lure her out. It was the same plan as at Vedrafjord, no deep cunning or wild assault on the walls, just a challenge. A challenge and an opportunity for the Witch-Queen, the völva who had tried to kill his wife and offspring, to come out and fight. The people of Vedrafjord knew Hundr was coming—men had lit a warning fire beacon on a spit of land to the southwest, and Hundr had sailed his seven ships past, unable to do anything to halt the warning. That had been the previous day. Hundr had beached and anchored his ships on a long strip of golden sand to the north of the fortress, making no effort to try to conceal his presence. The one-eye sigil emblazoned on his flag and sail would have been visible to everyone in Vedrafjord. Yet, no force had come out to meet or challenge them at the beach camp or on the march south that morning.

"Remember," said Hundr, turning to Bush, Thorgrim, Amundr and Sigvarth, who stood behind him, grim in mail brynjars and helmets, carrying shields, spears and axes. "When I give the signal, march the men out."

"Even if Bárid is with them?" asked Bush.

"Even if Bárid is with them," said Hundr. For it was too late to turn back now, even if the King of Dublin had brought his army of Finngaill Irish and Norse warriors south to fight alongside his ally, the Witch-Queen. And if the King had indeed brought his forces south, they outnumbered Hundr two to one, despite his own fleet of ships carrying a long four hundred Viking men to bring to war. Saoirse would have fewer warriors of her own, and Finn's army had been crushed at Vedrafjord. Yet Bárid could potentially bring an equal or greater number of warriors than Hundr, and then there was Erik, son of Bjorn Ironside and his warriors, who would also surely be in the fortress waiting to fight alongside his new Irish allies. Hundr glanced at Refil. He had put weight and muscle on, just like Einar, since his liberation. Refil sat on a roan mare, clad in a brynjar and wearing an eyehole-fronted helmet. Even though Erik had allied with Saoirse and Bárid, Hundr still hoped he would not fight against the man he had travelled so far to find, for the search for Refil was the reason Erik and Hundr had sailed to Ireland in the first place.

"What if we don't see the signal? What even is the signal?" asked Amundr, his broad face staring at Hundr, teeth chewing on his bottom lip.

"Is your head completely empty?" asked Bush.

"How am I supposed to know what the signal is?" Amundr frowned at the smaller man, his face reddening. The surrounding warriors laughed.

"If you see an arm or spear waving, that's it."

"But what if we go too early or too late?"

"I'll let you know when we have to go. Don't worry."

Amundr grinned and clapped Bush so hard on the back that his helmet slipped sideways, and he stumbled forward a few steps. The warriors laughed again, and Hundr smiled. Jokes and laughter always came before a fight. These were experienced men, the veterans of countless such fights on battlefields all across the Whale Road, and they knew that the best way to relieve the stomach-churning fear of an impending shield wall was in humour. So he left them, striding to where his horse waited. A bay gelding, taken from the stables at Vedrafjord, along with a dozen other mounts.

"Are you ready to pick a fight?" asked Einar. His scarred face was still gaunt around the cheekbones of his broad, flat skull, and, like Refil, he wore a brynjar despite his weakened state.

"Come on," said Hundr. He clicked his tongue and urged his mount forward. The horse picked its way through the shattered stubs of felled trees and snorted at the unsure footing amongst the sawdust. Einar, Refil, and Ragnhild rode with him, and Ragnhild carried the one-eye banner on a long pole. It was a still, warm day with little wind, and luckily, the banner was held aloft by a thin bracing spar; otherwise, it would have hung embarrassingly lank. They rode through a lush meadow of wild grass, deep and light greens dappled with yellow flowers. Bees hummed across the grass, and Vykyngelo's gates creaked open. Folk crowded on the battlements, their faces peering at the enemy coming to fight their queen and her black shield warriors. A line of ten horses thundered out of the gateway, cantering through the meadow as horns blared inside the fortress as if to awaken its warriors to the fight. "Hold here," said Hundr, and he reined his horse in.

Hundr patted his horse's muscled neck, his dead eye pulsing as the enemy came forward for the customary parlay. Ragnhild came to Hundr's left with the banner and Einar to his right, with Refil halting just behind, his helmeted head low. The enemy mounts came to a stop ten paces away, their hooves throwing up great clumps of earth as their riders kept the canter going until the last minute before hauling on bridle and bit to come to a dramatic stop. Saoirse wore a black cloak covering her from neck to boots, her long face tattooed and as sharp as an axe blade.

She wore a circlet of bronze over her grey hair. Finn Ivarsson rode a black stallion, his tousled chestnut hair falling loose about his youthful face. He had been handsome once but was now dark-eyed and malevolent, his smiling mouth now a thin slash of bitter hate. Erik Bjornsson was there, as was Bárid and a man beside him held his raven banner aloft. Hundr nodded and smiled at them all, even at Murrough, Bárid's Irish swordsmen, and Gjalandi, Erik's Svear shipmaster.

"King Bárid," said Hundr, inclining his head.

Bárid's horse skittered, and he grimaced, a hand jumping to the leg he had wounded in the battle at Cuan Loch. "You should leave, Jarl Hundr," he uttered through gritted teeth.

"We have come too far for that, Lord King. Your stinking witch here kept my friend, Jarl Einar of Vanylven, a prisoner for a winter and treated him like an animal."

"Dog!" Saoirse spat, her pale hands wrestling with her horse's bridle as it tried to turn.

"And," Hundr continued, ignoring her, "this man," he pointed at Finn, "was as a son to Jarl Einar, yet he betrayed him. How his father Ivar and grandfather Ragnar must look upon his deeds with disgust from Valhalla, knowing that their heir is a nithing, a slave to a völva, a betrayer and a coward."

"Bastard," Finn snarled, and his hand dropped to the hilt of his sword.

"Erik, son of Bjorn Ironside," said Hundr, smiling broadly at Erik, who nodded curtly. "Last year, you came to Einar and me for aid, asking if we would join you in your quest to find your lost brother. And we joined you, did we not?"

"You did," Erik answered, lifting his chin defiantly.

"You have grown rich in Ireland since that day. And though we left our home to help you, as a favour to our old friend Bjorn, you stood and watched whilst the witch and her whelp took Einar prisoner." Hundr pointed at the gold torc wrapped around Erik's thick neck and the arm rings as replete on his forearms as any king. "Have you found your brother?"

"Alas, no."

"I am here, brother," Refil spoke up, nudging his horse forward and removing his helmet so that Erik would recognise him.

"Refil?" gasped Erik, his jaw dropping as wide as a cow's yawn.

"Your friends here held him captive with Jarl Einar, starved and beaten. Your friends and allies imprisoned Einar with your brother. And you did nothing."

"She used his blood for a curse. A curse meant to kill Hundr's wife and unborn children. The witch killed Refil's men, your own kinsmen among them, whilst you feasted and fought beside her and her son. What would your father, Bjorn Ironside, say?" said Einar. He spoke softly at first, but then his voice rose to a bellow. "They cut us, flayed the skin from our bones, this Witch-Queen you follow and her cripple brother. Are you not a drengr, Erik Bjornsson?"

Erik looked from Refil to Einar, then from Saoirse to Bárid. His face flushed red as a rose, and the man could not speak with Einar's words spinning around in his thought cage.

"Your whore and your whelps died, I hope," Saoirse sneered, a smile creasing her hatchet-like face.

"They live, and I have twins now. Your power is nothing, a lie and a pretence like your switching devotion from the nailed god to Odin. A galdr-woman broke your curse, and she laughed at you from our home in Norway. She mocked your seiðr, and that old woman also laughed at you all for following a Witch-Queen like whipped dogs."

"When you die, I shall…"

"Enough talk," Hundr interrupted. "Einar and

I have brought our warriors here to Vykyngelo to fight you. We stand for drengskapr, the warriors' way, and for the Aesir. We stand with fewer warriors to fight your army of nithings and betrayers." He inclined his head to Ragnhild, who waved the one-eye banner from side to side. A roar went up from the forest, and Bush's war horn blared out, its sound rolling across the meadow as though blown by Thor himself. The army came forward from the treeline, four hundred warriors clashing axes on iron shield rims in a din to shake the rock on which Vykyngelo perched.

"I killed two of your husbands. One of those men was your father, Finn. I have killed two mighty sons of Ragnar, Eystein Longaxe, Prince Yaroslav of Novgorod and Dukes in Frankia." Hundr smiled at Saoirse and Finn. "I am the Man with the Dog's Name, Champion of the North. Come, fight with me and settle our saga. I am here for you to kill if you have the belly for it."

"All I have worked for has brought you here, to this place, to die," Saoirse uttered. Her horse pawed the earth and stomped a step forward so Hundr could see the malevolence in her eyes. "You are the luck stealer, a thing of Loki and the devil. Everywhere you go, people die, you steal their luck, and your fame grows, leaving others in your wake to suffer and struggle."

"I loved you once," Hundr said, not caring that the others could hear. "More than anything in Midgard, I wanted to spend my life with you. We could have been happy, living in peace together. But you chose Ivar and violence, and here we are."

"Fool!" She pointed a crooked finger at him. "I never loved you. What is love but a notion of children and simpletons? I was a princess, destined to marry for peace at my father's wish. I had to marry Hakon and then Ivar. You destroyed that, left me with nothing but my body and my cunning to scrape and whore my way up. I am Queen now, and I wish your wife had died, that your whelps had choked and rotted in her rancid womb. I hate you with all my being, and I call on the gods, all gods, Christ in Heaven and Odin in Asgard, to aid me in your destruction, for you are a pox on this world and must be killed."

"We can make peace here, still," Bárid interjected, and Saoirse shot him a look of such venom that, for a moment, Hundr thought she would attack him. "Go, take your men and your ships and leave Ireland in peace. Go home, Lord Hundr, and I will do the same."

"There must be a fight here, Lord King," Hundr replied. "But I would not wish to fight you, a man who was once my friend, and together we won a glorious victory over the great Halvdan Ragnarsson. So you should go. Take your men and leave this fight to the Witch-Queen."

"I wish it were so simple," said Bárid with a long sigh.

"He owes me his throne," Saoirse chimed, cackling. "My seiðr made him King, and he knows it."

"You convincing your son to give up his claim to the throne made Bárid King. When I killed Halvdan, that made Bárid King. When Erik and I brought our ships and warriors to the fight at Cuan Loch, that made Bárid King. My children are twins, which are always difficult to birth; you have no power, witch. Your seiðr is like a fart in the wind."

Bárid mac Ímair's face turned as white as the summer clouds in the sky, and the Witch-Queen just smiled.

"Finn," said Einar, his voice soft and warm amongst the hate and venom, and all eyes turned to him. "It's not too late, lad. Ride back to that hill with me now. Hildr is up there. Come back to Vanylven with me, and we can forget everything."

Finn's face softened for an instant, and he swallowed hard. His mother hissed, and Finn's mouth twisted again. Perhaps she had power after all, and Hundr wondered at the warp and weft of their lives, which had led them across battlefields, dead kings, and new kings crowned to reach this point.

"My place is here. I am still Jarl of Vedrafjord," Finn replied. He looked from his mother to Einar, and Hundr thought he saw a question there as though his conscience wrestled with his mind. Hundr believed memories of a joyful upbringing in Vanylven still lingered within Finn, yet his animosity and ambition battled against his once profound love for Einar and Hildr.

"So you would fight me? You would hack your sword into Hildr's face in the shield wall?" asked Einar.

"I would defend myself from those who attack me and from those complicit in my father's death."

Einar nodded slowly and chewed at the beard below his bottom lip. Then, he turned his horse and rode away. Saoirse, Finn, and Bárid followed suit, accompanied by their captains. But Refil and Erik stayed, and Hundr hoped Refil spoke to his brother as they had planned he would. Hundr also hoped he had provoked enough annoyance in Saoirse and the King so that they would march their army out to meet him. Finally, he prayed fervently to Odin for victory against the wicked völva who had tried to kill his wife and children.

TWENTY-EIGHT

lack shield fighters marched from Vykyngelo like ants in summer. They came in good order, two lines of warriors in leather or mail and bearing their black shields, until they reached the expansive meadow and spread out into two lines fifty shields across. Their blades glinted like the sun on a sea of shattered ice. Then came Finn's remaining black shield men, a meagre forty warriors who survived the battle at Vedrafjord and bore the black shield daubed with the white raven. Next, Bárid's warriors from Dublin came out of the gate and formed the following two ranks, spear points catching the sun and singing their songs of Irish heroes, and last of all, came the warriors of Erik Bjornsson. Bárid and Erik's men all fought under the raven banner that all men knew signified those born of Ragnar Lothbrok, the greatest of all Viking warlords.

"Looks like there'll be a fight then," said Amundr. Bush tutted at the big man's constant habit of stating the obvious, and Einar pulled Amundr away to organise and lead their left flank. Hildr stood with Ragnhild, the two Valkyries armed with an axe, shield and their recurved bows strung and hooked over their shoulders. Hildr was sullen, heartbroken that she must face and fight the boy she had loved, who had grown into a man swayed to betrayal by his twisted, hate-filled mother. She would not talk of it, keeping the pain to herself but ready to stand and fight.

"Will your brother fight?" asked Hundr, having to turn his head wide to look at Refil on his dead-eye side. It stretched the still-healing cut on his face, and he winced at the pain.

"My brother would never fight against me. His men will come over to us when the fighting starts," Refil replied.

"Watch where he stands in the line, and make sure you are there to remind him." Hundr turned to Ragnhild. "Send the horses away and prepare for battle." He rode his own horse out before the army. The enemy still formed up amidst a rolling thunder of boots, shouting, the clank of weapons and the occasional blare of a war horn. His horse was skittish amongst the noise and smelled of so many men, and the beast fought against him as Hundr wheeled it around to face his army. He took a deep breath to settle himself and searched across the faces of his warriors. He nodded recognition to some, remembering a face or a helmet from a previous fight. They were good men, brave men.

Hundr wasn't usually a man for grand speeches to his warriors before battle, but today was different. They faced a vastly larger foe, and even if Erik brought his crews over to Hundr's side, it would only swell his ranks by two hundred men. The black shield fighters formed the front rank of the Witch-Queen's army, with the King of Dublin's men behind them. Bárid was oath-bound to fight for his ally, the witch whom he believed had used her seiðr to grant him victory at Cuan Loch and make him King. Yet Hundr hoped that Bárid was not committed to the fight. Or, certainly not committed enough to risk losing his army in a fight for Vykyngelo, which Bárid could easily fill with another jarl under his own dominion if he so wished. Hundr faced his grim warriors, searched their fierce, bearded faces, and saw no fear, but still, he wanted them to know how they would win and burnish their reputations bright with a great shield wall victory.

"Warriors!" Hundr called, but only the front rankers fell silent. The rolling roar of hundreds of voices drowned him out as the rear rankers had neither heard nor noticed their leader was trying to speak. Bush took five of his hirpling, bow-legged paces forward and blew out a lengthy note on his war horn. The men fell silent, and Hundr drew Battle Fang to a mighty roar, the sound of his army shaking the meadow like a herd of wild horses. His mount bobbed its head, shifting from side to side, and Hundr fought with the reins and his thighs to keep the beast steady. "Warriors of the one-eye!" he called again, and this time, every face focused on him, mighty warriors standing ready to fight and die for their Lord. "They outnumbered us. They have many warriors, many shields and spears. But we fight under the banner of the one-eye, and men know of our fair fame across the Whale Road. We only have to beat the black shields—kill those ragged bastards, and the King's men won't fight. They serve a witch, caught like spiders in her dark seiðr. You are free men who have chosen to swear an oath to me, your Jarl. You fight for your own reputation and glory. Are you the finest warriors in Midgard?" They roared and clashed weapons together, and Hundr waited for the din to die down. "Are you fiercer, braver, more savage, weapon-loving killers than these black shield whoresons?" They cheered again, louder and longer, and Hundr waited for the noise to subside again. "Then kill them for me this day, kill them all, and drive their bones in the mud. Are you ready for war?" They bellowed, unbounded, red-faced and filled with war madness. Spears clashed on shield rims. The army edged forward, and Hundr felt the power of it, lifting his soul to touch the very gates of Valhalla itself. His pulse raced, and he leapt from the horse's back. Hundr slapped its rump and sent the beast running, and he turned to face his enemies.

The shield wall was where men died, and reputations were made. It was the horror that all men craved and all boys aspired to be a part of, but when it came to the fight, when the enemy was approaching in a wall of linden wood, iron and blades, men's hearts failed, and fear killed the minds of those who thought themselves brave. Hundr's army had seen more action than most. He was a sea Jarl, a warrior Lord whose crews were long since whittled of cravens and cowards. His men were fighters, so he knew they did not need the typical ale-drinking and boasting hours to fire them up for the battle. They were ready to stand and die if necessary, and so was he. Hundr turned to face the enemy, their shield wall lines forming. Spears wavered there like a forest in the wind, and he drew Fenristooth. Hundr held his two blades out wide, taunting his enemies, goading them on to battle, where Odin and the Norns would decide their fates. His own army surged forward, though he didn't turn to see because he could feel them lurching into motion like a great dragon erupting from its mountain lair.

The black shield fighters stayed still, waiting for orders, understanding the complexity of organising an army. With hundreds of warriors present, runners were necessary for relaying messages along the line, and the leaders in the front rank were crucial—men to lead the fighting line. Yet the Witch-Queen, for all her fierceness, could not stand and trade blows with Viking champions. Ragnhild, Einar, Amundr, Thorgrim, Sigvarth and Bush had followed Hundr's orders. He had told them he would speak to the men, that he would wait in the middle ground to goad on the enemy, and that they should not wait. This battle would not follow the usual way of war. There would be no archers, no spears thrown, no war music or battle songs. This was a fight concerning hate and retribution, so they would charge into an enemy who expected those things. The black shield warriors would be ready for arrows, prepared to take the shafts on their stout shields. They were trained to be ready for a barrage of spears, followed by the shield wall clash where the two opposing lines would crash together and heave at one another until a side broke. But not today.

In the black shield lines, warriors surged from the rear ranks, men in black armour, one of them limping. Finn Ivarsson, less the toes Hundr had cut from his foot. A roar rose, and the enemy surged forward like a great wave rolling into shore. Hundr set himself, no shield, just his swords. He risked a glance at the sky, stared into its hazy blueness, and felt the sun on his face.

Odin, I am here again on the field of war. Your hall is filled with the men I have slain. Grant me your favour today. Grant me victory and the witch's head.

The enemy broke into a run, as Hundr's warriors had moments earlier. No cautious approach, followed by the coming together of organised battle lines. This battle was a thing of madness, hate and courage. Hundr moved his feet to test the purchase on the soft grass. His chest heaved like a great wolf as countless warriors hurtled towards him, spears, axes and swords coming to tear and rend at him, to snatch his life and destroy his army. He could see their faces now, men with blonde beard plaits and iron helmets, warriors with bushy beards and scarred cheeks, others with a look of pure fear stretched across taut, screaming eyes. For a heartbeat, Hundr thought he had made a terrible mistake, that the black shields would reach him before his own warriors, that they would trample him and stab him to bloody ruin. But then his men roared past him, Viking warriors bent on violence and death, and the two armies collided in a monstrous clash of iron and steel, of wood and flesh. Hundr waited, allowing the lines to crash into each other, all semblance of a shield wall abandoned as the opposing warriors became embroiled in individual fights, man against man. Then, once the charge had halted in the maelstrom of battle, Hundr set off. He stalked through the melee, searching for his enemies. A giant black shield warrior chopped his axe into the skull of one of the men who had sworn to Hundr after Cuan Loch. Hundr darted forward, lunging with Fenristooth to take out the giant's throat and whet his blade with blood. He leapt away from a spear charging at him, turning to backswing Battle Fang across the spearman's hamstrings like Volund under King Niðhad's blade.

Hundr found Ragnhild hacking and screaming into the faces of the enemy. Men came for her because they saw a woman and thought her easy prey. However, they met their demise swiftly as Ragnhild effortlessly defeated them. She smiled as she cut through them, devoted to Odin and to the slaughter. Then, spotting Hundr, she threw her head back, laughing with the mad joy of it.

"This is how it will be, in Valhalla, every day!" she screamed, then charged full tilt into two black shield warriors. She was right. The glorious dead of Valhalla fought a mighty battle each day only to rise again each night to partake in a grand feast, and it would be just like this. No careful battle strategy, just furious carnage.

"Bastard!" came a bellowing voice, and Hundr saw Mundi coming for him with a snarl on his flat face. His bald head shone with sweat, and the silver wire woven into the thick braid of his beard glinted in the sunlight. Mundi was a warrior to fear. He was Finn's man, one who had served under Kvasir, the 'Burned Man'. Mundi came on with a short-hafted axe and a shield in his left hand. Hundr went for him, hacking and slashing at the tall warrior with his two swords, overhand, underhand, lunge and sweep. Mundi's face turned from anger to desperate horror, splinters flying from his shield under the assault. He tried to bring his axe to bear, but Hundr parried it, and without hesitation, he chopped Battle Fang's blade down onto Mundi's wrist, the crunch of his bones rattling up the blade. Mundi howled in pain and fell to his knees. He stared at Hundr with eyes as wide as a full moon. He opened his mouth as though to speak, but Hundr rammed Fenristooth's sword point into the red maw, smashing teeth and twisting the blade savagely. Mundi died, and Hundr moved on. He saw Amundr cleave a man's skull in two with his axe, splattering blood and gore across the battlefield. Thorgrim took a spear cut to his thigh but killed his attacker with an axe across the throat. The battle raged on. Men were cut, slashed, injured, and died. It was a savage spectacle, a wild battle where men faced off and fought tooth and nail for their lives.

Hundr parried a spear thrust and punched his sword point into the attacker's guts, quickly yanking the blade free before it became caught in the wounded man's innards.

"What news of Erik?" he shouted to Amundr.

"He came over to us. He fights alongside his brother," said Amundr. The huge Viking stalked off through the carnage, black shield fighters shrinking away from his size and the fearsome sight of his blood-drenched axe. So, Refil hadn't been wrong, and Erik had come over to his side to fight. The battle plan was proving successful thus far. Yet as soon as that notion entered Hundr's mind, the fighting ahead of him became fractured, men from both sides running in terror. Hundr peered around them and then froze as a pack of monstrous, slathering war dogs savaged black shield and Vanylven men alike. A dog, as tall as Hundr's waist, leapt at

Amundr, biting the warrior's arm with its bright white fangs. Amundr roared and hammered his axe into its flank to send the beast flying. Next, two came at Hundr with spiked collars and shining grey pelts. Fear gripped him, for the wild dogs, in their ferocity, was akin to Fenris, the wolf who guards the underworld. Hundr cut one down, and it yelped like a puppy. The other pounced on him, driving Hundr to the ground. He held its great head at bay with his swords crossed, and the dog snapped at him, dripping saliva from its jaws, barking and snarling. It snapped at his face, the foul breath engulfing him, and Hundr couldn't twist away. The dog yelped, then sprang off him, limping away and leaving a trail of thick blood.

"Cursed place this Ireland," remarked Einar, leaning over him with a bloody spear in his fist. "Where else would you use dogs for war? Are you going to lie there all day?" Einar held out his spear, and Hundr grabbed the shaft to haul himself upright. He shook himself down and made ready again with a sword in each hand. Einar was still thin and half the man he had been before his imprisonment, but he would never shirk from battle. With the dogs either dead or dispersed, the fighting resumed all around Hundr.

"Are we winning?" Hundr said, trying to regain his composure after the dog attack.

Einar shrugged. "Don't know." He raised his spear and pointed it across Hundr's shoulder. "But kill that bitch, and it's all over."

It was Saoirse, the völva, the Witch-Queen. She had shorn her head of hair and came clad in stiff, blackened leather. She fought like an animal, using her hooked fingers adorned with metal rings and iron bear-like claws to scratch and pierce through her opponents. Five black shield fighters surrounded her, protecting her with their shields as she leapt upon the backs of Hundr's warriors, tearing their faces and throats into bloody ribbons. Hundr ran for her, swords ready. She saw him then and screeched, howling like a wild animal. One of her guards tried to stop Hundr with his shield, but Einar threw his spear, and the warrior fell away with the leaf-shaped blade stuck in his shoulder. Saoirse leapt into the air like a cat pouncing upon a mouse, and Hundr fell away from her bloody claws, landing on his back. Then, with a thud and a rush of air escaping her mouth, Saoirse descended upon him. They lay together like the lovers they had once been, but when she raised her head, a line of blood and spittle poured from her thin lips to pool on the iron links of Hundr's brynjar. Fenristooth had pierced her body during their fall, and as the life drained from her, Saoirse fixed him with her eyes, which had once been so beautiful but were now dark pools of malice.

"Luck stealer," she whispered and then her slight, leather-clad body went limp. Hundr had the strange impulse to hold her at that moment, a wave of pity washing over him. Her life had been a grim climb to power, filled with suffering and misery. Perhaps it was his fault; maybe he had stolen her luck and that of the sons of Ragnar. He rolled her off and clambered to his feet. The fighting around him stopped. Men gaped at the dead Witch-Queen. Hundr's stomach lurched at what he must do next. He choked back a throatful of vomit and roared with anger and sadness as he chopped Fenristooth down into her thin, lifeless neck. He bent, picked up her head by its short tufts of grey hair, and held it aloft.

"Behold!" he bellowed. "The Witch-Queen's head." All turned to look at him. The black shield fighters simply lowered their weapons as Hundr strode through them, as though the power of her seiðr had been all that kept them fighting for her cause. Men fell back from him until he faced the lines of Bárid mac Ímair. Murrough flanked the King, his long two-handed sword strapped across his back. Bárid nodded as Hundr held the gore-dripping head before him. The warriors of Dublin had not joined the fight, and Hundr turned to show the head to the fighting armies. The battle stopped then as though a mighty hand waved across the battlefield. What had been a deafening roar of battle fell to an eerie silence, broken only by the moans and cries of the wounded.

"No!" came a cry, and a warrior stepped out of the clamour. A young warrior with tousled hair and a black shield emblazoned with a white raven. Finn Ivarsson. He tottered towards Hundr with his sword raised, limping, tears streaming down his face. His men came after him, three of the growlers sworn to Finn in Novgorod. The surrounding warriors paused, their attention captivated by a lithe figure who leapt from the crowd—a man with a thin sword, its tip red with blood. The slender man darted at the first of Finn's men, killing him in an instant, then he twirled to the second, and the warrior raised his axe to strike but moved too slow. The lithe warrior's arm snaked out, and his sword found its mark in the bigger man's armpit. Then, without hesitation, he swiftly came away to land at the throat of the next of Finn's men. It was Erik's renowned champion, Styrbjorn the Dancer. Styrbjorn, who had previously fought Amundr in Einar's hall on that fateful day when the son of Bjorn Ironside had first come to Vanylven.

"It's over," said Hundr, showing the grizzly head to Finn. "Bárid won't fight, and your men are beaten. Throw down your arms."

"I hate you. You killed my mother and father!" Finn spat, his voice cracked with sorrow and pain. This was true enough, and Hundr did not blame Finn for his hate. How could he not hate Hundr?

Finn roared and charged at Hundr, trying to run but impeded by his limp. Hundr let the head drop and reached for his sword, but Finn fell with a frustrated roar. An arrow sunk deep into the meat of his thigh. The son of Ivar the Boneless crumpled and wept, overwhelmed with sorrow, sobbing into the battlefield. His mother dead, foster father and mother betrayed by his own hand. Amid the turmoil, Hildr emerged from the battle line, still clutching her bow. In a cruel twist of the Norns weft, Hildr had shot the arrow to fell Finn and probably saved his life, for Hundr would have killed him for his betrayal of Einar. The Witch-Queen was dead, and Finn was defeated. Erik had found his brother, and Bárid remained King of Dublin. His warriors had not even raised their spears in anger at the battle outside Vykyngelo's walls. Hundr had succeeded in obtaining the völva's head to take back to Vanylven, and he would lay it at the mouth of the galdr-woman's cave. The head of a woman he once loved, tattooed with runes of power but now lifeless and emptied of hate and malice. Amongst the screaming of the wounded and the carnage of the battlefield, Hundr wondered again about his own luck. Indeed, he had been lucky, for he was a veteran of many battles and yet lived. Hundr realised for the first time that his good fortune was a gift from Odin. Filled with deep gratitude, he silently thanked the All-Father for it.

TWENTY-NINE

Einar stood in the Fjord Bear's prow, staring out at the receding Irish coast. He leant against the ship's curving timbers and held Hildr, his two arms around her waist. Her head rested on his shoulder, and the salt-dusted wind whipped her long hair away from her face.

"What will become of him?" Hildr murmured, raising her hand to tighten the fur-trimmed cloak about her neck.

"Hundr would have killed him," said Einar. Einar and Hundr had argued long into the night after the battle, and Hundr had finally allowed Finn to keep his ship. He wanted Finn's head to match that of his mother, but Einar had asked for mercy. Hundr relented in the end, even though he protested they should learn the lesson of not leaving so dreaded an enemy alive. Saoirse had plagued them for years, and Rollo still lurked in Frankia, growing ever more powerful. Nevertheless, Hundr gave in to Einar's request because he could not deny him; he could not see Einar hurt any more. Such was their bond, a true drengr brotherhood.

"Finn should stay in Ireland. Perhaps Bárid will find a place for him?"

"Maybe. Finn is lost to us now, anyway." Finn would not talk to either Hildr or Einar after the battle. Einar wasn't sure if shame, guilt, or hate drove Finn's silence, but the boy he had loved and cared for was now dead to him. On the night following the battle, Bárid had held a feast in Vykyngelo, whose stout defences had not fallen, and neither Hundr nor Einar had wished to take the town after so much bloodshed. The King of Dublin had welcomed Einar, Hundr, and Erik as jarls and friends, and it had been as though they had not fought on opposing sides. Hundr and Einar both accepted Erik's apology for not defending Einar at Vedrafjord. He was sincere and had been unaware of his brother's imprisonment by the völva, so all was forgiven. Erik had not taken part in Einar's capture and torture, but neither had he tried to stop it. Even so, Einar held no malice towards the man. On the contrary, they swore oaths of friendship, and Einar vowed to visit Erik, Refil and Bjorn in the Svear lands one day soon.

Refil and Einar had found a quiet moment in the feasting hall to talk of their ordeal and exchange gifts. Einar presented Refil with a beautifully crafted arm ring forged in the finest Frankish smithies, and Refil gave Einar a fine axe with a bearded blade intricately etched with interlocking dragons. Despite their efforts, no one found Saoirse's crippled brother following the fight, but both Refil and Einar vowed to send word out across the Whale Road offering a generous reward for his capture, one sizeable enough to make any warrior who succeeded wealthy.

"You will see the twins when we reach Vanylven," said Hildr, smiling up at him. Einar kissed her forehead, seeing the sadness tinged in her smile. She would never forget Finn, and she and Einar had no children of their own and were now too old to try. Some things were better left unsaid.

"We shall spoil them, my love," Einar reassured her. "We shall sit by our warm fire, drink strong ale, and listen to the skalds tell us stories of heroes."

"And what then?"

"Then we sail with Hundr once again. We shall take to the Whale Road. We are Vikings, after all. There are still enemies to kill, our reputations to burnish, and silver yet to be won."

MAILING LIST

If you enjoyed this book, why not join the authors mailing list and receive updates on new books and exciting news. No spam, just information on books.

Every sign up will receive a free download of one of Peter Gibbons' historical fiction novels.

https://petermgibbons.com/

THE VIKING BLOOD AND BLADE SAGA

Hundr, Einar and the crew of the warship Seaworm sail the whale road in thrilling adventures during the height of the Viking Age.

They face brutal enemies and vicious battles in their quest for honour, reputation, and glory.

Viking Blood And Blade

865 AD. The fierce Vikings stormed onto Saxon soil hungry for spoils, conquest, and vengeance for the death of Ragnar Lothbrok.

Hundr, a Northman with a dog's name... a crew of battle hardened warriors... and Ivar the Boneless.

Amidst the invasion of Saxon England by the sons of Ragnar Lothbrok, Hundr joins a crew of Viking warriors under the command of Einar the Brawler. Hundr fights to forge a warriors reputation under the glare of Ivar and his equally fearsome brothers, but to do that he must battle the Saxons and treachery from within the Viking army itself...

The Wrath Of Ivar

866 AD. Saxon England burns under attack from the Great Heathen Army. Vicious Viking adventurers land on the coast of Frankia hungry for spoils, conquest and glory.

Hundr and the crew of the warship Seaworm are hunted by Ivar the Boneless, a pitiless warrior of incomparable fury and weapon skill.

Amidst the invasion of Brittany and war with the Franks, Hundr allies with the armies of Haesten and Bjorn Ironside, two of the greatest warriors of the Viking Age. Ivar the Boneless hunts Hundr, desperate to avenge the death of his son at Hundr's hand. To survive, Hundr must battle against fearsome Lords of Frankia, navigate treachery within the Viking Army itself, and become a warrior of reputation in his own right.

Hundr must navigate the war, survive Ivar's brutal attacks, and find his place in the vicious world of the Vikings in this unputdownable, fast paced adventure with memorable characters.

Axes For Valhalla

873 AD. The Viking Age grips Northern Europe. Seven years have passed since the ferocious sea battle with Ivar the Boneless, and Hundr is now a Viking war leader of reputation and wealth. A voice from the past calls to Hundr for aid, and he must take his loyal crew and their feared warships across the Whale Road to Viking Dublin, in a vicious and brutal fight against Eystein Longaxe.

Hundr must fight against an implacable and powerful enemy, amidst brutal attacks, shield wall battles, and treachery. Will his skill and savagery be enough, and can Hundr and his crew survive? Find out in this unputdownable, fast paced adventure with memorable characters.

King Of War

874 AD, Norway. A brutal place, home of warriors where Odin holds sway. King Harald Fairhair fights to become king of the north.

Hundr, a Northman with a dog's name... a crew of battle hardened warriors... and a legendary war where the will of the gods will determine who is victorious.

After incurring the wrath of Ketil Flatnose, Jarl of the Orkney isles, Hundr and his crew become drawn into King Harald's fight for supremacy over all Norway. Hundr must retrieve the Yngling sword, a blade forged for the gods themselves, and find favor with an old friend, Bjorn Ironside, as he fights a vicious and deadly enemy, Black Gorm the Berserker.

Hundr must navigate the war, survive brutal attacks, and make Harald the King of War in this fast paced adventure with striking characters and bloodthirsty action.

Valkyrie Rising

878 AD, Norway. The fight to secure Harald Fairhair's throne is over, but one last battle sends a crew of Viking Warriors on a desperate, bloodsoaked quest.

Hundr, a Northman with a dog's name... a crew of battle hardened warriors... and a voyage that will determine the fate of Ragnarok itself.

The crew of the warship Seaworm sail the Whale Road across Viking Europe in search of a spear said to have been forged for Odin himself. Ragnhild, Hundr's sword-sister and Valkyrie Priestess, must recover the mythical weapon if she is to be restored to her order. The Burned Man stands in their way, a vicious warlord bent on vengeance who will stop at nothing to kill Hundr and his old friend Einar the Brawler.

Hundr must join the war for King Alfred's nascent Kingdom of England and venture home, to the great city of Novgorod. Can he survive brutal attacks and vicious shield wall battles in this fast paced adventure with striking characters and bloodthirsty action?

ABOUT THE AUTHOR

Peter Gibbons

Peter is the winner of the 2022 Kindle Storyteller Literary Award, and an author based in Kildare in Ireland, with a passion for Historical Fiction, Fantasy, Science Fiction, and of course writing!

Peter was born in Warrington in the UK and studied Law at Liverpool John Moores University, before taking up a career in Financial Services and is now a full time author.

Peter currently lives in Kildare Ireland, and is married with three children. Peter is an avid reader of both Historical Fiction and Fantasy novels, particularly those of Bernard Cornwell, Steven Pressfield, David Gemmell, and Brandon Sanderson. His books include the Viking Blood and Blade Saga and the first novel in his new Saxon Warrior Series.

You can visit Peter's website at www.petermgibbons.com.

Printed in Great Britain
by Amazon

39199139R00260